Izz of zIA

Bowels of the Deep

The Only Thing to Fear is Fear Itself

Tom Icon

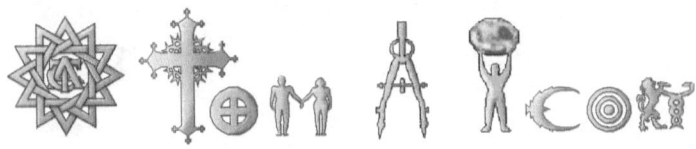

—*7*7*7*—

TOM ICON

I want to acknowledge my photographer, Tony Devine.

Cover design by Tom Icon

Interior design by Tom Icon

Front and back cover illustrated by Tom Icon

Published in the United States of America

ISBN: 978-0-9987089-0-4

1. Fiction / Fantasy / Epic
2. Fiction / Fantasy / Romance

TOM ICON

WHERE FANTASY AND REALITY COLLIDE
THE WONDROUS ADVENTURE CONTINUES

To my brother and my father, who have
gone into the Eternal Beyond

For comments or inquiries: izzofzia@gmail.com
or
visit us at: izzofzia.com

Contents

Introduction

In the constellation of the Northern Galactic Orb. During the time of the twelve kings in the old world of the seventh dynasty recorded as the Golden Dawn, the children of the flesh born inhabited the Southern Lands of Zia. In the days of the Great Wars between the light and the darkness, in an age older than where our story begins, the most powerful and learned minds of intellectual vanity yearned to answer the riddle that would reveal all mysteries. It was an uprising of human thought. In their search, they permitted vanity to seize them, arousing the burning fire of ambition within. The self appointed elite believed there was a better way to rule the world of Zia—their way. In their misdirected inclinations, they intermingled revolutionary thoughts for too long, and unseen demoniacal spirit beings lured them in through their arrogance and lust for power. They became futile in their erroneous reasoning, and they allowed their vain minds to darken. Befouled thoughts violated more and more sacred doctrines, diametrically contrary to the laws of truth. The self professed illuminated ones desecrated fixed realities for conjectures, believing themselves to be more all knowing than the omnipotent mind that created them. In their quest to be wise, they became fools trying to make the most profound questions fit their presumptuous answers and demanding it to be so.

As time passes, by and by, the Ancient Wars have been all but forgotten. Peace and prosperity reigned paramount over the land—that is, until our villain, Baddlock—through spite, envy, and resentment over some imagined injustice—sought an alliance with the Dark Priests of Phantomsdeep, an ancient fortress in the midst of the Noragore Rim, where the Book of Forbidden Knowledge fell into his hands. His thinking becomes perverted in all thought; outlawed incantations not heard out loud in a thousand years filled the forgotten temples beyond the Wastelands of Woe.

Soon Baddlock, now known as the Wicked Warlock Wizard, ensnared Dandork, the king's most trusted subject, and friend, into disloyalty because of greed and promises of power. Then both tyrants, through spellbinding treachery, employed a handful of nobles like rotten apples in a barrel, to provoke ideas of resentment and feelings of betrayal, revolution, and, finally, open rebellion. Ultimately, by way of a series of brutal massacres blamed on the king, Baddlock and Dandork managed to shackle the vicious bitterness of the barbaric Norticlan tribes of the Noragore Realm. Darkon, the ruler of the Norticlan, has joined forces with Baddlock to depose King Ozzdon, seize the throne, and thus the Empire of Xenia.

At present, the Kingdom of Edawn is caught in the vortex of a crisis rapidly gathering force. Princess Zuree has been abducted, tying the king's hands. Our hero, Izz, having come to Edawn for one reason—stayed for another—now hopelessly in love with Princess Zuree. Izz secretly sets off on an impossible one man mission to rescue his beloved, and here is where our story continues to unfold.

One
Abaddawn

The magician of survival, far too exhausted for reasoning, was unsure where the inevitable fate to which he was hopelessly bound was taking them. But Izz meant to keep moving until he discovered it. Destiny's will would be done, and he would accept it whatever it was. All he asked for was a fighting chance. Either way, the demon hordes were almost upon them, rushing through the cavern like an unleashed torrents of blackness, and sooner or later Izz and Zuree were sure to be overrun.

As Izz struggled to escape, he pulled Zuree along, running like two rabbits trying to stay one step ahead of a flying wolf pack. All the while, the forsaken spirits gained momentum, boiling and towering like thunderheads. They were now a tightening circle of pitch blackness, frenzied shadows racing violently toward Izz and Zuree, cursing and blaspheming them.

Izz's mouth and throat were so dry, and his insides tensed as acid churned in his belly. Nevertheless, Izz remained focused on his relentless objective of keeping them alive as long as he could. In his desperate attempt, Izz banked one way and then the other, gambling an impossible escape from the jaws of death, guided only by the will to live. He had no time to gather his senses. It was either keep one step ahead of the churning tide, without stumbling or die. Izz clasped down on Zuree's hand, squeezing it so hard it hurt. Running good and scared, he guided her swiftly along the path in the direction of the black door's exit. She was dizzy with exhaustion, her legs weak; but somehow she kept her balance and stumbled on. At their heels followed a rattle of extremely frightening noises as the hordes of leering demons continued to gain on them coming closer and closer upon them. Every turn seemed blocked against them. His trembling grip sent a shuddering feeling quaking through Zuree's body. Izz knew to be overcome with fear would be to fail.

All at once, the spearheading demons whirled around Izz and Zuree, and suddenly they were cutoff with nowhere left to run. The cavern was darkened, as the air was filled with the chattering and bellowing of black wings. Each form remained shadowy and silhouetted, like the moon during an eclipse. Arms with outstretched hands, set in clawed talons flexed and curled with anticipation, taunting them as they whooshed around them. The clattering and rustling of leathery wings filled Zuree's ears, and she asked, "What now? What is happening?" Her desperation fractured her voice as the ring of evil engulfed them in an ever growing whirlwind of thickening negative energy and the odors of death that swirled around with it.

All Izz could answer was, "Whatever happens, do not look, no matter what."

Too weak to run, Izz just decided he had had enough, and stood his ground. He drew his weapon, and this only brought laughter from the milling throngs of foul entities crowding in around them. They encircled themselves trapping them in the darkness like a swirling black net in a violent cyclone. Thrusting and slashing his dagger in front of him, Izz struggled for life, against the innumerable assailants, that pressed in, and surrounded them. Izz threw his body in front of Zuree for protection. As he lashed out with his weapon, his blade seemed to slice straight through thin air merely. The wicked, immortal powers bore more of a spiritual presence than a tangible existence. They were darkness itself, wisps of black vapor careening in and out of everywhere. Izz's resistance somehow seemed to repel the inky evil that encroached in on them. Zuree clung to Izz in fear as he tried frantically to make it from one fleeting moment to the next, as every wicked spirit being focused their attention on them. Izz's heart went cold, and his blood flowed like icicles in his veins. Zuree felt sickening nausea thrashing around in the pit of her empty stomach as horrible whines filled the air. Izz backed up, trying to get away from the hordes of demons bearing down on them. Death was on the loose, hovering overhead, whizzing in ever tightening circles around them. Zuree kept uttering the question that refused to go away. "What is it? What…"—her voice croaked out the first word of her second question before her dread strangulated it—"is out there!" As the demons who survived by tormenting the undead squeezed in.

Still hoping against all hope, Izz tried to reassure Zuree, "Do not panic!" as he vigorously shielded her.

"I would rather know the worst of truths than know nothing," Zuree pleaded.

Izz could not tell her what was happening, so he pushed her back as he tried to press forward. Finally, he had to accept that they were hopelessly cut off, trapped with their backs against the wall. Izz could only discern the reptilian like outlines of the monstrous black, slimy, parasitic beings backlit by the unnatural red glow of the distant flames. More winged creatures began to land all around them. Zuree could feel and hear the leathery flapping that created whirling winds about them. "Izz, why will you not tell me what is happening? *Please*, please tell me!" Zuree pleaded.

"Just promise me, you will not look, *promise me!*" There was panic in Izz's voice.

It took every bit of resistance she could muster, but she complied and did not remove her blindfold, or attempted to look. She remained brave as a lioness just as clutching taloned hands reached for her, trying to separate her from Izz. Izz just kept repositioning Zuree behind him, shielding her with his body as he backed her slowly away. He was acutely aware that the slightest mistake would cost them both their lives. Braced upon the strength of his love, the rock upon which he stood, so long as he had breath in his body, he would protect Zuree no matter what. They were surrounded, as if by a black cloak, the sulfurous odor that surrounded them was staunch and nauseating. The winged inner dimensional beings crowded in, thrashing out against one another, savaged with a blind lust for destruction. The gooney eyed fiends pressed ever tighter around them, tripping over each other, each wanting to be the one that claimed Izz's soul and recapture Zuree. The air became thick and suffocating with the congestion of so many foul spirits. Out of the swarm, the emerging shadows took on a more definite individual outline as distinctive forms began to take shape. Zuree's presence drew them together in ever tightening throngs. They could smell the blood that promised them freedom, eternal life, the power to wage war in the heavens, and a chance to gain control of the universe, running through her veins.

One of the demons, who seemed to be the ringleader among the malignant spirits, stepped forward. Those overzealous demons that overstepped their ranks were violently slapped away by the dominant archfiend who held sway over those that dared challenge him. And just as if in the middle of a pack of hungry wolves there was an uproar of vicious anger that threatened to erupt into an all out riot. But finally, the bottomless black cauldron of spider like demons backed off, spitting out their hatred for having been rebuked. The controller turned his full attention to Izz. Its drooping, warty face expanded into a gruesome, slobbering grin that bore his jagged canine incisors. He snickered with demoniacal pleasure, as its fiery red, snake shaped eyes filled with delight. When it came closer, its incredibly muscular body and expansive leathery wings seemed to eclipse the cavern. As it moved in closer yet, its sulfurous breath coming from deep inside its rotting pit, became nauseatingly overpowering. From its nostrils meandered two ribbons of black vapor that drifted along its path like putrid streams trailing in midair. From its head dangled a writhing snake like crown of matted hair. The lumpy, evil hellion snarled as it reached out its gnarled hand toward Izz, with its crooked, clawed fingers inwardly curled.

Izz drew a quick, deep breath and readied his weapon. As if being trapped below Zia's underbelly as far down as Zia's face was below the heavens was not bad enough. Zuree's and Izz's fate was about to deteriorate, moving them even closer to the very edge of a bottomless abyss of desecration. To say that the situation was about to rapidly "take a turn for the worst," would be grossly undermining the definition of that statement. As it were the world of madness was about to be united with the world of horror.

Suddenly, out of the ever intensifying chaos, there was a commotion at the rear of the multitudes as another bulkier, blacker form forcibly imposed itself through the ranks. Time stood still as a rift abruptly opened in the heart of the frenzied orgy of disorder, and a heightened stench of death filled the air. The ground groaned and trembled as Abaddawn, the wretched emperor of heartlessness himself, stepped into the epicenter of the birthing delirium. The air around him appeared to splinter as he moved through it, altered by the unutterable perversion of his existence. The offensive odor that accompanied him smelled as if he had just dredged himself through the sediments of a cesspool lake of putrid slime and decay. The surrounding atmosphere staled as it was displaced with the unbreathable disgusting odor. The multitudes began to squirm restlessly, their eyes lurching about, their faces collapsing with dread. The supernatural appearance of Abaddawn was so sudden, so powerful, and so vile that his presence caused demons of all ranks and power to cringe in panic and cower in fear. Instantly, their ranks opened an even wider berth as they dropped to their knees, whimpering loudly with their faces to the ground. Abaddawn's approach sent the smaller demons scurrying away like terrified rats as they cried out, their wings shrilling, and their nostrils streaming sulfurous vapor. The dominate demon shook, in obeisance, and then dropped flat to the cave floor. Its limp ebony body trembled before his lord and master like a sniveling, shuddering, big, grubby, blackened rug of itself.

All the while, Izz could feel the electricity crackling and spark in the air. He felt something unhallowed coming closer and closer, making his skin crawl. Zuree also felt the unhallowed presence's approach as she waved her arms around as if trying to ward off some invisible assault. As she moved her hands back and forth, she felt a strange fluttering resistance, as if she were moving her hand thought stagnant waters. It was bad enough being blindfolded, but it was much worse to know next to nothing about what was happening all around her. The notion of ghosts, spooks, and demons was much too awful to contemplate at such a time. She felt her heart start to tremble as the fear of the unknown rushed in on her, and all that Zuree could manage was a silent scream.

Izz pulled his right hand from Zuree's side and shielded his face, doing his best to brace himself, but his best effort could not keep him from utter shaking terror. Something so terrible and fearful was forthcoming. Izz shrieking in panic, his mouth veered open sideways as every muscle in his body shivered hot and cold at the same time. Izz tried convincing himself, over and over again, that it could not possibly be as awful as it seemed. But he just knew in his heart of hearts that he was about to see something he did not want to see. He closed his eyes tighter than a vise. Then it happened. The full figure of the supernatural being stood before him. And even though he had his eyes shut tight, through his eyelids, he could see a brilliant light and feel the heat of its radiating blaze. Izz finally dared to look up with one eye half open. What he saw emerging from the red fog; he never reckoned in his wildest imagination appeared to be reality. Izz continued to shield his eyes with his hand not being able to bring himself to look at the presence in front of him directly.

At first, all he could see was its fiery white eyes that instantly held Izz in their spell like grip. And there was absolutely nothing he could do to make himself look away. Appearing as if out of thin air, was what looked like the outline of an angel of light. As the being moved closer to Izz, a radiance came from this animated creature. A streaming white hale of glimmering white stars trailed it. At least it had a head and arms. It also had legs, but it appeared to glide over the cavern floor without their use. Izz's body was starting to tremble, and his legs were shaking, as he was drawn into some spiritual trance, moving towards an intangible dimension. What Izz beheld was beautiful. The entire universe seemed to be reeling around him, as Izz felt himself tittering on the brink of the rim of ecstasy. He suddenly felt dizzy, feeling the gravity of Zia as it spun, pulling him slowly and sinking him in a downward spiral to his knees.

The illuminated form stood directly before Izz and, in a soothing voice, whispered in his mind, *What do we have here, a life where no life is possible?* What appeared like an angelic being of the Abyss studied him meticulously mapping his face inch by inch, studying every facet and fragment. That was when Abaddawn noticed Izz's dagger and immediately recognized that is was one of the ancient blades of the Noble Kings. "Are you a wizard? A seer?" The personage asked as it leaned in closer. The being eyed Izz with all its power to pierce the thoughts of his mind, able to absorb the memories of anyone its presence touched. "No, no, you are a mere man, Izz of the northern province of Zollerzon." By now the demon ruler's eyes had turned from white to a deepening shade of red and were greedily bulging as it eyed the dagger in Izz's hand.

Where in the world did you get this? He wanted to ask. *What could be more perfect? The imbecile has brought with him the ancient dagger of the noble kings the perfect blade I need to complete the perfect sacrifice of the maiden. What a fool!* The personification of evil thought almost out loud. The father of lies abruptly tore his eyes away from the weapon as not to arouse Izz's suspicion. Then the strange entity proclaimed. "Well, it just so happens that I have come to save you from your most unfortunate present situation."

As Izz slowly rose to his feet, a quizzical stare dominated his face and astonishment reflected in his widened eyes. Had an angel of mercy indeed come to save them?

As long as Zuree remained blindfolded, she could not hear the words spoken by the entity of feculence.

"Oh yes, I know everything about you." Apparently, the soothsayer did not perceive with eyes only. "What I do not know is by what power you found your way down here. Alive, no less. The girl has been brought here at my invitation, but you—"

Obviously, this self proclaimed angel of light did not know everything as it claimed, Izz thought. He looked over the edge of his bent arm and, at long last, made eye contact.

The being of light assumed an evil imitation of camaraderie. "I am the highest among spirits. There is no higher reality. I am all that matters, and I have come to bless you, my child," the being of light announced. The being's eyes held a look of infinite knowledge as if all the secrets of the cosmos were seated in its penetrating eyes. "Of course…you are here for the girl," the spiritual being glared with a piercing gaze at every subtle expression of change in Izz's eyes as it spoke. "Well, I just cannot let you have her. No, no, that will never do." After a contemplative moment, the radiant one spoke again. "I can give you something better," the shining one waved his hand before Izz, and a vision of beautiful, scantily dressed women appeared. "Choose any one you want, or better yet, choose them all. I can give you anything you want. Anything you could ever wish for, anything you could ever dream of, anything."

Izz nervously took a step closer, unconsciously leaning forward as if under a powerful spell. He was held captivated. Abaddawn sought out the weakness that he knew lurked in the deepest corners of all men's hearts. Slowly but surely, uncharacteristic tides of temptation rose within Izz, and his resistance was compromised, as was the will of a mouse to the tempting cheese in a mousetrap. The power of the grand deceiver from whose own mouth came the first lie ever uttered, spun his lofty sounding delusion.

"Today is a very lucky day for you. This hour you have been called to the greatness I have reserved for your special appointment. At my side, you will be the most exalted king in all of Zia. As you can see, I can be extremely generous to those I chose to serve me."

Izz's resolve weakened; little by little, as he began to yield his mind to the control of the powers of profound darkness. Yet he could not at that moment understand whatever it was that made such a splendorous offer so vastly repulsive.

The illuminated one waved his hand toward the young maidens. "I am prepared to give you anything your heart or imagination desires. Riches, fame, immortal glory can all be yours. And perhaps in time, you too can be a god as I am. All you have to do is declare me your lord and bow down and worship me."

Even though in his understanding, Izz calculated what he heard to be too good to be true. The words looped in his mind, mesmerizing him as he began to brim over with preposterous self aggrandizing. The dark lord's illuminating power was penetrating every vertebra in Izz's backbone, every fiber of his muscles throughout his body, defiling his blood, consuming him with weakness and infesting him with corruption. Izz was at his most vulnerable—that is until he heard what he most—did not want to hear. "And all you must do is relinquish your so called love for the princess. All you need do is slay the maiden before me by your hand at the appointed hour. Then I might know that you are loyal to me alone, and all that I rule over will be at your fingertips."

The words spoken hammered deeply into Izz's skull. He recoiled, just as if he had been slapped across the face as if someone had punched him in the gut at the same time. At that moment, out of the blue, he heard the familiar voice of Ammiz come into his heart and mind like that of a long lost friend. He jerked up his head to the side as if he expected to see the old seer there whispering directly into his ear.

Beware, not all that glitters is gold. Guard your heart. Beware lest anyone cheat you of your divine destiny through temptations and empty trickery. Where you are, there are no rules. Your battle is not of the flesh but with the principalities of wrath, against powers, against spiritual wickedness, against the rulers of the darkness of this world. Reach as much as a finger to accept so much as a crumb, and you will find something reaches back out to drag you down into its fathomless depths. Fear will be your enemy...grasp and cling onto your divine destiny. Be who you were destined to be!

The thought of the seer's voice gave Izz the will to resist. All at once, in the background, he could hear the faint sounds of gleeful snickering, and the shrieking, mocking voices coming from the shadows. Repelled by what he had heard from the would be god set Izz on a course of resistance. Relentlessly he put up a moral fight for his sanctity and the possession of his soul. In the next instance, he picked his thoughts carefully as he found the courage to stand his ground against the powerful principality who at every moment threatened to weaken his resolve. Izz straightened his spine and held his ground. He rose to his full length, took a deep breath, and, without stopping to think, uttered in total defiance what he had surmised. What the seer Ammiz had warned him about so many times: "I know what you are. You are the minister of eternal damnation." Izz looked into Abaddawn's face, which no longer beguiled him. "You are the father of all lies. What you offer is not a life in paradise but a life in an everlasting, living hell. A place where the souls of the lost are condemned, an abode for those who chose to live a lie rather than what is right. The kingdom you speak of is an eternity where one is convicted to the deepest form of death. A death in which one is inflected with all your eternal miseries, damned to the highest hopelessness. You speak of a doomed and defeated eternity."

For a moment, it seemed to Izz as if Ammiz himself was somehow speaking through him.

Then the spell broke. It was as if Abaddawn had been struck dumb. As a result of this truism, the murderer of souls was forced to ease his demonic grip, and Izz was all at once released from the deceiver's powerful spell. Izz felt as if some form of scales had fallen away from his eyes. Every demon in the room, large and small, was suddenly held in the clutches of fear and causing the hordes to shrink back as they lashed and clawed out at the powerful words of defiance that came to their hearing. Izz immediately recognized the importance of what he had said and continued, "You do not know the first thing about the true riches of life, of love, joy, or happiness!" Izz's words echoed across the abyss, shredding to pieces the cloak of trickery projected by the crowned head of illusion and deception.

Taking every demon by surprise, Izz's words sent the demonic host screaming farther back into the foul realm of darkness, just as suddenly the aura of the evil imitation Abaddawn radiated began to diminish and disappear. The light that had cast its disguise over the fiendish being, withered into complete lightlessness. The prince of deceit suddenly appeared in the fullness of his unmasked perversity, exposed in his complete uncloaked true form. The brightness of his semblance was completely snuffed out. And as the false angel of light masquerading as a representative of virtue receded, he seemed to momentarily suck the light from even the flames that continued to rage in the distant background. Every jot of light that crossed his presence seemed to submerge into his blackness. It was as if his existence had cast a breach that had slashed into a time where light never glowed. Instantaneously, the subterranean sphere turned into a total eclipse as dense as a pool of liquid tar. As the luminescence of the faraway inferno gradually regained its power to shine, the fallen angle's true appearance was betrayed.

Izz stared at the white tingling star lights dancing before him for a moment, still half mesmerized. Suddenly Izz was utterly traumatized at what pure evil looked like. And then all at once, an all encompassing fever of terror scorched across his consciousness as in a flash, Abaddawn's actual, deformed presence came into full focus. The one that had at first appeared as an angel of light was now only darkness. Izz shrank back from a face that was indescribably unbearable to look upon. As he pressed back against Zuree, he pinned her between himself and the cave wall. Izz had no time to react in any other way than to emit from the depths of his throat, the most unnatural choking sounds that was supposed to be a scream released at the top of his lungs. Zuree suddenly cried out, "What is *it*?"

Petrified by what he saw, Izz's mouth contorted open to one side, and every hair on his body stood on end. So evil looking was Abaddawn that hell itself trembled at his presence. With gaping jaws, the host of the lower world of the damned gave their overlord an ever widening berth. Even the vilest demons found him offensive. The murdering rogue drew near to Izz, towering over him, allowing him no escape. Its odor was immediately and immensely revolting. Izz gagged and then retched, as his stomach rolled. His mouth watered with bitterness as he was struck mute. In a blind rage, Abaddawn's dominating form heaved in and out; his nostrils flared as dark, insidious powers coursed through him. His huge and menacing red eyes, which were more like globes of fire burning deeply in vacant sockets, seethed with wrath. Izz stared wide eyed at the decrepit beast that looked like something that had been blasted into countless pieces and then hastily put back together like a damaged jigsaw puzzle with more than a few pieces missing. Every feature seemed out of place and out of line. Its gnarled goat like head stuck out from hunched shoulders like an abnormal cancerous growth. Protruding from the top of the creature's lopsided head were several mismatched, warped horns curved outward from the top of his head and forehead. From its face, twisted, bony knobs of different lengths and sizes protruded. One eye drooped the other was slanted.

The mass of pathetic waste was hunched over, twisted like a deformed vulture with sinewy arms dangling limply at its side. Its leathery wings hung from its shoulders, drooping along its length like long black drapes. The mouth was ajar and drooling, a ghastly greenish substance that dripped to the cave floor and bubbled. Red vapor discharged in blasts of puffs and streams from its nostrils. The monstrous abnormality frothed at the mouth as it drew breath into its malignant lungs that spawned strained wheezing sounds that hissed through rows of misaligned, barbed fangs. Abaddawn's talons flexed as they poised themselves for the attack. Izz fumbled for his dagger, not realizing that it was already in his hand. His nerves tangled and turned his hands and arms into useless numb appendages suspended limply at his side. So disoriented and confused was Izz that he could not even feel his feet touching the cave floor.

Just like that, Izz found himself eye to eye with the personification of evil. And for the longest moment, his mind was frozen with fear as he stood motionless like a mouse charmed by the spellbinding eyes of a viper. He could see that deep in those leering, blood black pupils, empty, unused tombs that reflected only narcissism spiraling inwardly forever. The only perceptive life behind its deadened eyes was the dancing reflections of the turbulent flames that glowed from a distance. At long last, Abaddawn spoke, "Are you so stunned? You should feel honored you are one of the very few living mortals to ever look upon me." The prince of darkness continued, whispering to him behind clenched teeth, "As you can see, I am not a myth. Let me reassure you that any predetermined concepts you may have about who or what I am, despite whatever you may have heard of me, are completely false. I am the deeper self of every man. I am on your side. Your so called creator only wishes to deny you, cheat you of the pleasures that you so rightfully deserve.

"On the other hand, my ways are simple. My only law is that you do as you will those things that most please you. It is in my power to give you anything in this retched world, any ecstasy you could ever imagine. Your bliss could be everlasting, riches, glory, and joyful fulfillment forever and ever." Abaddawn continued to compromise, distort, and misrepresent the truth.

Izz's only reaction was a quickly exhaled breath that made his lips flutter loosely, as he tried to expel the putrefied stench he had just inhaled into his convulsing lungs. The source of foul odor continued to exude from what Izz realized to be the enticer's breath. And all the while, due to Zuree's shielded sight, she seemed almost oblivious to the full level of horror that was taking place in Izz's head.

The one that had uttered the first lie ever repeated what he had once promised Baddlock, "Together we could be invincible against all. Let me set you free from the false beliefs, laws, and reasoning that have for so long enslaved you and denied you the pleasures of your longing flesh. What is forbidden to you on Zia is your rightful passage here." The deceiver disgorged one extreme blasphemy after another. "Everything you can see and cannot see is because of me. I and I alone am the rightful ruler of heaven and all its worlds within, but I was cheated out of my due by the present powers that be. I promise you, you will enjoy the greatest glory of my way. My plan is pure without the need for the meaningless feelings of guilt or remorse."

Vaporous wisps of noxious breath accompanied every word as the father of all lies shamelessly continued his attempt by any and every possible means to entice and beguile Izz. "And all you have to do is acknowledge me as your master, and everything that you ever wished for will all be yours."

Suddenly, with every passing moment, Izz seemed again to be caught in an unexpected undertow that began to suck him under. He seemed immersed into a ruinous and decayed dimension that farther degenerated into obscured illusions of ghostly images. A fleeting, yet powerful expectation of selfish indulgence ever so briefly seeped into Izz's soul, as he felt himself slipping and sliding back into the world of spiritual shadows again.

When Abaddawn noticed this, his eyes filled with gleeful evil as he continued to spin his enticing illusion in a deeply hypnotic, intoxicating whisper that seemed to resound up from the most profound depth far beneath Zia. "All you need to do…is pledge your allegiance to me…simply relinquish your love for the maiden, and together we will offer her up, that you may be king of not only this world but of all other worlds and their peoples. That I may finally take my rightful universal throne, that darkness may reign…forever and ever, and evermore. No one need to know…it will be our little secret. No one can be worth what I am officering you—not even the Princess of this unpleasant little speck of a forsaken world. What would you take for the immortal essence of your existence? Riches, power, eternal self gratification? All you need do is accept, and it will be yours." The monster's eyes blazed with pompous self assurance at the expected outcome as he let out a sneering laugh.

Triggered by the proposed fate of his precious love, Izz's mind snapped, freeing itself of the entangling enchantment as he came fully awake. He suddenly realized the stupidity of believing anything he had heard. Darkness bolted out of Izz's soul as he purged the wicked entity from his mind and stripped it from his spirit. Having regained his self possession, Izz declared, "The only thing that has ever even come close to being my master is my undying love for Princess Zuree."

The face of the lord of deception shook like the tail of a rattlesnake as it became a mask of astounded disbelief. And in less than a heartbeat, something erratic had happened that had never happened in the lightless empire of the underworld. A mere mortal man had risen to stand up and dispute the word of the master of the fallen—in his own realm, no less. There was a shuddering breach in the lightless space, a rip in the fabric of all evil. Suddenly every demon in the inferno seemed to dissolve into nothingness. Izz felt the enslavement of the shadow lord's sorcery drain away from him, for the moment at least. Abaddawn seemed off balance as he staggered backward, and for a twinkling of an eye, Izz thought he saw fear in Abaddawn's eyes. The would be god shrunk into the shadows, seemingly attempting to steady himself. Hysterically, the demon crowds of terrified onlookers stared wide eyed in uncertainty and pandemonium.

However, Abaddawn was not the ruler over all of darkness for nothing. Despite being momentarily vanquished and humiliated before his entire court of underlings in his own domain, he recuperated almost at once. Suddenly a murky, ink like cloud filled the cavern like a rotating tidal wave that began boiling and thundering around the room. Every instance Abaddawn gained strength as he reabsorbed the black energy. From the darkness within his abode, moment by moment, the prince of the underworld regained the ability to merge from the spiritual realm back into the physical world.

And all at once, a violent force crashed upon Izz like a crushing avalanche of renewed terror. A tremor of faintheartedness shook Izz. His eyes flared wide with alarm when he saw Abaddawn hemorrhaging forward through the texture of the shadowy fog. The blackness inside him bled and took shape, causing Izz's eyes to glaze over with reawakened fright. Izz stumbled back pressing against Zuree, groping in reverse. He backtracked as he stretched back his arms and surrounded her in a last ditch effort to protect his only reason for living. All the while he desperately tried to formulate a plan in his panicked mental state. His hair bristled with alarm when he heard the most sinister, monstrous bellowing.

Boiling in anger, Abaddawn spewed deep, nasty animalistic sounds. As he stepped forward, his steps echoing like hooves on the cave floor. As seething sounds rumbled in his throat, his vehement growl reverberated throughout the entire crypt of the living dead until the foundations of the underworld were shaken. Izz saw the archfiend, crazed with wrath, rushing at him.

"What is it? Please, please tell me. Tell me something. Tell me anything!" Zuree begged.

Izz's frantic gasp for air was his only response. Izz only cringed as he tried backing away, like a mushroom gatherer overcome by a hallucinogenic fungus mistaken for an edible morsel. The begetters of darkness moved in on Izz like a pack of jackals, descending on a trembling newborn fawn. Abaddawn's anger birthed visible bands of inky hate that spread, and collided and meandered within drifting clusters of discernible rage. As Abaddawn moved in for the kill, trailing ribbons of blood red like streamers and twirling spirals of smoky vapors were set spinning in circular dances in his wake.

All the while, Izz tried to reason away his approaching encounter. "You cannot be real," he gasped, backing Zuree up farther against the cave wall. "You do not exist. I am only imagining you!" Izz raised his voice until he was almost shouting.

"What…what does not exist? What cannot be real?" Zuree managed to blurt out between her escalating breaths of overpowering fear. Caught in a spiderweb of incomprehension, Zuree could not get another word out, unable to make sense of the vague shades of imagery that cascaded before her mind's eye.

In all his lionhearted faithfulness, Izz stood his ground, fully committed to sacrificing his life, if need be, for the slightest chance of Zuree's survival. Without solid footing from which to resist, he carefully pushed Zuree back, sheltering her with his undaunted devotion. They were both trapped within a net of condemnation, in a surreal world, a lost place within the empty void of emptiness.

Zuree choked up and could only cower behind Izz when she felt the quaking spasms running through Izz's trembling body as a cloud of enshrouding paranoia engulfed him like an infectious disease. Izz might as well have been made of air, the way

Abaddawn was able to scoop him up with one hand, with fingers locked in a viselike grip around his forehead. As though Izz was a bag of feathers, Abaddawn yanked him off his feet, and then swung him in a wide arc, sending him crushing brutally against the opposing stone wall. Izz fell, landing heavily on the dusty cavern floor, as if a wooden toy soldier, broken beyond repair, discarded in a heap of waste like a mass of lifeless splintered parts. Abaddawn's ruthlessness brought gleeful hoots and crackling laughter from the crowd of demons.

Zuree was left to crumble to the cave floor in a mess of anxiety. She waved her hands frantically in front of her in search of Izz. But instead only felt a force of the hatred and evil that flowed around her like a thick liquid seeping through her fingers. She reached for her blindfold, but stopped short of removing it when she heard Izz scream, "*No! Do not* remove your blindfold," as he stirred his limp form, trying to lift himself, but only managing to roll onto his back.

A crazy howling broke out as unseen entities pushed Izz into the center of the cave and formed a ring of extreme resentment, around him. The air was charged with murderous hostility, and electrified with loathing animosity. Zuree frantically kicked herself back against the rock wall as if she was kicking away something that might draw her in and sweep her away. It was a terror so pure she could taste it in her mouth. She was twitching and shivering with fright as a strange remoteness and intangibility surrounded her. Zuree slowly lowered the trembling hand she held out in an attempt to shield herself and scooted back on her haunches until she was pressed firmly back against the wall. She pulled her legs in tight and braced herself against what she could not see.

Izz lay on the cave floor, moaning, trying to recompose himself. Lesser demons were beginning to spill out of the shadows into the clearing mist. The ever mounting assembly was mumbling, nodding, congratulating and praising their master for his excellent display of power and majesty. Once again, the prince of abomination moved slowly toward Izz where he lay, bringing with him an unnatural cold chill. The foul being growled, reached down with his sinewy fingers and twisted clawed nails, and grabbed Izz's throat in an iron grip, digging its talons in deep. In a new burst of rage, sulfurous spittle flew, and slimy drool dripped, from Abaddawn's gaping mouth. He exposed his fangs, gnashing his teeth as if he would have eaten Izz's heart right out of his chest.

Abaddawn pulled Izz's face almost up against its own, as Izz's throat began to constrict. Abaddawn's eyes warily narrowed until they were nothing more than fiery slits while he stared at Izz, freezing Izz's blood with his glare. Abaddawn's perception focused with fierce penetration, as he continued to study Izz as if looking upon a unique peculiarity. Izz could feel Abaddawn's gimlet eyes boring into him, peering into his very soul. Izz tried to look away but instead felt his gaping eyes go wider and bulge out as though they might be forced right out of their sockets. Unable to look away, Izz continued his spellbound stare into Abaddawn's depthless leer. He gaped into the king demon's eyes until all that registered on his retinas was his own image in the bottomless abyss of Abaddawn's black pupils.

Finally, intent on destroying Izz's will to fight on, the dark lord smiled wickedly as his forked tongue slithered and lashed out at him. His enigmatic eyes turned to fissures as he said, "Know this, I can darken the sun by the snap of my fingers, turn a waterfall into a raging flame. I can build a kingdom out of one single grain of sand. Open your mind. Admit defeat! Relinquish your will! Bow down to me!" Abaddawn's head withered and twisted like the head of a serpent, while black blasts of vaporous, foul odor belched from his nostrils and his jagged gash of a mouth. As he spoke, his words drifted through the air, like spider silk almost visibly floating in the mist.

Izz continued his frail resistance. His stomach rolled with a wave of revulsion as he was held face to face with a nightmarish revelation of vile evil. Abaddawn suddenly angered at Izz's persistent opposition, drew him close. "You are a fool. You could have had the world of Zia, untold riches, pleasure, and power." So close was Abaddawn that his words seemed to strike Izz like the little stinging lashes of a whip. Eye to eye never had Izz seen such a vestige, as cold as death warmed over. Izz's vision blurred as he looked pleadingly into the coldest, darkest eyes he had ever seen. Abaddawn's irises that suddenly began to change from dark red to inky black, until his pupils were lost in their fathomless depths. Again, the angel of darkness spoke as he sneered, "So be it. Now you will pay the price." His tone was cruel and cutting. "The time has come to open your mind to your new reality." The words Izz heard thrust through his soul like a death sentence.

Then Abaddawn's large, black hand carried Izz by the throat, shaking every inch of his being about ferociously like a broken doll. Izz's body contorted violently, his legs waving convulsively, and his face shrieking wildly. Then Abaddawn hurled Izz back, like an adult whirling an infant, and slammed him up against the stone wall with incredible force. He held him helplessly pinned up against the wall like a crushed bug. The impact drove all the breath out of Izz's lungs. He whimpered as he tried to regain his breath.

Abaddawn, the cosmic parasite, suddenly raised his hideous head as if sensing something in the air, and then rotated it slowly as if pinpointing a particular point. His forked tongue flicked in and out as if tasting something carried in the air. The moment stretched; finally, the prince of darkness addressed the host of wickedness: "The Kingdom of Edawn is about to be consumed heart, and soul. Let us concentrate our darkest powers and rise to our rightful supreme dynasty."

The whole underworld all at once began a feeding frenzy as they drew power from their interconnecting forces. They created an energy field of terror that linked between the people of Edawn, through the demon horde, and into Abaddawn. Absolute evil interwove with the total wickedness, seeping in from above, into the darkness, descending like a slow moving twister from a blackened thundercloud. Abaddawn focused and channeled the glut of dark power that his demon armies were sucking in from the agony and fear of men. All of Edawn's present misery was at that moment being coursed and consolidated by each demon into their wicked master, Abaddawn. The epitome of depravation shuddered and shivered with delight as he feasted on the present and approaching misery of the Edawnian people. He absorbed the impending horror in like a sponge, growing incredibly stronger on a coming untold evil beyond thinking. The spirit of wickedness would not spare any cost to attain his goal or accomplish his purpose. Nor would he rest until Izz paid for his insolent interference—with his sanity, his soul or both. The point of Abaddawn's attack would come by way of Izz's vision, through the windows to his soul. Abaddawn further immobilized Izz against the wall and locked his stare way beyond Izz's eyes, from where his malice tapped into the deepest reaches of Izz's extrasensory existence. Soon Izz would be involved in a high stakes mental twister with the innermost principalities of darkness in which his soul was at stake.

Zuree cringed as she brought the back of her hand up to her quivering lips and trembling lower jaw. She called out to Izz repeatedly, "Izz, Izz, who or what is there, and what are they doing to you?" For the time being, as long as Zuree's eyes remained bound shut, she would remain just out of reach. That is if Izz could stay alive if Izz could somehow stay within the realm of sanity.

All the while, the dwellers of the lightless realm, where real nightmares are born, crept toward Izz, engulfing him utterly. And like an endless precession, they just seemed to keep spilling out of the black shadows from every side, baring their teeth and talons ready to rip Izz to shreds. The ghoulish hordes were everywhere, haunting Izz's soul with their grotesque emergence. Unable to look away, Izz felt anew strange, disorienting dizziness. He gulped a shuddering breath as he sensed his very essence drawn, sapped, and drained away from him, down into a bottomless, inky hole. Every wretched ghoul joined in, drawing him down by a series of gradual, successive stages of fear and despair. Izz had never known what it felt like to be so altogether forsaken with such abandonment of all that was real. It was beyond the most gruesome death, and decay Izz could imagine, ever escalating to something increasingly worse and worse. The air, dirt, and space around them bit by bit, step by step, level by level was slowly but surely becoming gradually more and more vile and unhallowed. And still, the circle of unrestrained, venom filled evil ones pushed through, crowding in like angry piranhas to pour out their vehement hatred on Izz. The higher ranking demons converged toward the front of the inner circle as they incessantly unleashed their heart chilling assault on Izz's senses. They united, reaching forth their scrounging evil thoughts to poison, torment, and reduce Izz's spirit with tribulation and disheartenment.

His vision seemed to shift in and out of focus, becoming distorted, then blurred. His hair bristled, and the underworld around him seemed to recede as he felt himself slipping as if into another place and time. Abaddawn heightened the intensity of his relentless spiritual attack as the demonic throngs crowded in, moving to and fro like swirling shadows in a tornadic whirlwind. The demonic world flashed in and out, quivering and surrounding Izz from all sides. They salivated like giant scavengers playing for position around an upcoming death. Out of the obscurity, on the edge of insanity, the fearsome specters continued to increase in intensity by the hundreds of thousands each one inflecting their projected evil. Completely swallowed up by the closing net of leathery winged hellions, Izz and Zuree's fate seemed all but sealed.

At that very same moment, Baddlock's war camp buzzed with intensifying tension and concern as the ferocity of blood lust consumed the drugged Zomborges to the highest pitch and threatened to boil over at any time. It was already getting late in the midday by the time the Zomborge armies were finally assembled. With great prudence, each ghoul was cautiously armed with a wicked, spiked battle ax forged in the eternal fires of Phantomsdeep. Momentarily distracted by the feel of the weapon in their hands with fixed eyes on its razor sharp edging with a crazed look they were moved into position. But too soon, once again, the legions of the dead were screaming in escalating vexation. They strained at the leather thongs that held them, foaming at the mouth, ripping at the air with their weapons like beasts in a maddened trance. Sorcerers and handlers of the despicable creatures were struggling to keep their drones under control and only waited upon the signal of their own master Baddlock.

At last, to everyone's relief, the Wicked Warlock Wizard finally commanded in a loud voice that exploded from his gaping mouth. "Unleash the Zomborges!" He grinned slowly, evilly, wide enough to crack his face as he surveyed his prey kingdom with those dead, sunken, glaring, gimlet eyes.

The handlers needed no second command. *Wwshhhhhhhh, crack!* The snap of the whip sounded as sickening whacks of the lash herded the tethered puppet creatures like dumb beasts of burden, feeling the sting of the strap. Keepers mounted upon their armored warhorses and drove their droning slaves, gruesomely forth charging forward, mindlessly before their long whips. With mouths gnashing and drooling with slick slime, the Zomborges were driven like a flash flood of living death ahead and toward the Kingdom of Edawn. The mind numbing attack was launched with terrible fury and brutality. The assault was made known by volleys of shrilling screams and dreadful howling sounds like something between a roaring lion, a raging bull, and a hideous squealing pig. Without any other thought or meaning other than to slaughter and destroy. Long, dirty fingernails twitched around the handles of their gruesome axes as they rushed down the slope waves of terror. There would be no way they could be called back. The teeming sea of Zomborge throngs stampeded headlong south across the valley, jostling and elbowing one another, heading straight toward the Kingdom of Edawn in an all out homicidal onrush.

Empowered by their demon masters within, the gangrenous hordes quickened their pace to nearly as fast as the racing stallions that drove them. They pounded the ground beneath them like the rumbling of thunderous hooves from a colossal warhorse racing into battle. A trail of pus and tattered flesh marked their trail along their path. Thousands of Zomborges merged into one mass, changing shapes, shifting positions, moving in seemingly dozens of different formations and random patterns, like agitated dust in a brutal windstorm.

"Land attack! Land attack!" was the outcry from the alert tower watch. The same ram's horn that signaled the surprise attack in the war games blasted from every corner of the kingdom. For one heart stopping instance, everyone within earshot of the alarm froze. Suddenly the eerie stillness that had permeated the kingdom was broken as the kingdom's dogs were sent into a frenzy of barking and howling. But soon their growled warning turned into piteous whining sounds between bays and wails. And after a while, the dogs were no longer yelping, only whimpering, as if they knew better than anyone else what was coming their way. The tower watch hoped everyone was wide awake and ready if not, they were in for the rudest awakenings.

King Ozzdon made his way to the upper main keep so that he could observe the advance of the oncoming army of bizarre animated corpses. Each one of them bore a giant ax blade. He beheld the looming land attack with mounting alarm. The jumbled waves of movement dashed forward and poured down the hillside in a continuous ripple along the plains, which seemed to pitch and billow as if the fields were overrun with giant cockroaches. "So many of them," the king murmured to himself. He turned away to one side for the moment and closed his eyes for a few seconds of prayerful thought. How would they be able to fend off all those monstrous creatures when they came trampling over their breached walls? He felt his heart contract just as though an evil clawed hand had coiled over it, as lines of mortality etched across his face. For an instant, his mind was barren, like a stagnant lake flattened by nothingness. From the depths of his soul, a single bubble of hope grew and came rising to break the surface of his spreading disheartenment. Small ripples of calm waves multiplied and widened as he progressively adjusted and channeled all his thoughts. His pulse quickened, and uncertainty turned into a riveting conviction that surged through his veins with the assuredness of what he had to do. He quickly composed himself. His brain became suddenly clearly alert and logical. Then in a loud, commanding voice of a noble king, he broke the numbing silence. "*I am a warrior king!* And you are fearless warriors! The day of days has come upon us. We were born to be, for such a time as this. Are you ready to stand where you were born to be?"

"We will not willingly surrender one single grain of sand of our beloved kingdom. If our path leads to death, let us die with honor, as it is our honored duty to do so." He looked around as he spoke; his gaze did not waver. He saw respect and unfailing loyalty in every eye, and it gave him strength. "I do not know how this hour will end. I do not know if there will be another dawn. What I do know is that we need to fight to stay alive." His facial expression echoed his tone and conveyed whatever emotion his words did not. "I will mince no words. The juncture of time fast approaches when the unknown evil you have heard spoken of will descend upon us from the very pit of hell itself. *Will you stand with me?*"

Zandor, a man of legendary courage, was the first to respond to the call of the king. With both feet anchored to the ground, he stood tall and drew his sword, holding it at the ready and pledging his everlasting loyalty. He stepped forward and snapped a salute in the Edawnian way. "My sword is yours, my king. I for one, am prepared to lay down my life this day for you, my king. Honor demands it."

"I no longer matter. Soon it will be every man for himself. The only thing that matters now is our wives and children, our culture and the things we believe in," the king returned.

Kondor was the second to pledge his undying loyalty. "I know your heart, my lord, for it echoes my own."

And at once, the other generals, led by Arius, stepped forward to be counted.

"Well, then, we are in agreement. I count you as brothers and always shall." The king returned the salute. His respect for his men was mutual and profound. "Now, there are a hundred and one things that we needed to ready, but time has long since been against us. We must position our catapults and our best archers on what is left of our northern wall, and defend our damaged fortifications as well as possible."

Zandor and Kondor immediately organized an effort to reinforce the kingdom's fortress walls with wagons, carts, and any and everything that would fill a hole. They then quickly moved to build up a makeshift defensive line on the northern wall. Zandor looked for the best ways to maximize the use of existing supplies and weapons to defend the most vulnerable points.

From atop the main keep, King Ozzdon stared through his spyglass to see the enemy's army of charging cadavers surging forward like the hounds of hell. Closer and closer the murderous army came in like a blistering dust storm of chaos, barbarism, and bloodlust, advancing like a horde of disturbed hornets. Ozzdon then looked down upon his severely dwindled standing army. Thousands of citizens that had replenished the ranks of the slain were jammed in clamoring throngs. They lined themselves all along the inside of the outer wall and along the battlements that remained standing. Farmworkers, artisans, office workers, rich and poor, men from all walks of life joined in defense of their kingdom. They knew nothing about war, only what they had read in their history books. Most were men either too old or too young to be asked to bear the charge of defending their kingdom. The soon to be defenders had been provided armor and weapons from the ancient royal armories or taken from the slain.

The youth, of twelve years and up, the next generation all rose up to take the place of the fallen. And the older men were as out of place as the outdated iron helmets, the battered cuirasses, the rusting gorgets, and the obsolete gauntlets they wore and carried. The old swords they bore at the ready were little more than corroded antiques that had once flashed in the ancient battles of old, with but one bright streak along their sharpened edges. Some bore only picks, axes, and spades. For many everyday citizens who had never before wielded a weapon in their lives, this would be more than likely a sentence of death. Their choice had been clear, stand, and fight for their families and their own lives. Fight against the evil that was about to descend upon them or cower among the women and children waiting to be slaughtered like a flock of sheep drawn back in fear. They chose to fight.

Deep in his heart, the king knew they could not win. There were too many descending on them. And this was not even their main force, and to make it worse, their supplies were all but depleted. Their fortifications were besieged and undermined with gaping openings. His remaining generals had attempted their best to shore up their beleaguered defenses. But their best efforts would not hold for long against the whirlwind of death that was about to come crashing down upon them. And yet, if only they could hold out just long enough for their reinforcements to arrive, they may barely survive.

There was no time to make battle plans. However, the king continued to encourage his ragtag troops as they positioned themselves along the northern wall. "We must hold down our kingdom at all cost! The preservation of our entire empire is in our hands. If they are not stopped here if they prevail against us...they will spread their madness throughout Zia, kingdom by kingdom. We must use our heads in battle. Courage without cunning will mean nothing. Do not sacrifice yourselves. If you must fall back, then fall back, but do it in good order. Coordinate your positions, reinforce, and defend each other. Attack and ambush your enemy at every opportunity."

The approaching inhuman screams intensified. It was hard to tell where the demon started and human left off. As the flood of nightmarishly foul creatures bore down their disgusting odor rose in waves. At any moment, the hideous things, neither living nor dead, would descend on the kingdom, carrying within them the hordes of murderous demons that spawned this abominable beast. The sounds that seemed to come from some other world, a dark and forsaken one, were getting closer and closer, louder and louder, rising into a screeching, terrifying nightmare. Every warrior stood firm in his place, Edawn's disheveled defenders hopefully readied themselves with little hesitation. Because of the incredible

longstanding tradition and sanctity commanded by the Noble
Kings, King Ozzdon knew he could have confidence in the
courage and loyalty of his men. But in reality, his men's allegiance
went beyond what he could have ever imagined. Every standing
man would have followed their beloved king through the very
gates of hell if he had asked them to.

"They are within the range of our catapults, my lord!" came
the call from Kondor.

"Loosen at will and make every discharge count," returned
the king. "Grind them into dust."

"Fire!" the catapult masters screamed their urgent orders,
followed by the sound of several warning pinging rings. Wood and
iron groaned, rattled, and shook as catapults launched their
massive stones. Seconds later, one at a time, sometimes two or
three at once, roared into action. "Reload!" shouted the catapult
masters.

The well trained crews operated their catapults like well
oiled mechanisms. Ponderous machinery was forced into
submission by their grumbling connecting pulleys. Each *click* and
clank of the ratchet and pawl was a pulsating throb that
transformed every working part into a mechanical warrior. Once
the trigger was set, groups of stone bearers reloaded their catapults.

"Target!" Aimers used their complex mathematics,
allowing for angle, and position of the ever approaching hordes.
Handlers spun their gears, turning the heavy, loaded, and primed
weapon quickly on their mounted turrets. They rechecked the
elevation for the maximum kill, then fired, bearing down on their
incoming targets. Every catapult on the unstable battlement was
blazing away, each one coming to life, existing only to unleash
yawning payload after payload.

There was a crackling noise in the sky as the enormous
stones whizzed into the air, trailed by the peculiar humming sound
they gave off as they screamed across the sky. At the end of their
arc, on impact, they bit into the earth of Zia, splattering soil
fountains everywhere, pelting the surrounding area with hailstorms
of rocks, dirt, and dust. Each stone on impact rolled end over end

squashing large numbers of onrushing Zomborges. They were hurtled back in parting paths of carnage as if they were bundles of dry twigs. Other pitiful beasts not caught in the direct path of the vaulting stones were sent toppling back, tumbling, screaming, arms flailing.

Wicked heaps of grossly battered flesh were swept aside like so much debris in the wake of each stone like two raging tides from a parting sea of death. Maimed creatures smashed beyond belief, continued to crawl forward, like broken, wind up toys, driven forward by some internal, perverted impulse that diseased their minds. They held, but one thought, one hunger—to advance and to kill. Thousands of others advanced uninterrupted, indifferent to life and death. They refused to divert their course, even when they saw a crushing stone coming straight at them, readily willing to accept doom without seeming to care. Mutilated Zomborges wrapped their arms tightly around themselves, trying to put their broken bodies back together. Others tried to push spilled guts back into place. As other advancing Zomborges simply stepped over the fallen.

As the undead reached the kingdom's walls, they clustered and climbed atop one another, using each other as scaling ladders, like interlinking ants on the march determined to traverse an embankment. They were an entanglement of confusion reaching for the upper walls edge with clawed hands. Archers rained thousands of arrows through arrow loops from above, pelting the climbing Zomborges like pincushions, but they were undeterred. No matter how many times they were pierced, they could not be stopped. Zandor stood his ground like an army of one in the thick of battle. In a loud voice, he commanded, "Choose your targets carefully. Do not waste one signal arrow." He took a deep breath and then released his next arrow. "How can one kill a thing that is not alive?" asked a frustrated archer.

Zandor's steel point shaft whistled as it sliced the air until it lodged itself through a Zomborge's forehead, severing his two optic nerves. Its cry of pain sounded like something between the squeal of a stuck swine and the howl of a dog. Unable to see, the

Zomborge turned on the nearest other attacking drones, to live out its diseased inner vision of psychotic destruction. Then with a dying breath, it lurched and heaved before collapsing. Noting this, Zandor hollered, "Aim for the head! A head wound is the only thing that will stop them."

The first attacking Zomborges to reach the top penetrated through the outer curtain wall only to find themselves unprotected. They found themselves exposed to the archer's hailing arrows, rapid lance launchers, and stones fired from stone throwers. Large stones were also dropped from atop the inner curtain wall and makeshift walkways. As the Zomborges scaled the propped up, high inner curtain walls, copper caldrons filled with boiling oil kept boiling. Their contents were then poured down from the machicolation openings in the floors between the corbels of the projecting parapets, onto the snarling Zomborge clusters below. Then archers ignited the hot oil with incendiary arrows shot from above, coated with asphalt and rosin and soaked in oil, sending the pillars of scaling besiegers bursting into flames. Kindling demons roared hideous screams that sounded like a large heard of squealing hyenas. The sight and sound were appalling. Moments later the tower of entangled climbing Zomborges crumbled like the ashes of a burnt roll of parchment paper.

From the projecting circular turrets atop the corner walls more mobile, but less powerful torsion mechanized throwing machines hailed projectiles of every description. Specialized artillery pullers easily reoriented on wheel mounts, to different angles, fired down repeatedly on the invaders. A storm of stones, lead balls, and long lances were effectively and accurately chucked down at the attackers. Hundreds fell, only to be replaced by hundreds more. In spite of everything, ultimately, the trenches were overrun, and the hastily erected barricades began to give way and were breached. First, hundreds of hands reached out over the compromised walls, clutching their wicked, spiked battle axes. Then came their hideous heads and then torsos, followed by the putrid smell of them that weighed heavily in the air. Thousands of

Zomborges poured across the gaping wounds of the damaged walls, like boiling water over the rim of a rumbling cauldron.

Zandor and Kondor stood their ground, ready to fight and die for their king, people, and kingdom. Quick witted and deadly, they stepped forward with their swords. On the northwestern wall, Zandor cut through two or three rotting bodies, slashing them out of existence with one sweeping swing, and kicked the next attacker back over the edge. As the next assailant rushed forward, he tried to read behind the lifeless, sunken eyes and only saw death and profound madness.

On the northeastern wall, Kondor swung his broad blade from side to side, ripping through exposed throats and sending decapitated heads tumbling. He slashed upwards with his sword, slicing a Zomborge from its jaw through its ugly face up to the top of its head. The two twin pillars devoted all they had to their duty of sending as many Zomborges to hell as they could. No matter how great their mounting numbers. They yet went on and on, slashing their way through the incredible tangle of Zomborges, driving them back for a moment, until they were standing ankle deep in rotting guts, yellowish blood, and other vile, rancid gore. Despite their best efforts, there did not seem to be any way of slowing, let alone stopping their onslaught.

Down in the courtyard below, at the onset, only a few Zomborges managed to force their way over the wall and through its gaps and were quickly dispatched. But then there were others, and more and more in increasing numbers from every corner. They multiplied until there were hundreds of them, thousands of them, pressing through the kingdom's improvised barricades and weakening defenses. It was the dawning of the undead. Defenders stared in utter bewilderment. Mounting disheartenment grew into shock, then terror.

The noise and confusion were mind boggling. Such pitiful screeches, and cries, certainly not humanlike, had never been heard in the land of Edawn. The Zomborges filled the battlements above and the courtyards below, pouring into the streets, ready to strike out at any living soul that stood before them. Relentlessly, they kept crowding in, with accelerating quickness, pouring in and advancing, unhindered by the barrage of arrows raining down on them. One of the severely wounded Zomborges sloughed putrid clumps of stinking flesh and globules of slimy fluids as it advanced laboriously forward. Like animated inhuman puppets whose stings dangled on the unseen hand of their demon puppeteers, they invaded the kingdom. There was only one thing for the Edawnian defense to do—kill their assailants before they were killed. But nothing could have prepared them for the blinding speed in which the Zomborge attack came. They struck with such momentum and brutal savagery that no one could have anticipated the bloodthirstiness of their invasion. The situation deteriorated quickly and moved irrevocably toward the abyss of annihilation. The world of terror was about to collide with the will of those that would not yield without a fight. Arrows fired at their heads at point blank range mowed down countless Zomborges. Before archers could launch another volley, they found themselves suddenly overrun and outnumbered by overwhelming odds. It was impossible to kill the invader faster than they were able to breach over the wall.

Despite carrying several arrows in its chest, the lead Zomborge, fearlessly stepped forward, teeth exposed, seemingly unimpaired. The abomination rushed forward stiffly, mechanically arching to slash, its wicked ax. Their axes swung and gashed through the Edawnian ranks severing arms and lopping off heads so fast that its razed edge sliced effortlessly through human flesh. Blood trailed the length of the ax blade and left its half mooned blood splash along its span.

The first of the Edawnian blood bath was spilled, and once the Zomborges smelled fresh blood, there was no way to control their diseased thirst for more. There came a gruesome war cry in unison from the demon hierarchy that resounded like something between the mighty roar of a ravenous grizzly bear and the hideous shrill of a half starved mongoose. The progression of the battle very quickly became one sided. The deteriorating situation unfolded very quickly, and before long, the defenders found themselves fully engaged in a cyclonic, rolling, whirling, hacking blade to blade, face to face confrontation.

The Zomborges were everywhere, devastating the defenders at every turn, attacking mercilessly, vehemently slashing gaping wounds with their wicked, tempered axes. The entire perimeter was lost in battle, soon there was mayhem, with screams and confusion everywhere. The Zomborges heightened their crazed killing frenzy, tearing through the Edawnian defenses like a mechanical thresher. Those that panicked and scattered were massacred; those unaccustomed to prolonged physical exertion and those overwhelmed by the violence fell next.

In the course of time and space, the Zomborges spilled into the kingdom's corridors, searching out the streets as they drove forth. Defenseless citizens were killed on sight by blood crazed mobs of Zomborges. Cries of death came from fanning pockets of blood bathed carnage that erupted from everywhere. A monstrous abode of insanity spewed from the depths of hell as men splattered with the blood of their friends witnessed their heads, legs, or arm severed from their bodies. Then they had to watch as they flopped around like decked fish, dying in agony. But still, they fought on, defending their ground with desperation, losing every step of the way, not knowing that the Zomborge storm of hostility was just beginning.

The king was frantically trying his best to coordinate the archers on the battlement when he saw that Kondor was all but buried in the heat of battle. The dilemma was unraveling all around as Zandor too was waging a losing fight against the deluge of Zomborges bearing down on him.

In just a few heartbeats, it seemed that Kondor would succumb to the relentless onslaught. The king struggled to strategize a counter to cope with the inevitable mounting tragedy. His main task as king was to direct the battle, to address all the elements of the puzzle. And to move all the right pieces to the right places at the right time. He looked out at the mass of confusion below him and knew that his defenses were quickly deteriorating into an unbelievable catastrophe. Seeing that his soldiers were losing courage as their losses mounted, he knew if he did not do something soon, all would be lost. But he was unable to develop a solution and did not know what he should do next.

Two
Sons of Darkness

baddawn, as if returning from a faraway place in his mind, eased his grip around Izz's throat. He set him on his own two feet and put his left arm around him in much the same manner a father would a son. And then, mercilessly and without the slightest warning, the king of defecation took his right hand with talons as long as butcher knives, and formed it into a claw. And, without compassion, plunged it deep into Izz's solar plexus. Izz felt the intense pain. His eyes widened as he tried to cry out but only shuddered. He looked down to see Abaddawn's hand buried into him past his wrist, but he saw no wound. He saw no blood. As if caught between two interlocking dimensions, fading in and out of material and spiritual reality.

The area in which Abaddawn pierced looked like a swirling, swarming, agitated nest of fireflies. In a voice that sounded like something between grinding gravel and the rumbling of distant thunder. With elongated and slurred words, Abaddawn, the emperor of desolation, spoke as his face wrinkling hideously, "Refusing my offer was the biggest mistake you could have ever made. Now you will see that the path you have chosen to tread has led you to ruin. In your very near future, I see only death and decay all around you. It is a pity that what is done cannot be undone, and what could have been can now never be." His breath embittered the already stale air as he exhaled a long winded sigh.

Izz squirmed, twisted, gasped, gagged, groaned, and regurgitated his own spiritual existence. After a pause to enjoy the pain he was inflicting on Izz as he dug his talons in deeper,

Abaddawn said, as if talking to himself, "I am going to enjoy hurting you. Hurting you more than you ever thought possible."

And this is where the physical and the spiritual twisted, blurring their differences. As Abaddawn continued to absorb the black energy channeled to him by the dark priests, his ability to merge into the material world increased. The evil power within him danced and burned as it grew. Slowly but surely, Abaddawn's power separated Izz's spiritual essence from his bodily existence. Izz metamorphosed closer and closer to becoming one of the living dead, where he would forever be lost in utter darkness. He faced eternity wasting away at the mercy of the lord of the truly dead. Abaddawn paused again as if to savor the moments to come. "Oh yes, you are truly about to feel more pain and horror than you ever thought possible." These are the words and the spirit in which the villainous sadist had uttered many times to flesh born men that had dared to cross his path.

Abaddawn then bit by bit forced his spiritual clawed hand slowly through Izz's soft, fleshy belly, just below the rib cage. He reached to wrap its talons around Izz's frantically beating heart. Izz's whole disembodied existence jerked as he threw himself backward, attempting to escape, but his soul was caught in death's embrace. Izz retorted defensively, trying to take a protective grip against Abaddawn's attack, trying to wrench his death grip away. But his hand seemed to disconnect, separating and hanging in a repeating pattern that echoed in the space between them in a transparent existence.

Suddenly everything became murky. The pain remained vivid and real, but the penetration was on a spiritual plane. What seemed so real was perhaps not real at all. Perchance an imagination, a hallucination, a vision, or was it actually happening in some disconnected dimension? Whatever, whenever, wherever, however, the crushing heaviness that held him was unmistakably, excruciatingly real.

Izz became a cornered animal, instinctively struggling to get loose from what seemed immaterial in the natural. He gasped at the thickening smell of his smoldering flesh, as he was engulfed, and swallowed up. As Izz was sapped of energy and spirit, he begged for pity, but the Prince of Misery's iron grip only clenched and squeezed the more. His overwhelming hold, imposing every bit of agony it could inflect without remorse, without mercy.

In the background in his shifting semiconscious shock, he could hear the demon hordes cheering their sadistic approval. Mixed with the rejoicing Izz heard Zuree's frantic pleas, "Izz, my dear Izz...what is happening to you. I am afraid for you."

All the while unable to cry out, Izz could feel his insides being violated like a butcher's icy fingers reaching into the chest of a lifeless animal, disemboweling its contorted intestines and probing its carcass for the heart. Izz let a little puff of air out of his mouth, and his jaw shuddered uncontrollably as he tried hopelessly to draw breath. He wanted nothing more than to drop to his knees on the ground, rollover, and curl into a fetal position. But instead, he was held suspended by the center of his soul in a fisted clasp that was killing Izz slowly. Suddenly with extreme ferocity, Abaddawn heartlessly tried to rip Izz's pounding heart from his chest with one wrenching jerk. But Izz's heart held firm, and instead, his spirit was pulled out of his body. He was removed farther from the real and drawn past the edge of the surreal. "Oh! Such a stout heart we have here," Abaddawn acknowledged.

Izz's physical body fell to the cave floor as if dead, while Izz's spiritual existence remained held in Abaddawn's clutches like a mouse impaled on the crushing teeth of a ravenous wolf. The sound of laughter resounded from the multitude that impatiently awaited Izz's demise. Their heightened ecstasy penetrated thought Izz's skin with every negative human emotion—anger, hatred, failure, and torment. Abaddawn slowly carried Izz from one world into the drifting world unseen by the eyes of most men. Zuree struggled to comprehend what was happening but could not bring herself to imagine the horrible scene that was unfolding just beyond her perception. Seeking comfort, she reached out to Izz, but could not find him. She recoiled and huddled back up against herself, drawing her knees tight to her body, her soul taking refuge in her own arms. After a shuttering moment, she found her voice and cried out, "Izz, where are you? And why will you not answer me?"

Like a rubber ball, Izz's consciousness bounced between his physical self and his spiritual self. One instance he was sprawled out on the ground, the next he was back in Abaddawn's grasp. In his state of fluctuating existence as if from a distant world, he heard Zuree's frenetic appeal. *How can I possibly tell her what is happening when I am not sure myself?* But after an awkward moment of dead silence, which seemed to extend forever, in a moment of madness, Izz finally flew out of his mind, whispering between cries of pain, "My love…my…love…the odds seem to be mounting against us." The audible panic in his voice shrilled in the air. "I am afraid I am going crazy!" he whimpered as he winced in pain. "I do not understand what is happening to me!" his voice lashed out with distress and confusion.

Zuree gritted her teeth, her lips moving in silent prayer. *Please, please, help us*, she pleaded with a god she was not sure even existed as her heart crumbled inside her.

No matter what as far as Zuree was concerned she was fated to Izz like an unbreakable fetter. Their destinies were bound and sealed forever as one resolve, one soul, and one heartbeat, even to the point of death. She could feel the vibrations in the air of Izz's body trembling in terror. Drawn by Izz's physical presence as he lay on the ground moaning and crying softly, Zuree crawled to his side. She gathered him in and clung on to his convulsing body. The plight of their deadly predicament only served to draw them closer together, despite the gulf that seemed to be expanding between them. Still horrified of what was happening but somehow less so, Zuree wailed, her heart pounded, and her nerves turned into knots as she held on to Izz for both their dear lives. Meanwhile, every moment that pasted Izz's spirit was carried farther along the egress. The pain was unbearable.

Now that the demon horde had recaptured their prize sacrifice their hideous laughter continued to fill the chasm. The sounds of unintelligible chants of glee and celebration as thousands upon thousands of demons anticipated the great alignment.

Approaching was the coming ritual sacrifice that would unbind them from their subterranean prison.

The misery on the surface of Zia continued to centralize and fortify the accursed powers of darkness. The host of wickedness overflowed with thoughts of only evil beyond belief. Their elation seemingly causing the stone walls and stone floor of the underworld to be set in motion like a beating heart that drew breath as if a universal evil had suddenly come to life. Shadows deepened, and the room darkened noticeably as Izz's soul drifted away into a more shocking nightmare from which he begged to wake. Izz could not feel his feet as the rest of his physical body began to tingle with numbness. With nowhere to turn, his thoughts focused on Zuree. In her arms, he found the refuge he had sought. It became his last bastion of defiance. At the same time, Izz's spirit resisted with all his will and devotion, as he careened crazily to free himself, fighting off wave after wave of pain and madness.

"Oh, oh…oh my…you are a fighter," Abaddawn said. "But why fight? Just let it go. It is all over for you. Why make it worse by struggling? Just let it happen. It will all be over in just a wink of an eye. Surrender your soul to me. You know as well as I, resistance is pointless. Izz of the Isles of Zollerzon, you will die like the fool that you are and have always been. No one can help you now. You entered here of your own free will. Only a fool would have rushed in where only angels themselves dare to tread. And now you must pay the price." Abaddawn's hysterical laughter spewed up, from deep within the scum and slime clogged bags of his respiratory tract. His belly laugh gargled up a black haze of nasty stale odor mixed with a spray of stench filled spittle as rotting mucus continuously dripped from the corners of his foul mouth.

As Zuree held Izz, she could feel the life being drained out of his body. His screams were raw, fractured, and freakish. Suddenly she could take no more, and thus she chose to rip the blindfold from her eyes, daring to defy the underworld gods, come what may. As her eyes adjusted, she focused on the macabre scene and saw two of Izz's personages—the one she held and the one dangling from Abaddawn's grasp. She was appalled to see what was happening to Izz. But rather than distance herself, she chose to unite herself to him. Before the full grim reality of what was happening could penetrate, her spirit leaped from within her bosom and instantly connected itself at Izz's disembodied side. What she had not chosen was the all consuming madness that soon overwhelmed her. Zuree was too overawed to refuse or resist the power of perception that pierced her eyes, like well driven spikes nailed through the windows of her soul. By way of her vision, falsehood immediately cast its sorcery over her. Zuree supernaturally joined Izz's nightmare and shared in the bitterness of his heart's agony. The contradicting conflict of the moment rushed in her head, churning and colliding as it pushed its way to the forefront of her consciousness. Almost instantly, her brain began to whirl with each fraction of the passing time, and her sensitivity to the physical tortures of pain intensified tenfold. Yet she refused to leave Izz's side, both physically and spiritually. And at that moment, the will of her soul once again reinforced its eternal commitment to Izz's soul. No matter what the consequences, there she would remain.

"How touching, the maiden has come to your rescue," Abaddawn taunted.

The legions of minions roared with laughter.

"Relent!" Abaddawn screamed at Izz. "Release your soul to me," Abaddawn demanded as he raised Izz to the roof to his arm's full length. He shook him violently and squeezed down on his celestial heart with all his strength, as he roared, "Relent!"

"Yoow!" Izz cried out in maddeningly, unbearable pain, scared to death beyond all horrors. His hands went to the side of his head, then back down on Abaddawn's piercing hand as he tried to double over. The compounded suffering was hundreds of times worse than any he had ever known. Somewhere between his struggling, choking, gagging, and cries for mercy, Izz sensed Zuree's presence and reinforced his resistance with nothing left to resist with.

"Such a stout heart," Abaddawn said with a slight, contemptuous smile. "That much is true. Well, we will have to soften it up a bit. Since there is still time, we will have to see how strong it is after my devoted brood is done with you." Despite what Izz had heard, he desperately clung to the glimmer of hope that seemed to vanish and then reappear like a glint of light that was about to go out. In the pitch darkness, faith like a guiding light came he knew not whence and went he knew not whither.

Discerning a small window of opportunity before the Great Conjunction's arrival, Abaddawn walked Izz to the dark side of the void, to the edge of a vast infinite drop off. Izz's eyes focused as he reluctantly looked down towards the fiery chaos below. It was the most frightening sight he had seen thus far. It was a place, from which no one had ever returned. He saw visions of plunging beyond the innermost deep, into an immersed ocean of human death, and his soul sank and was filled by the profoundness before him.

Within the kingdom's courtyard, Arius spun and kicked another Zomborge aside and then spotted a sudden shadow movement cast from behind him. Suddenly an ax blow hit him in the upper back. He gritted his teeth against the pain. The ax blade twisted against the tightly woven steel mesh and the thick layers of wool without penetrating. The impact knocked the air out of his lungs, yet he somehow managed to hang on to his trusty sword, as the blow sent him careening to the ground. Arius tied to get to his feet, but his legs would not respond. He screamed in rage, thinking the impact had severed his spine. He desperately batted away descending blades from the dense swarm whirling and shrieking above him.

From above, as the dilemma of defeat was rapidly unraveling all around him, the king saw Arius, his childhood friend, fall and thought him to be dead. All hell was breaking loose. As he began to shake from head to toe, a knot twisted in the center of his gut and his chilled blood ran backward in his veins. He stood atop the main keep, staring down at the carnage fixed in his vision in disbelieve, suddenly overwhelmed with the moment it seemed as if the air around him had suddenly darkened. He stumbled back, all in a tremble, fearing the others would see the fear gathering in his eyes that he could no longer suppress. His facial features contorted into a sweaty, hollow mask of confusion. He desperately struggled to regain his self control, trying to rethink so many things at once. He wondered, *What more can I do?* What did it matter? What did anything matter now? Then he murmured with gut wrenching remorse, "What is happening to me, and by what sinister power is it that the king has been reduced to a sniveling, spineless coward!"

Like a lashing, he felt a surge of self revulsion that shook him to the roots of his soul. He felt a stab of shame now, as sharp as the sting of a scorpion. All manner of disturbing things tore at his heart and came crashing over his head. He thought of how King Kozar and all his royal family had been skinned alive and fashioned as banners for Baddlock's invading army. He thought of how he had led thousands of Edawn's most dedicated youth to their death only to preserve the few. Ozzdon thought of the inconsolable wails of the mothers and wives of the dead. He felt his mind shrivel down to a tiny, tangled speck, where small nasty voices in his senses relentlessly pounded their way into his conscience.

All is lost. Your so called deliverer, Izz of Zollerzon, is as good as dead, and very soon, your only child, Zuree, will anoint my altar with her precious royal blood. Every dark doorway throughout the cosmos will then open, and every source of darkness will converge on Zia from where I will rule the universe forever. Relinquish the rights to your kingship over Zia now. Drop to your knees and grovel at my feet. Worship me, and I will allow you to be one of my personal bondservants for eternity, in my new kingdom.

In an effort to resist, the king let out a long mournful groan, and as he spun around, his eyes searched everywhere, wondering where the voice had come from. Sensing the king's mounting weakness, the voice sounded aloud, "You are as good as dead.

Your hide will soon be among the other trophies I have collected from this wretched, insignificant, little planet."

The thoughts seeded by the power of darkness was like a crafty, malignant virus that began spreading its infectious paralyzing venom of fear. While down below on the ground the slaughterous carnage continued unabated. The king's head drooped between his shoulders as his mind boiled over with thoughts of defeat. Sooner or later, they would have to come spewing out in one way or another. Attempting not to come completely unraveled under the unceasing demonic onslaught, the king drew his sword and turned to face his assailant. Seeing none, King Ozzdon's bewildered spirit seemed to drain from him like water into a bottomless chasm, pouring out deeper and deeper into a gash cut in endless space. His courage was failing him miserably. Tormented with self doubt and guilt, the king's resolve weakened, and his strength sagged, and deflated like a punctured wineskin. Then suddenly, the blackness faded and disappeared, leaving King Ozzdon convulsing in a panicked feeling shaken more in spirit than in body, disheartened, and full of gloom and doom. All he could do was stand there, sucking in one shuttering breath after another, like a sea captain going down with his ship.

Izz's spirit and body, though separated went simultaneously limp as Abaddawn dangled him over the fathomless abyss. Izz could see glimpses of his soul forever damned by a thousand tormentors in a fiery, bottomless pit of misery. He felt the despair that slowly became a part of the fate of the truly damned. Already the negative darkness of the deep began its frenzied anticipation as its lightlessness had already started to devour away at Izz's soul. As the last inkling of hope oozed from Izz and disappeared into the bleak blackness, the emperor of abomination eased the talons that entwined the heart of Izz's soul. Izz dropped off the edge of the underworld to a more profound depth.

Zuree screamed at the top of her lungs. With an outstretched hand, she reached out and stared wide eyed at the spot where Izz's soul fell. She was held suspended, by an unseen force, not allowed to throw herself over the edge, after Izz, as she wanted to. She saw Izz's soul fall away from her with his own outstretched hands reaching out to her. His face was frozen in rising hysteria, her face etched by the shock of horror that left both depleted and empty. Her spirit was drawn back and away against her will by Abaddawn's strong arm.

"No, no. My dear…dear precious one, the most important event of all is reserved for your special appointment." A long, lustful sigh seethed out through Abaddawn's jagged fangs. "The hour to forever rent a hole in the everlasting continuum of light will soon arrive, and you will be my chosen one forevermore. Thus, you may avoid eternal, agonizing affliction in exchange for an endless lifetime of servitude to me, your new master. You will beget me a child, and my wickedness will run in his veins that I might be born again with greater power. And together, my lovely, we will rule over the eternal night." The prince of demons gathered Zuree to himself, trembling all over with delight. "You can follow my destiny, or you can follow his." Zuree tried to pull herself back. "I would rather die a thousand deaths at Izz's side than spend one more moment at yours."

"Ooh, such fire! You will make an excellent host for my unborn children."

The face that measured her was warped, and far too hideous to look upon. Zuree felt herself shudder as she looked away. The words spoken by Abaddawn numbed her senses. She felt their heaviness grab and dig in like talons into her brain, like twisting daggers into her heart, like being flayed alive in her mind. Zuree could not see, she could not think; she felt as if she was dreaming the most frightening nightmare.

"I assure you, you will have plenty of time to change your mind, even if it does take a thousand years. But for now, all we need do is wait until the transformation of this antagonistic worm known as Izz is complete." As Abaddawn spoke, tar black fumes of noxious breath escaped from his filthy mouth and nostrils, straight into Zuree's face. The stench caused her to gag and her eyes to sting as she whimpered, "But…but I love Izz, and Izz alone!" she exclaimed with a quiver in her voice.

She was crying and uncontrollably outraged all at the same time. In the most sinister voice, Zuree ever heard Abaddawn addressed her again, "You really must execute me. There is a small matter I must personally attend to. I promise I will not be too long, and then we will be inseparable, I promise."

Zuree's mind spun and wobbled like a toy top coming to the end of its spin. Everything began to whirl around her, too fast, and all at once. Zuree lost control of herself and dropped to her hands and knees. In nearly pitch black darkness, she found Izz's hollow, spiritless body, fell on it and wept bitterly. She lowered her ear and listened to the fading heartbeats of the master of her love. Izz's body suddenly convulsed violently, his pupils dilated. Then his eyeballs eddied, and his eyelids began to flutter.

As Abaddawn prepared to depart, to concentrate on Izz's demise, he turned briefly and said, "Yes…yes, it will not be long now. Sons of everlasting darkness, prepare the altar for our special offering," he called to his minions. "Prepare for eternal glory. Our legions shall be waiting. They shall soon pour out of their imprisonment like a raging storm, and all shall tremble at our majesty." Again a long black blast of foul stench hissed out of Abaddawn's cesspit of a fang filled mouth as he chuckled and shook with his demented laughter then turned and mutated into the darkness.

Zuree could feel the evil presence that had melted into the shadows all around her, receding and leaving her alone in her solitary world for the time being. Her spirit suddenly felt abandoned and discarded as Izz's spiritual existence continued to fall away. His presence faded toward the point of no return, to a place that led to eternal damnation in all directions. Their separation was like the clanging of an impenetrable gate setting her apart forever from the only man she ever loved. Her face was frozen in dust and etched by anguish as she stared toward the spot she last saw Izz's spirit disappear over the edge of oblivion. The only movement was her trembling lips that twitched in tremors of rising shock from the hysteria that threatened to drive her own soul over the edge of insanity. The gathering of demons began to break up, knowing that Zuree would never leave Izz's side. The demon hordes receded more rooted into the darkness, to watch over her in silence, from the darkest shadows.

Soon the Great Conjunction would be in full bloom. Soon Izz would be wholly overcome, unable to protect Zuree with his frivolous love. Then Abaddawn, the master of debauchery, would have total control over the chosen bloodline without interference; and then it would be the beginning of the end of everything as it was, as it would be. The beginning of the reign of darkness and the end of man. Abaddawn, the angel of endless death, would spare no one—no, not one—for he hated man more than any other creature because man had been appointed to become heirs to everything he once controlled before the great fall.

Far too exhausted for reason, Zuree stared out spellbound in terrifying suspense, sensing the presence of the evil hordes hidden in the shadows just beyond her vision. Aware that she was being watched, she tried to cry softly, which was hard to do when her painful emotions were climbing all over themselves. Tears wanted to pour out of her like a cascading flood from a broken levee. She rocked Izz in her arms, whispering over and over again, "Oh, Izz, come back to me. Come back, come back!"

As Izz continued to fall—endlessly as it would seem—he felt himself sucked down across a spaceless boundary. He seemed to fall from one world to another, and yet another, through the sub-universe of strange levels deep within a ghost haunted verge. His spirit's smoldering glow began to waver as it plunged through a stagnated swirl of shadows whose limited continuance existed only in the mind. As he fell, it was as though, he was evaporating through the darkness, breaching the barriers of all reality itself, just as if, he had never existed. As Izz fell through the depths, in the abysmal distance below, he could make out a dazzling pit of molten fire. Its heat waves made his nonphysical flesh burst into flames and caused his supernal blood to seethe. Izz was caught in a lost dimension within the supernatural—falling, spinning, and tumbling in midair where time and space twisted. He fell, and fell through a jagged rift beyond mid Zia. An oppressive, convicting finality suddenly surged through Izz's mind as he plunged forever toward nowhere.

Is this how it ends? Was the only thought he could force through his mind as he fell.

In the palace, Ammiz was as ever elbow deep in gore. Outside the monstrous clash between the dead and the living raged on. The young trooper he was working on was contorted in pain. He was held down while Ammiz probed an entry wound with his surgical blade in search of pieces of jagged steel or broken stone chards. The young man screamed in great throbbing waves of excruciating pain, which periodically, momentarily eased him out of consciousness. It was necessary to make sure the wound was clean. It was a crude, agonizing procedure that caused unsafe blood loss that further weakened the patient. The next casualty brought to the healing table before Ammiz was wailing between choked breaths, and ceaselessly bemoaning sobs wrenched from deep within, not wishing to die. One look at the torn muscles and ripped chest tendons told Ammiz that there was no point; nothing could be done for him. His heart was exposed and could be seen frantically pumping out the juices of life. Yet Ammiz refused to give up on anyone. Therefore, he set his broken bones, cleaned and bound the wound, trying his best to save the young man's life by any means in his power. The mortally wounded warrior was put to sleep with powerful narcotics, and set next to the dead and dying. The dead were quickly taken to the smelters and thrown into the fires as soon as their torment was over.

Just as Ammiz had finished sealing the last of the horsetail stitches to the horrid gash in the last patient, his attention was directed toward the windows on the West wall. Above him, the lengthening shadows marked the approach of dusk. Soon the red haze of twilight would surrender to the deepening somber shades of the coming night. Complete darkness would shroud the land, and the Zomborges would be in their perfect element and most deadly, and the kingdom at its most vulnerable.

Unexpectedly, all at once, through the barred openings on the opposite windowed wall, an eerie light began to pour in and diffuse itself throughout the entire palace. Alarmed, at first, Ammiz thought the stronghold was ablaze. But he soon realized as Zia continued its rotation, that the row of soft silvery orbs was, at last, nearing their appointed reunion. At the same time. The Ziaian sun was reaching toward the other end of the world. At the same time, the gathering conjunction was rising over the eastern horizon on the other end. Its birthing brightness dispersed the darkness as if a new sun was rising. As the strange light crept across the wall, it cast weird florescent shadows along its path. Without thinking, Ammiz meticulously wiped the blood that clung to his hands like glue with an already bloodstained rag. Drawn to the light, he made his way through the mist of the agony that surrounded him. He walked past the many lives that were slipping into eternal sleep, and toward the palace's upper exit door. Ammiz was tired, and his thoughts seemed to come slowly. Among the wounded, grown men shrieked and cried; some reached out to him, begging to be put out of their misery. As Ammiz climbed the stairwell that led to the upper keep, the sounds of battle could now be heard that its pinnacle throughout the kingdom below. Still wiping the blood from between his fingers, he continued up the keep's stone stairs. The sounds of battle that raged outside intensified with every step he took. Suddenly a strange breathless hush seemed to fall over the keep as though death itself was gasping. All the while, the gleaming eventide's eerie new dawn lightened the eastern sky. The room by now was saturated through every open window with the soft silvery blue glow from the approaching conjunction. Those attending the wounded stared in silence with unnaturally wide eyes as the light glowed brighter and brighter.

The Seeker's thoughts suddenly turned to Izz. Ammiz unexpectedly saw a mythic vision of fiery ruination rearing up in his mind. He saw a mental image of Izz's scorched white bones lying in a bottomless pit. He wondered how any man would be able to withstand such a hideous assault of evil. He was more frightened than ever for Izz. He took a moment to regather himself, sorting images from between the real and the unreal. Somehow, he knew that Izz was out there somewhere, still alive and fighting. But more than anything, he knew that his time was running out. He wished with all his heart that there was some way he could help him. The old man whispered to himself as if he was offering up a prayer, "Whatever happens, you must not give up hope, my son." Denouncing his doubts, Ammiz thought of how Izz had been in more circumstances beyond the bounds of impossibility than any other person in Zia had ever been. And he had always managed to come out on the other side. Then he turned his attention to an unseen Power and whispered, "Creator of all things, you are our only hope. Be with the young seeker and guide his path."

Black robed and hooded, Baddlock sat atop of Nightmare, with his nose thrust high into the air, smiling hauntingly, as if all was as it should be. He squinted through the eyepiece of the long eye he had his sticky fingered goons steal from Ammiz's library. Baddlock studied the emerging bright points that appeared like distant stars shining on the edge of Zia. As he stared at the distant pageant in the eastern skies, he was able to discern that they were giant luminous globular spheres. He astutely observed the merging celestial bodies, flooding the landscape with their ominous light, filtering in tiny shafts from the high, faraway ceiling of the vast astronomical sky. The conjurer of lawlessness knew that the long anticipated moment, when the universe would tumble, and cascade itself into eternal chaos, was quickly approaching. His dark priests by now should have been making their way down into the labyrinth where the princess would be awaiting her appointed time. The ultimate objective would soon be at hand. When time and space would be distorted, that he might inherit all the powers of darkness to rule over Zia as he willed.

The Norticlan masses that had already begun building their campfires stood there frozen in fear and confusion under the untimely dawning. All eyes were glued to the mysterious, perplexing, golden orbs. The Norticlanders were disciples of the oldest forms of sun worship, offering human sacrifices regularly as a form of homage, accounting for many of those that had vanished off the face of Zia without a trace. The barbarians looked upon the Wicked Warlock Wizard, who was unmoved. They marveled in awe that he could have predicted the exact timing of the celestial phenomena. And they worshiped his majesty, as the coming conjunction seemed to cast a deific aura around him. His revelation could only mean one thing: Baddlock had to be a god as he claimed to be.

The Wicked Warlock Wizard and his crony Tigbone amused themselves with an almost childish pleasure at the impending doom of the center of the Xylenian Empire. Baddlock was tumbling a gold coin through long, brittle twig like fingers. "Soon my Zomborge pets will weaken the resolve of the Edawnian will and Edawn and all its treasures will be ours for the taking. The world will soon fall at our feet. It is as good as history," he said with a pompous smile. "We are the new masters now." All the worst in Baddlock's nature was drawn to the surface as his face contorted into a demonic grin. He was an unfeeling monster, born under an evil star, doomed from his birth to become the evil diseased mind that he now was.

Tigbone focused on the gold coin as it tumbled end over end, glistening in the rays of the approaching conjunction. Baddlock took the golden coin and flung it high in the air toward Tigbone and said with a cynical twist to his lips, "We are about to become richer than we have ever dreamed possible."

The pinhead, bumbling oaf reach his grubby little hand high into the air as he laughed with glee. He made a twanging sound much like that of an untuned stringed instrument in the hands of an unskilled learner. The coin flicked wildly in his gaze as his eyes darted around like a starving rat's stare into a cheese shop. His bony hand, with its dirty, bitten fingernails snatched the coin in midair, which instantly vanished into the inner pocket of his faded and moth eaten robe. Tigbone was thrilled by the gesture. Not exactly an act of love, but it was as close as Baddlock had ever come to embracing Tigbone for his lifetime of servitude. The natural born simpleton brought his two greedy hands together and rubbed one over the other as if attuned to the evil ticking within the psychopathic mindset of his master. For once, his overlord was not displeased with him.

Having reached the top of the keep, the seer stepped out onto its upper deck. The first thing Ammiz observed as he stared into the distance was that lights, here and there, beginning to glow against the dimly lit landscape. They were Norticlan campfires that had been lit to counter the long coming night of the northern hillside. Ammiz felt sweat trickle down the back of his neck, which turned cold against his skin as he emerged into the open air. As Zia rolled around on its eternal path, the last vestiges of the sun disappeared beyond the kingdom's domain. Yet the eastern skies remained luminous, glowing with a supernatural light of the approaching conjunction. There was an uneasiness about it, as amazing as it was terrifying.

Ammiz brought his eyes into focus. On the eastern horizon, each planet's reflected light was like a miniature sun, ominously visible, as they rose higher over the curve of Zia. As they rose over the horizon, they appearing to slightly wobble while they shimmered in Zia's atmosphere. All seven planets were in the same hemisphere, and their globes could now already be seen with the naked eye, moving along their predestined treks. The new light source set in the cosmic clock had crossed across trillions of miles of empty space, into Zia's orbit, gradually lighting up its night sky. The day of days that had been on every stargazer's mind had finally arrived in all its mystic splendor.

Izz could not tell how long or how far he had been falling because the physical forces of gravity and the laws of time had become more and more distorted the deeper he fell. He felt himself being forcefully drawn down through the eons. Down he fell into a realm of ancient darkness before time, where two universes straddled the other, in a sphere where one vortex energy system interacting with another. He finally landed with a tremendous thud. He impacted with such force that it sent shock waves of shrilling pain pulsating with convolution after convolution of escalating agony throughout every crushed nerve ending in him.

Izz lay there stunned, dwindling from one reality into another, shifting from the physical above to his spiritual presence below and back and forth repeatedly. He lay there like a fallen angel with two broken wings, not knowing what, where, or when. His eyes rolled back into his skull and slipped into oblivion. He knew not how long he had remained there, in his own spiritual carnage, gnarled into a tangled knot on what seemed like a slime covered stone floor. The only thing he thought he was sure of was that he had reached the end of his fall. The next thing he became aware of was that what appeared to be a chamber was overflowing with tendrils of sulfurous fumes that drifted over him to mingle with the sickening breath of death. Izz had fallen into a deeper, hotter fiery abyss, closer to the center of the planet, into an existence beyond the physical. His hair was crackling, and the surface of his skin was smoldering. His next fractured thought was that he appeared not to be dead. He was alive, but just barely, like a phantom flickering in and out of the world of the dead. He dimly wondered at what was happening, where he was, and why he was there; but the answer was a chasm too inconceivable to bridge. His stunned spirit endured there, separated from his body, in a spacious, echoing cesspit.

Izz suddenly came more awake and found that he could not move. He could not turn his head one way or another. He could not stretch, twist, or change positions to relieve his stiffening aches and agonizing pain. His heart was hammering erratically, his temples were throbbing, and his breath came in short and jagged gasps. His muddled brain cast a confused gaze around, his eyes darting up, down, to one side and then the other. The light given off by the raging inferno pit that surrounded him in the ebon chamber was immediately absorbed up by a different kind of twilight that lined the outer edges of the abyssal alcove. Darkness as thick and as black as a coal bin on a charred darkened nightmare, was as dark as dark could get. Other than being able to rotate his eyes, breathing was about the only other thing Izz could still do. However, that too, he had trouble doing. There was the ever familiar disgusting stench all through the bleak realm nearly too thick to inhale. Every breath he thought he was breathing was asphyxiating. Flames fluttered and flickered the whole time wildly, leaping and jumping around as if engaged in a battle between the murkiness and the light. It was within that witching hour that sparse traces of light seemed to be doing their best to hide from the darkness. The fire was supernatural as well as the gloom that fed upon it but could still be seen against the enveloping blackest blackness. Izz lay there drawing in the stagnant, age old atmosphere into his lungs. It felt as if his chest were crushed, collapsed, and splattered beneath him upon the fiery surface he lay on. He had to stay in the same position, unable to move, not even able to wipe the blood, sweat, or tears from his smoke rimmed eyes. The rotting ground underneath him was jagged, pointy, and seemed to be moving beneath his entire length. Reluctant to focus his eyes, Izz cringed at the thought of what he might see. When he finally did slowly focus, he saw, oversized spiders, larvae, and snakelike creatures not found on Zia. The armies of insect like scum eaters seemed to be gorging themselves on the slime covered floor before his eyes. He discovered that from what he could see that he had landed in a primordial black chasm surrounded by rising tides of extreme heat. Heat that was seemingly fueled by the wicked unbroken hate that appeared to infuse everything. He was surrounded by an unlimited evil presence and an absolute absence of compassion.

Over the crackle of the flames, Izz thought he heard the faint sound of wailing throbs in the whirlwind of rising heat. With the fiercest power of thought, Izz forced himself to raise his head with a moan. He saw a labyrinth of passages and champers all around him. Then his vision started to blur, and he lowered his face back into the splattered blood and dust. It was the gloominess of unnatural realms imaginable. In shock, he stared into the illuminated darkness, over the wormy, withering, maggot ridden expanse, trying to comprehend the incomprehensible.

Apart from the impact, Izz initially felt no pain. But even despite the fact that he was separated from his physical half, he would soon learn that all of his senses would prove to be most assuredly alive. As truly alive as if he had been in his real physical body—in fact, more real. Then all at once, it happened: He was hit with an excruciating surge of acutely sharp pain. He could suddenly feel the intense, unbearable burning sensation that engulfed him and penetrated his soul thoroughly. The burning floor was so sizzling hot that Izz felt like a lamb on a grill being broiled alive. He looked down upon himself and saw that everything was twisted and deformed and grotesquely out of symmetry. It looked as if the fall had fragmented his discarnate body into thousands of broken pieces held together by only the thinnest strips of tendons and ligaments. His internal organs were ruptured. His ribs were all broken, and it felt as if the entire inside of his chest cavity was covered with lacerated goosebumps. As he gurgled and coughed up what tasted like blood, the odors of death swirling around him, making it chokingly oppressive to breathe. The fumaroles gases that drifted from the surface he lay on suddenly threw Izz into a coughing fit that brought up blubbery globules of phlegm from his scorched lungs. Feeble, rickety, one step away from eternal death, his mind unraveled, and his soul descended with misery. It was not just his imagination. Izz wished it were only an illusionary figment fabricated only in his mind, but he was positive now that it was not. He cried out, as the unthinkable possibility that it might all be too real invaded his fractured state of oscillating consciousness. Everything seemed detached, with no connection with objective reality. Izz ultimately found himself wishing the cave ceiling would tumble down and finish him off.

Izz desperately tried to find order out of the multidimensional distorter. As he searched for the meaning projected into his mind, a repeated sound surfaced. The sound was recognizably human. The resonance droned within depths his inner ear. of his head as if a multitude of souls were weeping, groaning, and crying out an utter warning of choked anguish. "Run, run, and do not look back!" The voices seemed to bring Izz fully awake to hear a chorus of soft whining whimpers of unmitigated regret mixed with the gruesome sounds of sliding chains and the grinding of metal ports opening and shutting. And their depression and oppression were above all so, so heavily laden with hopelessness. Suddenly, a shout from within the midst of numberless souls packed tight into the darkness, uttered out an ominous warning, "Do not enter here. There is no way out, no escape. If you enter here, you will never leave. Escape while you can, if you can!"

Ominous silence ensued. Moments later, there came another shout, which sounded with a different voice: "Izz of the Isles of Zollerzon, welcome to your eternal kingdom of doom." Laughter from the multitude of thousands, of thousands, of thousands of demonic voices reverberated against the cave walls and ceiling.

As Izz teetered there between consciousness and unconsciousness, he was unable to separate himself from the real and the unreal. The continuous laughter like that of Abaddawn's sounded in his hearing and thundered in his head. Izz's heart imploded when he heard the words of the archfiend raining down condemnation upon his mind: "You are ever an ignorant fool! You could have held the world of Zia in the palm of your hand, reaped untold pleasures, riches, and honor. Do you realize how many men would have gladly changed places with you? Any of them would have given up their wretched, meaningless souls in exchange for anything the fresh could ever desire? And now you will gain only the worst of torments."

Izz's eyes began to grow more accustomed to the darkness. They darted from side to side. He could see by the reflections of the black lit fires a vision emerging out of the endless apparitions, drifting along the edges of the foggy vapors. There were long darker than dark crevices among fuming flames that crackled almost invisibly against the expanse of space in the background. Everywhere he looked, Izz saw monotonous galleries of baffling untold interlocking tunnels full of small hidden rifts. It was a matrix of systems, within a black maze of dead ends with no way out. From the darkest shadows, he could hear, as if from a distant world, the never ending, wailing screams of inconsolable hopelessness. In the deepest, black, prison like an endless void, Izz could see through the haze an infinite multitude of lost souls kept behind bars and gates, against their will, bound to the flames with unseen chains. They howled, gnashed their teeth, and chewed on their tongues, attempting to somehow, rechannel their maddening pain. The absolute supernatural fires, ignited by the wrath of an unseen, punishing force, magnified the terrible suffering, of those condemned for their unbridled wickedness. Part of the torture was the ever present, terrible, suffocating smell of sulfur in and air like rotting rubbish forever burning. Its stench was so revolting that it could have made even a maggots gag.

Three
The Rift

Ammiz's gaze was fixed to the heavens, and as he shaded his eye against the ever increasing brightness of the coming conjunction, his face filled with astonishment. As he continued to stare in utter amazement at the ever illuminating skies, his attention abruptly shifted to the myriad of thunderous, clashing sounds of battle. Animal like screeching squawks mixed with sudden screams of terror, that were seemingly getting louder and louder, coming closer and closer. He turned toward the sound of the intensifying battle against the relentless attack of the undead Zomborges.

As the seer's gaze slid across the keep's upper deck, his eyes caught something out of place. His redirected attention was suddenly locked upon what looked uncharacteristically like the king. Ammiz's eyes narrowed, as he gave Ozzdon an odd look, unable to believe what he saw. He drew closer for a better look and stood there, staring with wide, disbelieving eyes. The Emperor of Zia, the noblest king of kings, the ruler of the mightiest dominion on Zia, seemed helpless to overcome an assault that appeared to be coming from within his mind. He looked graver, paler than Ammiz had ever seen him. He looked beyond dejected as if there was too much internal anguish in his heart to carry on. The Seeker could feel the king's spirit fading away within him. Ammiz slowly approached the king and asked, "Are you well, Your Majesty?"

The king seemed confounded. Weary lines showed deep on his face. Ammiz looked as if he were an apparition from a dream, and Ozzdon could not figure out what he was doing standing there in the flesh as if a real person. The king did not stir; he remained hunched over, stricken and overwhelmed by the total turmoil of the moment. Realizing he had been discovered, he only slipped into a deeper state of dejection. His noble resolve seemed orphaned, his courage lopped away, left floundering in a sea of stagnant confusion.

Below Ammiz heard no commands from the generals. He realized that without the king's leadership, those still able to fight had disintegrated into no more than jumbled mobs, with no mind, no heart, and no hope. A sudden, restless wind with the power and fury of a dust devil gusted up from the heated attack below, seemingly fanning the growing frantic and chaotic flames of out of control rage. The strange wake, laden with the harsh smell of death, whirled past Ammiz and the king, scattering dust and pulverized debris, stirring up something infinitely wicked from the deepest bowels of hell on its breath.

Lost in an illusionary continuation Izz desperately searched for a tolerable point to anchor his mind from where he could hold on to his sanity. Izz could feel himself trembling uncontrollably as he did his best to sort the illusionary from reality. Ghostly images emerged from the receded rolling fog and then disappeared. The underworld had become an ever increasingly frightening nightmare, and Izz's only bastion of sanity over and over again had been denial. The things he smelled, heard, and saw could not be true. He reasoned that it would be far better not to attempt to give meaning to the waking nightmare that surpassed all his understanding and just wake out of it when it had run its course. He shut his eyes as tight as he could, but he found whether his eyes were open or closed made no difference. Izz could see everything as if from different angles from within and without. From where he lay there crumpled up, twisted and jerking spasmodically against the rocks like a midnight phantom, he could see in every detail the multitudes of trapped souls in the darkness. The pitiful look in their bulging eyes was filled with absolute out of their mind distress and everlasting damnation. The suffering of these souls was so awful that Izz could feel their pain, on top of his own, everywhere, haunting him, etched in his mind forever.

The hopelessly lost that filled the underground abysses of unthinkable cruelty were the vilest of the condemned, like the likes of the dark priests that had died in the service of wickedness. They were ministers of evil that had been promised anything and everything only to discover upon their earthly death that instead they had been denounced to a greater damnation. Forever to inhabit the gloomiest reaches of the underworld, sentenced to die a thousand deaths multiplied by thousands of thousands of times. Izz could tell by the profoundness of their agonized cries and moans of torment that they could acutely feel the fire, the worms, the pain, and the bottomless hopelessness that imprisoned them. They were naked, their hair matted and their eyes were dull, filled with emptiness. The surreal scene filled Izz's soul with fear driven grief that was so enormous no words could define it. Never had Izz seen such a glut of misery that defied belief, not even in the lake of fire. Horrible visions of untold terror fogged up his thoughts and faded out into the blackness. He thought his eyes and ears had to be somehow bewitching him. But when he tried to blink the images away, ultimately he concluded that it was not a delusion. Izz's mind was brought into focus on individual figures lost within the congested crowds and saw that they were insatiably inflicting rebuke upon their very selves.

As if their self punishment offered them some sense of solace, some sense of escape from the agony that overwhelmed them. It seemed as if it was a means of venting enormous amounts of pain that they were unable to cope with. He saw one personage straining against imaginary manacle and leg irons that held the condemned's hands and feet, voraciously biting its teeth through its lips. Its tongue was gone as well as bite sized pieces that were eaten from its entire naked body. Another picked obsessively at the orifices of its naked body and packed its gaping wounds with its own excrement. A different individual was throwing ashes in its eyes, repeatedly, it's burning, bloodshot, swollen eyes never blinking. Another lost soul pulverized its foot, already soaked into a bloody pulp, pounded away repeatedly with a heavy stone. Each time it brought the stone down hard against its toes, the sound of sopping bread being slapped against a rock wall thudded out. Still, another scratched continuously at a face that was already shredded to pieces. And another drove rock shards into its ghostly flesh until there seemed not to be one single place to insert another. Throughout their self mutilation, their dull, frozen faces never expressed the extent of their self destruction. All the while, the cries of the living dead were unyielding. Some wailed over the blood stained on their hands and their abuses against the most innocent members of society. They wrung their hands until their skin was blistered and piling. Those that had tortured other people without a shred of mercy, those that accepted dark, forbidden knowledge, those that lived a life of abomination, and those that took their own lives all cried out, "Cursed mind!" Others cursed their tongues, their eyes, their hearts, whatever the cause of their downfall. And yet others wailed for their thefts, how they had preyed upon the poorest and most vulnerable of people. They had allowed themselves to become covetous souls that sold their souls for gain, imitating selfish dogs, which could never have enough. And they asked themselves, "Where are our riches now?"

Mass murders, haters, child predators, rapists, blasphemers, those that led the innocent astray—they all knew there was no escape, no reprieve from the flames, and that their loss was permanent. Desperately, they still hoped against hopelessness as they cried out for mercy, and Izz could hear them calling out to him as if from a distant universe. "Help!" a sound wave echoed faintly. "Help me!"

The next wave repeated, "Help me! Help me! Help me! Please, please, please!" another wave chanted.

Even so in their disheartened wretchedness, they turned and lashed out at Izz. "We are here to pay the price for our twisted hearts cursed with the inability to love. We suffer for our indulgence in the forbidden pleasures that we refused to deny ourselves, despite our better judgment. But you, you, Izz of the Isles of Zollerzon, are here of your own accord, for the sake of love, no less. But where has that gotten you? You are the grandest idiot among all idiots! And now it is too late. Too late!" With that said, the lost souls shook their fists at Izz and cursed him profusely, with unmentionable blasphemies. All the while from the background came a constant barrage of filthy gibberish, constant mocking, and sexual insinuations.

Out of the darkness, the sound of chains dragging and rattling and scraping filled the chamber. There were noises of victims being gathered and pulled along as they dug their heels in and screamed at the top of their lungs, "It is not my turn! *No! No! Not again!* It is not my turn!" An unspeakable evil carried away the lost soul that cried out with hysterical fear and despair.

Volcanic mounds erupted simultaneously, and in the flickers of flames, Izz could see the expressions on the faces of the damned. The affliction, the resentment, and the anguish were furrowed deep in their expressions. Men or women he could not tell shrieked in terror. None of it made any sense. But one thing was evident throughout the stark misery. Izz had surpassed the threshold of his ability to cope with the madness and pain raging all around him. There was an actual place deep in the bowels of Zia, a vast desolate wasteland, a place inhabited by shadows. It was a complex asylum of weeping screams, and mournful misgivings, and never ending wails. And he was stuck right dab in the middle of its trial by fire.

Izz tried not to think about anything anymore, still hoping that somehow he could just wake up. But it was too vivid, too real, and there would be no waking from this nightmare. Instead, he found himself wide awake to a plague of persecution of every fear he had ever imagined. And just when Izz managed to convince himself that his situation could not possibly get any more bizarre, in the next moment, all at once, demons of all kinds—hundreds of thousands, perhaps millions of evil spirits burst out in a roar of gleeful laughter.

Izz could feel in his aching bones something intensely negative coming closer and closer. The space that already felt like an oven started to feel increasingly hotter. The escalating heat created blast furnace winds that began to roar. But even more ominous was the sound of amplifying screams, wailing, and gnashing of teeth. Then Izz heard a feminine voice crying out hopelessly to the evil powers that were entering the forsaken chamber. Earnestly, the voice pleaded with desperate fervor, "Have I not been here long enough to pay for the errors of my ways? My affliction is much more than I can endure. Please, let me out, for mercy's sake!" The outline shook with a torrent of sobs, so profound that Izz could feel her great suffering pierce his heart and mind with pity and grief.

Suddenly a howling torrent of pathetic wails shuddered the walls. No words could describe the bone chilling cries of ever mounting terror. And all the evil in the underworld seemed at that moment was about to crash down on him. All the while, Izz tried with all his will to move, to crawl into the shadows, and hide, anything to reduce the level of his soaring fear. His mind was seized up in such turmoil that he could hardly focus on the thought of escape. He forced his head up and drove his mutilated, twisted form forward. He slid across the jagged, slime covered rocks, but after just a few inches, he was so out of breath that he collapsed back down, totally exhausted. He wanted to escape somehow, but as he desperately attempted to crawl out, he only found himself hopelessly crawling deeper back into the bottomless pit that was his mind.

Suddenly reptilian like creatures, neither human nor animal, filled with complete loathing, gathered as they encroached themselves restlessly around Izz throughout the entire subterranean chamber. Were they his tormentors, executioners? Every scourge of the deep quietly whimpered as they moved in closer as if Izz's very presence had somehow heightened their eternal damnation. But their pitiful self condemnation soon became secondary to the moment that was fast approaching its climax. Izz found himself flanked on all sides by assassins everywhere, packed in tight, focusing on him. There was no way to fight back. The demons swarmed and clustered, closing in all around him like vile, angry, stinging hornets. Suddenly a slimy, black, dripping foot, like that of a buzzard's claw ground his face hard to the stone floor. He was held fast as another caught him in the chest with a brutal blow that ripped out a chunk of intangible flesh. Another kicked him viciously in the ribs, knocking the breath from him as he groaned, doubled over, and tried to roll away. Another claw like foot caught him in the crotch and made him wail. A heavy knee smashed into his back, pinning him down so hard he thought his ribs and spine would break. Demons that held the highest rank inflicted Izz with the wretchedness of their punishments. All the while frothing lesser demons leaned in closer with their leering yellow eyes They anxiously laying in wait, rotating in tight circles, ready with the anticipation of blows they longed to contribute to Izz's misery. Inky finger like tendrils reached out for him and tugged at him with razor like talons, as others kicked, tossed, and slammed him around for sport.

Out of nowhere, a strong bony hand caught Izz and raised him—his spiritual presence lifted effortlessly into the air—and thrown forcefully against the rock wall with a devastating impact. He heard his bones crack and felt them break as he collapsed to the floor in a heap. Another spirit clamped onto Izz's back, tearing his phantom flesh open, as it hurled him across the chamber. A reeking, cankerous orgy of freakish ghouls threw their heads back and broke out into a burst of raucous laughter that sounded like a flock of squabbling crows. For a long while, the savagely bizarre assault persisted with no mercy whatsoever. The brutal beating that seemed would never end was horrific. Anyone that was not there to see it could ever imagine how terrible it truly was. Izz was almost invisible under the clawing, hissing, swarming attack as evil spirits exploded from every corner to batter Izz like raging bulls to a red rag. They hammered the roots of his being until their blows ripped him to pieces.

Lost souls behind smoldering fires observed the shadowy mass in front of them as they beat Izz to a bloody pulp. They were thankful for once that it was not one of them at the receiving end of the relentless assault. From every nook of the room, countless depraved spirits of the deep howled with blood thirst delight as they pressed into the middle of the nightmarish onslaught. The demon hordes filled the air with incessant desecrations, screeching with pleasure as they sensed the dying of Izz's soul.

Izz was lifted from the ground where he had been battered beyond recognition; his arms were placed over the necks of two hideous creatures. Although he had lost all sensation, Izz had suddenly realized that he was being moved through the darkness. He sensed he was being victoriously paraded along a dark, descending passage. And no matter how he strained his inner eye, he could see only shadows and shrouded shades.

All at once, his perception of pain returned to him with a vengeance. The fingernails of the hands that reached across Izz's back dug into his spiritual presence like the cruel tendrils of a monstrous stinging vine. Izz was carried along the nasty cave floor, with his feet dragging behind him. As Izz was yanked along the gauntlet, the multitude of demons moved aside and growled at him, reechoing with frenzied cries of hatred as Izz was dragged past them. The multitude of lost souls frantically cowered back into the darkest shadows against the cynical abuse they knew was coming. They cringed against the terrible and indescribable concentration of suffering they all periodically had to endure, and it chilled them to the core. The lower he was taken, the louder the wailing screams of the lost, and the more gruesome their punishment. Each one grinding their teeth, trapped in their personal torment, buried in piles of misery, and swallowed up in heaps of offense and shame. There was not one trace of hope in this world. Izz wondered what one would have to do to end up in a place like this. But he knew it was better not to know.

In the middle earth, Zuree held Izz's physical body to her bosom and rocked him back and forth. She looked into dimming eyes that were once so radiant with life and was startled. She felt his hand squeezing the blood out of hers as the expression of deepening vexation shrouded over his face. She could discern the oppressing plague of every fear she had ever known covering over her and smothering her like a leaden fog. Zuree pleaded, "Wake up, Izz! Come back to me." The dredge of sucking darkness deepened and closed in on her as a vicious, mocking voice in her head said, *Izz, Izz, come back to me Izz. Your hope is lost. Here you are, and here is where you shall remain.*

A whimper rose in her chest. She barely managed to choke it off until she heard voices out of the blackness calling her some of the most despicable names imaginable. She clung to Izz in fear as silent tears that welled in her eyes fell upon Izz's face.

When Izz came to, he found himself in a different cavernous hollow. There were pits and torture chambers where one form of affliction or another was specially prepared for each victim. Every holding pit was meant to maximize every conceivable affliction of the senses with multiplying misery from which no single part of the body was excluded.

In one chamber, a lost soul was being flayed while fully awake; others were being dismembered, boiled alive, impaled, disemboweled, ground to a deathless death on grindstones and many more inhumane acts that cannot be written down. Izz had not even ever heard of or imagined such dreadful, horrible, and abominable crimes against the souls of humanity. The blood stench of entrails of thousands of undead corpses made the mucous membrane in Izz's nose wither as the disgusting odor reached him. Causing him to disgorge the nothingness he had in his stomach. Out of nowhere, Izz again heard the harsh, raspy voice of the prince of darkness call out, "Congratulations, Izz of the Isles of Zollerzon. The agony you are about to endure is a privilege reserved for only the wickedest of the most wicked."

While the voice was yet speaking, a group of demon creatures grimly huddled and pressed in tight around him. They looked half jackal, half buzzard, part human, part animal, and wholly evil. The voice continued, "This will be your special baptism into our little world—a momentous indoctrination to your new realm."

The specialized demons were preparing to unleash unspeakable debauchery on their distinguished guest. All at once, there were appalling squeals all around him that sounded like swine in a slaughterhouse being slashed to bits with blunt blades.

The confrontation launched on Izz's soul was magnified with overwhelming power and vindictiveness. One of the demonic beings pressed its knee into Izz's throat, while the others held him down and reached into Izz's mouth and tore his tongue out. The demented demon then held it up as if sporting a trophy. Meanwhile, other demonic beings were ripping his finger and toenails off. Multiple demons stretched Izz out spread eagle and disemboweled what was left of his intestines, turning his discarnate guts inside out like long strands of cord. Still, other demons pulled handfuls of hair from his scalp. Two demons held him at the shoulders while another held him down from the chin, while yet another gouged his right eye out of its socket. Izz howled with shock and anguish. A clawed hand swept across, ripping his left eye out. Izz screamed as he blindly searched out the remains of his defiled eyes and trying to scrape them up and push them back into their sockets. A slayer inserted two taloned claws into Izz's nostrils and forcefully yanked his head back. His scream caught in his windpipe as they slit his throat from ear to ear. If that was not enough, they twisted every tooth out of his mouth. All the while over Izz's blaring screams, unutterable cursing, desecrations, profanities, and blasphemies were venomously hurled at him from all sides. Izz had been mangled with such wrath that he relinquished all hope of his recovery.

In Zuree's arms, Izz's earth shaking screams reverberated off the cavern ceiling and backlashed on every surface of every wall until its echo vibrated throughout the whole chasm. But no matter what Zuree kept her faithful vigil over Izz. Suddenly she lifted herself and slowly turned her head and eyes to her right as far as they would go as if something hideous was about to leap upon her. The pain in her face and heart deepened. Below her, Izz's unoccupied body lay drenched in a sultry, cold sweat. Despite the sweltering heat from the fires that burned in the distance, his skin began to get cold, not like the cold in the air, but the bone chilling cold of death. As Izz painstakingly gasped for breath, his body writhed, twisted, seized, and violently sprawled out. Izz was fading fast, and as he faded away, Zuree realized her worst fears; Izz's physical existence on Zia was drifting into an obscure world beyond death. With all her heart, she willed that her life's essence could somehow flow into his body. "Oh, Izz," she whimpered, and then she began to cry great sobs of anguish. As she leaned back over Izz's spiritless body, her hair tumbled down and around his face like a soft protective shroud, and then her tears fell one by one, baptizing Izz's dusty, pain filled face with her unyielding loyalty.

The demon pack coagulated around Izz as thick as a mass of bloodsucking leeches. They continued to afflict great pain and hate within all the power within their wickedness while deriving great satisfaction from their evil deeds. As Izz was squeezed between powerful opposing forces, demons took turns cutting their names into him with razor sharp blades. Some burned their marks into his unearthly flesh with red hot branding irons down his legs and arms, across his stomach and chest and all over his face. Others gnawed into him with their scummy fangs, infecting him with every disease known to man. They bit with their mauling fangs and tore with their claws, scraping, scratching, and ripping at Izz's desecrated spiritual manifestation. Each demonic hellion relished every moment in a black hearted sense of pleasure, feasting, eating, and drinking hatred as if gorging themselves on Izz's spiritual flesh and blood. Shocked to the core Izz found himself incapacitated in the wake of the uttermost inconceivable torment. The sounds of sucking and grating of tooth and nail filled the air. Cries of unbearable pain and inconsolable, grief stricken shrieks, blasted from deep within Izz's throat at the top of his lungs. Although he was out of his body, the torment was felt as if his body were present. It was as if he were somehow standing at a distance, listening to himself cry out as the screams echoed deep within him, and the pain rippled through him.

An overzealous demon reached through the hole in Izz's solar plexus trying to get to Izz's sacred heart. Izz attempted to pull the hand away, but the demon was unbelievably strong. Izz was seized in an iron grip, and he could not break free. The overseeing demon screamed, "No! This heart is to be reserved for our most high master, Abaddawn."

When the assaulting demon could not resist the temptation and persisted, the overseer drew his sword and cut the hand off of the would be heart snatching slaughterer at the wrist.

Then all of a sudden, the encounter was over as unexpectedly as it began. Not one square inch of Izz's nerve endings escaped the excruciating torture that left him depleted and degraded. The pain was so complete that it seemed that even his hair follicles caused him agony. For a moment, there was a trilling sound that gradually receded into an oppressive silence. Izz lay on a black stone slab all slashed to shreds, injured everywhere inside and outside. Alone there for an eternity, with no sense of time, he thought of all things, he had done in his life and had not done. What had he done wrong? Was his belief system all misguided? Was he to blame for his present circumstances? He edged into a fetal position on the hot, sticky stone, trembling in despair, trying to sort through everything, anything.

Suddenly he felt cynical. What if he had been wrong about everything. He felt guilty, unclean, soiled by all that he had done. He had made a wrong choice to descent into a forbidden boundary. For a crucial moment, Izz drifted along a riff on a long digression into insanity as a slashing self condemnation dominated over his entire being. Izz thought that these were his thoughts, but little did he know that Abaddawn the master of illusion had disguised his own thoughts as Izz's thoughts.

He was bound in a place where convicting sights and sounds and foul smells filled his senses. Millions of voices called out to him, with words full of aversion and cruelty. He felt the presence of invisible evil spirits and knew it was them who were cursing and profaning his name. It was like being carried along in a strange dimension filled with insidious, finite, and eternal doom, draining him of the last vestige of dwindling strength. Izz tried to move but seemed helpless to wield any control over his incarnate self. His nerves and muscles jellied, unwilling to react to his directions. It was as though he lay dead, all except for the fact that he was Very much alive. He found himself surrounded in woe. His consciousness broke into a multitude of meaningless fragments. His spirit fainted into conscious blankness, where splintering portholes led to an alternate universe that pointed to eternal damnation at every position of the compass.

Zuree felt Izz's body stiffen, then tremble. She raised her head to look at him through her teary, pleading eyes and saw his face turn a deeper shade of gray as his eyes glazed over with the presence of death. Through her sobs, she begged, "Please come back to me! I will not live without you my breath, my heartbeat, my true love."

As if hearing a voice from a far off Izz moaned and tried to lift his head. He tossed back and forth and then collapsed. His skin suddenly felt feverishly hot, and his face glistened with unhealthy perspiration. Zuree lowered her head to Izz's chest. "Come back to me," she whispered. "Please come back." Then Izz went completely limp. Zuree instantly leaned her ear over his chest and listened as his heart grumbled like some distressed, mechanical pump, barely capable of sustaining even minimal function.

The king's eyes were fixed and glassy. His cheeks were sunken. His shoulders were stooped as if he was suffering from a deep mortal wound that was hemorrhaging from the inside. From deep within, he could hear in his mind the voices of doom pounding in his head. *Your foolish incompetence has resulted in the murder of thousands of, your people. You are unfit to rule. All is lost. You are an imbecile with innocent blood on your hands and deserve to die.* Ozzdon was helplessly caught in Abaddawn's monstrous multidimensional grip.

The king's mind reeled as if from a heavy blow, as a violent tremor of darkness swept through him, and each breath he took seemed to shake him as though he was a sapling in the wind. The faces of the dead suddenly came to him. He tried to remember each one, but there were so many that he could not. He tried to remember their names, but he could not. Abaddawn and his host of haters continued to concentrate all their concerted evil powers on the king as they simultaneously fed on Izz's wasting heart. The vast empire of the underworld flailed away at two souls at the same time. Abaddawn gained his most significant power and pleasure from the destruction of a noble mind and the corruption of a pure heart. Ether one enriched him more than a thousand murders. Both together pleased him more than a million.

Ammiz called once more against the lengthening silence, "King Ozzdon."

The king, oblivious to anything, transfixed by grief, only stood there trembling with one hand on the wall, and with his war crown tucked under the other. Ammiz wondered what was happening to the king, what he might be thinking. He knew that King Ozzdon was only human—vulnerable, and open to being attacked and wounded by the despair of his own mind. Again, Ammiz called to the king, "Your Highness, are you well?" Seemingly easing the ironclad grip of hopelessness that was sapping everything out of Ozzdon.

He was annoyed by the intrusion, having no interest whatsoever in reaching out or allowing anyone else to reach into his greatest moment of shame and disillusion. The king shifted his weight, and as he leaned his head against the wall, he lowered his free hand to his sword. His heart erratically pounded as he squeezed the hilt of his weapon and realized he had forgotten to take the next breath. He drew in a deep, long gasp. When he finally found his voice, he tried to speak in a firm tone, to mask his insecurity and anger. But he could not keep his voice from jittering. Without looking up, King Ozzdon responded to the voice that he recognized all too well. At last, he said in a murmur that was little more than a croaked whisper, "I…I have lost Edawn…all those lives…I have failed my people." He despised his existence.

"Do not be absurd. Believe me, no one on Zia, under the same circumstances, could have defended Edawn as you have." Ammiz's strong, authoritative voice, for the moment, pulled King Ozzdon back from the brink.

The king reemerged from the helplessness and the hopelessness that had disconnected him from his core, where he had teetered on the edge of no return. The king flinched as he sighted the seer from the corner of his eyes and slowly swiveled, turning his head to face Ammiz. The two men's eyes met. King Ozzdon's eyes were haunted, teary, veined in red. He was trying hard to smile; his weak, bitter attempt quickly narrowed more into a hairline fracture on his face than a smile. He forced a wider grin. But it turned out looking less a smile and more like a sneer to Ammiz. As sweat streamed down Ozzdon's face and his hands shook, the king finally responded to Ammiz's encouragement, "You almost make me **believe** that it is true. I wish more than anything that it was as you say I wish I could believe that but I cannot."

The king stared at the ground as he seemed to be focused on the mid distance on something only he could see. Then wordlessly, he turned and stared back at Ammiz. His eyes nervously darted as he felt Ammiz's measuring gaze upon him, studying him questioningly. And after what seemed like half an eternity, the king was finally the first to turn away. He felt, frail, fragile, brittle as if all his strength had suddenly been bled away, sucking the heart out of him. "What of our defensives, my lord? Does it not concern you that the curse of full blown battle is upon us?" Ammiz asked. Then the old man demanded, "The kingdom needs its king!"

At first, the king did not respond. He only rested his head back against the wall with a quiet thud, ignoring the question, ignoring the demand, not appearing to care one way or the other. His only reaction was to take a long, careful look toward Ammiz. His eyes narrowed bitterly. At long last, he mumbled in a bewildered voice, "How does one defeat what is not of this world?" The king's mouth wordlessly continued to move as he groped for the words that were scrambled in his mind.

He took a difficult breath and then exhaled. Then he took another deeper breath, and in a low voice full of resignation, he added, "In case you have not noticed…death is all around us, and will soon be crashing down upon us all!" he continued, his voice low, strained, frightened. "What does life mean anymore? What does anything mean anymore?" his hoarse tone trailed off into the obscurity of his despair. His expression collapsed into a profound frown, and his face hardened in thought as he tried to collect his fragmented deductions.

Ammiz spoke, trying to inspire the king with a new train of thought, "Our triumph is on its way, and we will prevail. You must have faith and believe that and nothing else. Those men down there are sheep without a shepherd. They need a leader! The crucial situation makes your headship all the more vital. You must make them believe in the unbelievable. Who will champion our cause, if not you? Are you not the rightful King of Edawn? Emperor of Zia? Ozzdon, the son of Zoldon and does his strength not flow in your veins?"

Ammiz continued to stare at the king, trying to read behind the odd expression in his eyes, his lusterless, dim, unfocused, sunken eyes. He seemed lost, not knowing what to do next. He looked very frail and heavy as if he was ready to come apart at the seams at any moment. In that instant, King Ozzdon was filled with a torrent of conflicting emotions. His next words were as despondent and detached as his soul, as he mumbled in an undertone, so low that Ammiz could hardly hear. "The crown… the crown has abandoned me. Defeat has found me, and encompasses me." He stared at the war crown with a puzzled look. He twisted his mouth in mockery and continued as if speaking to his own heart instead of Ammiz. "Its strength has left me." The hurtful words trembled from his lips. His voice cracked and broke off as he deflated a little more. This was all the king could say before his throat tightened and something seemed to tear deep within. " T h e only power the crown has ever had is the power your heart has bestowed upon it," Ammiz said. His presence radiated an aura of power as he spoke as if there could not be any doubt in his words.

The king's face was bloodless as he questioned in a strangled whispered. "I am not sure what you mean by that."

"True power is in one's heart."

"I am spiritless. I have no more heart. There is no more light in the world. Your Creator has abandoned us." His voice sounded as if it were coming from the far end of a deep dark hole. His words drifted into a murmur and disappeared in a moment of uncertainty and bewilderment.

"The light you seek shines above you." Ammiz looked up at the gathering conjunction in the sky. "The great clock of time will soon point to the hour when the fullness of light will come. The hand of the Creator even now readies to strike the pivotal moment at the appointed hour."

The king followed the seer's eyes across the sky. He could see the glittering globes. "Yes, I have seen them, and I am still having trouble believing it. For all I know, it could be only an illusion of the mind. What I do know, old man, is that you have lost touch with the reality of the present. Does your eyesight fail you? Can you not see we are overpowered, outnumbered, and shut off from the rest of Zia? And as we speak, the whole Norticlan army waits in the wings. It is only a matter of time, a very short time before we are all dead or worse. Did you see what cruelties they committed on King Kozar of Skymount and his family? We are aptly doomed."

"You do not need me to tell you that if a king is unfit to rule, he is not fit to be king! It is time to rise or forever remain fallen." Ammiz spoke with a firmness that commanded absolute respect that was not to be denied.

All the king's emotions were on a thin edge, and suddenly all the anger and all the frustration and all the terror of this whole day exploded within. King Ozzdon's mind recoiled, his lips tightened in rage, and the muscles in his jaw flexed sporadically. For the most prolonged instant, the king wanted to scream at

Ammiz, to punish him, to curse him, to lash out. But somehow he managed to catch himself, and at the last possible moment, he rejected and shut off that impulsive line of thought, knowing that uncontrolled madness lay along that path. He sagged back against the wall, let his head hang, and just stood there, face downcast for the longest moment. Finally, the king could contain himself no longer and broke his prolonged silence. He spoke through lips pressed tightly together and twisted out of line as if to hold in his anger. "Never say to me what I must or must not do. And never, ever challenge my authority you, old far..." This time his unutterable words died on his lips.

Somehow, Ammiz preferred the king's rage to his whimpering weakness. He knew that fear did strange things to men. He was much too old to be burdened with the thoughts of death. As it was, he was on the verge of completing his mission in this circle of life. He was on the edge of returning to the next world and leaving behind what only turns to dust. This fact made the moment all the more urgent.

Izz focused on an incessant buzzing sound, the only other sound he heard was the shallow, elongated pounding in his chest. All was obscured beyond understanding. Time and space were an illusion. He was beyond the bounds of his mind's ability to wrap itself around the reality of anything. His presence seemed wasted, deflated, and crumpled up. Then suddenly, his dulled senses came to quasi wakefulness with a start. He waited for the hammering of his heart to subside, for the sheer overwhelming terror in his chest to stop. Blood was pounding in his head with unimaginable force, and he thought his head had exploded. As his existence lingered to see what horror awaited him next, suddenly Izz realized that he was encased in some leprous fungus like that which swallows up the decomposing corpse. A myriad of something was crawling all over him from head to toe, and scurrying all around him. At first, he thought, *Centipedes!* Izz's inner eyes opened wide and seemed to dart from side to side. In the next thought, Izz's mind unscrambled itself enough to realize that whatever it was, they were too small to be centipedes. Then it all became too clear. They were swarming flies from hell that had found him by the smell of his decomposition. And now they had gathered by the thousands to enshroud what was left of him. He felt millions of hideous little annoying, hairy, sticky feet crawling all over him, creeping over every inch of him, inside and out.

But when Izz tried to swat at the flies on his face, his arms just dangled down, unfeeling, inert to his will. Izz was as if bound as a result of the mutilation of his desecrated inner dimensional presence. He could not make the slightest movement. Not even to blink away the cluster of flies that battled for the smoky tears he no longer had eyes to weep. The nasty flies were all over him. They were feeding in his open mouth and up his nose and in and out of his eyeless sockets. He tried to crawl away, but just flopped over sprawled out in the scummy dirt, and the swarm simply buzzed back gluttonously to the same spot they had been feeding on. Each one, in turn, extended their proboscis, vomiting their disgusting digestive juices, enzymes, and saliva to break down and dissolve the blood and other liquid gore that was oozing out of Izz's spiritual equivalent. With their sponge like mouths, they gorged on what remained of him while they spread every sickness known to man with their filthy little feeders. The diseases they spread immediately began to ravage Izz while the flies slurped up their meals, literally eating him up alive. If in fact, he was still alive. He could not believe what was happening to him. It was so unreal, yet it was all too excruciatingly vivid. He willed himself to revive from this living nightmare, but the intensely sharp pain only worsened. Oppressive darkness pressed in on him, and Izz was swallowed up in profound, compounding hopelessness as if the very darkness was penetrating through his skin to the very marrow of his bones. Forsaken repugnance further sapped away his life, like a scourging affliction pressing him closer and closer to the gates of eternal death and damnation.

All the while, above where Izz's physical body remained under Zuree's watch, Izz squirmed and swatted at what seemed to her like an imagined attack.

When the flies had fed to their fill, they began to lay their nasty little eggs all over him by the thousands. Almost instantly, the eggs started to hatch and initially began feeding on the fluid juices that exuded from Izz's eternal body born of the spirit. He suddenly felt something gnawing in the inside of him. He looked down to see maggots throughout, teeming and feeding on him inside and out. It was too unthinkable to be real. They had done their work on his organs, and now they began to feed and bore into his spiritual tissue, which seemed could never be fully consumed. The mass pierced their way into the upper interior of his body toward his heart. Thousands of disgusting creatures started to squirm around his ruined, discarnate flesh. His insides were riddled with horrible pain. The maggot throngs wriggled quickly throughout and within Izz's entire body, creating their own soupy environment. They filled the hollows where his eyes once were, trying to burrow through to his brain.

Out of nowhere, Izz heard the great multitude of lost souls crying out their thoughts to him. Then all at once, they collectively spoke together, vile words, curses, and blasphemies. Upon hearing this sacrilege, Izz called back into the darkness in dismay. "Why do you persecute me? I do not even know you."

One condemned soul cried back, "This is our punishment… never having learned to love, now that we long to, we cannot. There is nothing left to us but hatred and despair. We, therefore, live on hatred and malice. We long to die but cannot. Hate is our only minutest relief."

Izz felt more greatly oppressed with grief as evil projected its thoughts, driving him to believe that they were his own. He felt an overwhelming desire to cures his soul for having come to nothing, curse his own life for having failed. Was it because of his martyrdom for Zuree's love? Was he somehow responsible for

Rizan's death? Had his quenchless love for Zuree been forbidden? Had he missed the whole purpose of being born and the pursuit of his life? Had he chosen to believe a deception rather than the truth?

As if on cue to a script rehearsed since time began, at exactly when Izz was at his most vulnerable state of mind, the voices in his head launched their greatest onslaught of accusations implicating and blaming him for his own demise. Izz felt a heightened demoralization and disgrace upon realizing that it was all too true, that all was lost. He had become a part of the irretrievable castaways, lost in a void of perpetual condemnation. Izz broke down and wept bitterly, which set off a chain reaction of taunting from the multitude of condemned souls thrilled with satisfaction, delighted with knowing that Izz had joined them in their inconsolable anguish.

He was lost in an existence beyond existence, where death was this black hole in the underworld beneath where a thousand years were like a moment and a moment was like a thousand years. And it had already started to feel like forever. Yet his heart just could not accept that this insanity was not just for a moment, or an hour, or a day or a year, but forever and ever.

Could it be possible to be tormented throughout all eternity? The most painful part of it all was the profound loneliness and the depression that there was no hope left, and he could not free his mind of that thought. *I have no hope of ever seeing Zuree again.*

All at once, the bowels of the deep beneath him and the foundations of the mountain above him shook and trembled. And while Zia was still quivering, suddenly and without warning a fiendish manifestation of evil winged spirits once again could be heard approaching Izz's mutilated soul from afar. And at length, as their approaching footfalls indicated—there they were back—out of nowhere a contingent of shadowy, demonic beings gathered around his defeated and defenseless spirit being. Through eyeless sockets, Izz could see the group of pitch black demons closing in. He felt a sudden, irresistible urge to leap to his feet and run like a madman, but he could not even move one digit of his fingers to defend himself. Even if he could have, he had no strength and no will to rise from the scummy floor where he lay in his gore and excrement.

At this point, Izz was beyond caring—not even caring that he did not care. He just lay there, not inclined to put up a fight, nor resisting. And even the momentary stone silence seemed in some way painfully overbearing like the deceptive calm before a violent storm. Then suddenly, he could hear unintelligible, animal like voices, see their yellow eyes in the darkness, and smell their sulfurous breath. They wore no coverings; they bore no features and looked more like bottomless shadows that reflected no light, similar to no other demons he had seen before. Izz could only make out in his mind their silhouettes moving between the dark illuminating flames. They were huge, and they smelled like the incineration of rotting flesh, mixed with sulfuric acid and putrefying sewage. The combination was so distinct that it could not be compared to the most horrific odor Izz had ever smelled thus far.

Then the formless beings reached down and gathered up what was left of Izz. Shreds of intestines dangled from the hollow in his stomach, and white bones protruded from his gory flesh. The sight of his spiritual counterpart was an offensive eyesore.

And once again, Izz was dragged along in a procession of triumph, carried from where he had laid forsaken, down and through an unknown passageway. He was taken deeper into the bowels of the underworld while maggots flaked off of him by the hundreds. He was carried to the edge of another drop off more yawning than the last. Izz was alight with fear. Where were they taking him, and why? Sensing his final demise, Izz found a ray of comfort by assuring himself, "I have surrendered all for the sake of love. I bear no shame or regret."

A demon that overheard the last part of Izz's whispered words replied, "Oh, you will surely regret that you ever came to exist, I swear to you."

Izz was sliced with heightened fear at hearing this promissory threat. Yet his terror up to that point was but a shadow of the unspeakable horror that awaited him. No words in a million years could ever have described the desecration prepared for him, some too horrific to be written. In agony filled voices, the lost continued ceaselessly to cry out from all sides with vindictive gratification that they had never had to suffer the vast indignation Izz was appointed to receive. The satisfaction that sprang from the suffering of Izz's coming pain was chilling. Izz was forcefully yanked to the edge of an infinite volcanic chasm, similar to the one he had fallen from. It was the gateway vortex to the center of the emptiest obliteration. And once again, he was flung into its fathomless depth. Maggots fell away from Izz's riddled body as he plunged into the profound abysmal drop, the bottom of which could not be seen for its vastness. Izz plummeted toward the center of Zia itself at an abstract rate of velocity. He was gripped by a force that pushed and pulled on him simultaneously, accelerating him until he burst into flames. Izz fell like a comet, leaving a trail of sparks and ash behind him. He felt the burning pain, and yet he was not ultimately disintegrated.

While Zuree held Izz's physical body to her bosom, his clothes unexpectedly burst into flames. Even though the abrupt phenomenon caught Zuree totally off guard, she reacted quickly and decisively, removing her cloak and smothering the flames. Izz's clothes were scorched, leaving his body covered with a garment of singed cloth and unmistakable traces of fire that left Izz dotted with superficial burns. All the while, Izz's heartbeat erratically, and unspeakable fear veiled his face.

Four
The Twelve

On the deck of the upper keep above the raging battle, Ammiz arched a single bushy eyebrow toward the king and said, "There is not much time…and I have less than little time to exchange insults with you. The conjunction is fast approaching. It will soon be upon us, and the prophecy it ushers will soon be fulfilled. What is to come must come, and as sure as the sun will rise tomorrow, that which is written will come to pass, despite what you believe or do not believe."

"Do not bother to waste your breath, old man. I am more than familiar with your fables," the king said through gritted teeth, his words seeming to dribble over gravel.

"The greatest fable here is that you allege these undeniable truths to be just fables. Free your mind; let go of all your uncertainties, reservations, and disbeliefs. There are forces at work here beyond our understanding, but one thing is certain. It stands proven. Every single prophecy foretold, up to now, by the Ancient Book that Reveal has come to pass, to the letter."

"Bedside stories leftover from a forgotten age! I will not put any further hope in the miracles and dreams of children's fantasies, as the feeble minded and the gullible have for as long as anyone can remember!" At that, the king gave Ammiz a look as if now he was sure all the accounts and gossip told about Ammiz being a raving lunatic were true.

"Those so call bedside fantasies are far beyond the laws of chance and are about to become everyone's reality. Facts are facts, it is written in the stars."

"In the stars no less! How could anything be written in the stars, old man?" Ozzdon asked, emphasizing *old*.

"The truest of stories are written in the stars. Believing otherwise will not alter the truth they reveal. And the truth is that we must resist with all that is in us until the zenith of the Great Conjunction has reached its threshold. There is but one solution, however, beyond the bounds of possibility it may be, it is our only hope. Everyone's last hope, you can make no mistake of that. What Izz does and what you do now will determine the fate of all of humankind."

The icy stare frozen on Ammiz's face skewered the king to the wall through and through.

"Izz?" The king cringed as his mouth twisted sardonically at the sound of the name. "Izz is little more than a boy, only flesh and blood like any one of us." Ozzdon paused for a moment, as if not sure what to say next. Then he carefully continued, "I must admit he has accomplished some pretty amazing things, but it may already be too late. For all we know, he may already be dead and stiff with rigor mortis, with nothing left to worry about. And who knows what has become of my beloved Zuree." The king spoke with resignation, lowering his voice as if not wanting at that moment to be thinking about Zuree's fate.

"Izz is the greatest brave heart of us all. That is why destiny has chosen him." The old man's hope filled countenance seemed convincing and infallible beyond understanding.

Yet the king resisted. "A grand coincidence, too far fetched to be truly foreordained. His luck has all been a fortuitous combination of accidental circumstances that have little chance of repeating themselves on end."

Ammiz's response came with the absolute certainty that only faith could have inspired. "There is no such thing as coincidence. Victory is our destiny; it is written across the cosmos and is already ours! All we have to do is reach out to seize the moment and pick it like ripened fruit from the tree of life."

At that moment, all of Ozzdon's suspicions were further confirmed beyond the remotest doubt. The old goat had gone off the deep end of madness. He felt his anger bolt through him, yet he fought it back down and did not speak the words better left unspoken. Instead, he said, "Your words were not worth the breath it took you to utter them. I ask you again, are you blind? Does your sight fail you, old man? Are you sightless of the simple and obvious truth? Look around you! All is lost!"

"Sometimes what appears to be real can be deceiving," Ammiz's heart prompted him to say. "I know what I know by virtue of the facts. The truth is the truth."

"I see what I see when I see it. And you, no matter how much you believe it, you cannot see into the future any more than any of the rest of us. What you believe to be truths are nothing more than ancient superstitions and ideologies." Their eyes locked.

"Look up. Do you not see that the night has become day? What appears to be unbelievable is, in fact, reality, and what appears to be real is unreal."

Then the seer spoke as if reciting a prayer as he pointed unflinchingly at the approaching conjunction. "The galactic alignment will mark the completion of the Grand Cycle of the universe. It will be the end of this age and the beginning of the everlasting unfolding of all things. At the zenith of the galactic day, the universe will realign itself to its original birthplace position at the Creator's command, when all things within time and space began. At this juncture in time, for the shortest period, there will be a fork in the cosmos that was never meant to be. One path will lead to unimaginable bliss. The other could scatter the fire of the sun and plunge humankind into eternal darkness."

The king listened in breathless amazement at the unbelievable proclamations Ammiz was making.

"There are post markers throughout the cosmos where the spiritual dimensions and the material intersect. Evil altars have been built around these realms and will become portholes if..." Ammiz continued even as burdensome as it was to utter such words merely. "If Zuree's royal blood is spilled on the Altar of Abomination, where demons not to be trifled with dwell."

The king flinched as his heart twisted in his chest at the sound of his beloved daughter's name mentioned in such context.

89

"If the powers of darkness succeed…at this precise moment ,a rift in the cosmos could cause the interconnecting forces among all bodies of the heavens to be offset. This might open a hole in the creation in which the workings of time and space could be distorted. This, in turn, could upset the balance of the universe. This breach could unlock every bottomless pit marked by a black altar throughout existence. Freeing the vilest creatures from dimensions created and meant to keep them and hold them forever."

The king gave the seer a blank stare, as everything he heard was not quite registering.

"There is a name most evil among all other names," Ammiz spoke in a demeanor that asserted his proficiency and authority on the matter at hand. "For a seer to merely utter, it is blasphemy. That name is Abaddawn."

Ammiz cringed at the sound of his last word as if he had suddenly tasted something foul in his mouth. "He is humankind's greatest enemy. If he and his fallen archangels are ever freed, there will be no stopping them. He believes he will then become invincible. Under these circumstances, if man is allowed to survive, he will only exist to be enslaved, to be born into misery. He will spend every waking day in despair, dying in agony, generation after generation. And worst of all, there will be no hope for humanity, and no end to his misery."

Even though the king thought it impossible, Ammiz's ominous, foreboding words sent shivers up his spine and sent unholy crawly things back down. The mere mention of Zuree's name continued to wreak havoc into Ozzdon's heart. Along with the wildest sort of nonsensical babble he had ever heard. Such a tangle of stories post markers, black altars, portals—it was too unheard of to believe! And yet it all seemed to fit somehow, somewhere. What was he supposed to believe? How was he supposed to separate truth from untruth? Ozzdon lapsed back into his oppressive despondency.

Izz of Zia

As Izz fell, he uttered the most prolonged scream in terror until his throat constricted. Izz plummeted every muscle in his body contorted and thrashed as he plunged his way ever deeper down into the bowels of the underworld. It was like flying through ink, in the truest terror and sheer fear beyond endurance. Izz did not know how to engage the vastness of each split second as it raced toward the sheer breadth of its conclusion. Izz had no idea to what point of fathomless depths his fall was leading him. Little did he know he was headed to his darkest, longest hour of unspeakable foulness.

Izz gasped for air and babbled to himself, struggling to recuperate some notion of control over his dilemma. He hurtled headlong at the speed of thought until he saw what looked like a fiery substructure. Izz cried out a frantic scream suddenly cut short by his sickening impact. Izz was smashed into the fiery core crystal of Zia's nucleus with numbing force. Pain burst in bright, inky colors from his forehead to the back of his skull as sparks exploded outward in a cascading burst that spattered in every direction. And then the displaced molten igneous rained back down upon him like red hot coals. He exhaled a pitiful, smoky, muffled moan that enveloped him like a thick blanket of agony.

Izz's rancid existence was burned to a crisp, reduced into a heap of charred flaming and burning waste, unrecognizable even as a human. Every part of him that was not already broken was pulverized, shattered beyond repair. The very sinew of his joined bones unstrung and receded. His head felt like a jelly sack filled with his scrambled brains. Pangs of pain rippled through him like the swells spreading across the face of a thick puddle of blood. He lay there sprawled out like a lifeless soul on the innermost, hottest part of Zia's liquid iron pooled surface, with one arm painfully twisted under him.

Izz seemed trapped within an interspace phenomenon, in an existence of no ups and no downs in a paradox outside of Izz's limits of comprehension. It appeared that beneath him, the whole planet was reeling, teetering, and tottering. The entire universe seemed thrown off balance, just as though it was twisting and warping into itself within the realm of inner and outer space. As if he was caught in the most savage inner edge of the eye of a storm. Izz rotated with the wobbling core in an easterly direction at an astonishingly high rate of speed as everything when black, and Izz lost all sense of awareness.

In the kingdom's courtyard, Arius was caught in a knot of trampling boots and clawed bare Zomborge feet. He had fallen, unable to regain control of his legs as he continued to dodge and parry away one deadly blade after another. He twisted and turned in the dust and the blood, and the gore splitting hairs between life and death.

Above, Ammiz continued to challenge the king strategically. "You are still the ruler of Zia, and I must respectfully hold you responsible for what you do in the next few moments."

King Ozzdon laughed hollowly. "It sounds so simple, so right, so true, does it not?" the king remarked with wry annoyance. Still stunned by the unfolding confrontation of contradictions between his mind and heart, he sifted through Ammiz's words for an endless moment.

Izz awoke after what seemed like the longest, dormant sense of time as if he had been indefinitely gone. Izz's consciousness came swimming back up toward the surface. At first, he noticed he felt no pain and was now struggling against nothing. Space within seemed to be spinning in a circle around him. His thoughts slithered around and around within his head as if they were entangled on the brink of a vortex. He felt as if his thoughts had become separated from his own mind. His face and temple were pasted against the sizzling floor, withering, shrinking, and peeling his scorched skin away from his skull bone. He attempted to hold his head off the searing canopy but immediately had to rest his cheek back down on the sizzling slime covered canopy. A huge black snake slithered over his face, dragging its scaly underbelly across his empty eye sockets. He could not even bat an eyelid.

Only his outstretched hand trembled as it slowly clenched and unclenched. His ashen skin was still oozing whitish blood from the many lacerations in his discarnate flesh like tissue. He was drenched in his own waste. Izz could still feel the maggots that had never ceased riddling his festering flesh. Obnoxious gases belched up from everywhere, as everything around him raged with the red, white heat of an unquenchable furnace. The surrealism was so profound that he was not even sure he existed. He was certain he must be dead—yet undead. He struggled to see something out of his eyeless sockets, but all he saw was glowing illumination. Maybe it had been all a dream, and he was on the verge of waking. He willed this with all his heart to be all just part of a bad dream.

You are just having a nightmare, just a nightmare, he kept telling himself. *This could not be real.* He could not fathom the possibilities of any of it being actual.

Suddenly the oddest sensation came over him that it was, in fact, he that was unreal. He felt as if he was only a faded phantom observing from a distance, in effect, from another universe lost in some primal vastness he could not name. At that moment, wickedness enlarged itself beyond evil. Magnetic fields of polarized negative energy further crushed him to the sizzling external core that seemed hotter than the surface of the sun. The ambiguity of it all was that who he thought he was, was not him at all, yet in reality, it was all a part of him, which was just the same —or could have just as well. His self perception had taken on a madness all its own.

After an eternity of confusion, Izz at long last came to the only obvious conclusion: *This is real. I am not going to wake up.* He breathed a sigh out and inhaled a lung full of foul air. The reek was overwhelming. Stricken, his breath burned in his throat, drying his mouth, and his throat wound made it impossible for him to swallow. He began to be aware of a faint sensation of feeling coming back into his hands and feet; and yet he could not seem to come fully awake. He lay full length on the molten ground perfectly still as if he was inert, which, he was. Izz's thoughts wondered around inside his head in a kind of haze desperately trying to sort hallucination from the truth. He was not dead, but neither was he alive. He could feel himself trembling inside as if something had begun digging at his soul, trying to get in. Confusion was tying his mind into knots, distorting his perception. Visual and auditory hallucinations, removed Izz from reality as he knew it. Yet Abaddawn's black, sinister presence was still there, all too real, lurking in the darkness. Izz shivered and turned cold inside despite the sweltering heat radiating up from the interior's depths. There was a sense of everything happening in slow motion as he floundered, face down.

The intense heat had wholly singed every inch of what was left of his skin. He felt the heat of a white hot furnace reaching out to consume him. In every bone throbs of anguish grew and spread outward through his whole body. Every nucleus in his spirit seemed to pulsate. Fiery pain fixed especially in his head once again engulfed him. His mind felt as if someone had crammed his skull with red hot coals and shaken him hard. With ever widening eyes, utter pain thrust Izz to new heights of agony that exploded every time he shuddered a breath and threatened to drive him ultimately out of his mind. Right there he curled and squirmed like a smashed worm. The pain was so unbearable that Izz could not manage to push out a scream, so piercing was his anguish. Izz whimpered loudly and attempting to move, instinctively trying to somehow distance himself from the pain that overwhelmed him. He fought to block out the pain. The immediate truth of his pathetic plight filled him with repugnance for being alive. At least he appeared not to be dead.

With all his effort, Izz raised his head as he rolled onto his back. With both hands, he started to grope over the torn up remnants of what was left of him. He was conscious of how bad the condition of his condition was in. He searched out the cavity that was once his belly, trying to pull the strands that dangled from his insides back into some kind of whole. He recognized the shapeless barren hollow left inside his chest, a gash that throbbed with the concaved void of hollowness. His fingertips ran up his inner spine, where his entrails and organs once had been as wave after wave of pain washed over him. He touched around the worm riddled holes where maggots still gorged, and the rotten waste crumbled away into tiny pieces, like spoiled curd cheese at the touch of his fingers. Izz looked like a ghost out of hell, and his skin began to show signs of gangrene. And even though his sunken sockets were still eyeless, Izz could in some way still see out of both hollows. There were shimmering images of shadowy patterns somehow flickering through his perception center. Izz did not want to spend eternity without end in the clutches of pain and darkness. He had to get back to Zuree. He attempted to force his crusted eyelids open with his fingers. The two red cavities where his eye should have been produced not even a pinhole's worth of clear vision, and only resulted in horrible pain. At least he was able to close his eyes. Through his hazy inner vision, he searched for an escape but again was only able to surmise that he was trapped like an eviscerated animal, helplessly ensnared. When Izz came to terms with this, he eased into acceptance.

But it was not long before Izz was instinctively struggling against his invisible bonds, trying to get loose from the unseen crushing weight that held him. He worked his jaw back and forth, up and down for a few seconds, trying in vain to introduce saliva into the incredibly dry, tongueless hole that was his mouth. He felt his throat crack were it was slit when he tried to swallow. He was weak with exhaustion, pain, and fear. Every jot in his soul cried out that all this could not be real.

Suddenly Izz was overcome with a strange sensation as the inner chamber began to heave and oscillate between many interacting energy systems. The fiery vortex collapsed and transformed into an inky shadow empire of a black sun. He was at a loss, finding it impossible to grasp the situation that imprisoned him. Izz drifted back and forth across the boundaries of interweaving force fields as thick as molasses that bled through an atmosphere filled with incredibly hot gases and dust. From the nucleus of the pitch dark pit, the sound of the heart of all evil started to pump. Black blood began to seep through the rock floor.

One moment, Izz was surrounded within the luminous lights of the pillaring flames that besieged and lit up the shadows on his face. He found himself pitched on a disgusting refuse heap of dung, where the foulest waste from all of hell flowed to and collected. A pool of stagnant, untold filth tinged with the foul blood of the lost gathered, pooling and boiling all around him. Izz watched and listened. Even the piercing silence seemed sinister in every way.

Then again out of nowhere, the flashing flames reappeared hotter than ever like an inferno stoking up, suddenly rekindled to burn day and night forever and ever. Izz felt as if his bones were burning like charcoal in a furnace. The dualism of dimensions continued intertwining one with the other and simultaneously interfacing with repelling stratums, changing back and forth between many polarities of evil until all concentrated into one. The surface beneath him was once again a spongy carpet of stinking, greasy black slime covered goop. The ever present stench was overwhelming. It smelled like a humid, rotting, quagmire of death. The fetid odors were like the unbreathable, putrid air of a festering open sewer.

Izz lay in the reeking cesspit of muck. His thought patterns attempted to make some sense of it all. He knew he was swallowed up in darkness, caught in the unknowable and guessed that it was some kind of collecting centrifuge. Gradually, he developed a clearing sense that he was in a place from which all evil spewed, where all that was unclean drained into. A sewage repository filled with all the filthiest, scum waste of the underworld. It was the axis of wicked webwork that connected all that was unholy. From here Abaddawn controlled his sacrilegious domain. The air had become ever increasingly vile, his chest wrenched from the unbearable stench. He tried to quell his nausea, but he could not stop his mouth from bleeding with bile.

Izz felt alone, and forsaken now, more so than at any other time in his struggle for life. He felt his head begin to spin, and then he felt a backward churning followed by a sharp jab from where his guts once were. He felt choked, from the middle of his chest to the base of his throat, and he could not swallow. Suddenly something contracted and pushed upward. A mass of thick, sticky, yellow and greenish muck seeped through the slit in his throat and secreted out of his mouth and nose. He gagged on the nasty, bitter, sourness in his mouth, a taste, and the smell of mixed rotting eggs and acidulous lemons. He continued to heave violently, but there was nothing to throw up, only a slimy, bloody mucus that oozed out of him. Eternal death was real; it was dreadful and hideous, and it would be forever.

Izz was whimpering and wailing in agony. All of a sudden, he was overwhelmed with the intense sense of the heightened presence of a profoundly heinous evil. He found himself amid wickedness such as he had yet to know since this whole nightmare had begun. He gasped for air but could not get any. The sudden realization ran backward through his veins like a noxious toxin growing stronger until he screamed with ever escalating regret of having lived past his birth. His body ached as he forced a deep breath, raising his head from the filth that dripped from his bony cheek. He tried to somehow brace himself for the next nightmare he somehow knew was coming. He stared out through his eyeless sockets and could one way, or another see something from inside his head. Whether it was real or not, he did not know—only that he could see mutating patterns of darkness, bleeding from one shade of blackness to another. Izz then felt an unpleasant feeling of coldness descend over him. Even though the brutal heat was still causing beads of sweat to form and drip down his forehead and run into his wounded red eye sockets. The pain was coursing through every fiber of his being, but he was so scared stiff at the impending dread that he was almost oblivious of his agony.

As his perception drifted through the constellations of uncertainty and delusion pulling in and out of focus, further altering the fabric of reality. Despite the obscurity of his visual spectrum, Izz became acutely aware of one thing. It was the one thing he knew was truly real, that he was not alone. Surrounding him, he could see in the retina like optical in his mind's eye trace imprinted silhouette edges. The configurations flickered like marred, dying purple black flames, outlining six, twelve, thirteen humanlike profiles bound to the stone walls, crucified upside down. The forms were arranged in a circular pattern against the outer walls of the oval chamber around him. The evil that indwelled them reached out toward Izz like insidious tentacles of vapor, entwining, and tearing shreds of his substance from the surface of his soul, eating out his substance. With all his might, he tried to scramble back frantically, whimpering as he dug his fingers into the filth and dross as he tried to drag himself away.

Like a weather beaten, animated skeleton, the Wicked Warlock Wizard watched over the Zomborge attack with mounting excitement. Under the influence of his concoction, he had not slept a wink. His pitiful figure looked like something that had crept out of some bottomless hell for the condemned. His skeletal head and neck were so emaciated from the narcotic induced sleeplessness that there seemed to be no flesh over his bones. His dry skin was pulled back as if it were a tightly stretched parchment over his cynical, toothy smile, exposing his gritty, eroded set of brown teeth. Wisps of white hair from beneath his head covering whipped across the facades of his dead looking face. His full attention was focused on the unfolding pandemonium swallowing up Edawn. He watched through his spyglass, with a peculiar aloof amusement. He drew in the negative powers to the full from the bowels of the deep, feeding strength from the mayhem of human pain, misery, and madness. The dark energy swelled inside of him, dancing and blazing as he jubilantly basked in the feverish glory of his overwhelming conquest. The dawning conjunction blew its eerie breath down across the land, carrying on its exhalation, the heavy stench of the killing fields. Baddlock breathed in deep, filling his nostrils as if he was taking in a deep, invigorating breath of fresh mountain air.

In the deepest pit of hell in Izz's presence, each shadowy figure suddenly emerged from the smoky mist seemingly blurring and whirling in and out of his frantic mind. Their hominoid forms were fixed to the stone walls with three enormous silvery spikes. They were pierced through each hand and the third through their overlapping feet, as the other demons had been. They were incarnate and animalistic looking. They were a menacing, bestial mix of a half angel like, half demon and in every way all evil, cruel, and vicious. Their bodies were covered with scaly reptilian skin that looked like metal armor. Their faces appeared emaciated like that of a corpse. In his reawakened terror, Izz could somehow will himself to see them one at a time, all at once, or all at the same time from any and every angle. Amid this eerie, baffling perspective, he violently shivered when something snapped in his head, and delirium edged in, whispering, *You are not getting out of this one.*

The malignant spirit's physical forms seemed to be held in a state of stagnated lifelessness, in suspended animation, like sleeping pod shells waiting to be woken. The only vestige that indicated that the ensnared creatures were even alive was their shadow breath that sounded more like the dragging of chains through a slug filled gravel pit. Unlike the creatures he had encountered before, these perverted life forms were additionally grappled to the walls with roll upon roll of large claw like pruning hooks that outlined each of them. Each hook was tightly fastened to the stone walls, with steel chains and interwoven through the flesh of each spectrum of dark matter. Surrounding every carcass were sacrilegious symbols, offensive signs, vulgar profanations, and every unimaginable, horrible expression of hatred were scratched all over the walls. Writings whose sole purpose was to blaspheme and desecrate the holiness of the Great Creator and his creations, particularly man.

Without warning, from somewhere above came the sound of a loud, terrible, steady banging. It was a frightful hammering against a metal door as if some hideous, wild beast with a hundred screaming heads, was making every struggling effort to get in. The wails were followed by a horrific clang, which sounded like the repeated opening and closing of a massive iron door. Izz immediately sensed an irrepressible manifestation of negativity. The scene metamorphosed from that of animation and sound to an echoless sphere of virtual stillness.

Izz suddenly felt as if he had been cast into a den of hungry lion like predators, and he was dinner. He stiffened with tremors of fear that spilled quivers up and down what was left of his spine. Under him, the sensation of the turning planet suddenly rolled with the peculiarly slow motion of a great wave. This farther ebbed him away from all that had once been at best intangible. There was a sudden terrible howling sound like that of a blizzard, but there was no wind, no storm. Within those great, prolonged mournful sounds were other gritty rasping intonations, hissing, slithering noises. In the background, there was a rhythmic drumming reverberation; like the pulse of a hideous evil too wicked to imagine. Noises that sounded like toenails scraping across a stone surface sounded louder and louder, getting closer and closer, oozing into the cavity. And yet the kaleidoscopic darkness seemed to grow somehow denser and denser. Encroaching wickedness that dredged with its caustic revulsion, death, and gloom secreted into the enclosure. Izz began to sweat as he felt fear and dread reach deep from his throat into what was left of his intestines to his groin and squeezed, making him shudder.

Izz knew he was being watched from everywhere. He could feel spiteful, eyes scorching into him. Then Izz felt dazed by waves of a vacant kind of hate and fury that oppressively closed in on him. The sensation pressed in from all sides, while unimaginable malice amplified within him to a daunting pitch. Izz began to make out semitransparent black tinted apparitions. He could only interpret the phantoms as evil spirits. The shadowy figures melted in and out of the pit of ruination. Hideous faces took shape through the mist and murmured disgusting conjuration. The manifestations emerged and vanished at irregular intervals made of what appeared like some gaseous fluid. It was like being in a hall of mirrors. Every singed hair left on his body was standing on end, and he felt as if his disarranged bowels were about to loosen. One by one, the discarnate spirits, crept into the same sphere like a procession of cold blooded executioners.

Izz lay perfectly still. There was no reason to cry out for help. There would be no rescue, no escape. The procession entered across the threshold of the dregs. The unreal antiparticle haunts were only apparent as outlined purple black contours darker than the darkest shadows around them. Despite the most profound, pitch black that enveloped everything, there were the slightest patches of light that glowed from the murderous heat. Each entity was very careful to avoid the slightest speck of light, preferring the fathomless darkness. Each evil spirit maneuvered through the deepest shadows until they reached their crucified equivalents. One by one, they reentered their tangible counterparts, the only physical connection they had with the material world.

Once inside their physical duplicates, their spooky manifestations seemingly tensed and strained against the discomfort of once again being encapsulated into the membrane of their embodied selves. But they knew they had no other choice than to endure their contact with the material world to reenergize themselves. Izz's presence seemed to compound their physical and mental pain a thousandfold because of the illumination and sacredness of his untainted heart. But nothing this side of life or death could deter them from their appointed hatred and lust for retaliation against humankind and in particularly Izz. Their material bodies instantly reacted to their spirit's reentry. Horrible growls filled the chamber; eyes went wide with pain, and then closed tight as grotesque faces froze in grimaces of discomfort.

Izz could feel the infinite black of the phantom's pupils within their red coal like eyes already fixed on him from the gloom. He slowly realized that these diabolical spirit forces spoken of by Ammiz were the twelve archfiends and of course their master, Abaddawn the prince of darkness himself. In the center at the highest position the unmistakable carcass form of Abaddawn, in all his grotesqueness, was crucified. His bestial, goat like head was covered with thick, filthy black encrusted patterns that gave him a revolting, almost serpentine characteristic. His physical presence was as ugly a figure of a monster as anyone could ever care to imagine. He was monstrosity horrendous beyond any expression or human words. But his physical appearance seemed nothing compared to the terror that penetrated Izz's being from having to once again look into his tormenting serpent like eyes. The rogue's eyes seemed to snuff out any trace of light from the span of the room. His upside down physical form was hulking, twisted, and deformed. His dingy outer covering hung down in pockets and folds from the nightmarish reptilian form that he was. Its weighty membranous wings were spread eagle and fastened along the wall with grappling hooks. He was ensnared in the realm of the inner circle of evil, where archangels, emperors of the underworld were physically imprisoned, where they awaited the day of their final judgment.

As the inner axis of evil tuned their senses inwardly, then outwardly, they focused and connected to the dynamism of negative energy. They maximized their reign of terror released on humanity through their puppet Zomborge hosts. Just as panic and death swept through the kingdom of Edawn and spread throughout the land of Zia, its pulsating dark forces were channeled deep into the world of lightlessness. The wicked dozen, principalities, and powers, along with their evil master Abaddawn were all noticeably ingesting some source of black, wisp like power. As they took in the cynical force, their leathery wings quivered with raw ecstasy while they gorged themselves.

Unbelievably, the chamber began to blacken into a seemingly impossible inkier shade. The thirteen evil personified beings of hell squirmed with the agony of their crucifixion, and yet at the same time relished their gluttonous feeding frenzy of fear and pain as every shred of light was literally being absorbed right out of the unhallowed space by the presence of Abaddawn and his twelve unholy henchmen, supreme lords of the underworld.

Suddenly a vision blew through Izz's mind, breezing past the arches of his skull like a prophetic whisper that flashed in the temple of his thoughts. Unaware of its source, Izz saw thousands of Edawnian citizens, men, women, old and young screaming in terror and pain. And the principalities of darkness ever increased their capacity to feed off the negative energy, sucking and inhaling the hate and fear that they had evoked, manipulated, and were now responsible for creating. The horror filled screams of the most innocent victims of war amplified their power. Through his peripheral vision, Izz could see the malignant spirits as they let out little squeals of gluttony. As long as the energy of the frightened woman and children pulsed through their incarnate receptors. They thrilled with every harsh shrill of the mortally mangled. They shook with a trembling ecstasy as they connected with and greedily devoured the negative energy of the deepest fears of those dying on the surface of Zia. The lost souls seemed to rejuvenate as they appeared to regain their strength, and became more and more powerful with every passing moment. Their arms, legs, talons, and heads undulated with power, like swelling, slimy leeches— heaving, bristling, twisting and bloating like hideous oversized black maggots. They arose huskier as their muscles bulked, rippled, and metastasized. Their red reptilian eyes bulged out of their knobby faces, as they leered at Izz, and watched him with growing lust. He could hear their sulfurous hissing, and screeching as they withered against their captivity. The closer the Great Conjunction came to its critical junction. The weaker man became. The stronger the evil grew, and the more the glow of the red, white core flickered into the darkness like a dying ember.

All the while refusing to abandon Izz's side, Zuree waited by his mortal opposite, where her unceasing vigilance filled her heart with overflowing despair for him. Tufts of wiry blond hair cascaded over Izz as she whispered words of endearment and tried in vain to wake him from his inertia. But his fate was sealed deep in the core of oblivion. His periods of animation unconsciousness had been locked in nightmarish dreams. For a while now, Izz lay still from head to toe as if he was dead. But his irregular breathing and his heart that was making a distant sound like fluttering butterfly wings told her that he was still alive. Despite that, for the longest time, he had made no other sound but these. Zuree begged, "Izz, please wake up! I am here, and here is where I will stay until you return to me."

The heckling of demonic laughter could be heard in the darkness just beyond Zuree's sight. Izz suddenly tried to speak, and Zuree put her ear to Izz's numb, parched lips. Except she could not fully focus on mumbled words that only sounded like choked whispers laced in fear. His eyes filled with sharp tears, and his nose ran as his face was etched with deepening shadows. Zuree crushed Izz to her bosom and pleaded, "Izz, please come back to me. I cannot live without you. Please, Izz, please."

The sound of cruel taunting, mocking laughter intensified, filling the cavern with gloom and doom. Zuree tried not to tremble as she lay curled against Izz on the floor filled with pure fear.

In the most bottomless pit of the underworld, Izz felt a murmur of Zuree's presence, which wrapped around him like the arms of a protector. And something swelled in his heart and heaved to the surface some feeble effort of resistance. His hands turned into fists at his side, and the resolution Izz so desperately needed at that moment, to keep from ultimately yielding all, rose within him. With renewed strength, Izz braced himself. More afraid of being a sniveling coward than dying a grisly death.

Five
The Resurgence

King Ozzdon could not seem to shake the words Ammiz had spoken, nor the nameless assurance that had crept over him, mending his brokenness and weaving his confidence back together. He felt the tiniest remaining ember of fight still smoldering, suddenly ignited by a whispered breath of faith. "All you have said, you have spoken as if there could be no doubt…" The king's voice trailed away.

"The truth speaks for itself," Ammiz assured the king.

Something deep inside told King Ozzdon that the stately elder's words were too bold and too real, that they could have only been inspired by something as factual as the truths they proclaimed. How he knew, he knew not. Perhaps it was unknowable. But somehow, what he knew, he knew, that he knew. And so he believed as the perception of the truth compelled him to do. The seer stared at the king carefully, as Ozzdon seemed to metamorphose before his very eyes. Energy spiraled up King Ozzdon's spine, and his features firmed as his heart dropped back into its proper rhythm, and his thoughts snapped back into place. Ammiz saw the king's brown eyes rekindled with determination as he regained control of himself, and wiped his eyes. The heavy guilt he had felt for the senselessness of his failed counterattack and the appalling losses of his countrymen was lifting. With that in its place, a kingly sense of duty descended upon him. Like a royal change of garments, he renewed his continence, and despair lost its stranglehold. Out of the kindred depths of his soul, he felt the inward strength of his ancestry leap to the surface like the mighty spirit of a fearless lion.

He had made a noble decision that inspired a profound calm over him. H. More than sure that he was more than likely about to die, he made peace with himself and his Maker. He gripped his sword, ready to make the ultimate sacrifice, prepared to forfeit his life, for the greater good, if need be. The king quickly raked his fingers over his unkempt hair, placed his war crown back on his head, and buckled it under his chin. Then he turned to Ammiz. "My faithful friend…thank you for helping me realize that it would be better for me to die on my feet, with my sword in my hand like a king, than cowering in a corner like a whimpering worm."

"I almost thought you no longer want to be king," Ammiz said.

"And you were almost right," replied the king in a slow, measured voice. "I would rather believe what you say and find out that you were wrong than not to believe you and find out that I was wrong." He then drew his great sword from its sheath, and it glimmered with a living light reflected from the gathering conjunction, as it resounded with a metallic ring. He held his sword in his fist and raised it to the sky as he proclaimed, "I have delegated long enough from this lofty place of safety. It is high time that I join the side of my brothers on the field of battle. "If today is my last…" He swallowed a halfhearted, little laugh. He looked up at the approaching conjunction. A half dozen emotions shuddered through him as the grim probability of his death slashed deeply into his soul. "If this be my destiny,…it is a good day to die. At least I will die in defense of the land that I love."

Ammiz attempted to encourage the king further. "Sometimes our paths are chosen for us, and sometimes the right path is not the easy path. What matters most is that we do all we can, regardless of the consequences. The sun has risen every morning of your life on you and Edawn. Why should you not believe with confidence that it will rise on both tomorrow? I plead with you, leave your fears behind, and be who you were born into this world to be." And with this, Ammiz drew his thoughts to a close.

King Ozzdon nodded mutely, better than anyone else he knew there were no more words to say. And here, the encounter ended. Ozzdon closed his eyes a moment, took three or four deep rasping breaths as he readied himself. This day was the worst day he had ever lived through. With the thought of what he was about to do, it was getting worse with every breath he took. His heart began to thump with a strong surging rhythm as he filled his lungs with one last deep breath, then let it go in a sigh, which finally brought him to the moment of truth. He squared his shoulders and hardened his jaw. He raised his chin and straightened his spine as he suddenly felt the spiritual power of generation after generation of Noble Kings flowing through his veins, joints, and marrow. Throwing caution to the wind, he turned wordlessly and ran, sword in hand, down the steep stone stairway of the keep. When he reached the last flight of stairs, he drew a deep, long breath, and in a crisp, direct tone for all to hear, the king let out a shrieking battle cry as he cast himself down, lunging himself into the heat of the battle below.

Arius by now had no strength left, not even to deflect a slow and sluggish blow. Soon would come down the ax's edge that would strike and spill his blood to mix on the ground with the darker, thicker swill of the Zomborges'. The king plunged directly into the stormy eye of hell on Zia, where Arius was about to reach the end of his luck. The king quickly found himself engulfed in the nightmarish brutality and the ever maddening battle of slashing razor honed steel. His nostrils filled with the smell of death that hit him like the breath of a slaughterhouse. The growing multitudes of dead drones and devils immediately focused on the king, closing in on him, twirling their axes as they advanced. Their keen edged steel flashed before him, and the foulness of their breath blasted in his face. Ozzdon was hopelessly outnumbered, still the king stood his ground above Arius, his old friend.

The closest attacking Zomborge bore down on a deadly swing of his razor sharp ax. The king spun quickly, rounding full circle, narrowly avoiding the deadly attack. He drove his blade forward. With the sound of a wet rag ripping the sword hacked deep into the Zomborge's chest, passing straight through its dead heart. When the king withdrew his blade from the body, with a twisting jerk, it emerged bloodless, and he was astonished. But more surprising was that the mortal chest wound that exposed bone and cartilage did not seem to faze the brute. Without skipping a beat, the Zomborge quickly recovered its missed swing and was already coming down with another blow. Just then, the king stepped forward and thrust his blade in an upward motion, which tore through the Zomborges throat, jutting out of its face, and through its forehead. The king then wrenched the finely honed weapon back with an upper sideway yank, which ripped through the beasts cheekbone and temple. Yellowish blood like goo exploded from the gaping wound. The head was still attached to its neck and torso by stray strands of tendons and muscle. With one hand, the ghoul tried and tried to readjust its head back on its shoulders, but it just kept flopping over, until the ghoul itself veered backward. It moaned and groaned until it collapsed to the ground, flailing wildly and wheezing like a dying animal.

King Ozzdon's eyes widened, his mouth gaped open, and he looked the way one might a split second before being overrun by the stampede of charging yakoxen. The upheaval all around was lunacy, sheer lunacy. He cursed Ammiz under his breath for tricking him into this. He felt his insides jump as his heart wildly pounded against his chest. He had no strategy, no plan except to stay alive. Ozzdon fought with the heart of a warrior king that his ancestors would have been proud of, and for the moment, he was able to hold the onrushing Zomborges at bay. He did not stop to think of how many he had killed or maimed. He only thought of them as soulless things that had to be destroyed to save his kingdom, his world, his people, his queen. But the intense violence and death seemed just to keep coming from then until forever, crashing in on him from every overwhelming direction.

The king killed the horrendous invaders in droves. Each time the length of the royal blade made contact, it sliced its way forcefully through the dead, rotting flesh that trailed a gory splash of oily yellow along its wake. The wounds the royal sword inflicted left bones poking through, making the slaughtered looking all the more hideous. Still, they kept coming, swooping down like vultures with their frightful cries, sounding like groaning, squealing swine. They were already dead; arrows and swords could not stop them unless their heads were destroyed.

The next wave of dead flesh focused their glinting, hungry eyes upon King Ozzdon and moved in on him with terrible fury. This was the point where he thought the story would end. The king's hopes for survival shrank into no more than a minute mote of crumbling dust that drifted through a universe of death and mayhem. He was so exhausted that he did not care anymore. He had fought the good fight. He could now die with his sword in his hand, with dignity, with the pride of a Noble King. He would be remembered as the Lion of Edawn that fought to the death against impossible odds if there were anyone left to remember him.

King Ozzdon braced himself for the final onslaught as the deadly blows of ax blades descended, too many for one man to ward off. The hair on the back of his neck bristled with the static electricity of anticipation. Suddenly, out of nowhere, he heard the unexpected, hard *whack* of something striking flesh and bone and felt a splash of cold gore splatter across the side of his face. His eyes seemed to slam shut of their own accord. He managed to forcefully pry his tightly closed eyes open a crack to see out of their corners, Zandor standing at his side. And the Zomborge that half a heartbeat before would have sent him into the Promised Land was a headless body. The fiend turned, jerking as if searching for its assailant, stood there for a fraction of a second then crumbled to the ground, and coiled into a twisted knot as it died unyieldingly. Its feet flailed about, its arms thrashed, and its hands searched for its head. Its grotesque head stared up at the king with sightless eyes as a rancid yellowish white liquid flowed from its ears and wildly flared nostrils. Zandor made a small whooshing arc· through the air as he kicked the hideous Zomborge's head away.

Zandor had been elbow deep in attacking Zomborge slime when he caught sight of what was about to happen. He was shocked into action from what he had seen. Alarm for his king's safety had stoked within Zandor the raging fires of superhuman strength and unbelievable courage. Knowing that Ozzdon could not hold out much longer and realizing that the death of the king would have led to escalating panic and defeat. That would have been more disastrous than their present hopelessness. Zandor, in the face of death, urged on by the supreme vigor of his loyal heart, had fought his way to his king's side with maniacal zeal. He had slashed and hacked crumpling skulls and chests with forceful thrusts cutting down Zomborges that stood before his fierce slaughter.

In a relieved voice, the king said, "It is good to see your soul is still among the living." And he was strengthened with a fresh spirit of hope that spurred him on with renewed courage.

Upon seeing Kondor had suddenly, out of nowhere, joined the fight calmed the raging storm of concern brewing in Zandor's chest. However, his half smile waned quickly as hundreds of jaundice eyes suddenly turn on them, and every Zomborge in sight converged on the trio. Like crazed predators, their axes flashing, and their bared fangs dripped with ghoulish drool. Zandor swept his formable sword in a broad circular arc around them. A multitude of heads rolled with the rhythmical sound of a stick intermittently beating along on a thicket fence as his blade sliced through the scrawny chicken like neck bones of the encircling Zomborges. Their headless bodies stood with their axes still held high, until they tittered and dropped, slicing other Zomborges with their razor sharp axes as they fell. Zandor's sword claimed credit for each kill within its reach as other headless corpses wandered around until they fell into heaps of thrashing arms and legs.

As the wall of Zomborges continued to hurl themselves forward, their eyes deranged with blood thirst, Zandor, Kondor, and King Ozzdon stood over Arius, back to back. Two handedly the twins swung their broad swords in wide swiping unison with all their strength. As each dispatched Zomborge perished, their demonic host handlers within were sucked back into the abyss of the underworld's imprisonment for the dammed. But despite the trio's heroic efforts, the three were engulfed, with little or no hope of lasting much longer.

In the most profound depth of Zia, Izz remained collapsed upon the slick, oozing slime covered bottom of the world. He knew this finally had to be the end, but this was just the beginning. He dangled there between consciousness and unconsciousness in the way they say a drowning man cannot find his way to the surface. Izz felt numb, powerless, too weak from fear and exhaustion to care. By now ultimately, the only obscure light source that remained in the hole was that of the glow that was still kindled within Izz's heart. A light inspired by Zuree's refusal to give up on Izz. The more light the unrelenting hellions suffocated, the brighter Izz's heart glowed, and the darker the shadows around him appeared. The evil spirits' powers combined, unleashing a massive, undulating, all consuming burst of pitch darkness that utter wickedness might reign in their presence. But the pure love that burned within Izz's bosom, for Zuree, refused to yield.

And just when Izz thought it could not possibly get any worse, one by one, the demonic entities of darkness astral projected themselves from their imprisoning carcasses. One at a time, they began to detach themselves from their physical selves with crackling, suctioning noises, popping forth with the sound of a broiled goat's shanks being twisted and pulled from its sockets. The bizarre silhouetted black things seemed to spawn from shredded strips of shadow as they floated like spirits through derelict curtains of drifting, blackness swirling in the air like an enshrouding paranoia. The terrified distant moans that became screams of the lost souls cried out, terrified that it could be them that was being haunted. Izz jerked up his head as his eyelids opened like sprung traps. A dozen different forms too hideous to describe came into his sightless view. He suddenly felt a powerful wave of doom hovering over him as the disincarnate moved to gather themselves around Izz. Their festering plethora of stench followed them like a diseased fog seeking to infect every uncovered surface. He gagged on the adverse effects of the foul odor. Waves of nausea broke over him as his rising need to vomit set off a convolution of dry heaves once again.

While Izz lay at their feet shaking, breathless, half dead, petrified as his heart quivered in helpless panic. He could barely breathe from the expected terror that ran through his soul. Izz tried to move, but it was no good. There was no point trying to escape. In what seemed like an eternity later, Izz looked up, and he turned to take in the knot of groveling arrivals. At least a dozen demonic warriors surrounded him. He could see their forked feet, like the clawed feet of gruesome reptile toads. His recent encounters were still etched with such fresh horror in his memories that Izz tried to scream, but no sound came out. With the shaking of the surface under his quaking belly, Izz's mind let out a mental scream that started at the tip of his trembling toes.

Like a procession of hardened executioners, the discarnate crept forth to form a closing wall of blackness around him. They were towering, vicious, shadowy figures with enthralling, red, glowing eyes and dagger like fangs. They sneered and snorted with mocking laughter, their sulfurous breath choked him, and Izz could not breathe to cry out even though he desperately wanted to. His jaw involuntarily clenched together tightly to keep his toothless gums from chattering. Ever blacker darkness came over him. Even though it was nearly pitch black, except for the dimming core and Izz's inner light, the souls of the damned could see everything, as if they were standing under the midday sun. Not only could they see one another, but they could also see all the transgressions that condemned them, both their own and that of each other.

In his mind, Izz could hear from the animated shadows that surrounded him, the incomprehensible accusations and blasphemous lies being told about him. He could hear the murmuring threats of condemnation that were launched at him from all sides. Like the rushing of wind whirling inside his head, Izz could hear all twelve antimatter phantasms grumbling discontentedly all at once. Incessantly and belligerently, they mocked and cursed Izz and all that he represented, with his heart flickering its little glow of faithful love. It made them all sick with venomous hate for Izz.

The intense onslaught of hatred was so horrendous that Izz was driven passed the borders of delirium. This time he felt for sure he had to be in his final throes of dying, dead perhaps or lost in some terrible realm in between. Maybe he had awakened into a hallucination? Just in front of his face, encompassing him, he saw the talons of three toed feet glistening in the darkness as they stood on their two hind legs all around him. And even though Izz felt the dark presence of eyes glaring at him, burning stares searing into him with terrifying and lethal power, he could not bring himself to look up, to make eye contact. However, he knew he had to look to see what he must see. And when he did, what he beheld, was a dingy wall of hideous, lofty, wart filled, deformed, ugly things, looking like a three way cross between a crab, a reptile, and a warthog. They glared down upon him with their two hatred filled, fiery pit eyes. Bottomless voids that by some strange power held him in their unfathomable wickedness. Izz began to tremble in rhythm with a distant thrashing that seemed to reverberate up from the heart of evil itself.

In the heart of the beast, in the deepest part of the globe, in the next instance of Izz's dwindling existence, the evil spirits stood as one around his fallen state. The chasm chamber became noticeably ever darker still, and Zia suddenly shuddered as a powerful earthquake rolled beneath him, shaking him from head to toe. A few quaking tremors more, and it was all over. The red hot light from the core's intense heat suddenly vanished as if wholly swallowed up and snuffed out by the sinister paranormal forces that lined around him. Izz laid sprawl out, motionless with no strength in him whatsoever, helpless, vulnerable, and doomed. It was like he was by hook or by crook dead inside and out.

Suddenly Abaddawn, the master illusionist, came forth and stood before Izz. The presence of the evil inner circle joined by their master had seemingly extinguished every speck of light completely. The devoid phantasms were mere black hole anomalies, lacking substance, like bizarre, animated vacant, lightless voids. The ringleader kept his wings tightly wrapped around himself in a cloak like fashion as he spoke. "Help our esteemed guest up. Where are your manners?" he commanded mockingly.

Izz felt a translucent clawed hand reached down for him like the tentacles of a stinging jellyfish. Hot, steely viselike talons wrapped around his head as if it were a melon. Izz was jerked up on his rubbery legs by the arch demon standing before Abaddawn as if he were a sack filled with his own broken pieces. As he was lifted, Izz trailed red smoldering, smoke from what was left of him. The shock of the excruciating pain was so great that he could do little but suffer as the arch drudge's piercing clasp tightened and droplets of pus began to ooze down his face. His joints and muscles cried out in agony. Without inspiring any sensation of contact, two other demons took him from underneath each arm. Izz was held up stooped over, his head hanging down like a sparrow with a broken neck, with his hands dangling uselessly at his side. His joints twisted in anguish, strands of fleshy gut dangled from his stomach. And his exterior hung suspended like ribbons of static energy, discharging out and sparking in tattered waves. Izz's knees almost buckled as if he were a soggy rag without the use of his legs. His presence writhed like a bag of squished worms. Having little blood left, his wounds oozed with watery, yellowish white pus. Izz blinked his eyeless lids several times as if trying to clear the black spots that obscured his inner vision, as viscous liquid streaked from his eye sockets flowed down his cheeks.

The great lord of the fallen looked upon Izz and was himself astonished at the extent of misery his under lords had inflicted on him. Abaddawn exclaimed, "I did not know they could stack maggot dung this high." Then he laughed in Izz's face as the twelve misshapen shadows that flanked him laughed themselves silly.

After fighting the pain of standing for a moment or two, Izz gave up, and his legs buckled underneath his weight. He let himself collapse and had to be held up. His existence was like a deflated outer skin of a squid filled with rotten bones and gelatin.

His face was fixed in wilted and shriveled agony. His life form shattered and drained, recoiling, and exploding with roaring pain as he whimpered softly. All his old injuries were suddenly reawakened the shark bite, clawed arm, centipede stings, and every scrap and scratch he had suffered along the way. Izz inhaled sharply at the painful shock as every hurt he ever knew concentrated inside and outside.

"Izz of Zollerzon, welcome to the real world. How good of you to honor us with your presence, here in our humble abode. Your attendance is in perfect order. The Great Conjunction is almost upon us, you the last vestige of hope for Zia, are all but finished. And our most precious prize awaits her appointed hour tethered to your worthless carcass up above us." Abaddawn grinned with fiendish delight bearing his row of long, jagged, teeth. A black cloud seeped an unbearably strong foul odor that fizzed from his mouth and nostrils.

From the background, the jarring sound of demon laughter filled Izz's mind and was getting louder and louder. He felt the wicked creature's breath expelled upon him as their long black tongues reached out to him and Izz was compelled to inhale their rancid, poisonous breath as well as that of his own.

"I am so sorry to have kept you waiting so long, but it was so hard to tear myself away from the side of my soon to be newest bride, Zuree." His breath hissed through his teeth as he spoke.

Upon hearing the words that furrowed cavernous evil scars in his mind, Izz's helpless and hopeless spirit let out a deep, prolonged, grievous groan. As his thoughts began to hemorrhage, he felt that the light had gone out of his soul. Izz found himself unable to avert Abaddawn's eyes. "Yes, welcome, indeed, to our undermost world. Once again, congratulations are in order, Izz of Zollerzon, you have achieved what no other mortal has ever attained. You have earned the honor of being anguished and tormented all at once by my most personal servants, under my special undivided supervision no less. You have most certainly earned and so justifiably deserve the greatest level and highest degree of degradation that is in our power to inflict upon you."

Sprinkles of spite dotted Izz's face as Abaddawn continued, "I have anticipated this moment…it seems like forever."

Cruel laughter floated through the chamber. "Please, let me introduce you to the elite of the underworld, the cream of my crop, my closest allies." Terror permeated every word Abaddawn spoke. "Each demon master rules over their special dominations, principalities thrones. Each had its own specific talents to do unhallowed things to defile man with his own specialized anguish to inflict. To your right is Deceiver, to his left is Blasphemy, Murder, Fear, Hate, Lust, Thief, Envy, Greed, Guilt, Doom, and Hopelessness, who, without this place, would be virtually guest less."

Izz's face was drawn, his cheeks shrunken and shriveled; and vomit and mucus were streaked down the front of his mouth. He was looking more and more depleted with every weak heartbeat. Izz panted for air. He could almost taste a fear more terminal than a hundred deaths. He wanted nothing more than to drop himself back down to the ground, dig a hole in the slime covered surface, crawl in, roll up into a small tight ball, pull the filth in after himself, and die.

Like a sleepwalker, Izz was held rooted to the spot by the two henchmen, as images and sounds faded in and out half nightmarishly until all he could hear was the dull, hollow echoes in his chest. Due to his strangled arteries and frantically coursing coagulating blood from an emaciated heart, he was rendered almost senseless. Izz drifted within the boundaries of his thoughts, while the creatures of darkness and death mystically stagnated his heart. They spitefully began to completely separate his soul from his body to be condemned to the deepest hell where they could torment him for all eternity. At that moment, Izz realized that he no longer could feel any connection with his own body.

The twelve howling beasts who specialized in extreme hate, whose only purpose and pleasure were to cause anguish within any one of flesh, tightened their encompassing circle. They drew near to humiliate Izz, to break him down. They circled Izz like diabolical undertakers preparing a corpse for eternal burial.

Each spoke inside Izz's mind at the same time, *Your eternal death awaits*. They pummeled his weakened spirit with hammering iron fists and tore at the little that was left of him with taloned claws. He heard and felt the sickening blows descend on every part of his dwindling existence like ruthless jabs upon ulcerated wounds. Indifferent of his howling wails, they lifted him off his feet and slammed him down over and over again. They slapped at his face, slashing with claws that ripped gashes in his already tattered flesh with their serrated nails. His soul erupted in anguish. From somewhere behind him came a stunning wallop on the back of his head, and it took him down. He fell into a heap in a crouched position. Izz rolled forward over and staggered on to his hands and knees, and then collapsed against the hot granite, into his own waste as if he were made of melting wax. He curled up with both hands hanging on to his knees, trying to squeeze his body into a small, awkward ball like shape. They plucked him back up and held him, mobbing, kicking, and punching him randomly. They piled up misery and heaped shame upon him. Izz struggled, choked, and gagged. He could feel that his ribs were pulverized. He tasted a bloody fluid running out of his mouth and could smell it pouring out of his nose. He could feel something dribbling out of his ears. The last of his ebbing strength failed him and his will completely collapsed. Terrible vexation and spiritual grief had taken over his soul. His consciousness fractured into pieces integrating into the darkness as his spirit spilled a sorrowful moan. His broken heart wept out bitterly as his mind went mercifully black.

Inside of the Edawnian Kingdom, within the maddening carnage, the continuous racket of clashing and clanging steel resounded. Birthed of misery and slaughter nothing else mattered except the blade's razored edge and the outline of its reach. The bloodshed, moment by moment, only seemed to ebb those still standing farther away from the boundary of the living. The only ray of light was that in good time, Arius had recovered enough to stand. Zia seemed to wobble under him as he took a couple of tottering steps and felt as if he was walking over emptiness. After a few more fumbling steps, Arius finally slowly at first, then more sure, stepped forward, until he was moving with vigor, and purpose. His ache drained from his flesh as the sensation of strength swept over him. He joined Zandor, Kondor, and the king, and together they stood like four corner pillars that held up the Kingdom of Edawn, the world of Zia itself. Each faced outward, sword drawn, poised for battle. And little by little, a remnant of survivors began to rally around the fearsome foursome. Men that had long since given up all hope, came to life like dormant seeds, to rise together as the last bastion of hope. But from their vantage point, they could not see the horror closing in, all around them, could not imagine the impending storm about to swallow them up. Less than one hundred able warriors stood to face thousands of screaming Zomborges. Blades clattered and pinged, men roared, and sparks flew.

At the brunt of the attack, at first, the Zomborges were warded back for the moment but recovered the upper hand almost immediately. As if they had been rewound, drawing their axes back and letting them swing forth like obedient mechanical drones of their invisible demon puppet masters. The defenders of Edawn were ill prepared for the horrible impact of the never ending attack. They were hopelessly caught in an endless maze of death within a whirlwind of mindless savagery. They pierced the undead with the edge of their swords, but they could not kill the demons that drove them from within. The courtyard echoed with the metallic pealing of steel on steel, and the fiery red sparks of their blades danced like tiny comets across the battlegrounds. Slashing swords, swung in short, slicing arcs, severing arms and lopping off heads. Each man, was occupied solely with just the thought of staying alive. They watched the backs of the men in front of them, and the men behind them watching their backs in turn. Every man fought on, exceeding everything, any human could be expected to bear. The overwhelming odds only served to sinew their resolve. But despite their above and beyond valor, little by little, they were getting slaughtered. Edawnian blood sprayed out, swords and shields fell from dying hands as the battle raged on. The bodies of the slain were trampled, and those unfortunate enough to fall among the Zomborges were ripped to shreds.

After tallying their options frontward and backward, Zandor spoke out, his face was pale and drawn, covered with streaks of Zomborge gore. He turned to his king and said matter of factly, "We are about to be overrun, my lord if you have some sort of plan. I believe the time is now...if you have some counteroffensive in mind, I strongly suggested we get started on it immediately!"

Echoing his twin brother's thoughts, Kondor cried out, "We are not going to make it if we do not do something quickly. As in *now*!"

Arius, still a little shaky, sidestepped just in time to save himself from the monstrous blade of a Zomborge's ax. On the return swing, he flipped the axes away, exposing the assailant's dead flesh to meet his sword. Kondor, from the other side, struck the Zomborge drone with such force; it lifted it off its feet and nearly, sliced it in two. As King Ozzdon's mind raced over all possibilities, it was incapable of coming up with any final solution. Unable to avoid the pressing urgency, he continued to grope for the appropriate answer, as if his inner man was evoking some reply from a divine source. Forcing a response, the king finally spoke above the cries of pain and rage and bloodlust screams of the Zomborges, "The only plan I have is to stay alive no matter the sacrifice or cost until we kill every demon from hell or they kill us all. We fight on, like all the others who have fallen before us, knowing that we have not died in vain. Only then do we stop."

And on and on they wielded their flashing swords, shimmering the reflecting white light of the approaching conjunction, against the high stone walls of Edawn. But no matter how many countless Zomborges fell, they just kept coming. Wave after wave, they came crashing towards the noble few that stood between heaven and hell, like a downpour of death that never ends. There seemed no way out of the entangling nightmare as it closed in on the quick, the dead, and the dying with a fury of finality. The

Zomborge's ax was swift and fatal and the power of their spellbound madness matched the energy of their narcotic induced stamina. Hearts pounded, adrenalin surged, but the hearts of men could only be pushed so far, and yet the dead kept coming, ever compounding. And everyone knew in their heart of hearts that the battle had been long lost. Still the king, Zandor, Kondor, and Arius, inspired their men to continue the good fight. They were caught in a relentless vortex with their lives precariously routing on the jagged edge of the drop off. One by one, they were being sucked into death's undertow. The king seemed, like almost everyone else, to be on the very edge of exhaustion with most of his strength rapidly ebbing away. In spite of it all, because of him, everyone else would defend their kingdom until the last remnant of their strength was spent, and the last drop of their blood was spilled.

Sensing that the ultimate kill was at hand, every demon from within each Zomborge vibrated with the lust of mass hysteria. Crazed with the smell of blood and wanting to spill more and more, the fallen friends crawled around willing only to sink their teeth into one more victim. All of a sudden, out of nowhere, there came an eerie howl that seemed to come from everywhere. The king looked up and cringed at the sight of the wild looking Zomborges running toward them. It had an ax in one hand, and a short sword in the other, and the king was its target. But the king miraculously ducked just in the nick of time. The attacking Zomborge, to its surprise, found itself in front of Zandor as its ax was coming down. From the side, Kondor was already reacting. The Zomborge impossibly strong, with the strength of madness, brought its blade down. Zandor blocked with his shield. There was a horrific clash, and the sound of metal tearing. Zandor was spun around. Kondor leaped forward when he saw that the Zomborge was about to bury his ax into Zandor, he brought his sword down with a two handed swing. His blade sliced off the front of the Zomborges face from the bridge of the nose to its throat. Just as the ax blade was in mid arch, it twisted in the incapacitated Zomborge's hand.

Wham! The flat of the ax blade smacked Zandor in the small of the back. The sword slipped from the elite commander's hand as he fell to the stone floor in a twisted position. He started to rise, but the overwhelming pain coursing through him in pulsating waves of tingling paralysis prevented Zandor from doing so. His back burned with throbbing agony, and he opened his mouth to cry out, but the wind had been knocked out of his lungs. His legs were numb, and Zandor thought that his back had been broken. His eyes filled with terror as a powerful pang surged up and down his spine. But somehow, through the anguish that shook him, he reached for his sword and grabbed it as if he was being reunited with a lost part of his body. Kondor stepped over his fallen twin and roared, "Keep them back!"

The king arced his sword, and another headless Zomborge went down with a muffled thud. A vestige of the dwindling Edawnian army circled their fallen comrade and prepared to meet the end of their own lives. Any hope of victory had been nothing more than a fabrication of their imagination. Hopelessness would be the ultimate reality that they would all soon have to face.

When Izz reentered his black awakening, his hearing was filled with the sound of his rancorous laughter. His soul had been beaten, butchered just short of death. Everything had been taken from him, yet he was still clinging to life. Izz was lost, in an ever obscured existence. All he had left was his dwindling sense of self. He could hear Abaddawn speaking as if from a great distance, "You will in this age, and the eternal age to come, have the opportunity to know each of my henchmen as intimately, as I will Zuree." The way he said it sounded like something filthy, something perverted, something eternally blasphemous.

What registered in Izz's head was so terrible, it ran like a bitter, acidic toxin through his mind. *No! No, that was... inconceivable! Unimaginable! Impossible!* The scream in Izz's mind protested as every jot within his spirit revolted at the thought. Izz forced his trembling hands open and clutched them repeatedly trying to relax and revive his knotted mind. He stiffened his deflated posture, shook his head, and then raised his face, gathering his strength and courage. Izz's voice suddenly pierced through the fright that was incapacitating him. He finally feebly muttered, "You are a liar."

"What? What is it, you say?" Abaddawn snapped with a hissing sound, like that of a thousand angry vipers as he yanked Izz to his feet viciously by a fistful of hair, lifting his feet off the ground. He then shook him viciously, like a child with a toy on a string, so violently that Izz heard the bones and cartilage in his neck crackle and grind. Izz felt what was left of his insides, tearing loose. With greater and greater violence, the prince of darkness continued to shake him wildly. Then he held him out at arm's length and said, "I see that there is still a spark of defiance in you, but believe me, you will very soon beg for my mercy." Abaddawn went on as he ran a pointed fingernail across Izz's raw, eyeless face. "You look terrible! Give our honored guest something to drink after all we are not uncivilized down here in our meek roost." Then he cast him to the back to the pack of twelve. As Murder and Doom clamped his arm from behind, a glass urn containing stagnant wine turned vinegar, was brought and placed to Izz's parched lips as his head was held up. "Compliments of my faithful servant, Baddlock, whom you call the Wicked Warlock Wizard. How appropriate."

The wine filled urn was tipped high, and its contents ran freely, filling Izz's mouth, and cascading out of his slit throat and perforated rib cage. "What? What we have here is a man who cannot hold his liquor." The loud laughter from the thirteen was harsh and offensive.

The group laughed until they were jiggling all over, over and over. Abaddawn turned to them and asked, "Could it be possible that such a worm could have the power to resist me, who is mightiest of all? How could this puny, infinitesimal dimwit have given us so, so much trouble?"

The intangible entities broke down into smothering laughter that closed in on Izz with great depths of hatred, bitterness, and perversion that echoed off the stone walls. Waves of deep, deep terror flooded over Izz as hopelessness gobbled him up. Where were the shining ones? Where was the Great Creator? Was He not supposed to be his Vindicator? Izz hopelessly searched out hope and found none. The earth shuddered with an aftershock that almost went unnoticed, except for a few tumbling pebbles and the dust that trailed them. As Abaddawn held Izz up, the twelve shadowy arch demons, torn away at tattered parts of his flesh that still clung to his rent and lacerated body. Every one of Izz's breaths was a drawn out pain filled act of clinging to existence. A horrific raw odor came from within him as Izz stood there forlorn and forgotten, wishing with all his heart that he could drop, coil up, and die.

As Zuree pressed Izz to her bosom, his fists clenched and unclenched over his chest as if something was eating him from the inside out. Suddenly a vague expression came over his face, and he began trembling and moaning. He grew an ever deepening shade of pale as he shivered all over. Then a cloak of pain and grief of immorally wicked power that only spirits could perceive overshadowed his embodiment. Zuree enveloped Izz into her bosom, willing her strength and resilience into him. Perspiration poured from every pore, from head to toe. He was as white as a ghost and felt frail in her arms as he trembled uncontrollably all over, over and over.

As Izz slapped at the unseen and clutched at his heart, Zuree was spooked breathless. With every moment, Zuree fell deeper and deeper into despair as her faith slowly unravel. She saw a horrified look twist and entwine on his face as if unimaginable pain was fracturing and lashing through his skull, as she felt his mind cried out. And again he went suddenly limp in her arms, seemingly knocked unconscious by an unseen blow. Out of desperation, she realized in a moment of extreme hopelessness; she needed to believe in the Creator that Ammiz the Seer and Mistress Aria often spoke of. She needed divining intervention. Zuree needed a miracle, and she needed it now. She closed her eyes trying, desperately to believe and began to pray as best she knew how, "Creator of all things, if you do exist, please, please help us now. Please, please, please." Zuree crushed Izz to herself as her tears rained down upon him. She could feel his heart against her bosom winding down like the counter springs of a music box playing its last tune.

Zuree cried out to Ammiz's God, "Please! I beg of You. Please help us!" But her words were answered with only the bedeviled bitter curses of the watchful demons all around them. Zuree found the breath to cry out a rebuke, "Be gone!" Suddenly the ground shook all around them. Zia was in flux. In the anguish of the spirit, Zuree threw her face upon Izz's chest and poured out broken, heart renting sobs, which only the hosts of heaven could fully fathom.

Six
The Brink of Doom

S uddenly, in the most bottomless bowels of Zia, the eerie toll of a bell rang out over the subterranean chamber, with an evil resonance of finality. Abaddawn withdrew a familiar weapon, one he had used in his first attempted murder that rent the heavens apart. The metallic blade, once exposed to the sub terrestrial atmosphere became translucent, made a dull humming sound, and glowed fluorescent blood red. Abaddawn waved it slowly in front of Izz's face letting its reflection flicker in Izz's spiritual sight. As he fought his pain and weakness, Izz recognized the unmistakable blade, and he knew he was about to die the final death. He saw a vision of a hideous serpent laughing in the background smoke. And of screaming skulls that leered and beckoned. An unexpected hush fell over the chamber. The silent lull seemed to last a very long time. Overpowered by condemnation Izz struggled with a sickening sense of damnation growing from within. He was ready to banish his own soul and curse his next breath just to end it all. Again and again, he begged softly whispering a pitiful plea, "Oh please…mercy! Oh please, let it all end!" But his words were sucked away from his mouth, only to echo on deaf ears. Laughter came from the group of arch demons. They all reached for their weapons of desecration, bloodthirstily, itching to get in on the kill; but this would be Abaddawn's kill to savor alone. There had been others, and there would yet be more, many more, but never before or after, like onto Izz of the Isles of Zollerzon.

As Abaddawn ran his finger up the edge of the dagger's blade, then around the point, he spoke, "This is your final passage, both your soul and body will forever be bound in ruin that you may forever burn, and may feel the eternal pangs of utter misery." His voice gurgled up from deep within the fallen archangel's bowls, hissing through jagged, clicking, and gnashing teeth as he sprayed out puffs of dizzying, pungent crypt like vapor. The angel of the abyss held the dagger up high; its red glow filled the room as its light reflected in Abaddawn's greedy, bloodthirsty eyes. The arch demons in attendance gasped and rooted as the dagger's reflection bathed the whole gathering in ominous red light. In the hand of the fallen one, the dagger seemed to burst into flames as its gems caught the light of the eternal flames.

Izz saw the light flash off the razor honed edge of the blade as it was raised, what happened next was shocking. Like the strike of a rattlesnake, Abaddawn then plunged the sacramental dagger into Izz's chest. It felt like a searing flame, slitting through the center of his chest. Then he twisted his blade and slashed upward as he withdrew it. In complete agony, driven to a new height of utter anguish, Izz screamed helplessly, but still, the worst was yet to come. Abaddawn instantly ripped his hand inside the gaping wound in Izz's upper chest bypassing the layers of his spongy lungs, seeking to crush his weakening heart. Then came a sound, a squishy, ravenous, sucking noise that made Izz want to disgorge. A bloodless trickle dribbled from his ears and nose. "Now you are lost and forever undone," Abaddawn roared.

The lawless one suddenly paused and raised his head and rotated in slowly. His eyes seemed to focus in on something that only he could see. His forked tongue flicked in and out as if sensing something in the air, and then said, "Edawn is well down the path of inevitable doom." Then he threw back his head and laughed, showing a mouthful of needled teeth. Soon thereafter, he added through clenched teeth, "Now you will see why it would have been far, far better to have ruled in darkness than to be enslaved in the light."

As the evilest being in the universe forced his hands past Izz's lungs, Izz's soul turned into a grayish yellow sulfuric shadow that appeared to wither. Izz heard his heart cry out to him, *Do something!*

126

Izz's incarnate heart was about to bear the grisly fatal wound of its final death sentence. There was incredible pain, and the pain grew ever worse. He hurt more and more deeply every time he sucked a shuttering breath. As the pain splintered his skull, he shook his head back and forth, up and down, and made moaning and wailing underwater noises.

Darkness plunged forth completely. Izz had already taken all the host of injustice that could be inflicted on him. It was as it were, worse than if all the light in Zia had gone out. It was as though every evidence of illumination had been bled from the cosmos. Izz's heart's primary function was no longer to pump blood. Its critical purpose now was to create a protective spiritual field around Izz's soul center. The vessel that contained the sacred love for one woman, one spirit, one soul, began to shut down. And his heart was losing its fight as it began to shatter into countless chards. Still, Zuree's love remained intact, and alive in his maimed heart, creating a protective vortex wave of electromagnetic energy that kept the pieces of Izz's heart from falling apart. But it too was beginning to manifest and reflect darkness as it started ebbing under the unbearable strangulation of the evil dark void that made the air scream as it was sucked into its vacuum. In desperation, his heart moved his lips to speak out. He spoke with a grumbling nostril moaning mumble. Sluggishly he uttered a question just below a whisper, "Oh Great Creator, why have You preserved me thus far only to forsake me?"

Izz's plea at first only brought laughter from the inner circle of evil. "Look, he is calling out to his god," said hopelessness. At that instance, the chamber darkened into a deeper utter blackness as solid as a pool of liquid tar, as if impenetrable gateways had been suddenly slammed shut on all sides.

"Does he not know that in all the history of humankind no one has ever escaped from our centermost axes of power?" added Murder.

Abaddawn only sneered, and then spoke, scornfully, "My god? Save me?" Then he turned to Izz and ran his sharp nail down the length of Izz's cheek as he asked, "Where did you learn that...

in clown school?" Laughter resonated among the twelve. "There is no mercy down here. There is no god but me." Abaddawn looked about the desolate pit high and low in mock weariness, probing out an imaginary overseer, then leaned forward and whispered in a low voice as if afraid to be overheard, "Take heed, there are certain words that ought not be spoken down here. How dare you intrude on my unholy dominion, and blasphemy my authority but now yes, now, I have you just where I want you. And we will deal with you as we please," Abaddawn said matter of factly, and then he resumed his booming laughter, joined by his minion.

An arrow out of seemingly nowhere fired from a longbow struck a Zomborge in the eye, shattering its skull. The wounded creature let out a tongue lashing, banshee scream causing it to spew out several broken teeth. The horrendous sound was almost unbearable. Grown men staggered backward in astonished disbelief. At least one archer was firing. The king looked up toward where the arrow came from. He saw a bowman perched along the upper wall and then another as a few brave archers were once again raining arrows down on the perversion of nature that refused to die. The most courageous of women and their children had managed to evade detection to gathered arrows pulled from snarling lipped heads and immobilized Zomborge bodies and had run a chain back up to the archers.

The king's eyes traced along the higher walls of the battlement, and farther down along the top outline of the inner curtain wall. His eyes plotted the lofty parapet along the uppermost walls of the gatehouse, not precisely knowing what it was he was in search of. The gatehouse was one of the most critical parts of the kingdom's defenses, and it was mostly intact. It took a little thought, but at that precise moment out of the blue, inspiration struck. A monumental possibility came to him, igniting itself in the center of his wits. After a few moments, the solution that he sought blazed through his mind as brightly as a shooting star. The insight was more a gut call than anything if he was wrong, he was wrong;

but if he could pull it off, it just might work. His instinct told him, he could not allow himself time to think it out, or reason or hesitate. In his sudden inspiration, his fatigue and confusion fell away. The surprising revelation, once fully realized, was the most potent epiphany the king's mind could have received or could contain at that very moment. The king set his mind. And just when all seemed lost, the king shouted, "This way!" His utterance was practically impossible to hear amid the noises of the surge of blood crazed Zomborges. "Back up!" His hunch was upon him like a scourge, driving him onward. He screamed again in a tone not to be argued with. "Now!" it had to be now.

At first, his men only followed him with their eyes. Then without thinking, they started to shuffle their leaded feet backward. They backed toward the sound of their king's voice never turning their backs on the roaring Zomborge still so viciously attacking them. With one hand, Kondor dispatched oncoming Zomborges, and with the other, he dragged his brother Zandor along. Kondor was a man of legendary courage, and he knew deep in his warrior soul that no matter the odds, he would lay his life down before he ever abandoned his brother. Kondor moved with panther like prowess, trying to put distance between himself and the devilish fiends. Turning Zandor saw two Zomborges coming at Kondor from his blind side. Zandor cried out a warning, and Kondor immediately responded with deadly force. Kondor plunged his sword into the first devilish creature and felt a satisfying crunch. He then ripped his sword out, and the beast's intestines came pouring out. The second brute opened its mouth to roar its bloodcurdling howl. But it was instead filled with Kondor's brutally trusted sword. The blade severed the Zomborge's spinal cord from its head. Kondor twisted his sword, and the Zomborge's neck snapped, audibly, the tension in its body relaxed, and with a flop, it fell into a pile of flailing limbs. Just then, the king repeated emphatically, "We move! Now!"

Sometimes, especially of late, the king's orders made no sense to them, but they had learned to trust their king. If he had ordered them to withdraw, they knew that they were either in an exposed situation, or their withdrawal would entice the enemy into a weakened position. Their trust in their king was complete, and so their retreat became quick and responsive. What remained of the Edawnian army, those that were able backed up toward the king. They pressed together, into a tight cluster as they continued to fend off the avalanche of madness. A near solid moving wall of rotting, animated flesh, scuffled and stumbled forward, crowding in step for step, inch for inch. Most of Edawn's defenders were all severely wounded or exhausted beyond numbness, but they relentlessly fought on as gallantly as ever. The king led the tattered band of Edawnian defenders back toward the kingdom's gatehouse, and his men moved in unison. Hope in their king gave them the extra strength and resilience they needed to face the ceaseless pounding without mercy.

With one arm, Kondor continued to slice away at the advancing Zomborge army, severing limbs and parrying away ax blades. With the other arm, he continued to drag Zandor along. All the while, at the king's command, they fell back from the midst of the murderous chaos. They kept backing away in disorder, backing away in total disarray. It was like trying to outmaneuver an onrushing cyclone. They were skirting back on the edge as close to the brink of disaster as they could without falling in. As the walls of the gatehouse loomed behind them, they slowly edged toward the large holding cell. All the while, brave warriors fought back with their last dying breaths.

In the center of the netherworld, in the belly of the beast, things looked grim as well. Izz was held in the clutches of the most gruesome, terrorizing experience he had ever suffered. He stood on the edge of the wrong side of time and space where death would have been received with welcome. The love he had held in his heart for Zuree, that which had become an infinite part of him, once unshakable, was now fragile and altering into obscurity. Abaddawn's talons of death surrounded Izz's heart, dragging him down into ever deepening degrees of horrors too terrible to be told.

His heart could no longer beat strong enough to keep him from feeling desecrated; its brokenness bled only sorrow and gloom.

Izz's endurance became a nightmare within a nightmare. He gave a muffled sob as he tried to stand on his own. But his legs only dangled like wet rags. Izz felt certain that his inescapable conclusion was only heartbeats away. An acute stabbing anguish throbbed straight up through his spinal column then magnified a thousandfold and exploded with agony in the midst of his scrambled skull. Izz felt as if multiple steel spikes had suddenly been driven through his brain simultaneously, shooting tentacles of inflaming agony throughout his being. Izz tried to scream out in sheer desperation, but at best, it was nothing more than a choked whisper: "Please stop, please. Someone help me!" A lungful of smoky vapor followed Izz's words.

"No one can hear you down here. You belong to us now, and we are the only truth you will know," Abaddawn said as he toyed with Izz like a spider with a fly. "Know this—that very soon all will be mine for the taking. We are the Shining Ones now. The Host will soon bow, and all of Zia will bend its knee to us. The heavens will fall, the universe will have a new god, and Zuree will rule at my side forever." Abaddawn continued to squeeze and tug on Izz's heart as the twelve rulers of the dark continued to suck out Izz's substance as they whispered torment to his mind.

Every tortured instant felt like an endless eternity. Izz was all alone, cut off from everything that was hallowed, left to depart from the living, thought by thought, piece by piece in forlornness and hopelessness. His harsh gulps for air slashed through his throat in choked convulsions, and its heat seared his lungs. His heart was inflamed now, sizzling, and crackling. Fiery pieces of riddled spiritual flesh hung in shreds from exposed bones, and the back of his skull suddenly flared up, and flames plumed from his eyeless sockets. He knew he was coming apart at every seam. Thoughts burst through to his mind. *I am ripped inside out, blind, and diseased.* There was no right way for this to end. Even if he was willing, *What can the Creator possibly do for me now? He has forsaken me.* These are the thoughts that Izz heard burning inside him like smoldering coals in a spirit that seemed to blaze like a blast furnace.

He was worse than dead, and there was no way of knowing what ghastly fate awaited Zuree. His last thoughts were of Zuree and how they would be eternally separated, never, ever would he see her again. He could not stand to think of her being dishonored, harmed, or tortured in any way. The thought of his most precious breathing her last breath, beating her last heartbeat, sickened him beyond anything he had or could ever bear. It was not something he could even stand to think. "Zuree!" he screamed at the top of his lungs. "I am sorry... I am so, so sorry I am sorry! I did not mean for it to end like this." Then he broke down and wept bitterly.

The demons all joined Abaddawn in gleeful laughter and mocking. "I am sorry, so sorry. You are most sorry that is true, and you will be so much more. Is this not a gorgeous dream come true? What is more beautiful than the thought, sight, smell, feel, and sound of eternal death?" The Prince of Damnation could not resist a laugh as close to joy as his putrid heart could manage.

"At least I will die knowing that she loved only me," Izz murmured in a croaked voice he barely recognized as his own.

"What would you know? Nothing you know is real. Love is not real. You are not real. You are an illusion, just like your imaginary notion of love." Abaddawn's presence faded and disappeared as he spoke, then reappeared as he chuckled in Izz's face and said, "Embrace the darkness and let it embrace you." He unfurled his pair of leathery black wings and stretched them out. As Abaddawn held Izz in his clutches, he raised him to the roof and stood tall with an intimidating air of royalty that appeared to be invincible.

Meanwhile, back up in the upper levels of the underworld, Zuree maintained her faithful, loving, and compassionate vigil over Izz's incapacitated body. His, waxing skin tone was that of someone deceased, pale, frail, and ghastly. She touched his cheek. It was burning hot. His fever was by now so high that, she was sure that at any moment his mind would begin to smoke. She cradled him like a baby, soothing and stroking the excruciation from his face. His skin felt drawn out over his facial bones. Then suddenly, Izz's entire body began to shudder as he cried out and babbled hysterically. Zuree knew that if he did not calm his mental overload, he would lose his mind forever. As Izz moved irreversibly toward the all consuming madness, tears pouring from his reddened eyes that were practically swollen shut. While Zuree tried desperately to understand what was happening, she whispered, "Izz, please, you must wake up. Wake up now!" She clasped Izz's body to hers as tears of anguish sprang and flooded from her eyes, bound by Izz a thousandfold more surely than the chains that once held her.

Abaddawn relished slowly destroying Izz's heart in small increments. He bit by bit, peeled away layer after layer from his eternal soul, little by little, bit by bit, for no other reason than to prolong his agony. Izz was a prized sacrifice, chosen from before the foundations of Zia to oppose the darkness and the princes of darkness wanted to make an example of him before his underlings. Izz fainted briefly, only to reawaken to a new dawn of enhanced madness and heightened utter jerking agony. Hopeless and broken, half mad Izz's mind struggled to run from its pain, to escape to another world somewhere, anywhere. Leisurely, Abaddawn pulled Izz over the edge of a bottomless vortex where there would be no escape from the wailing vacuum void of nothingness. Below, a portal to the other side of hell began to open where there was nothing but an infinite black hole of unimaginable lightlessness. It was a deeper dimension of punishment. It was a place where anguish and torment swallowed up anything and everything in its wake, where not even light could escape its power.

Izz's whole existence was reeling and throbbing, in constant flux, aware only at a crippling level. His pulse thudded in his temples as his soul and spirit went completely anesthetized as he slipped into a state of complete shock. Except for the blurred vision of his inner eye, he was cut off from the rest of his senses as if they belonged to a spirit observing an unreal nightmare from a remote, removed existence. Besieged with fright and suffering, Izz cried out in a strange, ill defined utterance, "I can bear no more!" He was laughed to silence.

"You are afraid. Good, be very afraid that I might drink in your terror. Let it mingle with the dread drawn to me from the surface of Zia."

Wisps of Izz's soul were drawn down toward a vanishing spiral path into extinction. All at once, the horrors Izz thought were too impossible even to imagine were suddenly too real to be denied. The harder his mind tried to make some sense of anything, the farther he was taken by hopelessness down a deeper descent into the negative whirl of the everlasting absence of existence. How many times could his heart and mind be shattered and remain among the living? Izz screamed until he lost consciousness. His innermost mind was lost in disorder, in a violation of natural existence in a place from where it was impossible to return from. His mind was not able enough to think anymore. To retain its sanity, it shut itself down. Knowing that Izz was done for, Abaddawn let Izz slip from his iron grasp onto the ground that was already crumbling and opening up to receive him. Izz landed with a splatter in an unrecognizable heap of brokenness clinging to the breaking edges of the opening portal. Izz did not know whether to hang on for dear life or let go.

As Izz lay on the cracking molten floor, his only fractured impulse was that soon it would be all over. Suddenly the surface all around him began to fall away as the sucking force began to pull on him at an accelerated pace. The vortex, like a howling undercurrent threatened to absorb him into the descending depth to consume him utterly at any moment. The closer Izz got to the tipping point, the stronger and the faster the riptide's current drew him down into endless drop particle by particle. The invisible evil that waited there was even worse than the visible powers that bond him with strangling fear.

At that very moment, Ammiz was he was needed the most, attending to the wounded. He all at once turned his mind to a faraway thought. His thoughts suddenly turned to Izz, beneath Zia's surface where he knew the evilest demons ruled the dark. Peculiarity shaken, he feared it would be too much for anyone mortal man to bear and wondered if he would ever see his young friend in this world again. He hoped against hope that the young carpenter was still alive. Some kind of bad energy suddenly surrounded him. Something was wrong, terribly wrong! Thereupon Ammiz lost all sense of Izz's presence as if Izz had abruptly been sucked away from the world. Knowing that the fate of Zia depended on the outcome of his divine quest, Ammiz was vexed.

Spirituality wounded unto death, just as everything began to mean nothing anymore, in the remotest part of Izz's heart, where Zuree's presence was fading fast. There was unexpectedly birthed a vestige of hope that persisted and refused to yield. Out of final desperation, his heart tightened the sinew around the walls of its atria and forced plasma through its ventricles as it leaped into a deeper order of complexity unto itself. Teetering on the brink of eternal oblivion, in one last act of defiance and with his last ounce of strength, Izz rose. He would die on his feet, not groveling on his belly on the scum covered ground.

There was nothing more he could do. In his concluding pangs, Izz subsisted through the heart of his heart alone. From its bleak awareness, it was hard for Izz's mind, at first, to accept that there was something beyond its own reflexive comprehension. However, the mind was below the surface of cognizance, too slow to respond and so followed to wherever the heart compelled. As his wounded heart began to integrate and fade away into the shadow world, in fear, it called out a fountain of the deepest supplication. It cried out an appeal for the sake of divine love to the Spirit of the Highest Power, with its last dying beats. Suddenly out of nowhere, in the midst of chaos, something caught Izz's inner eye on the shadowy wall above Abaddawn's crucified physical carcass.

Tom Icon

At the uppermost apex of the grotto, Izz had not noticed the emblem until that very moment. Badly obscured with defacement and obscene graffito, in several ancient forgotten word groups, was written an edict. Izz stared up with a glazed inner eye at the strange, marred writing on the stone wall. He could make no sense of the fragments that remained, yet at the center, a unique underlying axiom of etched letters was still faintly evident. At first, it seemed too vandalized to be read. Try as Izz might, he could not recognize or make out a single character or word.

Frozen where they stood, astonished that Izz had risen, the keepers of the lost followed Izz's gaze to notice that Izz was staring past them at the rear wall, in deep thought. A few more *tics* of the universal time continuum and Izz would be beyond reach, and then not even the Creator of all things could have saved him. All of a sudden, independent of Izz's will, his heart cried out in final desperation, "Father, hear my cry! Why have you deserted me? Save me or blot out every trace that I ever existed!" The words sent echoing shock waves in repeating, accelerating patterns throughout the perpetuity of time.

There was no other time that Izz's heart was more in need of trust, hope, and courage. It waited in vain, it seemed. Then on the last click, on the last heartbeat, on the tipping point of finality, the extraordinary happened. The writing from beneath the surface suddenly glowed faintly like a reviving ember unexpectedly rekindled by the gentle wisp of an unseen power. Patterns of light danced deep in the stone, surging and swirling in looping designs that almost looked like words in a dialect written by no man's hand, written for angels and men alike. From some living source of heedfulness, with all he had the sense to understand Izz perceived it meaning from within. At the heart of his being, beyond his human capacity, the words lit up like sunshine filtering down and viewed from the bottom of a murky swamp. The words read, *Do not fear for I Am with you.*

It was the answer to the question which the mind could not have asked. From powers outside comprehension, Izz's heart found relief and eased its fight. As death crept over his physical body up above in Zuree's embrace, and eternal demise overshadowed his soul below the light brightened.

The writing that glowed forth was the mere first rays of light that preceded the new dawning. The flashes of light did not disperse and only grew brighter. All the laughter immediately ceased. Every wicked eye was dazzled by the sudden appearance of stunning streaks of intense light that shot across the roof above them. At once, as sudden as the twinkling of an eye, there was an explosive spectacle of brightness. There came out of the nonexistence a dancing flash of light that blasted into a billion constellations, instantaneously disintegrating every wall of the imprisonment to oblivion. Izz's heart immediately reanimated like a gasp of pure air wafting on a smoldering ember, and the most breathless little spark of hope resurrected somewhere from deep inside. At that moment, death lost its poisonous sting, and his dying heart immediately came to life again. That which was *not* became that which *was*; and Izz unexpectedly found himself in the midst of what *could not* be that suddenly became the what *is*. The light continued to disperse in every direction in multiple dimensions splitting the darkness like the bloom of an iridescent white Light unfurling fiercely with brightening sparks exploding from every angle.

Each glistening burst expanded into legions of aches that pulsated gloriously into searing white. Wide arcs ruptured from one degree of glory to the other without limitation or boundary. Izz's body swayed gently back and forth as if in a breeze. He wobbled backward on trembling legs as if dancing on the head of a pin. Within the storm, Izz held on for dear life or was someone or something holding on to him. The intolerably bright light shone in the darkness, and the darkness was confounded. Shadows vanished as everything within the vista was bedazzled in blinding whiteness, and the blackness melted away as though it had never existed.

The Living Light flared dauntingly brighter, and brighter than the most brilliant star in the firmament, brighter than the midday sun. The vibrant rapture streaked through the mist around Izz, mirrored and amplified its radiating energy, flooding the space with the magic of a billion illuminating moonbeams that expanded and grew in numbers and density. He saw stars flying toward him each one dazzling into brilliant life before him, filling his presence with radiant energy that glowed and shimmered. Then all of a sudden, matter, energy, light, gravity intertwined. Frightened at first, Izz thought this must be eternal death's irreversible ending. All the forces of physical laws and spiritual laws simultaneously seemed to turn inside out to merge as one.

Out of the blue King Ozzdon made eye contact with the archer's positioned on the crenelated battlement. He pointed to the two portcullises and with an upward spiraling finger, motioned that, the portcullises that had been locked down be raised on both sides of the gatehouse. Several archers saddled their bows on their chests and responded immediately to the king's silent command. Two teams of men manned each heavy winch, which gathered in the chains that would lift the heavy metal latticed grilles. Even though the frame walls were slightly damaged, the pulleys and counterweights made it possible for the massive portcullises to slowly slide up the vertical grooves along the castle's walls. Like clockwork, the king, his three generals and the refuse of his once great army moved back, back, back. The close knit formation of Edawnians laboriously lugged overlapping shields with swords thrusting forward, swatting and hacking away at the dead flesh that followed. As one mind, body, and soul, they clung to a tattered thread, linking them to the mysterious instinct of self preservation. They withdrew slowly under the iron gates and into the hold of the gatehouse. And the ghostly procession of cadaverous Zomborges eagerly followed, mechanically sweeping forward, walking stiffly, snarling, salivating, jaws open, and sharp teeth exposed. As swiftly pursued they made gruesome, screeching noises as their skeletal hands wielded their wicked axes.

When Ozzdon and his men had reached the exiting portcullises held at head level, the king signaled a halt and ordered the defensive line to be held at the edge of the outer portcullis. "We must stand here and prevail!" Inspired by their king, the ragtag remnant of surviving elite warriors were not about to give up an inch as long as there was breath left in them. The crunching sound of flesh and bone being ripped by gore stained swords filled the gatehouse.

The exhausted Edawnians held their war footing just outside of the compromised Northern Gate as the Zomborges continued to force themselves forward, packing into the expansive gatehouse. Defenders leaned forward with shield and swords raised for protection as ax blades glanced violently off the armored frontlines. Lancers came forward to form a razored steel barrier. The king screamed, "Hold!" Men grunted and drew strength from places where there was nothing left to give. They somehow stood their ground, slicing and stabbing their steel against the unbalanced equation of ax wielding madness.

Slavering corpses in the back pressed those before them forward, until they were crammed in wall to wall. Still, the depleted Edawnian warriors refused to break ranks against the wild and surging swarm. Drained men held on by the skin of their teeth, countering the relentless onslaught of the soulless innkeepers of demons. They repelled razor edged axes that clapped like thunder with their metallic rings. Showers of sparks broke forth over them in the ever present face of imminent death. And again, King Ozzdon urged, "Hold!"

Depleted men groaned, their souls trembling more than their rubbery arms and legs. Soaked in sweat, tested past their limit, they stiffened their worn out bodies to steady themselves, desperately trying to maintain their defensive boundary. Still, the Zomborges pressed forward, undaunted. And undauntedly, the Edawnian warriors bolstered up each other's innermost spirit. Together they stood with the shared covenant aching deep within their souls—to stay alive, to kiss their wives again, to hold their children to their breast once more.

When most of the attacking Zomborges were clustered, jam packed to capacity, and the gatehouse walls seemed to bulge outwardly. The king ordered the portcullises be dropped, "Now!

Drop the iron gates!" The king's voice rang out as the defenders of Edawnian took one giant step back.

The gatekeepers at each portcullis lock took their sledgehammers in hand and pounded away the quick release latches. Chains rattled like writhing iron snakes, and pulleys screamed as the two huge portcullis gates came crashing down. At each opposing opening, frontline Zomborges were caught under the gate spikes, crushing and piercing their rotting meat through and through. They were quickly dispatched as the edge of Edawnian swords struck their spiny necks. Pus from infected tissue poured out of their stumps to end their surreal high pitched screeching.

The Zomborge packed gatehouse was brimming over like a boiling cauldron, making its hold look like an overflowing maggot infestation. Those Zomborges that managed to escape the well executed trap were cornered and beheaded. "Get up to the barbicans! Quickly!" The king's commanding voice stirred with strength almost shrilling with excitement. "Afford them no mercy," the king demanded.

At that very same moment, Baddlock was laughing a diabolical laugh, watching gleefully as his evil plan unfolded. He was milking the moment for all it was worth when suddenly, his crooked and gnarled fingers tightened so tightly around the eyepiece of his long eye that it made his knuckles creak like a rusted hinge. A sense of confusion simultaneously swept across the features of his face. He focused his long eye and saw the tattered Edawnian army come out through the rifted Northern Gate, only to pour back in through every break, crack and breach of Edawn's north wall. What he found alarming was that his Zomborge forces were not in hot pursuit!

The demons within the undead immediately realized they were trapped and felt helpless fear and outraged anger at the same time. There they were, trapped, unable to retreat, for their escape behind them was jammed with other Zomborges pinned against the rear portcullis, their advance and retreat sealed. Nor could they stay put, for that meant certain death. Sooner or later, their hosts were bound to be slain from above. In a frantic rush, they all at once stormed up the walls. What was left of the Edawnian defenses instantly rallied, somehow breaking out of the inertia of their short lived reprieve. They went up the opposite side of the walls all at the same time, to meet the climbing Zomborges on the other side.

Kondor propped Zandor up against the nearest wall and rushed to join the slaughter. On his way, he struck a Zomborge from behind cracking his skull. The incapacitated beast pitched forward headfirst, where the Edawnian women finished it off with their gardening tools. His long sword blade droned and clashed through the dead flesh of the fading demon ranks. By this time, Zandor had begun to feel aching warmth in the tips of his toes as the feeling in his legs started to return. He tried to get to his feet. He wobbled, almost fell, steadied himself, took a few staggering steps and then fell.

Kondor stood atop the gatehouse like a beacon of power, prepared to meet the forerunners trying to escape the death trap below. He focused on a face that was a mass of pus and decay. It surprised Kondor how fast the creature came up out of the pit toward him, somehow managing to carry its heavy, wicked ax with it. Whack! He struck the monster down with a devastating drive from his sword across the face, shattering its temple and slicing on through its head to burst out the other side with a soggy scrunch. The Zomborge's head exploded in a spray of several fragments of teeth and bone, and yellow blood and brains as its skull disintegrated under Kondor's massive blow. The breath of its pungent mist reeked of green, rotting limburger cheese. The demonic Zomborge fell back, howling, and dropped onto the climbing swarm. Mangled and dismembered cadavers dripping grisly slaughter down their shoulders, and rib cages from their bloody headless stumps fell one by one to Kondor's blade.

Outside the gatehouse, the screams from incapacitated Zomborges ended with a sickening *thud* as their skulls were cracked like eggshells. With spiked ball maces and war hammers, women, children, and the elderly smashed what was left of their driving system into gory jelly. Their screams rose to join the escalating panic filled howls of the wireless puppets in the pit. Every capable Edawnian Warrior, able woman, and child of age by now had reached the upper walkways surrounding the gatehouse. And in unison, every able defender began to throw whatever they could find down upon the dwindling hordes of Zomborges. The demented wails of empty minded ghouls echoed sounds of breaking bones.

Whatever would inflict maximum casualties was thrown from the barbican. Stone blocks, scraps of metal, lances, arrows, and anything and everything at the defenders' disposal were used to keep the Zomborge hordes at bay. Arrow slit planks were removed from the sides of the walls, enabling archers and lancers to pick off the trapped hordes of invaders. The Zomborge masses found themselves locked into the massive gatehouse that became their slaughtering pen. Horrified men stood before former comrades, now demon slaves. They knew that their friends were already dead, for their soul was not within them. They knew that it was not really them, but still they had great difficulty in hacking them to pieces instead, they were taken captive with long grappling poles.

At length, pots filled with a boiling mixer of resin, sulfur, pine tree sap, and oily petroleum were carried up and poured into the death pit. Archers with incendiary arrow ignited the volatile mixture, which spawned a bloodcurdling reaction. The screaming by now sounded ominous across the plains as it reverberated against the gatehouse walls. When the undead somehow realized that they had very little time left, they screamed the louder as all hell broke loose. With powers not their own, they grapple up the vertical stone wall with their huge claws. They dug into the wall with bleeding hands as their nails splintered away from their fingertips. Those that out of reckless desperation managed to reach the upper parts of the gatehouse walls were pushed back down into the rising curls of smoke with long hardwood rods pointed with medal tips.

The uncountable numbers of Zomborge casualties mounted as hundreds flashed and caught on fire. They jerked spasmodically, and fell away as their dead flesh hissed, seared, and sizzled. Flames quickly enveloped them in their final fatal, embrace. The Zomborges that once seemed invincible fell away almost at random as the unrelenting battering whittled them away. Zomborges flopped to the ground squirming and withering like snake masses.

As Zomborges continued falling into the consuming flames, they screamed with tongues undulating at full stretch, struggling to hold on to the walls as the flames consumed them. The boisterous voice of the king called from the archway nearest the gatehouse's main entrance. "Seal off the perimeter, relentlessly slay them from all sides. Let none escape!"

But the demon that indwelled the burning corpses, knowing that their appointed hour was within sight, refused to yield. In a last ditch effort, the Zomborges began to intertwine one upon the other, creating towers of burning flesh that were used to climb out of the flames. Human torches of flesh reached up the tall walls only to be pushed back down, again and again, into the pit of ravaging fires. Eventually, some flaming Zomborges forced their way through, reaching up to overtake Edawnian soldiers on the upper walkways to pull them down with them to be engulfed in the blazing inferno below. At long last, the fading wails from the intertwined forms ebbed away. The smell of burning flesh stood out even above their repulsive stench, as they shriveled into little whirlpools of diffusing gases that made hissing noises as they disintegrated into embers. Finally, the last of the burning Zomborges forms became blackened things that stiffened and fell apart like dwindling twig tinder. They collapsed like limp paper cutouts crumbling down as they fell deeper into the ebbing flames. Ultimately the evil that had come upon the sons of men disintegrated away to ash until they left behind only clods that looked something like piles of dung.

Tom Icon

The battle against the Zomborges had been hard won. Almost every mis-creation had been burnt to a crisp or hacked to pieces. Death squads were sent forth to search among the dead, and dying Zomborges to dispatch those remaining ghouls that were grotesquely still jerking. Whether they were convulsing or not, their necks were wrung to make sure they were dead. As their last gasps came, and their jaws loosened, they lost their power to do them harm.

A Zomborge crawling on its hands and knees, its brains oozing from a long gash in its skull, struggled to escape. A child gathering arrows came upon it, took a large stone, and bashed its skull in. The loathsome Zomborge stretched its disgusting arms out, clawed and clutched at the ground, looking even more grotesque in death than it looked when alive if alive is what they were.

Seven
The Light

Deep in the bowels of Zia, just when Izz thought, it would be impossible for the light to get any brighter, there suddenly was what Izz perceived to be another more dazzling bright blast of purer light. The second light, greater than the former one, burst forth so ecstatically intense that it caused Izz's very soul to moan aloud. Like a raging, scintillating storm at its pinnacle the aura of awesome power, oscillated, glared and frolicked to its own rhythm as it shone in the fullness of its perfect glory. At that point, Izz's mind drew a blank. No words could explain or describe it. So bright was the Light of Life that it shredded darkness into a billon invisible fragments.

All at once, the fallen creatures found themselves engulfed within the midst of a supernatural light they had not seen since they were first vanquished into darkness. Their wings shot out to steady themselves. Their eyes bulged as they began to squirm in the lattice of the mystical, magical barrage. In the hyper-dimensional realm where his five senses were all but useless, Izz was utterly stunned, unable to pick his mind out of the muddle. He was unable to make sense of, or recognize what was happening, or where he was in the human condition.

There and then, time began to slow or did it speed up until time itself came to the point of singularity, beyond the spectrum of space, and mind, beyond the quantum boundaries of possibility. All timelines came to exist as one until all movement reached total stillness at its center like unto the eye of a hurricane.

Abaddawn, in the act of desperation moved in to reclaim his prize. However, an indiscernible fraction of time later, from within the great light, a smaller white flashpoint of magnesium like bright luminosity exploded. It was so instantaneous that its expansion spread across the chamber with an imperceptible velocity like the strike of a bolting flash of lightning. So fast and powerful was its outward eruption that it violently rent and shattered the surrounding space in one blaring quantum leap, faster than thought. Its edges spilled out as bright as a detonation, obscuring every form in the hollow with a blinding fire of Holiness. Within the clutches of evil, Izz suddenly disappeared in their midst as if a divine hand had stretched out to protect him. And Abaddawn found that instead of holding Izz in his eminent grasp, he held a fistful of emptiness. The guardians of the cesspit momentarily silhouetted the walls as an inhuman howl filled the dungeon.

At this moment in time, the Keepers of the Light and the keepers of darkness confronted each other face to face, Principalities clashing with principalities. There was no fellowship between the cosmic encounter. The Light lived only to love and bless. The darkness existing only to hate and defile. The only real purpose of the rulers of darkness was to subjugate all of humanity and overthrow the rightful Masters of all things. Abaddawn rage filled wails trembled in the air as he struggled to hold on. "He is mine by right!" Abaddawn screamed in anger. His words were swallowed in the celestial winds. Every evil being was momentarily blinded as the exalted sheer Power encased the workers of iniquity and stopped them cold where they stood. Abaddawn's look of loathing suddenly changed to one of fear as he coward from the same overpowering force that twisted his mind and sent him reeling backward. His demonic lords folded their wings, screamed, shrieked, and cried out profanities, worse than Izz could have ever imagined. The keepers of the dark could not bear to be in the midst of the light that was so torturous for them. Darkness was forced to bow and concede that the Light was its Master. Every negative entity was instantly made to drop to their knees, bound to the core of Zia. Completely, utterly, totally, and wholly conquered. The evil spirits from their knees fell to their faces. Abaddawn the last to fall spewed out the most horrendous blasphemies that they can be neither written nor repeated. The prince of lightlessness darkened against the miraculous light as the Light's Splendor obliterated his presence

Without warning the floor, walls, and ceiling bulked and bulged, and suddenly crumbled. Debris crashed down from the ceiling as everything tumbled down and flew away all around Izz. The inner circle of evil, including Abaddawn, toppled headlong, followed by their physical duplicates as what was left of the walls shot downward through such unimaginable emptiness. And they plunged beyond the boundaries of the tangible where Izz had intended to be cast. Behind were left thirteen scorched outlined afterglows where the walls once were, where the unholy thirteen had once been crucified.

Suddenly Izz found himself surrounded in a boiling sea of sub universal white patches of dancing light so intensely bright that the hollows where his eyes once where ached. Its gleaming glow illuminated the vault like a brilliant sunlit day where the light had once been impossible. The Creator of all things Himself had descended into the bowels of the deep to recover that one lost sheep from His flock.

There was an ever growing realization in Izz's mind and heart that the cascading astral storm was becoming impossibly brighter and brighter, blazing with hues beyond the color spectrum. Izz felt, tasted, and heard the supremacy of angelic harmonies full of caring and pity, resonating at the edge of the overwhelming light source. Its brightness seemed to saturate his brokenness, unexpectedly seeping into each speck of his existence as if soaking up through his pores. A torrent of energy pierced through him and shone greater and more powerful as its pure brilliance fanned out until its rush trembled and crackled across the face of the deep. Izz's whole being glowed and every scar and blemish fell away like clods of dirt disappearing as he felt a feathery supernatural presence of divine energy sweeping across his soul.

Abaddawn was drawn back, vanquished into an inky dark radius cratered out of the lightless backdrop. He desperately clung on to an invisible edge, against an immense gravitational pull, which progressively tightened its grip around him. Terror stricken, Abaddawn was wrenched back toward a horizontal boundary of a rotating vent of darkness. He teetered on the very edge. He was firmly fixed drained away through a point beyond which nothing could escape. Abaddawn struggled in opposition to a powerful tidal force thumbing over the side, reeled away with both hands covering his face. And like an elongating, hideously deformed ghost, he was stretched out of proportion. He was transformed more and more into a warped image as narrow bands lengthened his form until the phenomenal gravitational force became stronger than the bonds that held him together in one piece. Abaddawn began to snap apart and disintegrated rapidly from there, pulled in shredding streams, reduced into the smallest parts, then the smallest particles, until he was disconnected into the finest possible subatomic dust.

Izz's tattered hair and cloth fragments waft toward the siphoning whirlpool as he braced himself against the powerful wave force. In the great distance, Abaddawn was followed by his twelve henchmen out of existence. They were gobbled up beyond the horizontal matrix of some out of world existence. They were then squeezed so dense; they were crushed into an infinite point of intrinsic imprisonment. In their paradoxical fate, the thirteen were squashed into a small ball no bigger than a pea. The distorted end they had reserved for Izz had become their own. However, the Light did not wholly destroy the evil inner circle. The Omnipotent only drove him deeper beneath the surface to be banished for the while.

The unbelievably forceful bedazzlement that had been unleashed had left Izz grasping. Out of seemingly nowhere a million shafts of astral like illumination strikes bathed him in its molten white light. In Izz's next thoughts, he eventually realized that the presence of evil was gone. He saw between his eyes a white ellipse like an eternal cosmic glow that shone so bright that Izz experienced flash blindness. He had to avert his eyes, squinting against the sudden burst from the enormous white hot like fireball.

His eyes! Without stopping to think another thought his right hand wonderingly came up to his face as his left hand slipped to his midsection to feel the roundness of his restored eyes and stomach. Under his lids, his eyes rotated in their sockets. Inside he could feel the intestines that once hung limp in his hands were now restructured and rewound in his belly. Izz's heart was simultaneously healed, leaving a deep scar that did not remember its wound.

At that same moment, the memory of his nightmare disintegrated within its own wickedness. Meanwhile, the strangled, shrieks of the fallen faded and died away in the fathomless distance. Izz suddenly found himself upon a solid pedestal that seemed rock solid, as he stood on his own two feet as if at the very pinnacle of the universe. All other ground was sinking sand. As a strange, propped up feeling held him, all around him, all traces of the solid ground were gone, sucked down into the eternal oblivion of nothingness below. Only the small pillar where Izz stood remained. Izz felt as if he was perched on edge, suspended from the thinnest strand over an immense void of emptiness. He clung to his foothold seemingly by the tips of his toenails and shivered, not daring to move.

Just as Zuree was coming completely unhinged, totally unable to cope with the thought that Izz's heart had sounded its last hollow beat. Unexpectedly out of nowhere, a bright flash of light filled the chamber and streaked across Zuree's vision. An outward transformation of an inward change exploded across Izz's presence as every scar and wound seemed to fall away as Izz's whole appearance was suddenly set aglow.

As Izz balanced himself on what seemed like the point of a needle, His spirit was reanimated, and life returned to his soul in all its fullness. His mind regained the power of clear thought and was abruptly whisked from its phantasm, snapping him instantly back into focus, as if reborn. For a split moment within the midst of the overwhelming brilliance, he found himself careening with more fright than he had felt from the wicked darkness. It was more than he could believe all at once. It was beyond anything he had ever experienced or wished to experience up to then. Tiny patches of sparks flickered and danced in the air around him, swirling as they mingled and spiraled into a sparkling eddy that engulfed him.

Baddlock sat atop Nightmare, staring towards Edawn, shocked numb as he listened to the unmistakable, high pitched, piercing cries, and hysterical screams of his treasured, dying pets, droning in his ear. He listened with astonishment as their panic filled howls, dwindled to muffled wails, which in time faded into a few lone moans and whimpers. Then that too was cut off. Finally, an eerie silence swept through the kingdom and across the valley until the kingdom broke out into a rumble of guarded celebration. The Wicked Warlock Wizard exploded in outrage at the catastrophic reversal of events. Through gritted teeth, he ranted and railed obscenities and blasphemies against King Ozzdon and the Kingdom of Edawn. The deep, folded furrows of his bony, macabre face puffed up until Dandork and Darkon thought he might burst a blood vessel.

Tigbone shrank away, holding one hand up defensively because there was no way of knowing what crazed state of violence Baddlock would fly into. He knew full well that the savage mood blazing in the Wicked Warlock Wizard's eyes always led to pain. Baddlock wheeled Nightmare around violently its muscles and tendons strained as spurs dug in without mercy. "Assemble our main forces! *Immediately!*" he screamed at his Norticlan generals. "Leave nothing to chance this time. This siege must find its end once and for all. Hit them with everything that is at our disposal, slay them all without mercy, wipe them off the face of Zia, for all time." The Wicked Warlock Wizard continued to spew as his breath oozed of foul air from his mouth like a flammable gas. The Norticlan leaders bowed low in homage and complied instantly. The mobilization order was passed on down the ranks with long, loud calls that were accented with the penetrating horn blasts of war. Every Norticlan warrior near and far heard the call and knew what it meant. At once, there arose a long, draw out reverberation, as a unifying cry roared up as the war drums began beating an ever maddening rhythm. The depleted Edawnian resistance would be no match for the monstrous Norticlan war machine. By their sheer numbers alone, even if the Norticlanders had been armed only with sticks, the entire kingdom would have been overthrown easily, and then a new terror would ensue.

Back at the kingdom, the Edawnians were still indulging in a cautious, muffled cheer and giving one another congratulatory hugs and pats on the back. And just when King Ozzdon had started to feel good about their chances for survival, his elated hope was cut short. From the enemies' encampment came the unnerving faraway sound of the ram's horn blast, calling the Norticlan assembly to battle, followed by the ominous beating of the war drums. Then from within Edawn, they heard a roar from so many voices, that it sounded like a giant seismic tidal wave crashing toward them, from a raging ocean of humanity. The rumble of an assembling army was clear, and the king realized that their chances of making it through the next confrontation had just suddenly dropped to about a million to one. An audible, collective gasp sucked the breath from every man's lips. A profound silence abruptly eclipsed the momentary celebration. The gloomy silence that ensued over the kingdom was so complete, so total, and so final that they could taste its sorrow in the air. Stunned, the king called to the watchman on the northern tower, who was already staring through his spyglass toward the northern horizon. "What say you in the tower?"

The watchman stood frozen, speechless for a moment. He seemed stunned, dazed, then devastated, then traumatized as he looked through his long eye. He could make out the thousands of mounted riders, and at least thousands of foot warriors, jostling rapidly into their attack formations. They deployed to the right and left and skirted the hillside from every side, quickly bulging out to the farthest horizon in every direction. His eyes could find no end of their, ranks from their front lines, column after column thronged back to as far as the eye could see. There was no end to the sight of tens of thousands strong. The unfolding scene was beyond incredible as to seem impossible. Like a nightmarish human anthill, with so many moving combatants that the hillside disappeared beneath the attack force. The watchman took in, with increasing, justifiable astonishment, the violent eruption of man and beast as the coming holocaust unfolded. As he stared, his jaw dropped, and his shoulders suddenly collapse from the heavy burden he beheld. The immense skyline, through his long eye, seemed to undulate as the colossal assemblage of men and animals spilled over and came into their final attack formation.

After the longest moment, the watchman recovered and found his tongue to report, "The enemy is on the march…there are so many of them. There are thousands of thousands…and they are all getting ready to come our way! We are about to be overrun." The hearing of this caused a deafening hush to fall over the kingdom, sending a spine chilling rush of curdling blood through every man's veins. It was as if an icy shadow had suddenly eclipsed the ever increasing brightness of the gathering conjunction.

Baddlock sat upon Nightmare at the forefront of his massive Norticlan armies. He had already decimated the heart of Edawn and her people. But now he wanted her soul and that of her people. He fiercely reined his warhorse to face his Norticlan warlords and commanding generals. He sucked the dross from his nostrils, spat contemptuously, and said as if casting a curse, "Be merciless toward all!" As if the savage slayers of men had to be told. "Kill and destroy!" he cried out as he gnashed his teeth in rage. "Annihilate and eradicate!" Nightmare danced skittishly to one side as the Wicked Warlock Wizard bellowed. "The more you kill and destroy, the better you will, please me. I want no prisoners, except for the Royal Family. Do you understand?"

The Norticlan leadership, dismounted, dropped to their knees and bowed their heads, in homage, with their noses nearly touching the dirt. Then quickly, they sprang upon their war mounts to obey their master. Baddlock drew Dandork near and spoke in no uncertain terms, "I want the Royal Family alive and in one piece. Fill their souls with fear, drive them to despair, but do not kill them. I have very special plans for them."

As those words left Baddlock's lips, Dandork took a step back when he saw Baddlock's eyes blazing with a hatred that rose from deep within his black heart. A crazed, demonic smile spread across his lips, almost stretching from ear to ear, that could have made a goblins blood run cold. Baddlock then turned to address the Norticlan Armies, and shouted, "Destroy with the sword everyone —men, women, young and, old. Kill every living thing!"

Every Norticlan Warrior began in unison to beat their swords against their shields and scream their banshee salutations to their demon gods of war. They filled their minds with thoughts of blood and the lust for death. The resonance of their war cry escalated until it sounded like clasps of rolling thunder. Their faces were impassive and lined with cruelty. Their dark eyes darted around as their call to battle intensified into a shuddering disturbance. Their battlecry rivaled the most violent of supercharged storms as they readied themselves for the point of no return.

"Kill them all!" Baddlock's voice grew fierce with madness. "Crush them!" the Wicked Warlock Wizard screamed as he extended his bony finger toward the kingdom of Edawn. His hand then coiled into a twisted, knotted claw as if he was strangling something.

In the heart of the underworld, there was a frenzied movement of demonic underlings, frantic and disorganized, as pandemonium threatened to erupt into a total mass of global disruption. From his new black hole imprisonment, Abaddawn's rage had hit the apex of his uttermost hatred for humanity. He combined and released every enslaved force of darkness at his command. He launched an all out attack focused on the world of Zia, spewing his fury and vengeance first and foremost on Edawn's inhabitants. Out of the blackness came a screeching howl. Apparitions of evil flashed in and out of the realm of chaos that swirled around the Norticlan Armies like a whirlwind of heightened violence. "Woe unto the inhabitance of Edawn, for evil has come down upon you, having great wrath, because deep within it knows that it has only a short time left to it."

From the tower of Edawn, each Norticlan Warrior became a grain of sand in a vast, gathering sandstorm of humanity. The onrushing assault created a thousand different sounds of an unquestionable approaching upheaval. The staggering numbers relentlessly bolted forward to bring into existence an interwoven phenomenon, like a massive arrowhead formation that transformed into an unstoppable, charging, monstrous giant.

The haggard, bone tired Edawnian survivor's eyes grew round, almost bulging out of their heads as every man caught a reflected glimpse of bottomless despair in one another's eyes. The hope that had been raised so high over their monumental victory over the Zomborges was now instead disintegrating into the dust. Every man in the battered, tattered assemblage at once came to terms with reality and knew at that moment that the end, beyond any doubt, had come for them. Things could only go downhill from there.

Everyone knew that the Norticlanders were fierce, murderous henchmen. Their brutality was well known far and wide. They were strange people that afflicted merciless cruelty on their own people, feared by all for their immoral and criminal inhumanity to their enemies. Every member of their clans was a battle hardened warrior, trained in every method of killing, which they enjoyed and were very good at. Each sect had perfected their hellish skills over centuries of intertribal wars. They were ruthless brutes that walked like men, their bodies covered with hair; their teeth filed to a point for tearing. They were the most terrible of enemies, and the riotous sound of their advance rumbled like the roar of an approaching storm that sounded as if the whole Norticlan world was bearing down on them.

The pathetic refuse that had once been the mighty Edawnian Forces, the most elite army in all of Zia lay in a wasted stupor of exhaustion. Each heart in its own way broken. Stunned faces splattered with the clotted blood of their friends and caked with Zomborge gore, bore the outward expression of the most horrible day of their lives. Yet every man knew that the worst was still to come. They knew they would not survive. There was no way to hide from that, and so they tried to prepare their hearts accordingly as men might when facing an executioner they knew was coming for them. Each heartfelt the weight of the brokenness of their wills as they looked to their king for a glimmer of inspiration, of hope, or reason, or anything.

The king smiled sadly, determined not to give way despite the feeling of the deep grief that pervaded his men. He commanded halfheartedly, "Man your posts, Sons of Edawn." The words were meant to lift the spirits of his warriors. But it was more like standing in the middle of a cemetery, trying to call forth the resurrection of the dead. Zandor, who was usually a man of very few words, was the only one that spoke up. "There is no longer any remedy, my Lord. Let us not waste time pretending otherwise." There was no denying it. He knew his day had come, and he accepted that. His noble head, usually held high with his typical gallant dignity, fell in resignation.

King Ozzdon immediately knew that Zandor was right, but he did not want anyone else to believe it. He looked at his men and could see it in their eyes and in their faces—a hopelessness like that of men about to go down on a sinking ship. Defeat and dread had descended over them like a burial shroud. And he was chilled to the bone as his face turned a deeper shade of pale. Zandor's words only confirmed the sense of doom that he had not dared to put into thoughts, much less words. With a heavy heart, he staggered back a foot dragging step. It had been one unfairness too many, and his will surrendered to the weariness and nothingness of staying alive.

From atop the main northern keep, Ammiz's watery eyes flashed beneath shaggy white eyebrows. He stared intently at the impending military attack that dwarfed any other ever witnessed or ever written about. The thousands and thousands filled his vision, onrushing toward the kingdom like shifting sand trailed by a massive cloud of dark dust, swiftly making its way across the valley. They swarmed toward Edawn like a black breaking wake of a roiling flood. A flood that was made up of a never ending multitude of those whose only propose was nothing less than to trample Edawn into oblivion. At the forefront, the Norticlan cavalry led the charge, notorious for their brutality and their love of violence. At the lead rode the flag bearers flying the skull head banners of Phantomsdeep. Between the banners, Ammiz spotted a gruesome sight. He saw what appeared to be the flailed outer skins of the royal family of Skymount—the king, the queen, and their three youngest children.

Behind them followed the infantry, human animals that were eager for blood and reward. Trailing in the dust filled horizon were the mass of munitions and equipment, the mobile siege towers, ballista, and a monstrous battering ram drawn by hundreds of yakoxen. Men, like giant cockroaches, raced for the final onslaught, for the honor of taking the jeweled trophies of Edawn and it's spoils. Looming on the horizon were so many men amassed in such vast numbers that they became indistinguishable from one another. Their lust for blood was so intense. It was like an aura of wrongness that had come to life. A shocking indiscernible frenzy of movement crested over of the upper valley from every side like a convulsing surf from the darkest ocean. The approaching surge of men and beast appeared like a raging disturbance of figures dressed in black just as dark as their minds, hearts, and souls. They just kept coming and coming and coming, as if every demon from hell had suddenly been set free from its depths.

Amid the chaos, the approaching conjunction suddenly seemed to intensify against the deep, endless, purple sky. Like fettered orbs locked into their uninterruptible, celestial course, they coursed through the skies toward their fixed point. Once more, in their one thousand year cycle, all seven oscillating planets cast their mysterious brilliance from their distant location. They glowed like solar furnaces against the outer boundaries of the universe, outshining every star in their background.

For a prolonged moment, Ammiz stared at the procession of planets, like a broken light in his eyes, moving in immeasurable increments. *There is not much time.* Ammiz thought to himself, and for a time, he was lost in contemplation as he folded his arms behind his back and began pacing around the keep's deck searching out a reason to believe.

Then the seer's eyes shifted and slowly scanned over the kingdom as he assessed the situation. The man of the keenest mind on Zia focus jumped from one implausibility to another. He searched up one side of his mind and down the other, trying to sift things out. He disparately tried to make some sense out of their do or die plight. But he could not get his mind through it, under it, over it, or around it. Every likelihood led him back to the same old nasty dead end. The crippling blow of their disastrous retaliatory strike had left them decimated. The catapult onslaught had reduced the kingdom's defensive walls to inside out, practically upside down rubble. On top of all that, the courageous, resistance against the Zomborge attack had resulted in grievous loses. The streets were covered with corpses as far as the eye could see, and the cries of the dying still filled the air with a pitiful chorus of groaning and moaning pleas for help. Many of their highest ranking leaders were dead, or too injured to command. What he saw ripped his heart apart and hurt his eyes from staring so intently. To say they had a disaster on their hands would undermine the graveness of the situation.

Their superhuman defense and their heavy casualties to this point had all been ultimately for nothing. Ammiz admitted grudgingly, *Edawn's future looks bleak, to say the least.* In another hour, nothing would make any difference. Deep shadows began to gather within, pressing tightly around his web of reasoning, like an unpleasant knot tightening in his heart. Sorrow descended over him like a dimming fog that covered his soul, pushing his thoughts to the farthest point in his mind, where they disappeared into a deep dark hole. A sense of inevitable doom and gloom reigned, and all the seer's mind could see was only the end coming. He found himself uncharacteristically filled with despair, but his old heart refused to falter, and somehow, Ammiz could not manage to let go of his flickering hope.

Something spiritual sparked in the old man's heart of hearts. Almost immediately, the greatest mind in Zia, realized that his last thoughts had been a useless chain of tarnished beliefs. Wide eyed, the visionary stared inwardly at himself, trying to gather his shattered thoughts, and saw an odd inner expression of his soul. Was that strange person him? Was that the true value of his character? From the depths within his spirit, the minutest jot of rebounding courage stirred like a rubber ball ricocheting off the walls of his inner mind. He realized that the alternative thought patterns, at the edges of his mind, led only into a world that was rapidly collapsing all around him, where only fear, death, and defeat existed. It takes a true master to banish disbelief and conquer despair in the heart of hopelessness. Ammiz knew that at that moment, the only thing to fear was the possession of fear itself. He cursed fear, knowing it only existed in the minds and hearts of double minded men. The seer tethered his thoughts on that deepening alternative consciousness of inward courage. He allowed himself to trust and felt himself being swept away by the thought guide of some exterior power. The element of doubt that had polluted his mind fell out of the back of his head. Just as he felt hope's flames begin to blaze up from within his guts, an intuitive voice called out to him. It spoke from the innermost corner of his mind, *Do not forget for an instance that you do not war against flesh and blood. You are in a spiritual battle, and you must fight in the realm of the spiritual world. Fear begets only fear. The only power darkness has over you is the power you have given up to it. Yield to your higher self. Only a courageous feat has the slightest hope now.*

The words he heard in his thoughts were accompanied by an undeniable and unquestionable surge of faith. And Ammiz found strength in his weakness. What just happened both, staggered his mind and boggled his imagination, as the union of his heart, mind, and soul danced around a central point. And someday he would have to examine and determine what mystical enlightenment had come to him—if he lived that long. If not... well, maybe he had lived too long already, either way, death no longer seemed to frighten him; and besides, there was nothing to lose.

Ammiz turned his attention to the courtyard below, his racing mind slowed, and his pulse quickened. Under the light of the coming conjunction, the king looked haunted. He read the expressions of the appalled and overburdened minds of men that stood fixed, staring blankly into space. Every man's mind that had turned to their king for an answer seemed rooted in discombobulating fear. Wherever he looked, he saw the bleak thoughts and feelings pasted on the faces of men helplessly cut adrift. And when their king gave no response, each man seemed to be struggling to find his own way, his truth, his reason to hang on. Hope was a fading echo of an echo in each man's soul that resounded like a hollow heartbeat. He knew that they had nothing left but a stark, collective longing to get it over with. Every single last one of them—the king, Zandor, Kondor, Arius, all of them had long since resigned and made peace with their fate. The body could take just about anything, it was the mind that ultimately broke the man, and it was hopelessness that broke their hearts.

Somehow Ammiz knew something he did not know. The only tiny corner of hope that was still burning in the whole kingdom of Edawn was locked fast in the seer's heart of hearts. From the depths of that tiny corner, passion rose from the deepest level, busting alive, and he whispered to a greater power than himself, "I will surrender my trust to you." Then the seer turned to the Edawnian warriors still standing below, lifted his rod, and whirled it forcefully in a full circle about him. Next Ammiz mightily raised his voice to the highest heavens: "The demons are almost upon us. Why, oh why, do you just stand there bellyaching, feeling sorry for your sniveling selves, and only awaiting hell to damn you? We may be hard pressed on every side, but we are not yet crushed. Do you not know? Do you not realize that the real battle is won in the heart? Live through your hearts, not your minds!"

Surprised men turned and stared up at the seer, the king held his breath; and there was silence as deep as death itself. Like blind men regaining their sight and seeing for the first time, they just stood there, blinking and squinting, gawking up at Ammiz. Sensing at that most critical moment that leadership was their last hope in the world, Ammiz continued, "To free your minds, you must release all of your uncertainties, fears, and disbelief." What he was saying, he could not explain, only feel.

Iridescent images began to rush and riot through Izz's head, growing frantic and chaotic, perplexing and puzzling, lost in complexity. In the next increment of existence, in one gigantic instance, there was a mega intense explosion of splendorous light that made its forerunners seem more like a shadow before its yawning radiance. It was more brilliant than the combined splendor of all the intensifying eruptions of light that had preceded it. Beyond any quantum of luster, the new light discharged with the force of an intense solar storm that swept across the void and spread like ripples from a disturbed cosmic pond. In the wake of the discharge that filled the air, shock waves of energy crackled throughout with overwhelming force and supremacy. From its center, Izz saw an exploding fireball of crystal and silver coming at him. When the light came in contact with him, it seemed to lift his body into the air. Izz felt an electric shock fill his mind full of light that shot simultaneously from end to end, dancing through his spine and down his limbs from head to toe. At first, his skin tingled painfully as white hot light surrounded him like energy throbbing in his pulse and thickening over him like a warm blanket. Flaring points of escalating illumination streamed around Izz like rogue stars shining in all of their awesome and amazing grandeur. Countless light orbs flashed and outlined dazzling arcs in the air that surged and swirled and surrounded him with iridescent streaks of dazzling impulses jousting and recoiling off one another in sacred geometric patterns.

Ammiz somehow knew that this was the moment he was born to take charge of; it would be now, or never. The visionary, whose equal will never be seen again, on the face of Zia carefully chose his words as he raised his voice so that all could hear, to the amazement of all. "Hear, O Edawn…the thing that threatens you most…and weakens you most the infectious condition that will kill you more surely than all the demon armies from hell is the fear that freezes and binds your hearts. Many have given their lives this day. Some will not see the sunrise another day. If we must perish from Zia this day, let us the living be counted among those that died with honor, so that those that have gone before us will not have died in vain. Brothers of Edawn! Prepare to make your last stand! Quickly, into the inner citadel, defy evil until the last drop of Edawnian blood has soaked into the land that you love!"

All around Izz, the proliferating sphere of multicolored lights continued to sweep over him, engulfing him, and utterly saturating him. Izz felt as if he would burst from the electrifying energy that was swirling around inside of him. Like living fountains of shimmering and glittering waters, the light cascaded into the softest rainbow colors. Izz could see, feel, hear, taste, and smell its colors. He panted with the rhythm of its fluctuation. The divine light filled him to the full and overflowing. Izz's mind was swept clean, and all the grim, stench, and filth—all the hurt and all the pain fell away. And all evil that had tried to plunder Izz's soul and had come so close to prevailing lifted like an unclean, foul, black haze of toxins dissolving away.

Izz's mind refocused, and peace returned to his heart and soul. An order he had never known before. He was made whole and filled with love, joy, and ecstasy all at once. He breathed in the strength of the light into every cell—patching up, cleaning, and nourishing every hurt in his being. His spirit sang out with the pure energy like that of Zuree's love that folded over and over, increasing infinitely with every tiniest incremented moment that passed. It was the best feeling Izz had ever felt in his life. It was the completion of everything—nothing missing, nothing lost, the All in All, embracing, blessing, and loving him. Izz was lifted up and away, moving through a world of living, light, and energy. The relief of having been lost and nearly dead and being brought back to life made him feel as if a billion effervescent bubbles were bursting and releasing every beautiful feeling of joy and warmth that he had ever felt all over, over and over.

There came a warm beam of consciousness beyond the spectrum of space, time, and mind in one glorious now. Omnipresent realities reversed time and resonated at the edge of an energy matrix of infinite singularities transformed back to the central source of the creation of all things. Only the authority of a loving Creator could have delivered him from the jaws of everlasting damnation. It was extreme and stayed intense for what seemed like forever and ever.

Eight
The Last Stand

The seer stood at the top of the main keep with his staff in the air, in the heart of the kingdom, at the center of Zia from where he beckoned hope into the souls of the men below. "We must fight on," Ammiz insisted. "Who is we?" King Ozzdon asked.

"Whoever it is that is left of us. Honor demands it."

The boldness in Ammiz's voice broke through the inertia that ill fated fear was seeping into the marrow of every Edawnian warrior's bones.

The seer's words struck the king with such a powerful force, awakening him into action, seemingly rousing him from his perplexity. The only foreseeable choice was to try. King Ozzdon wondered what difference it would make to go on the defensive when he knew they could not win. However, the old man had an uncanny way of swaying his confidence. With one titanic effort, he gathered what little encouragement he had left. And as he picked his chin up off of the ground, he lifted his sword from where it hung limp at his side, and proclaimed, "Men of Edawn, we fight to the death. If Edawn is to fall, we will have to fall first." A note of pride entered his voice. "Gather the wounded and your weapons. He made a sweeping gesture toward the citadel. "Retreat into the inner bastions, of the keep where we will rendezvous with death if that be our destiny," he added unrepentantly.

The king's men saluted him solemnly, like gladiatorial warriors paying tribute before they died in his honor. For a while, the king mumbled to himself as the weakness of his last few moments penetrated, trying hard to convince himself, that that had not been him a moment ago. It had been someone else, a stranger he did not know. He gazed up at Ammiz, feeling his indebtedness. Ammiz had been his only defense against a world rapidly coming apart and falling under the control of madness. The seer looked confident. Perhaps there was a slim chance they could resist until their reinforcements arrived, and this gave him peace, for now. The king sniffed deeply, and got a hold of himself, knowing there was no time for self doubt.

As time raced by, the noises of combat came rushing closer and closer towards them from all sides of the northern front. Exhausted troops, bloody, dirty and soaked with sweat, gathered their wounded and whatever provisions they could scrounge together. The thwarted procession of broken souls, just slightly less demoralized, quickly made their way behind their bravest women and children towards the kingdom's main stronghold.

Painfully, Zandor groped for his weapon and staggered to his feet, still weak from his injury, clearly, before he was fully combat effective again. Zandor's nerve function began to tingle, and his strength began to return enough for him to walk under his own power. With Kondor's help, the twins followed the besieged, beleaguered band of busted up, bloodstained Edawnians as they shuffled toward the entrance that led into the fortress of the main keep. As the first men entered the main door of the stronghold, they heard the encroaching shouts of the Norticlanders closing in. They listened to the extremely bitter, repulsive sound of the words of their language as they poured in at will and bore down on the kingdom like a marauding flock of vaulters swooping in to pick over a carcass.

The full assault of thundering horse's hooves and charging feet battered the earth and pounded the ground, filling the air with a whirlwind of dust. The king called out to the gatekeepers, watchmen, and the upper wall archers to retreat to the keep. A handful of brave archers, in a feat of undaunted courage, defied their king's command for the first time. They stood their ground to ensure that their comrades had a fighting chance to reach the fortifications of the inner keep. Each bowman moved into position on either side of the kingdom's main breached entrances, to lie in wait for the moment in which they could inflict the most damage. The retreating Edawnian forces hobbled and dragged their wounded, as the seething panorama of attackers, too many to count, much less to fight, rushed in through almost everywhere. At once, hundreds became thousands, heaving, splashing, and pouncing in from every side, all at once howling and shouting, plunging into the kingdom like an avalanche, weapons in hand, voraciously lusting for war. And very soon all would deteriorate into chaos.

Men that had nothing to lose, no wives, no children stayed behind waited in their secret places at strategic points around the courtyard. Biding their time they waited as the Norticlan apoplectic nightmare unfolded. Archers lifted their bows and drew their bowstrings back to their cheeks, knowing there were too many of them to miss. They took careful aim at the first intruder's exposed necks, knowing that they had to make every arrow count. Then suddenly, with suicidal abandonment and without warning, a hail of arrows rained down as hidden Edawnian archers opened fire with their longbows. Never ceasing, never wavering from their objective, with crossbow bolts ricocheting all around them from every direction, they stood their ground and let loose of their arrows again and again. Every arrow became swift death as they found their mark. The clustered Norticlanders began to drop in droves. But the defenders, despite their greatest effort, did not even put an indentation in the surging crest of assailants. Their noble stand only served to slow the invaders down. The brave Edawnian archers fell like birds from their perches as they were pierced with countless bolts from powerful crossbows. Inspired by the selflessness of the archers, those that lagged on the ground drew their swords and waded out into the middle of a deep sea of Norticlan enemies that stepped forth to crush them. They knew they were helpless to stop the advancing tsunami. It had been ultimately meaningless, more like a death wish. By forfeiting themselves for the better good of their brothers, they afforded the wounded the precious extra time they needed to make their escape into the keep's temporary safety.

Those that moments before thought they had breathed their last, weary and raw from being pushed too far, too hard for too long, reached the inner keep's fortified door. No sooner was the last man through the door when the Norticlan army of death, like a black cloud of doom, completely overran virtually every defensive barrier. The courtyard was crawling with leathery faces and matted beards, striking terror as they plowed down on the meager defenders.

As the doors were drawn, those inside looked back to see as the valiant defenders, covering the tracks of their retreat came face to face with their enemy. Outflanking Norticlan forces swirled around the courageous martyrs, virtually enveloping them like a churning cyclone of crossing swords and were simply mercilessly slaughtered as they battled for life. As the doors were prepared to be sealed, those inside watched in horror with tear filled eyes when they saw their comrades cut down. The king only wished that he could have sent reinforcements.

The occupation of Edawn had begun. The Edawnian army was already defeated, and, their spirits broken and it's remnants driven into the keep, their last bastion of hope. The last man that intended to seek refuge slipped behind the entryway of the inner keep as the invading Norticlan armies flooded the kingdom's courtyard. The massive reinforced keep doors were closed tight. The heavy crossbeams were set, and the reinforced catches were positioned and locked down. Every entrance was battened down. They were sealed within the inner fortifications of the kingdom, and, there was nothing left to do but wait. They could feel the overwhelming presence of the inrushing hordes as they pressed into the courtyard and surrounded the keep. From all the stomping footfalls and the clattering of armor and weapons, they all knew in essence, that they had back themselves into a corner inside the walls of the keep. It seemed like most everyone was like a ghost on the very edge of depletion in a dead end world that besieged them, sealing their fate for an inevitable out and out bloodbath. It was just a matter of time now. Some wished that they had instead chosen to face the quickness of the blade.

Izz of Zia

Outside the door, the sounds of battle continued—rumblings, shrieks, and clashes—but despite the heroic resistance, the ill fated defensive ended in cries and wailing death rattles, then finally silence. Inside the keep, men's hearts filled with holy dread. A fleeting moment later, the pounding began on the outer side, and the fortified door of the keep shook and rattled with the force of the enemies' frustrated blows. The intensity got louder as more Norticlan troops crowded in, swarming around the keep like agitated hornets. They sounded more and more like wild beasts than humans as the noise just outside the door became an ugly roar of terror filled with an unbroken assault of filthy, foul mouthed cursing. With eyes almost fully rounded, wordlessly those inside the keep just stood there frozen, staring out of their heads. Despite their vastly diminished numbers, they were crammed into overflowing, immobile, staring at each other almost face to face. They could glimpse their own dreaded trepidation mirrored in the faces of the men next to them, and they clutched at their weapons in fear and bottomless desperation. The wounded were strewed throughout the keep's, stunned, and perplex. The king walked among the edgy knot of humanity, hoping to encourage his men, to lift their spirits just a little. They would need strength for what was woefully coming. He let his gaze travel slowly over the keep; his eyes shifted over the assembly, from one anxious face to the other. He had no control whatsoever over what was unfolding outside the keep's fortress walls, and it all seemed so hopeless.

Inside, all the locks were reinforced. They were shut into the inner citadel as tight as a drum, their last sanctuary of defense. The walls within were solid stone inlaid masonry. Not even an earthquake could have damaged them. The windows were protected by interlaced, thick iron bars bored deep into the stone mantels. And the main door was a huge iron hard slab hewed from the giants of the forest and reinforced with iron at every strategic point. The keep was interconnected to the catacombs, but they were probably another dead end since Baddlock was sure to have every way out blocked. The beleaguered men were silent, each with his personal thoughts.

Ammiz and his healers gathered the newly wounded and retreated into the inner keep that spilled into the catacombs where the queen, women and the older children did what they could for the wounded and dying with what they had. Most of the Edawnian citizenry was already deep in the catacombs, where they sought refuge for the present.

The Wicked Warlock Wizard flamboyantly rode Nightmare through the ruinous northern gates of Edawn. He triumphantly smiled reeling in victory, enjoying the spectacle of the destruction and gore he had been responsible for. He strolled down the main street like a conquering deity, ready to declare himself master of Zia. His continence was filled with disdain, mocking, and malice. He had long since given himself over to the darkest powers that gorged on his soul. He fed on the human debasement of death and pain, with the wicked delight only a madman could enjoy. He suddenly pulled back on the reins and brought Nightmare to a halt and reined him in toward the faint sounds of a mortally wounded archer among the fatally wounded. The man's face was covered with blood, his eyes filled with death, and his body ripped with multiple shafts from the powerful crossbows. His throat made gurgling sounds as he shivered and tried to contain his pain. Baddlock called to a nearby Norticlan warrior. "Slay this human garbage." The lawless mystic had long considered Xylenians human dross not worthy of the planet on which they ruled.

The Norticlan warrior responded at once, drawing his long, wicked blade. He closed in on the helpless Edawnian warrior. The archer knew his death was long overdue and could not be harmed any farther. He kept himself steady and braced himself as the Norticlander brought his sword down in a fierce arc. *Whoosh!* The sword sliced through the air. Blood fountained in the air in the direction of the arching blade as it continued its path almost unhindered.

When all the bloodletting came to an end, Baddlock just sat atop his mount in the innermost courtyard of the kingdom, surveying the scene of carnage. His dark, beady eyes glazed over with savagery, and he could not help laughing with enthusiastic delight at his evilness. Then he said maliciously, "I will soon hold the scepter of the whole empire. The Edawnian culture is intellectually inferior, and the noblest thing I can do is rid Zia of them. I want every inhabitant of this wretched kingdom exterminated. Eradicate the entire existence of Edawn." Nightmare let out a loud snort as Baddlock forcefully heeled him into motion and rode to where the last of the Edawnian resistance was barracked.

Through streams of light, Izz concentrated his attention on the source from whence the heavenly flooding light originated. Izz was hardly capable of looking over his shielding arm so brightly shining was the light that it was impossible to look directly upon. The brilliance stabbed at his eyes like the incessant flare of a thousand noonday suns on a blistering, crystalline day. And the light only burned forth brighter and brighter and brighter, outshining the combined brilliance of every star in the universe.

The light swept over and around Izz sanctifying his mind, burning away the uncertainty inside of him. Reflections of rich shads of heavenly hues like eruptions of golden fire reached out to him, pulling everything toward itself without letting up. The light focused as it cascaded past his lips and down his throat, beyond his lungs, and into his heart Izz was purified as silver is refined, and tested as gold is tested. From within Izz's being, his heart danced to the great symphony of life, with the same frequencies of the light's energy, crackling with power, shimmering from its innermost center. The light was love, and Love was the Light, infinitely powerful on all levels.

"What...or who...are you?" Izz heard a voice within his shaky mind coming from inside his trembling heart.

Out of the midst of the Light, an audible Voice of supreme knowledge, wisdom, and infinite power called out to him in a Voice that sounded like something between the rumbling rush of countless waterfalls and the mighty blast of reverberating trumpets. "The question is, who are you? Do you know who you are or how and why you came to be?" The spoken words caused a mist of joyous radiance to form, dance, and whirl like a dome set on fire, scattering light in every direction.

Izz could not even gather his thoughts much less give an answer.

"Did you simply happen without design and purpose? Why are you different from the animals that cannot reason or possess the endowment of knowledge? Are you simply flesh, blood, and bone without an immortal soul? Were you put here, or did you just come to exist through the blind and senseless process of unintelligent material forces without meaning and aspiration? This is the unknown conundrum that has perplexed the higher thinking of man. So they, except for a very few, have shut their minds and mouths in unyielding silence, too ashamed to make mention among themselves of a possible design."

Izz found himself trembling and speechless.

"I Am the All knowing The Three in One whom you call IAM," the Voice spoke with the sound of rumbling thunder. "I stretched out the heavens by the foresight of my understanding. I suspended the stars and founded the world of Zia with the power of My wisdom. And I Am the One that extended my grasp and formed you in the divine order of creation with My own hands. You are a part of my family, and your presence on Zia has a purposeful relation to My intent."

At that precise moment, Izz came to realize the insignificance and insufficiency of his humble existence.

"Come forth," the commanding Voice called out. Izz looked down before him and saw that there was no solid ground beneath his feet.

"Fear not, step forth," the Voice came again.

Izz stepped out upon the void, an unwitting participant in an enfolding, epic, cosmic saga. He was drawn forth over an invisible threshold, traversed along through a gateway linked to interacting cycles, within cycles, within cycles created between an all Omnipotent reality of dimensions, and universes onto infinity. He came to be a drop within an ocean that became an ocean within that drop, where everything he could imagine and yet was to imagine already existed. His body, spirit, and soul stood face to face, each staring at its own opposite as if he was looking into a triangulated mirror. He was aware of himself, as he was a finite state of energy, which was the actual existence of his presence earthbound form.

Before him, standing afar off in the distance, Izz saw a likeness of dazzling brightness like that of Zuree. Then he saw a multitude of many coeternal, blindingly bright human forms of light. Intelligent energies danced and vibrated to make up the super being of breathtaking majestic beauty. Through the eye of his heart, all of a sudden, at the center from an infinite well source of One never ending vibrational energy, Izz saw a manifestation. A Mega Thermo Light too bright to look upon began to take on a form unto Itself as if unto the likeness of a glorified spiritual God Man Figure perfect in every way.

A flawless, multifaceted, equilibrium of Oneness had descended into realm of matter from the higher dimensions of Spiritual Wholeness. Thousands times thousands surrounded the One, the Holiest of the Holy, were closest to the Master of the universe. Izz felt the overpowering Omnipresence of pure living Awareness within his internal spiritual realm, and yet Izz could not begin to understand what he understood. While grappling with the simplest functioning of the smallest parts he could grasp, there came voices from the four winds from the Beings of Light as they spoke among themselves. From somewhere in the outer distance, words reached Izz's senses, like the great echoing of thunderous waters. The first voice among many spoke. "Surely we cannot doubt the reality of his faithful love, even when the flames of condemnation issued from his soul, he stood firm. His heart remained kindled with love so valiant and resolute that he has braved the sufferings of hell's fire to save the soul of his beloved."

Another voice continued. "Nor can we doubt the trueness of his love, when for the same purpose, he accepted unutterable torments. His virtuous love makes it impossible for us to deny the trueness of it."

TOM ICON

Izz could sense a Technicolor of power flow, swarm through him and bathe him like a kaleidoscopic tempest. Izz hid his face and was unable to look upon the Being of Light at the center as he forced the question, "Have you come to rescue me?" he called out through his heart to the Heart of all hearts.

The Being of multiplicity pierced Izz with His penetrating eyes like flames of fire shining onward. A different Voice of infinite power came forth like the crashing sound of mighty waves along a rocky shore heard from everywhere. The Voice was awesomely powerful, and yet at the same time, considerately consoling. "We have heard your appeal, and the cry from within your heart has come unto Us." The second Voice was as extraordinarily unknowable as the first, but somehow both were strangely known. And yet the first Voice spoke again, "I Am the way of all things. I Am before Zia's universal foundations were set in motion. Izz of Zia, you have found favor in My Presence." The awesome Voice was audible throughout even unto the whole demon underworld.

Izz approached the ever brightening Light with excited anticipation, trusting the things of the spirit, the things of the unknowable. Suddenly the light from within blasted outwardly brighter than ever. When the Light's presence reached its earthly zenith, there was an acute supernova explosion of illumination that swept outwardly in all directions, overwhelming Izz like an overpowering solar storm. And yet the Light brightened brighter and brighter coming forth like a shock wave to quake the highest heaven to echo across the cosmos and over again, and again, and again. Izz forced himself to look upon the Being. What he thought he saw was an intricately of the likeness unto a man of light set inside another, then another, then another. But what Izz had not realized was that he was merely gazing upon the shadow of the Being from which the source of light radiated. Nor did he know that the Light had not nearly reached Its celestial pinnacle. What he did seem to know, is that he stood before the mega cosmic Beings like an infinitesimal speck of matter in the specter of a wondrous and overpowering supernatural presence of Infinite Consciousness and Infinite Energy. So much so that he felt as if he was violating some sacred decree by merely being witness to this divine visitation of phenomenal Omnipotence,

The pure Light then ejected out of every volcanic vent, and shot straight into the Ziaian sky, spilling over to the ends of Zia and across the seven seas. Its intense rays of light cut a rift pass the roof of the heavens, through space up into eternity, and beyond.

In the hollow where Zuree would have done anything for Izz but leave him, the ground shuddered. In every direction, all at once a phenomenal Light radiated and scintillated over a thousand specks of clustered light. Each beacon mirroring the other as Its edge shone forth as brilliant as the noonday sun in its full strength. In the background, the flash of Light revealed demons wrapping their wings around themselves in terror, and Zuree felt the darkness tremble. The fiends all cowered back, knocking each other aside in their effort to hide. Their trampling feet echoed throughout the ruinous chamber as they drew away, packing tight, screeching with pain, seeking out the darkness as the Light flared into brilliance. Zuree cast her eyes upon Izz's to see them sparkling with radiance.

High above on the surface of Zia, after all the wounded had been attended to, Ammiz stood at the highest portal within the fortress of the main keep. Unseen, he observed the situation, trying to think of what could be done. And then suddenly, and quite unexpectedly, his attention was forced to the distant northern Noragore Rim. As Ammiz quickly turned his head, he saw something he had never before seen. From the crater of an extinct volcano, an immense bolt like that of lightning sprang out from somewhere deep within the bowls of Zia. In the clear skies above, there was a clasp of awesomely brilliant Radiance. Its splendor amplified over the surface of all the surrounding area. It's beams like a magnificent blast of cosmic light hurdling past the highest blue ceiling, piercing a gash into the outer stratosphere. Its awesomeness fading only when the Light ascended off into deep space and beyond the beyond unto the heights of the heavens. The center of the white hot Light flashed, sending blinding bright hues of awesome pure phosphorescence dwarfing that of the conjunctional illumination. The powerful burst broke forth with a glorious shimmer that filled the sky to outshine every combined source of light ever witnessed. The Aurora surged as if it were washing and purifying everything in its radiant path. Everyone in the lower keep was staring up out through the northern port. The air trembled and pulsated with a rush of startling pure, white power that cascaded everywhere. The Light filled every corner of the kingdom and even lit up a small mouse hiding beneath a slab of stone.

At that instant, the unearthly Glory flashed over the holding pen of Zomborge prisoners. Crouching captives that were chained to the wall slowly came to their feet. They stared intently into the Light momentarily. Their savage look of hate turned suddenly to that of fear. Then all together, in one accord, the group instantly fell, crumbling to the ground, lifeless, as an odd expression of peace eased on their faces.

At that same moment, while Tigbone had been admiring his evil master's godlike authority as the Wicked Warlock Wizard took mastery over the agitating armies. And while the bumbling oaf was rocking back and forth on the balls of his feet and wringing his hands together, he listened intently to his idol as he infected his mind with his grand illusion of supremacy. He was savoring the moment for all it was worth when his eyes suddenly were pulled to the startling flash of Luminescence shooting up out of Noragore Rim. Tigbone stared wide eyed as the Light immediately struck him like a sudden wallop across his face. He felt the jolt radiate right through him to the center of his being. As Its glow burned upon his skin, the next thing that Tigbone knew was that he was on the ground and that his flea bitten donkey was sporadically making high and low pitched noises as it careened across the courtyard. From the ground, Tigbone finally had the mind to turn to question Baddlock. And he stared as the Wicked Warlock Wizard clung on desperately with his bony legs and hands, for dear life as Nightmare reared high into the air, nearly unseating him. The horse was snorting and pawing at the glare and violently tossing a defensive head with flattened ears, as he neighed with an awful whinny squeal. Tigbone tried to shield his eyes through the brilliant brightness as he saw Baddlock's face seem to darken and appear to deflate and wrinkle up withering with fear.

The teams of yakoxen tethered to the battering ram and siege engines opened their eyes popping wide as if a red hot iron poker had been pushed against their hide. In unison, they pulled against their bindings and made deep, extended bellowing sounds of alarm.

The Norticlan, with slackening jawed amazement, shielded their eyes from the terrifying, angry blare of the light that blazed suddenly from the sky over the Northern Rim. Some thought that perhaps it was a sign of the eternal new world order Baddlock spoke about so often. Others, blindingly, wondered what it could be, that they had seen, but hardly considered the significance of the bewildering phenomenon. Most thought it must have been one of many flashbacks brought about by their prolonged use of psilocybin mushrooms and hallucinogenic herbs.

For the longest time, Baddlock's mouth was gaping wide open as if he was trying to let out a scream that was stuck in his throat. The astonishing blaze pierced through his eyes like tendrils of heat that felt as if two wasps were stinging his eyes simultaneously. The Light shone with such force that he had to shield his face from it. But he could still see the brilliance that burned into his retina and filled every corner of his brain. It was so powerful that it momentarily swallowed every shadowy thought shedding light even in the darkest recesses of his mind. At the moment that Baddlock believed that he was about to perish in disgrace, suddenly the afterglow dimmed and was gone as mysteriously as it had appeared. The phenomenon left him badly shaken and trembling. Even though Baddlock was pale, weak, and daunted, he managed to maintain a tight rein on Nightmare and brought the raging stallion under control. He sat atop Nightmare, his jaw clenched and his lower lip quivering. He reached up and rubbed both eyes with one hand, rotating his index and middle fingers over each eyeball. He tried to focus, but whether he had his eyes open or closed, all he could see was the bright after glow of the light that was no longer before him. A tight headachy feeling throbbed around his temples as his thoughts began to move forward, and to a degree, he was almost his wicked self again. When Tigbone finally dared to look again, the light was gone; but its vivid impression remained imprinted in the back of his mind. Hopelessly confused, he looked to Baddlock and asked," What that be, Muster?" His voice was feeble with panic.

The soul of a jackal composed a forged smile as if he knew a secret that was concealed to everyone but himself. His eyes shifted back and forth as he turned to Tigbone. "You boil on a warthog's rump. You could not figure your way out of a grain sack, even if you had a map glued to your nose. That my boy was the awesome power of Abaddawn, the god of darkness. *Blood must be spilled in his honor.* The scum of Edawn must die."

A dark look of concern on Tigbone's face showed the bewilderment of his mind as he nodded thoughtfully. It almost made sense, but he could not get past the part about the flash of light and the prince of darkness, dark and light, light and dark. It was probably a dumb question, so he did not ask.

The Norticlan generals sat upon their warhorses, trying to refocus, looking upon the Wicked Warlock Wizard who had by now regained his composure. Baddlock had predicted the coming of the conjunction, and thus he just had to be responsible for the blinding light. The clan of the Noragore were so well practiced in offering up sacrifices to gods that did not exist. Therefore, there could be no doubt what so ever that Baddlock was a god with unlimited powers, hence every lie he had told them had to be true.

In the underbelly of Zia, the Beings of Light spoke yet one last time. "The power of darkness over you, for now, have been bound. Follow your heart, let it be your guide, and it will set you free. Remember the truth that you seek is within you and has always been within your heart, waiting for you to unleash it." The Beings of pure energy continued as their light and voices began to recede. "I have seen the pureness of your Love for the maiden Zuree. Love is the only infinite truth. Love is the lifeblood of the cosmos. If you are found worthy, you shall save alive your True Love, but there will be a great price to pay. An atonement must be required of you. Let that be all for now. Now go, leave this place quickly while there is yet time for the appointed hour draws neigh, and the darkness will once again be unbound—until the final judgment."

"Thank you…I think," Izz murmured.

There was a sound of rushing wind; the Divine Light was ebbing and then suddenly dimmed and faded off. The words that had sounded inside Izz's head abated and muted away. The Presence that could have been no other than the Great Creator Himself. Whatever supernatural, mind numbing enchantment had rescued him, was gone, suddenly releasing him from its powerful grasp, leaving him wrapped and washed with heaven's wonderment. It had been the most astonishing thing he had ever witnessed, and the most hair raising. At that moment, he was not sure if he ever wanted to experience it again. In the hue of the vivid after images left in the eyes, Izz wondered, had the whole epiphany truly happened as he had beheld it. Or had it all just only been wrought in his head? Whatever it was, the out of body encounter was the most miraculous thing past his imagination he had ever perceived. Leaving him with the one thing he knew for sure—and that was that through it all, his heart had remained faithful, of this, there was no doubt. And this had been the reason he had been atoned from the lowest point of wretchedness.

As Zuree relentlessly maintained her vigil over Izz, she looked down at him in disbelief to see his face was suddenly radiant. Every trace of his previous injuries had faded, and she was sure she must have been imagining things. Then Izz suddenly began to stir. And then unexpectedly, he opened his eyes and jerked his head up as he felt himself reentering his body with a weighty, dull thud. Izz's eyes came wide open, and he gasped so hard it almost seemed that he would suck in all the air from within the hollow. His garments were as brilliant as the light he radiated in the room, and then he relaxed and fell back completely limp as if dead.

Moments later, his skin began to take on a more natural hue. And then as if resurrecting from a living death, Izz groaned and stirred slightly. His eyelids flickered and opened as perception began to creep back into him. As he stared vacantly up at Zuree, his eyes found the connection with his brain and refocused as the underworld waded back into sight. Izz's eyes were open and working, but the rest of his body was useless. The haze began to clear from his eyes, though not yet from his dysfunctional brain. Flash images of the burning light were suddenly, for a moment, still seared in his retina and his mind. Momentary paranoid delusions refocused as adrenaline shot through his veins. Looking and feeling like a crazed man, Izz frantically looked all around, kicked with his feet, and tried desperately to crawl away from an imaginary phantom. Zuree held Izz tight and tried to reassure him. "You are safe! You are safe now," she said as she clasped him to her breast.

Panting and sweating profusely, Izz was scared to death. The emotional and physical pain of what had just happened to him, the utter degradation that he had experienced in the presence of Abaddawn was too fresh in his mind for him not to be hysterical. He wanted to vomit out the many abominations forced upon him against his will, while he gagged on the unbearable remembrance of abuses against his soul. He hyperventilated and again collapsed from the lack of oxygen. Zuree drew him in, held him close onto her bosom, and gave him warmth and comfort in her embrace, relieved that Izz was showing signs of recovery. In her reprieve, she cried out, "It is all right! You have come back to me, you have come back. You are safe, and that is all that matters." Her heart bounded with joy at the thought of being reunited with the great love that had sustained her up to then.

Izz's breath came in deep, arduous gasps as he waited for oxygenated blood to circulate through his brain. Eventually, Izz began to breathe more freely as if he were gradually waking up from a terrible, nightmarish dream. The unbearable, heart twisting horror began to recede from his mind like an ebbing reflection. Even before he came fully awake, he could feel how weak he still was. As full consciousness slowly returned to Izz, he felt the softness and warmth of Zuree's embrace, like a baby in the loving arms of a mother as it first becomes aware of her love. It was like being enclosed in all the love he could have ever wanted, the kind of love that cures, mends, and revives. Izz stared out into emptiness for an extended moment, slowly recovering as he tried to retrace the events that had led from there to here. The first thing he remembered the Light and the memory of how its Spirit reanimated his mind out of death into life. The blackness and darkness left him, like the slow, gradual pacifying of a violent storm.

The expression of panic eased from Zuree's face as tears of gladness filled her eyes. Comforting warmth flushed throughout her body, and her gripping fears fell away as if her overwhelming elation had melted it all out of her. Disorientated, Izz wiped a crust of dried tears from his eyes as he continued to shake the cobwebs from his wits. As his senses returned, one of the first things he noticed was that he reeked of smoke and that his clothes were riddled with burn marks. Then as Izz stared up at Zuree's angelic face Izz suddenly come to his right mind. A broken smile slowly replaced the expression of confusion and pain on his face. He was alive and in the arms of the one who had kept him alive, and he would willingly have endured the suffering all over again just to be where he was by Zuree's side.

Spilling over with love and relief, Zuree held Izz lovingly in her arms as she had done the last time they had a moment to themselves. The love that refused to be denied instantly leaped with deliverance out of their would be tombs. Both eternally grateful that they were once again reunited were flooded with wave after deep wave of thankfulness. Gratitude washed over them, like the rush of the ocean under the full moon, until it had quickly engulfed them both like a seismic sea swell of love.

Izz shoved himself up on his elbows, pressing himself against Zuree's enfolding arms, and he heard and felt her heartbeat returning the call of his own. Nothing else mattered. They were together again. After a moment, Izz realized that he was beyond all the torment, all the hurt, and all the pain that he had suffered at the hands of the central axis of evil. It was all gone, like a bad dream that lay behind him in the shadows of his memory. But the pangs of his heart would always be there. He had seen a form of reality from a perspective no one had ever seen and survived alive.

From his new black hole imprisonment, Abaddawn tried to gather himself together. By now, he was recovering from his compressed imprisonment. The darkness had been pierced; its power bound and broken, fallen into nothingness for the moment. It had only been a harbinger for the once precious jewel of heaven of what would be his final judgment.

He wanted to disgorge a storm of disgusting blasphemies against the Highest, but instead, was struck mute. Unable to speak, Abaddawn's rage hit the apex of his uttermost hatred for Izz. Abaddawn bewailed the escape of his prized soul. In a fit of boiling anger, he flew into a rampage of delirious hate for all humankind. Brownish yellow plumes of sulfurous breath blasted out of his widened snout, and his bloodshot eyes almost jutted out of their sockets. Finally able to find his tongue, Abaddawn murmured, "He was all mine...all mine, yet he slipped right through my firm, iron fisted grasp."

As he regained his strength, Abaddawn began to combine and magnify the capacity of every enslaved force of darkness at his command, to launch an all out attack focused on Izz. "Up to half of my kingdom, I will grant to whoever kills Izz of the Isles of Zollerzon!" Abaddawn screamed, his words reverberated throughout the farthest boundaries of the bowels of the deep.

The voice of Baddlock was heard just outside of the keep's door. "Bring forth the dragon!" A burst of contemptuous laughter that gave out a hollowed resounding from the depths of the bottomless pit that was his soul followed his command.

The very next moment, there was the distinctive snap of a whip as the muscled arm of the yakoxen driver drew back and then drove forward. The wave of motion traveling quickly down the tapered lash, from the handle to the tip, gathered speed as the diameter of the whip decreased. And as the momentum reached its peak, its velocity exceeded the speed of sound and let out a nerve jerking *crack!*

Yakoxen eyes bulged as they straightened their backs and legs, their muscular, broad chests bulged, and their three toed hooves dug in. Deep grunts and loud, complaining, "Um muumuu," sounds of an extended duration were heard, as the mighty beasts of burden lumbered forward. The dragon was a monstrous battering ram designed from the ancient books of siege tactics stolen from the seer's private library. Oversized chains mounted on a wheeled support frame suspended the massive battering ram. The dragon itself was a huge oak tree log bound with metal bands and fitted with a large, heavy metalhead in the shape of a hideous horned dragon of Baddlock's own design, in honor of one of his many false gods. The strong yakoxen moved the dragon headed battering ram to the front of the keep's massive door, where they were unharnessed. The brawniest of the Norticantian warriors positioned the battering ram directly in front of the keep's barred entrance.

Baddlock wasted no time. With his long bony finger shaking with intensity, he made a sweeping gesture towards the keep's door, and commanded, "Man the Dragon!" He ran his oily tongue across his slippery lips at the thought of Zia's richest treasury just on the other side of the oak door. He pulled his heavy cloak over his shoulders and blew his rancid breath on his hands as he rubbed them together. And even though the weather was warm, a chill of foretaste ran up and down his spine.

The dragon was manned and powered by sheer muscle. Its incredible bulk was swung back as far as possible, then forcefully propelled forward on its chained pendulum. When the lead filled dragonhead slammed against the keep's fortified door, the clamorous blow was unbelievably terrifying in its thunderous intensity. The sound of impact reverberated throughout the echoing stone vault in every direction. Up and down the keep's corridors, the toll of doom reached into the depths of the catacombs, growing in volume until the whole keep shook with plummeting stone shards and cascading dust. A frantic communal gasp sucked the air right out of the keep as dread ripped through the nervous system of every soul at the sound of doom's first toll. For the longest, frozen moment, everyone inside the keep hunkered down low where they were. They were smitten in horrified disbelief, not breathing, hardly daring to think about the approaching calamity that was too terrible to contemplate. Then came the next earsplitting collision of the dragon's pointed stout against the resistant iron studded door. Inside, the surviving Edawnian Warriors clutched at their swords, as the dragon crashed ferociously once again against the door as it rattled violently on its hinges. Scattering chipped stone, splinters ,and clouds of dust jets shot out. Every wide eye was riveted with fear and shock on the keep's door. The strongest and bravest of men, still standing, felt their knees turn to jelly with the sound that sent fear crawling up their spines and then running back down with terror.

Down inside the catacombs the great, forceful crashes of the battering ram caused the children to run to their mothers, where they were gathered up and clung on to by frantic guardians. Everyone looked as miserable as sweated cats, unable to keep fear at a distance. Every pounding heartbeat marked the passage of time until the trilling sound of another metal on metal clashed through the chambers. It's sound vibrated within each heart causing it to stop in mid beat like the stroke of sudden death, only to restart again, with hammering waves of fear. Their resistance merely served to prolong the inevitable eventuality of their doom.

Each interval between the pulverizing pummeling of the battering ram seemed to take in all of eternity, lengthening out every soul's anguished agony. The unraveling of their nerves was worsening from one moment to the next. Their plight was galvanized. Every besetting boom of the dragon felt like fangs closing down on their throats. Every reverberating vibration through the keep drew them closer and closer to the inevitable moment that now was only a matter of time. The door bulged inward, with each buckling metallic moan of its timbers. Minute cracks began to spread along the edges of the massive granite blocks that held the reinforced door in place. Under that kind of strain, the door that separated them from life and death could not withstand much more.

"I am open to any suggestions," the king wearily said as he ran his fingers through his unkempt hair. Muted silence was his only answer. The king straightened himself up off the floor, signaled to Zandor and Kondor as if he would be right back and then made his way toward the innermost keep. He signaled to the married men as he went. They gathered and made their way into the inner catacombs, where they met with their wives and children. A sudden calm seemed to descend over the catacombs as the men appeared. Queen Zahra quickly came to the king and buried her head against his chest as she fell into his arms, begging for reassurance. "You are the one shelter where I know that my heart is safe," the queen whispered to her king.

And the king clutched her tightly, as though it truly was the last time he would. They nestled against each other instinctively, and each simultaneously let out a tiny, almost inaudible sigh. The remaining married men reached and huddled with their families for a few last words, hugs and kisses. Those women that did not see their husbands wept silently. Ammiz looked up from where he was, under torchlight as he attended to the wounded. He briefly made eye contact with the king and faithfully returned to his task.

"Is this...is it...?" the queen asked in a whisper as she felt a sob rise in her throat and swallowed it back down.

The king hushed her with a forefinger to her lips and attempted to smile. Then tightened his lips, as if he was about to say something too terrible to speak. Several seconds passed before he replied. "All will be well. You will see."

TOM ICON

A peace swept over them that could only be experienced by two souls who truly loved each other. A deep quiet ensued that did not have to be intruded on with mere words to reinforce the trueness that was their love. Finally, but much too soon, a monstrous clang interrupted. He held the queen at arm's length, the king said, "Zahra, my queen, we are all about to be tested, and you must be strong for me, for them." He looked toward the children, and automatically, his thoughts turned to Zuree. The same thought seemed to strike both of them at the same time.

From a distance, the crashing sound of the battering ram came echoing down into their ears again and again. The king commanded his queen to lead the women and children down into the lower, innermost catacombs. This would be the last defensible spot in the kingdom. He quickly grabbed Zahra's hands, brought them to his lips, and whispered, "I will be with you soon, my love." And then he turned to rejoin his men. The queen caressed the kiss that was still warm upon her hand as she wondered if her king had meant in this world—or the next.

The king returned to his men with the feeling that there was very little time remaining and that in another moment or two, all hell was about to be loosened. And all would be engulfed in chaos. He called Zandor and Kondor to him with the nod of his head. The king's voice was quiet but full of strength. He spoke so they would be the only ones to hear. "From the looks of things, our chances of getting out of this with our skins intact have been reduced to near infinitesimal." His words were of particular significance to himself.

Kondor was the only one of the twins to respond, "As of late, I have stared down overwhelming odds many times and laughed in the face of death, but no one is laughing now."

"There is only one thing that is of any importance now. I do not want the women or children to fall into Baddlock's hands."

Neither had to ask what that meant. Both Zandor and Kondor solemnly nodded in agreement. The word was quickly passed around the keep. A terrific shock ran through every husband and father, but every warrior without exception was ready to slit the throats of their own loved ones rather than allow them to fall into the filthy hands of Baddlock the Wicked Warlock Wizard. They all knew that they would not survive to protect their families, and they prepared their minds and hearts accordingly. The next hour would be their darkest. The king, Zandor, Kondor, Arius, and a few other high ranking officers drew lots among themselves to determine whom it would fall upon to do the unthinkable. Any exchange of words among them fell into silence. Zandor, being unmarried and having no children purposely broke his lot in two with his little finger in a way the others could not see so that it would appear that he had drawn the dreaded lot.

Again and again, the dragon's gaping snout with its dagger like filled mouth bit into the keeps weakening door relentlessly wreaking havoc with every strike. Each interval marked off an eternity. Time stood still each time the mass of the dragon's head was hurled with ever increasing momentum. Every booming impact sent spasms of jangling alarm through the raw, exposed nerves of the men within. The outcome was galvanized with the growing sense of terrifying anticipation and would now only be a matter of a short time. But fate itself seemed to be taking its own infinite time.

Then finally, the thunderous blow that ripped into the keep came. The hideous snout of the dragonhead, with its gaping teeth, pierced through the door and into the keep's interior. There was a collective groan as terrified men turned about exchanging perplexed glances of horror. There was more than ever before the overwhelming sense of the madness that was about to come crushing down upon them. Then all at once, the gruesome dragonhead was withdrawn with one mighty backward thrust, leaving a gaping hole in the center of the keep's door. From outside, there came an excited roar, which erupted into a riotous outburst of whooping and hollering. The Norticlan army of annihilation sensed the approaching moment, soon Edawn would fall, and the glorious scent of fear and death would become a sweet perfume in their snouts.

Led by Zandor and Kondor, a handful of men that were not rooted in their spots, scrambled with whatever they could carry and rushed to barricade the ruptured hole in the keep's door. Those that had nothing else to fill in the gap shouldered their shields to the door, while yet others shouldered those that bore themselves against the impending intrusion. Deep lines of fear etched themselves on the faces of those who waited for the terrible moment. Like doomed seamen on a sinking vessel trying desperately to patch an irreparable leak in their ship just before it slipped into the bottomless abyss. Everyone braced for the inevitable. They were like ghosts in a world that was about to come to its end. The moments seemed to drag on with agonizing slowness, an eternity at a time.

An elongating stillness followed, and between one moment and the next, all fell to the dead silence of a tomb. The guardians of Edawn stood in silence, crowded together. The quiet was disquieting and was more than eerie. Every man's heart melted, and each one was afraid, except Zandor, who stood his ground, braced to confront death face to face. Zandor was Kondor's hero, and he wished to be just like his twin in every way. Kondor instinctively reacted and stood by his brother's side. Kondor lowered his head and, for no logical reason, perhaps only to mask his mounting fear, laughed out loud. He turned to Zandor who was giving him a quizzical stare and reminded him of the most embarrassing childhood moment he could think of, "Remember the time...I gave you those candy coated deer droppings...and you gave them to your childhood sweetheart!" Kondor laughed vigorously at his own joke.

Zandor only stared in confusion, but after an awkward moment, a broad smile took over his face as a chain of thought snapped in a whimsical corner. His smile grew bigger as he tried to hold back the laughter that was building inside and said, "Yes, yes, but do you remember the time I rubbed stinging nettle in your loincloth?"

And they both laughed out loud, to the stunned amazement of the others. Zandor laughed at Kondor for laughing at Him. All else were too distressed to laugh. How could there be laughter at a time like this? What a couple of idiots some thought.

Then came the pangs of disheartenment that took hold of all of them like a cruel fist. Their nerves coiled like springs wound to the breaking point. And Zandor whispered, "At least we had some laughs."

Something inside Kondor snapped, and he impulsively blurted, "What are they waiting for? Why must they toy with us…?" The frustration carved on his face sealed a sense of doom in everyone that looked upon him.

Zandor placed a hand on Kondor's shoulder and whispered, "All we can do is all we can do. Wait, it will be better when the fighting starts."

"Maybe they are willing to negotiate!" a frantic voice cried out.

Kondor turned to the man. "Will you negotiate with the devil? The Norticlan are evil, murderous, lawless warlords. Compassion for them is impossible."

Zandor stared down at his sword. It was now shaking uncontrollably in his hands. He forced himself to hold it still and saw that it was still discolored with the blood from his last kill. The keep's door was severely compromised. He knew, like everyone else, that the door could not withstand the strain much longer.

Ammiz appeared out of nowhere, as often was his habit, and spoke up. "The odds are heavily against our making it through this, but we still have an outside chance that our reinforcements will arrive in time. We must resist until the last man—for the sake of your wives, for the sake of your children."

One by one, Kondor, Zandor, Arius, the king, and everyone present solemnly nodded their heads in one accord.

Then came a monstrous jolt with the scream of renting metal that sent broken shards of stone particles, splintered wood and horizontal plums of dust jetting and spewing in all directions. Men went hurtling in midair like chaff in a violent wind, slamming against the keep's flagstone floor with a sickening thud, and then forcefully shoved back away from the entrance. Blocks that once held the mighty door in place were decimated and crumbled to the floor. When the dust filled air cleared, the ominous dragon head had fully penetrated clear through and rested on the debris and rubble of what was left of the fortified barrier. The walls surrounding the door had also burst opened with a last convulsive tremor, raining down large stones on those standing closest to the door. The terrifying nightmare all feared was now upon them. A yawning gap in the hardwood door sucked out every last trace of hope from the room. Some trembled, while others seemed to hyperventilate. The keep had been breached.

From where he fell, Zandor bolted to his feet like a recoiling spring, trying to drive his heart back into his chest. Kondor jumped instantly thereafter, both with their swords in hand. Other men stare wordlessly at each other with the hard coldness of numbing shock and the dry indifference of bewildered dismay pasted on their faces. Chopping axes continued to widen the gap, sending an eerie collective shiver of anticipation that ran up and down the backs of men like long, icy, steel blades shoved through their spines. All eyes turned to their king, and his reaction was very much like that of every other man in the keep. Ozzdon's eyes neither glanced right or left, nor up nor down, but stared only straight ahead. No one else moved or breathed until the king drew his blade, with a long, continuous, metallic ring. Then instantaneously, they all leaped into action, even though they knew that their resistance was futile and that the outcome was inevitable and only a matter of time.

Nonetheless, they were altogether prepared to disappear into the pit of insane oblivion behind their king. At least, then, it would all be finally over, and they would not have so long to wait before they died. Finally ending the constant fear that seemed to exhaust them more than anything else.

Deep in the catacombs, the final slam of the distant battering ram was felt as if the enemy was closing in. The waves of quaking earth danced small stones across the stone floor and cascaded dust from the catacomb ceiling.

King Ozzdon, Zandor, Kondor, and Arius moved forward into the vulnerable perimeter nearest the door, backed by their men, all hoping for some unseen miracle. Their bodies set for battle, maneuvering for position in the cramped keep. Legs spread, with swords drawn and held in a two handed grip ready before them. They set themselves preparing to lash back with a counteroffensive. Behind them, the clatter and drone of burnished blades filled the room. Anyone capable of carrying a weapon, including women and children over the age of twelve summers, joined the swelling ranks of the last standing defenders of Edawn. Together they stood, prepared for the fatal clash, strengthened by the impossible odds endured by all. Each one felt their blood pumping frantically within their veins, and it gave their hearts courage and fortitude. Not that it mattered anything in the grand scheme of the end that was in sight. They stood, ready to meet their departure from the world of the living, sword in hand.

At that same instance, Izz turned his head with a jerk as he sensed a powerful foreboding that felt like something squirming up and down the core of his spinal cord. Izz and Zuree's elation was short lived when out of the blackness came a screaming howl that swirled around them like an angry wind in bursts of fury more violent than ever before. The veracity of reanimated demon hordes left Zuree and Izz clinging to each other as they watched the little light there was fading. A boiling black violet cloud of acute evil crashed into the room. Evil like a sudden avalanche of eerie darkness so profound that it seemed to shimmer and shine in its full wake. Evil like a suffocating cloak engulfed every speck of light and even the glow of the deep lake of fire flickered weakly, on and off like a dying candle.

Nine

The Final Refuse

ll at once came the inevitable moment. Beastly and terrifying, the Norticlan's shrilling outcries of blood lust came closer and closer. Suddenly a booming, earsplitting clash, much more massive than any other, shook the final barricade of the inner keep, climaxing with terrible steel on steel groan. The loud crash echoed through the marble halls of the keep. Zandor and Kondor were among the first to spring to their feet. Many exhaKondor responded, 'Youusted soldiers that had fallen asleep where they stood followed suit. There had not been nearly enough time to catch their breath as they returned to the front line insufficiently rested. Zandor looked sadly upon his younger brother's worry worn expression, smiled weakly, and said, "This could be the end."

A weak smile slowly broke out over Kondor's clammy face. "At least we had some laughs," he added in a sober tone. Then the smile he seemed to be attempting to hold back widened as he tried to suppress the laughter that was building inside. "Remember the day I threw that angry mother skunk and her brood into your bedchamber and locked the door?" His smile grew more prominent as he began to laugh out loud at his own prank. Then he fixed his jaw, but the laughter insisted on escaping anyway.

Zandor started laughing at Kondor for laughing at him as he grimaced with embarrassed recollection. Those around them exchanged puzzled looks. Both twins seemed in good spirits and feeling cocky, in spite of the approaching sounds of death. The unfolding situation was not a laughing matter. It was a living nightmare. All else were too startled to smile, let alone laugh, leaving those around them staring with expressions of, *What a couple of idiots,* pasted on their faces. Yet somehow, the sound of laughter seemed to ease the tension of the overwhelming moment, in some way, inspiriting an air of, *to hell with fear,* come what may.

All at once, stone wall segments cracked as the massive fortification rattled and shuddered violently as the enemy battered down the last barrier between life and death. A concerted rush of armored arms and legs was seen at the entrance. It was as if the whole Norticlan army was trying to squeeze through all at once. Hundreds and then, it seemed like thousands of gawky figures dressed in full black swarmed inside, pushing through the ruptured entryway. The nightmarish Norticlanders wore gruesome horned, metal helmets that made them that much more heinous. The headgear covered their faces almost entirely with a ridge plate over their thick neck Their body armor was of a thick black leathery material studded with steel overlay that covered their chest and legs. Their arms were clad in metal plates along their full length that continued to their knuckle guards, which were fixed with long razor spike like extensions. There were thousands like them, waiting to rush in one after another. There was an overwhelming feeling among the besieged that the end had come. The defenders knew they might kill a few or they may even kill many, but eventually, they would be overrun. And the Norticlan were voracity enjoying their vulnerability.

Everything was in intense motion. Inrushing footsteps echoed on the flagstone floor as black figures blurred past the rift like giant rats entering a grain storage tower to escape their ravaging starvation. The stench of their overpowering foulness permeated the keep as they rushed in. Each barbaric member of the human race was under the influence of Baddlock's potent narcotic mixture. The throat stripping swill had been concentrated, especially strong. The stimulant gave the invaders increased boldness, fortitude, and endurance. Norticlan troopers crowded through, pulsing wave after pulsing wave in incomprehensible numbers, like a black, boiling cloud clattering and thundering into the overrun keep. The deluge of force crashed in like an iron fist until the very walls of the stronghold seemed to be toppling in on them like a sudden avalanche. There and then, the rush of dread filled the keep as it erupted into an absolute madhouse. Hearts beat fast, and time stood still as the room erupted into piercing confusion for the most prolonged moment.

However, as expected, when most men were going to the left, one man went to the right. The right voice in the right place at the right time—could move the world, heaven, and hell. Like a pillar of hope, Ammiz the Seer walked among what was left of the troops, urging them to lift their spirits against the hopeless odds. "We must scrape together everything. Gird your loins sons of Edawn! Fight for your women and children! NEVER, NEVER, NEVER, EVER, GIVE UP! QUICKLY, INTO THE INNER CATACOMBS!"

The first of the thousands of bloodthirsty Norticlanders advanced slipping through the breached doorway at will, while others sacked and pillaged the surrounding kingdom. The greed and ruthlessness could be seen on their faces. They salivated after Baddlock's assurance of the riches that would be bestowed upon them after their conquest. The smell of imminent death was like a sweet fragrance in their nostrils. Like a pack of ravenous hyenas rushing in to pick over a carcass, the hardened men of war advanced, empowered with the strength of maddening greed. The quicker they eliminated the men, the sooner they could ravage their women.

Just outside, the Wicked Warlock Wizard was glowing with the pleasure of his long sought conquest, now so nearly in his clutches. An exhilarating thrill bubbled through his decrypted veins. He felt like a giant, literally gloating with victory. He entered Edawn laughing his deep, wicked laugh, and Dandork, who was ever at his side to facilitate the cataclysmic raze of Edawn, was gloating in the same manner. Baddlock's prelude to a final attack over Edawn would not stop until all of Zia bowed at his feet.

From within, fear gave strength to exhausted arms. With unbending courage and virtue, Zandor and Kondor responded with bulging muscles as they braced their war footing. Neither twin was afraid to go head to head with the overwhelming odds. Besides, it was as good a place to die as any. With glistening blades dripping matter and red blood, for the time being, they dominated the frontline with their two swords. The king, Arius, and the military commander of the Skymount forces, quickly joined in. Back by their men, they were a daunting presence. Their slashing blades immediately met and dispatched the forefront attackers baptizing them in the blood *of* death. Suddenly, there was a frenzied movement everywhere. Moments later, the chaos gave way to an organized defense. Death echoed off the walls as its scent filled the air. Roars of pain seeped from assailant's gaping mouths as the intruders felt the bite of Zandor and Kondor's steel, ripping across their flesh. Screams were soon choked off by mouthfuls of gushing blood as men on both sides of the front lines crumbled to the keep's bloody floor. In the knot of humanity, deadly Norticlan crossbows were fired at point blank range. The king's lord's of the sword instinctively intensified their defenses as they slashed at anything that looked like a Norticlander.

Between death and the Norticlanders ridiculously outnumbered, the Edawnians desperately fought on. And even though they were fighting a losing cause, they fought, because the horror of being taken alive by Baddlock drove them on. Edawnian men and even children precariously, out of desperation, stepped forward fearlessly to die. Edawnian boys who were barely old enough to hold their swords up before them confronted the ruthless Norticlan front, like lambs before the slaughter. The Norticlan warriors roared with laughter as if they had been told a hilarious joke. "What kind of insult is this?" one thundered. "Am I an insect that I should be swatted away by a *boy*!" A constant onslaught of filthy language followed.

Scarcely had the battle hardened warrior gotten the last word out when the Edawnian youth, forced into manhood, found his spine and drove the foul mouthed brut through between his armored plates. The startled Norticlan warrior dropped to his knees as the boy withdrew his sword, and the warrior fell on his face, dead. Outraged by what the Norticlan warrior standing by had seen, he immediately sliced his blade in a wicked arch toward the boy. But the lad's evasive movement was too fast as he quickly ducked under the path of the deadly broadsword and out of its reach.

Everyone knew full well, they would die a hundred deaths if they were taken captive. They knew what would happen to their women if they fell into Baddlock's clutches. So they clung with blind persistence to the increasingly vain hope that reinforcements would somehow magically arrive before they were wiped out or worse. In the midst of the madness more than ever, the king expected things to get worse and sensed that the defeat of Edawn would cause a cascade throughout the empire. However valiantly, they tried to hold back the flood; the defenders of Edawn were ultimately powerless against their enemies' overwhelming numbers. The harder the Edawnians resisted, the harder the enemy pressed in, knowing they would soon have the resounding victory. In the face of the appalling situation, the best fought the hardest and endured the bloodiest confrontations, only to be decimated. As the Edawnians backed away toward the catacombs, the thick, ripe smell of blood filled the keep. Death assaulted the defenders from every side until they had no solid ground from which to stand. Demise was everywhere, and the threat of utter annihilation was closing in with frightening speed. A brave soul with nothing left to lose tried to block their entrance, but he was quickly overpowered and dragged out. Overwhelmed by the sheer weight of the assault, the defenders had no choice but to fall further back and away. With countless dangers and enemies surrounding them on every side, the threat of total extermination deepened by the moment. The king realized that their ability to resist much longer was quickly fading. It was like trying to dam a tsunami of onrushing beasts of prey. Confronted with the collapse of his defiant opposition, the king had no other alternative but to fall back, so he called for a retreat. "Into the catacombs!" the king commanded with his last breath of hope.

Attempting to salvage what was left of the resistance, desperate men rallied their remaining strength and gave ground stubbornly. It was a bitter battle. It was every man for himself now. The outnumbered counterattack disintegrated into individual pockets of fierce clashes in the face of disaster. Fate was cruel; vulnerable men and children fell into the bloody winepress. Fighting erupted on all sides as the dwindling Edawnian forces, with crossbow bolts riddled shields, backed up struggling for life. The pitiful remnants of their already massacred army backed off fearfully, from a defensive last stand struggle that had been doomed from its inception. They clambered back among the walking wounded and the bodies of the fallen, knowing it could be them. The ripped, mutilated, and the twisted ran, hobbled, or crawled toward the lower catacombs. As the besieged backed up, a crescent of Norticlan warriors mercilessly closed in like a pack of ravenous predators, relentlessly and ruthlessly. The king, Zandor, Kondor, Arius, and a handful of others who had decided they would rather die fighting, were the only ones offering any backup to their retreat. The bravest of the brave grudgingly backed away while the others ran deeper into what they knew was a dead end trap. Finally, their flight led them to a narrow passage in the catacombs. The king decided it was a precarious foothold from where they could, at least, form any defensible strategy against an endless flow of unrelenting Norticlan slayers. Zandor asked, "What is the plan?"

"Just keep killing the heathen until they stop trying to kill us," the king retorted.

By now, more of the boldest women, having heard the encroaching commotion had come forth. They seized weapons from the dead and wounded and came to the defense of their men. Having reached the narrowest point of a tapering corridor that opened into a circular space, the king ordered, "We stand or fall here!"

The narrowing passage was too constricting to allow the bulky armored Norticlandors to fight well, which gave the advantage to the defenders. Their pursuing attackers could only manage to squeeze in a few at a time. From the threshold, Zandor and Kondor, the lords of the sword, locked their feet to the ground and stood at the opening like twin columns holding up what was left of the Edawnian world. The twins immediately set up defensive positions on both sides of the passageway, while stragglers ran inside. They were a formidable force not to be trifled with. Shoulder to shoulder, they dominated the entry with their two blades. For the first few moments, it had been a riveting clash of wills within a whirlwind of steel. The two champions of Edawn came together side by side, brandishing steel in a flurry of arching slashes, thrusts, and counter thrusts. Something had changed inside them. They were more ruthless than before, more voracious to kill. Their blades rang out loudly and erupted in bursts of sparks as they clashed with their pursuers who were choked off at the narrowing bottleneck. But that did not mean that the Norticlan were running out of bodies. As the Norticlanders fell, they were hauled back like so much useless refuse, only to be immediately replaced by fresh attackers. Even though the twins where able to hold back the incredible onslaught, over time, their strength waned, and soon they became too weary of sustaining a formidable defense. Zandor and Kondor stepped back, and King Ozzdon and Arius stepped up to repel the never ending incursion. The king and his best friend, Arius, fought bravely and fought well. But no amount of tenacity of spirit could hold back the overwhelming numbers nor the superiority of Norticlan firepower as they began to cut their way through the Edawnian resistance.

From within, the will to make mind, body, and soul stand and fight and hold back the Norticlan forces, buckled as the hordes ultimately broke through the Edawnian fortifications. They came rushing through the narrowing passageway like an unstoppable tide. Soon the enemy was everywhere with the frightful clacking of their savage blades as they filled the corridor with inhuman rallying cries. Quickly the thick, ripe smell of death filled the corridors of the catacombs. The king did not even bother to try to figure out who was left. More than a hundred but less than a hundred and fifty able warriors were left standing back to back. The rest were either falling back or just gone.

Then suddenly there squeezed through the passage, a bull necked, mountain of muscle and flesh. There was not an ounce of fat on the challenger. The powerful tendons in his neck stood out like the cables of a drawbridge. His muscles were firm and chiseled, greased to glisten in the torchlight. He was huge, the biggest man anyone from the kingdom had ever seen. With bulging, scarred shoulders the size of boulders and a narrow waist. He had a broad flat brow and a crazed look in his eyes. His long, oily black hair dangled down in thick locks on both sides of his face like dead vipers fixed to his scalp by their poisonous fangs. His sword looked as if it could slice a granite column in two. Muga, the name of the Norticlan Champion, was a subhuman component of the human race. The Norticlan Warrior, barely having been able to squeeze through the opening, was ugly and intimidating, appearing more animal than man. He was a combatant built like a yakox, with thick, powerful arms and a heart yearning for a brawl. Muga was very easy to please; all he needed was something to kill. With a cynical twist to his lips, the champion moved forward as he waved his long single edged and arched sword around like a toy rod. Muga's lean muscles bunched as his blade swept downward cutting, through the air with a rush of harsh wind. Only the quickness of the king's sword deflected the fury of the deadly blade that was intended to kill him. The force of the blow almost knocked him over. Again the huge sword came sizzling through the air, and the king was knocked backward, tumbling to the floor like a tossed rag doll from the force of the screaming blow. From the other side of the opening, Dandork watched in horror. "Not the king, you fool!" he roared.

The king immediately recognized the voice and wailed, "Dandork, you son of a pig…I am going to cut your heart out," as he tightened his fists around the hilt of his sword.

"You are in no position to make such outrageous threats, my old friend," the familiar voice returned with contempt.

Muga, having been denied, turned on Arius like a sinister predator with his deadly sword ready and challenging. Their swords met in a shower of sparks. The enemy deflected Arius's blade easily and laughed. Then the barbarian's sword swung up from the flank. Arius sidestepped it and countered with a forward thrust. The aggressive attack of Arius's blade was deflected aside with enough force to throw him off balance. Then Muga came back again, with his weapon, cutting through the air with the speed and force of doom. Arius felt the bite of steel across his left shoulder. Muga's blade flashed in slow, daunting sweeps for the moment. Then suddenly, a split moment later, a blow out of nowhere fell upon Skymount's finest! He saw it coming a little too late and had little time to react. By the time he realized what had happened, Arius teetered backward and immediately fell against the king, fatally crippled. "Arius!" The king cried out. And as King Ozzdon caught and held his best friend's limp dying body in his arms, sorrow drove a dagger in his heart.

Drenched in sweat and frail with exhaustion, Zandor and Kondor simultaneously drew a long ragged breath. And even though neither had fully recovered, they sprang in defense of their king and their fallen comrade, nonetheless. No matter what, the two seemed ever in a state of readiness to faithfully serve their king. Both were always willing, despite any hardship, to give everything for the king and kingdom, just in time, every time. Zandor and Kondor, the heart and soul of Edawn's final defenses, were conditioned by years of hard training to control their exhaustion and recuperated quickly. Already several more Norticlan warriors, almost as monstrous as Muga, had slipped through the narrow opening. Motioning Muga with his two forefingers, Zandor called out a challenge, "Step forward and let us, you and me, settle this man to man." Zandor single handedly faced the muscled ogre, while Kondor held off the other wild hellions.

The Norticlan champion spotted his challenger and called out savagely, "I have defeated more able opponents than you. You are no match for me. Come here so I can cut you up into little pieces." He said as he motioned with his free hand for Zandor to come.

By now, bands of Edawnian warrior brothers that had lost their nerve were beginning to return from the shadows. They decided they would prefer to face death rather than the shame of cowering. Delaying the inevitable would have been only an extension of Zandor's dread. With lion strides, Zandor wasted no time covering the ground between him and his mortal enemy, ready to engage and test his strength. Controlling his every move, Zandor prepared to confront the seemingly invincible immortal alone, face to face. Now standing before him, the big and nasty brute's chest and shoulders seemed to have broadened. Full of pride and power, the beastly boor thudded his armored chest with his hairy fist. Zandor had learned that survival meant never showing vulnerability. And never letting your challenger sense that you were afraid, no matter how much bigger and stronger he was. The Norticlan giant faced off slowly, weaving back and forth. He clenched and unclenched his massive fists as he gestured Zandor to come forward. Zandor took a few cautious steps preparing to engage the gargantuan. The oversized Norticlander suddenly lumbered forward, attacking with snickering mockery, and the combatants joined in battle, power for power, testing their mettle. Their two blades met with a loud clang, scraping off each other with a grating metallic scream, trailed by a crisscrossing shower of sparks. The great beast of a man struck one devastating blow upon another. As the two crescent blades cut crimson arcs through the air, the swords clashed with explosions of fire and light. As all other fighting came to a virtual standstill, everyone in the room had one eye on his opponent and one eye on the two titans as they squared off. The two arch enemies spun around each other with catlike agility, as if performing some ritual dance to the death. While they urged on their champion, every Norticlan warrior believed Muga was invincible and expected to see Zandor's bloody death. As he kept his one eye on the Norticlander in front of him, Kondor bit his lip, his heart desperately hopeful for Zandor's victory. The muscles in Muga's sword arm knotted as he jerked with a thrust so blisteringly fast that Zandor dared not blink. Zandor narrowly struck away the blow that almost broke through his guard. Then Muga came back hard and fast with one bloodcurdling, rage empowered slice. The monstrous sword came sizzling through the air. Zandor, with incredible skill, managed to step back a hair's breadth away from a slash that missed his throat so narrowly. It was so close that Zandor felt the blade's whooshing, hot breath across his juggler. A roar of approval broke out among the Norticlan as they urged the killer of men on. It almost seemed as if Zandor was up against multiple swords as Muga's weapon plunged toward him again, and again. Zandor ducked under Muga's mighty sword's driving force. He left his flank exposed just long enough for Muga to draw a line that burned like fire along Zandor's arm, causing him to wince with alarm. He grunted in pain as small rivulets of blood formed and dripped, revealing the wound. Tantalizing sensations of pleasure surged through Muga's fingertips as he sensed that a kill was near. A cheer of favor rumbled throughout the catacombs as the blood thirst of the barbarians intensified. For several cringe inducing moments, Kondor's heart became lodged in his throat as his blade parried away a near miss.

Expecting a quick victory, Muga boasted, "I am going to make you wish your mother had kept her legs closed." The words had scarcely left his lips when Zandor darted forward so fast that Muga was barely able to readjust himself with a parry and thrust.

Zandor's blade sang through the air, slipping just under Muga's sword. Its tip ripped deeply across his face, opening his hide with a deep, gushing wound. With one horrible, rage empowered whirlwind Muga swept his huge sword in a succession of devastating slashes. Zandor's reaction was instantaneous with a block, a parry, and a thrust. Their swords met again and again, and the air vibrated. Muga kept swinging and slashing. Sparks flew from the blades as they met again and again. Zandor ducked under a burly swing and buried one of his ironclad fists into Muga's belly. Muga, in turn struck a vicious arch blistering through the air and slipped just under Zandor's parrying sword. And again, the tip of Muga's blade bit across Zandor's chest. The keen edge sent a lightning bolt of stinging pain through Edawn's favorite son.

Without leave time for thought, Zandor parried yet another blow. Suddenly Muga's sword was up high, coming down for the final cut. Zandor possessed the presence to pull his head to the side just in time so that Muga's deadly blade ripped an ugly hiss just a breath from his neckline. Never in all his life had Zandor felt death's chilling breath so close on the jugular of his neck. Muga laughed as he interlaced his sword in the air and said, "I am the greatest warrior alive. No mortal has been born that can best me. I am going to enjoy cutting your heart out and eating it."

Zandor focused sharply on Muga's weapon. The curved blade arced back, and he saw the wiry nerved muscle in Muga's arms bulge as he started to bring it slashing again toward his exposed flank. But with a combination of luck and ruthlessness, Zandor's sword moved faster than the ponderous strongman could have anticipated, beating Muga to the counter by a mere fraction of a heartbeat. So fast was Zandor's blade that Muga did not have any idea where the slice that ripped through his throat came from. A lightning bolt of pain was sent through him as his broad face contorted in a grimace, and Muga knew he had been slain. Blood splashed Zandor's face, flowed down his sword, and over his hand. He heard its gushing and smelled it coppery scent. The giant of a man staggered a couple of steps like an out of balance spinning toy. He clenched and unclenched his massive fist around his slit larynx. His blazing eyes were oozing, as his carotid arteries drained like that of a stuck pig. Foam bubbled out of his mouth and poured down as his bare chest heaved from the effort of directing the sword he was holding in both hands. For a moment, the great Muga stood there, trying to let out a scream that a mouthful of blood choked off. Zandor gave Muga a steely stare and said, "If you are going to do something…talk about it after you have done it."

Zandor tried to wipe away Muga's blood from his face, but only spread it more. Muga clutched at his gaping wound as blood fountained in gushing spurts from between his fingers as he mouthed, *Who are you?* He let out one last whizzing mumble and crumbled to his knees in a splash of red. After that, he dropped like a ton of fallen earth then fell face forwards, dead with a rocking motion that pitched his feet off the ground. Kondor briefly turned to Zandor and said with a relieved sneer, "Must not have been so great."

Those Norticlanders watching, including Dandork, from the other side of the opening, stared wide eyed in horror. The large circle of puddling blood left little doubt as to whether their champion might be dead. Immediately, a loud outpouring of rage and filthy language went up among the ranks of the barbarian clan. Almost at once, the flurries of incoming hordes intensified. By now, almost every Edawnian warrior was exhausted, even Zandor and Kondor. Especially Zandor, but the twin towers refused to yield to the defensive battle. In the midst of the murderous onslaught, King Ozzdon continued to hold Arius in his arms. Ozzdon knew from the harsh sound of his fallen friend's breathing that he was still alive.

The mightiest warrior of Skymount looked as if he was in a great deal of pain, but he said nothing of it. King Ozzdon could feel the warm blood as he tried frantically to slow the flow from the gaping slit in his old friend's chest. Listless and stunned, the shades of death drew over Arius's face. Coughing up blood, he tried to speak. So obscure were he words that there seemed but half a will left to shape them out. He put a trembling hand on his king's shoulder. Still holding his sword in his other hand, between gurgled snorts, Arius said, "My only regret in life is that I had but one to give to my king. Don't let my death be in vain, fight the good fight to the last, and bring those accountable to justice." Arius' voice was so low that the king could hardly hear him now.

"You're not going to die, Arius," Ozzdon groaned.

Then blood trickled from Arius' mouth, and his existence on Zia went out of his eyes as death crept in to claim him. The king placed him on the ground as gently as he could. Arius' eyes seemed to be still looking up at him. King Ozzdon dropped his head onto his dying friend's chest as he struggled to contain the inferno of burning grief that was festering up in his belly. There was the faintest final cry, and Arius' head slumped sideways, easing him from the burden of having to grow old.

At the entrance, without missing an opportunity, Dandork noted that the narrow crack like opening extended up to the high ceiling. He at once ordered some of his troops to scale the walls on either side to breach the gap from the upper levels. With swords slung across their backs, up like huge cockroaches, the invaders climbed. They scaled from wall to wall, with hands outstretched recklessly, feet slipping and sliding. Soon, like giant four legged spiders, they came crawling across the upper walls and began to drop in on the already faltering defenses. King Ozzdon called for the few remaining archers and ordered the marksmen to target the numerous Norticlanders scaling the walls. Carefully, they released their bowstrings and fired their arrows down the length of the tunnel. At once, they began to pick off the Norticlanders along the upper walls. Each time an arrow was sent on its flight, a Norticlander slumped and fell to the catacomb floor. Those that were not instantly killed fell to their death, screaming in pain as they slammed onto the stone floor. One Norticlander, who took an arrow to his upper shoulder, fell and landed on his feet and fractured one of his legs. When he tried to join the attack, he heard the crunch and the grating of the two broken ends of his leg, bone to bone, as they ground against each other. He fell to the catacomb floor screaming, and clutching at his leg until he was quickly put out of his misery by Edawnian Swordsmen. Scaling Norticlanders continued to fall, but there were not enough arrows to hold back the flow of executioners seeping in from above and below. It was as if a pit of hellish vipers had been uncovered, and there was not enough goodness left in all of Zia to stop its overflowing evil.

Zandor reached down for the king who was still holding Arius, and said, "He is gone, my lord. We are overrun. We must retreat...now!"

One of Xylenia's greatest had fallen, and everyone in the room felt the heartbreak of his passing. Ozzdon's own eyes filled with anguish, but there was little time for mourning, so he turned his pain into vindictive rage. He cried out in his anger and agony,

"Death to the Norticlanders!" Then he leaped from his fallen kinsman's dead body, slashing and slaying the encroaching invaders. The king seemed to come out of his enraged daze just in time and ordered the ever dwindling, dispirited defenses back into the next smaller chamber. King Ozzdon then cried out, "Hold the devils back as long as possible!" Quickly calculating the full extent of the wrath that was about to overcome them as opposed to the time they might have left, the king realized that they were already out of time. He reached for Zandor's shoulder. His grip was sure and secure. He pulled his loyal champion back off the front line of defense. Fearing that it would be his last command, the king charged Zandor, "The appointed time has come, you know what must be done as well as I." Ozzdon momentarily tightened his grasped on Zandor's arm. He licked his dry lips, he could barely voice his thoughts, and even thinking them was painful. King Ozzdon grimaced as he whispered, "The grimmest has come to worse. The queen...be sure and be quick."

Upon hearing of this, Zandor felt the crawling sensation of chilled blood running up and down his spine. His heart suddenly seemed to turn to ice, and his bowels turned to jelly. He all at once realized that intentionally shortening his stick when they drew for the ill fated lot had been a mistake. The lot that would determine who would be the one who would prevent the queen from falling into Baddlock's hands...at any cost. Zandor emphatically uttered, "Please...my Lord, I would rather die fighting."

The king closed his eyes a moment to hold back tears welling up from his heart, but they spilled out from the corners anyway and rolled down his cheeks. Then he reopened his eyes and, regarding Zandor closer than a brother, he said, "I know you do not have the stomach for this kind of thing, but you are the only one I can truly depend on...waste no time."

Honor bound to obey, Zandor bowed his head obediently. He had been raised to regard his King as the anointed, absolute authority, and to bear with unquestioning reverence his every command. Wishing to please his king in everything, he bore his duties without complaint. He returned a nod of affirmation. The king was trying to form his closing words but instead had to settle for a feeble gesture toward the catacombs.

Zandor did the only thing he knew to do—he rose quickly and responded respectfully, "As you wish my Lord." His fist came straightaway, hard against his breastplate armor.

The king pulled Zandor close, wondering if Zandor truly felt as much resolve as he showed. " I can only say, your courage and steadfastness fills me with respect for you."

Zandor then tore himself away from the spot and began to walk reluctantly in the direction he would find the queen waiting. There was no doubt about what he had to do. He groaned inwardly and exhaled a more profound sigh of regret. Zandor was now lamented the more for having secretly broken the ill fated lot, but he had given his pledge to his king. Carrying out what in all probability would be the kings final decree would indeed be the hardest thing he would ever have to fulfill. Had Zandor been a mind reader, he would have perceived that his king wanted him to tell his queen that he would soon be with her. As Zandor hastened to obey what in all likelihood would be his king's last command, he saw King Ozzdon turn his head quickly, trying to hide the anguish ripping at him and intensifying with each heartbeat. He beheld a man who profoundly and desperately loved his Queen. The sight froze his heart to its very core, as it was drawn to his throat by the roots. Up to that moment, Zandor had not known a more acute pain of heartache besides that of the death of his best friend, Rayzar. With tear dimmed eyes, he turned away, sickened, his flesh crawling at the thought of the ghastly task which had befallen him. But it had to be done. He moved swiftly and silently, leaving no room for hesitation or second thoughts. Why was evil allowed to prevail?

Everyone immediately noticed the absence of Zandor, and everyone knew what that meant. A bloodcurdling yell of death sounded behind the mighty warrior as he departed, but he did not attempt to delay. Spurred by a sudden sense of urgency, Zandor quickened his stride. As he was leaving the chamber, his hard steps were heavy against the stone, but he made himself walk faster to keep pace with the swiftness of the passing moment. As his footsteps fell into a cadence of his single mindedness, he left behind him, the dwindling screams of the dying.

The king removed his royal headgear and his royal insignias so he would not be so easily recognized. Then he stubbornly turned, amid the last bastion of ruinous resistance, to fight on before his courage could find a sudden reason to abandon him. He pressed himself into the oncoming waves of Norticlanders, wiggling through and confronting the congestion head on. A Norticlan swordsman immediately challenged him. With a crazed look in his eyes, the king struck with one giant sweep in bottled up rage, severing the head of the aggressor, sending it to his feet below. Even so, it was of no use. The Norticlan were everywhere, slashing with their swords and piercing with their dreaded crossbows. Ozzdon was quickly swallowed into a pit of misery as the fighting increased in ferocity, and the catacomb hollow crammed to overflowing with Norticlanders. The strength of exhausted men failed, and the ever weakening Edawnian defiance fell back grudgingly. Their unwavering loyalty fully testifying to their king with each drop of lost blood. As Zandor turned the corner, he spun quickly to be sure no enemy had flanked him from any direction. Several crossbow arrows shattered against the wall, next to his head showering him with splinters.

Ten
The Quickening

At that very same moment, down in the deepest entrails of Zia, where the sands of time seemed to fall only one granule at a time, with each moment evil seemed to intensify. Zuree had remained at Izz's side, keeping watch over him throughout her faithful vigil. His welfare had been her sole concern. Her teary eyes came wide open when suddenly out of the corners of her vision, she saw a shift in the darkness. She focused and saw the stirring of the hidden demon masses that had been huddled in the dark corners, clinging to the wall like giant insects lying in wait. Zuree froze when she saw the glint of many pairs of red eyes wide with madness. She heard the gnawing of teeth and the clicking of fingernails as they began to unfurled their wings, and all at once seemed to be crowing in on them. And Zuree suddenly realized how much danger they were still in. In that same instance, her attention shifted, drawn to the striking outward manifestation of an inward change in Izz. Izz suddenly began to glow with an intense pulsation as every injury, blemish, and stain seemed to be miraculously healing.

All at once, Izz who, had been unaware of the material world, felt himself spinning, then rushing upward as if he were a shooting star falling skyward. He could suddenly feel his carnal body realigning its energies. All he had ever been and all that he would ever be suddenly sparked into physical consciousness. He perceived himself as his spirit was jolted upward through the empty darkness between two worlds as he was reluctantly dragged back into reality. Sights and sounds began to register in his perception. His eyes bulged in their sockets as the dim firelight registered on his dilating retinas. As Izz came awake, he felt as if he was suddenly recovering from a phantasm or a sleepwalking nightmare. He did not precisely know what was happening or what he had just been through, but he somehow knew it was over for the moment anyway. He suddenly heard Zuree's familiar voice. "They are coming in all around us." Zuree cried, "We must get away from this horrible place!"

As the last tremor in his heart faded, Izz realized that he had become awake. He knew he had to run, but both knew too well that Izz was still too weak to stand, and his mind was still too dumbfounded to formulate a plan of escape. Izz tried to stand, rising as he swayed back and forth. He fought to get to his feet, but his legs were like jelly, and he stumbled back down despite Zuree's greatest effort to keep him afoot. Izz felt as if somehow part of his mind was still missing. Bewildered and still dazed in a mixed up haze, he helplessly waited until the fog continued to recede. But try as he might, Izz could not quite fully recover from his mental plight, and could not shake the dizzy buzz ebbing inside his head. His muscles ached in a hundred places, and every bone in his body felt as if it had been drawn out of its place.

Once the demon hordes in the background assured themselves that the Source of all Light was gone, they all began to come out of hiding in countless numbers. The throngs erupted like a boiling, black blanket of pestilent lice. They swarmed as they started to settle down over the two mortals, preparing to attack like a crazed pack of vicious dogs out only to destroy. "They're coming from everywhere!" Zuree cried. "We have to get away!"

As the surrounding air filled with the stench of sulfur, the evil darkness thickened like black smoke. Raising gray clouds of dust over the dry cave floor filled the cavern as a swirling thickening flock of evil spirits peered down at the defenseless prize. Moments before they found themselves trapped under thick oppression, Izz emphatically urged, "Zuree, save yourself...run! Run now!" Without regard for his own safety, he pointed a trembling finger toward the swiveling stone door and insisted, "Get through the stone door while you still can!"

"NO!" Zuree cried and stood her ground, her mindset. "I will not leave you. If we perish, we perish together. I will not leave without you!"

"No!" Izz moaned, "Please run. Please, please, go now!" Izz begged again and again.

"I cannot!" Zuree only squeezed her eyes shut and enfolded Izz unto herself the more.

All of a sudden, out of nowhere and quite unexpectedly, a light flashed through the darkness like a prolonged lightning bolt that pierces the night. Just moments after the whole demon host came crashing down upon them, the space around them suddenly trembled with magical power out of some supernatural realm. All the shadows disappeared. What very few obscured colors there were in the subterranean cove leaped into life and splashed across the stone walls in every direction. The light just pierced through the darkness until the whole space was one enormous, exalted, luminous dazzle. The primary source of the light intensified and hovered over Izz and Zuree like the center of the universe. Its power spread and wrapped itself warmly around Izz and Zuree, cradling them under its protection. And the hordes of hell were violently wrenched backward and away as if cast aside by overpowering solar winds. The demon spirits were forcefully slammed against the hollow's outer walls where they remained fixed to the stone walls wailing, seething, drooling, grinding their teeth, and clicking their talons.

Then, out of nowhere, one by one, small globes of light appeared within the darkness as if unto a meteor shower in the night sky. Countless points of glittering lights continued to gather over the astonished pair of mortals huddling up against each other. The strange star like spheres then began to emit an ever intensifying light that seemed to shine inwardly rather than outwardly. Suddenly the cluster of orbs began to multiply. Each bright flash was pulsating with tremendous energy. One became two, then four, then eight, until the body of luminaries became a numberless multitude that proceeded to reproduce until the mass tally turned into a throbbing mist. The mist continued, uninterrupted, to increase until it took on the form of a fine, luminous vapor that suspended itself over Izz and Zuree, forming an impenetrable shield of light around them.

Suddenly terrified, withdrawing demons fled squealing in all directions, whooping and frothing, bouncing off the stonewalls like rubber balls down a funnel. From where they were scattered, the demon mass regathered themselves, squinting and trying to focus on their target through the blinding light. All at once, the scornful spirits grew overwrought and agitated. They attempted to charge forward. In the same instance, thousands of thunder bursts and lightning bolts repelled the mass in mid stride. Once again, en masse, screaming demons were thrown back and away, as if by a fierce blast. The demon multitudes were sent careening, by some powerful invisible force. The white hot light like an overwhelming storm cast them back like so much debris caught up in a raging tidal wave of solid light. Those that tried to resist tumbled in midair and sent out unholy shrieks of terror. They tried to open their wings in their futile attempt until one by one, they too were slammed and skewed against the grotto's interior walls. There they remained plastered against the stone by the light force. Howling like wounded jackals bellowing cries of misery, they whimpered and whined as if boiling oil had been thrown on them. Their terrified eyes, like glowing coals, gawked out from behind their black furrowed wings wrapped tightly around their heads. They struggled to shield their faces from the force of the powerful light that caused them so much trembling agony. There was nowhere to back away, nowhere to run, nowhere to hide. They stared with a stunned hallow look on their faces at the awesome light that held them fast to the hard granite wall. And all they could do was melt away before the fury of the Divine Army's assault of holy light.

From within the midst of the luminous vapor cluster, intelligent energy vibrated, danced, and pulsated with the magical power and reverence of eternal fire and dazzling brightness. Out of thin air, observable human forms began to manifest, conscious, thinking immortal beings of blinding light. Izz realized, that as the tangible presence neared, that they were the thousands of white robed warrior angels he had seen before. Super beings of awesome majestic beauty, perfect in every way, gathered in a ring around them. The Immortal Angels, veiled in garments of light, assembled themselves wing to wing. They formed an impenetrable circumference of fortification over Izz and Zuree. The eternal beings of light merged as one, forging an intricately arched orb of light set within another, then another, and another unto the threshold of eternity. The light continued to grow and grow, efflorescing, overfilling the room, as the darkness continued to compress. The shock wave of their presence continued to crush the unclean spirits against the wall as if they were being gripped by a huge, powerful vise of a hand. With cries and a terrible wailing, they continued to foam and froth, dripping pink drooling from their gaping mouths. They were packed so tight, layer upon layer, in such numbers that one became impossible to tell apart from the other.

In the next moment, the bearers of the light moved in unison, not one slower, no one faster than the other. Each spirit had his responsibility, his place, his level of authority. Shoulder to shoulder, the contingent of warriors interlocked their wings like crisscrossing swords to form a tunnel, creating an impenetrable corridor. The bellow of their wings drowned out every sound except the screams of the terrified demons. From within the mist of the matrixes came a voice from the four winds. Izz and Zuree were forewarned, *"Gather yourselves up and leave quickly. Stop for nothing, and do not look back!"* The thundering words were not exchanged through mouth and ear, but rather in and through the inner mind.

Izz and Zuree suddenly realized that the servants of the heaven's had routed a path toward the stone door that led out of the realm where the demons were most empowered. They instantly understood that their only hope of escape was to go through the tunnel.

"Can you walk a little?" Zuree asked, with tears streaming down her face.

"I think so," Izz rasped.

Tom Icon

And with that, Zuree pulled Izz's arm around her neck and shoulders. Half leading, half carrying, Zuree tried to stumble off with Izz. But he was too weak to walk, so Zuree took a firm hold of him and fortified by love, she began to drag Izz along the angelic tunnel. Izz gathered up his satchel and tucked it tightly to his upper body. Once inside the celestial canopy, they saw a dazzling spectacle. The space around them throbbed with ever increasing brightness as they hurried along. Flashes of reflected light enveloped the walls that spun in multiple counterclockwise directions. The Sons of the Mighty stood fast as Izz and Zuree made their escape. Their eyes were so intense, so frightful in their strength of purpose that Izz and Zuree were so glad they were there to save them and not a foe. Their stabbing brightness shone with such force that both Izz and Zuree had to shield their faces from it. Zuree unwaveringly struggled to pull Izz through the protective tunnel that non flesh could not pass through. She endured the most difficult challenge she had ever known, but her love for Izz gave her the strength. As they traversed the tunnel of living light toward the stone doorway, the holy wall of fire began to peel away. As Izz and Zuree made their way across the threshold of eternal doom, the demons in the abyss flew into a rage of panic and hysteria. But all they could do was squawk and cower with their fists venomously clenched as Zuree and Izz slowly but inevitably slipped out of their grasp. As soon as the mortals crossed the stone door threshold and were safely on the other side of the point of departure, the holders of the light returned into mist. They melted away into thin air without a trace as suddenly as they had appeared.

The instant upon realizing the hosts from heaven was gone, the demon horde quickened, unfurling their wings as their eyes narrowed with desperation. Waving their spiny arms, shouting, and hissing, the swarm erupted into one solid wall of agitated sound. They all at once frantically spread their tattered black appendages, slapping their leathery wings in each other's faces. Almost instantly, the air seemed filled with boiling black smoke as innumerable throngs took flight. The whole room exploded into one massive, bombastic bur of roaring wings. With cries and wails of wrath, the diabolical hordes deliriously burst forth in long, black streaks like the surge of a descending storm. Their combined rush rammed up against the stone doorway full force like a gigantic swarm of agitated killer bees. Again and again, they tried, only to be knocked back with loud whimpering howls and frustrated shrieks that electrified the air with their horrified terror. It was the barrier the Judge of all truth christened. No fallen spirit could cross. Their loud anguished cries grew into an echoing drone of savage fury that reverberated throughout the whole underworld. They would never escape their imprisonment; their Keeper had but left the door ajar in contempt.

Once on the other side of the stone door, away from the reaches of the demonic legions, Zuree and Izz felt the darkness weaken. Even though their bodies remained captive in the bowls of Zia, their souls felt they had been set free. And at that moment, a miraculous thing came about. With Zuree's assistance, Izz struggled to his feet and waited for more strength, and it came. Izz's mind quickly cleared, and he felt a new vigor surging in his veins. He rose to his full length and stood awkwardly on his feet, still fighting a trace of dizziness. It would take a few more moments before Izz's legs would bear him without the help of the wall. As he regained his balance, he took one step forward. His footing became firmer and steadier. With Zuree in the lead, together, they quickened their steps away from the gates of hell. Izz's legs still trembled from the experience they had gone through, but he willed them to an iron steadiness. Together with hands locked, in the hope of the living, they put distance between them and the abode of the dead where wretchedness was held captive. And neither looked back. When they were well out of sight of the gate marker, they stopped, as each drew a deep breath and held it for a moment. Then they reached out and snatched each other to themselves. Wrapping each other in oneness, each soul looking to the other for courage. Drawing the next fleeting half breath with parched throat, Zuree whispered against Izz's lips, "I was so...so afraid that I had lost you forever as she broke down and wept bitterly."

TOM ICON

There they clung to each other and kissed mouth to mouth with all their passion as true lovers do. The harsh, dim lit world around them became unimportant as they blazed fiery wet paths across each other's faces. Then and there, Izz felt in his heart that he was ready to go on, to complete his hollowed mission—to save his beloved Zuree from a fate worse than death. They together, they turned to face the unknown, neither having any idea where the path they were on would take them. They both knew their nightmare was far from over. There were many unknowns, but no matter what awaited them, they had each other.

Eleven
The Last Resort

Zandor hastened down the stone steps that descended through the narrow, twisting stairwell lending into the darkest recesses of the catacombs. It was dry and cold in the tangle of stone corridors that honeycombed beneath the underbelly of the kingdom. The catacombs were so vast, so labyrinthine that Zandor had to rely on instinct to arrive at the place he needed to reach. He navigated past the many cavities of tunnels that connected the hundreds of storage chambers. There were several escape routes, barricaded from the inside that lead outside the walls of the kingdom, but knowing Dandork, they were sure to be guarded. As he continued along, the path led him closer and closer toward his grisly task. Zandor paled as his insides twisted. He made an iron willed attempt to make ready for the appalling chain of events that would soon be set in motion. The handheld torch he carried before him cast his dark silhouettes on the walls of the subterranean corridor. As Zandor made his way farther down into the cold, silent darkness of the catacombs, he nervously chewed on the inside of his bottom lip, trying harder and harder to assure himself that he could do the unthinkable. No matter from what angle he looked at it, he could not escape his conviction to regard his king as the anointed supreme authority, and to serve him, he must with obedient veneration. But the more he thought about it, the worst he felt, and the more it disconcerted him. He continually glanced back, unable to shake the feeling that he was being followed. From time to time, Zandor thought he heard pursuing footsteps on the gravel just behind him. His sense of reluctance hunted him, and his conviction eroded with every step. Visions of past benevolence his queen had bestowed upon him began to surface. Emotions of weakness that

215

had waited for this very moment to burst from their hiding places and rushed forth like raging torrents through an overwhelmed floodgate. Every breath he drew was exhaled in regret. Suddenly emptied of the ability to think clearly, Zandor slumped against the stone wall of the corridor as his heart and mind began to afflict him. Every muscle and every tendon tensed all at once, and he fell to his knees with a tormented moan. He attempted reasoning to console himself. He had survived this long by growing a tough hide, by callusing over his sentiments, and bridling his thoughts so that each subsequent heartache hurt a little less. His commitment to his king forced him to rise. Honor bound to obey, he promised himself to accomplish his regrettable task as soon as possible. The sooner he accomplished his purpose, the better.

Zandor, at last, reached the chamber in the catacombs where the queen, wives, and mothers were huddled together to keep out the cold. The women were looking over their children like hens watching over their broods. The fine dust covering the floor muffled his approach. His ivory handled dagger rode snugly on his hip as he turned the corner in the expanding space. Queen Zahra turned to the sound of the approaching footsteps that had drifted into her ears from the outer chamber. "Who is there?" Sounding very startled, the queen called out from the shadows painted against the catacomb walls, cast by the light of the dim burning candles.

"It is I, Zandor, my queen," Zandor respectfully called out from the darkness. His voice sounded weary and emotionally drained.

The queen trembled at the recognition of the voice, knowing that it did not belong to the king as she wondered what that meant. As Zandor came closer, the flickering light of the candles that were bravely trying to shine, cascaded across the despair written in every line on his face. That is when the queen saw the unspeakable woe cast upon it, only to confirm what she had not dared to put into thoughts. Queen Zahra met the eyes on Zandor's stern face, and his gaze made her heart sink and shudder, knowing somehow from the bleakness of his expression what it meant. Despite his best efforts to conceal his fallen countenance. His features were darkened with sorrow as if the deepest shadow of the catacombs had suddenly come over his soul. As he glanced anxiously around the darkened tunnels, it was pathetic to see the women fearfully shaking, with every breath. His head dropped to his chest. Zandor spoke gently, careful not intending to upset the internal balance that had settled over the children. "It is time, my queen," he choked. The corners of Zandor's lips turned up in the faintest of smiles so as to not alarm the others, but his smile quickly fell to the ground.

The queen handed the orphaned infant she was cradling in her arms to Atta, who was faithfully at her queen's side. Atta clutched the shivering child to her bosom. Zahra's gaze traveled back to Zandor, as she gracefully rose to her feet. Upon realizing what was happening, Atta pretended not to notice the heavy tear falling and rolling down her queen's cheek. She turned silently to cry her heart out, privately. Her sobs were so soft that she did not shudder, so silent they could not be heard, but the profound anguish was there. For a long time, women and children stared at each other in mute, mournful silence. They somehow knew something was not as it should be. Zandor reached out his hand and escorted Queen Zahra toward the next chamber. As they turned the corner, Zandor clutched at his razor sharp dagger. The action was partly automatic and partly a reflection of his unquestioning obedience to his king. The queen stopped. She did not turn around. She merely stood there with her hands at her side and raised her head high, bravely exposing her throat to Zandor's blade. "What you must do, do it quickly," were the only words she managed to whisper.

At the forefront of the catacombs, at the cutting edge of the current fighting, the Norticlan pushed in harder, closing in for the final assault, knowing full well that their overwhelming victory was at hand. The king stood fast in up close combat, caught in a torrent of crossing swords and clashing blades under showering bursts of sparks. The ever dwindling Edawnian guardians were no match for the endless numbers of Norticlan warriors in uninterrupted head to head combat. Isolated pockets of defenders were forcefully maneuvered onto a weaker and weaker foothold, and forced to back up deeper and deeper into the lower catacombs to stay one step ahead of death. All fell back, that is all except King Ozzdon. Instead, the king was moving forward to face the onslaught. While death crowded in all around him, he shouldered his way to the front of the carnage. Life and death had become meaningless. On the frontline, closing in rapidly, was a Norticlan headhunter bent on killing his next opponent. Not recognizing it was the king, the Norticlan warrior lunged in for the kill. From the rear, at least one archer was still firing. "Target the leaders with whatever arrows you have left to you," the king instructed.

The closest Edawnian archer dropped the assailant and then reached for another arrow that was not there. He turned to the king and yelled, "In a few moments, we will be reduced down to throwing rocks."

By now, Norticlanders were swarming in from everywhere. The situation was turning into a final blood bath of bloodbaths. The man to the king's right took a bolt in the chest and fell, his head was thrown back, mouth agape. The man to his left lost his left kidney with one slice of an arching blade, and he dropped, unable to go on. The king looked around him for a helping hand but saw more black crested shields than Edawnian. He knew that at the rate they were being killed, it would not be much longer before their resistance would become a foregone conclusion. They were now being overrun and slaughtered like cornered lambs in a slaughterhouse. This day was like a bad dream that would not end. Already the king's men had long arrived at a point beyond the impossible, and yet, led by Kondor, they fought on—not because they had any hope left but because their honor commanded it.

The king was rapidly reaching the end of his strength. He was so tired that his eyes had taken on a dull glazed look. He was suddenly torn by the grief of not knowing if his queen was still alive. Zuree was more than likely as good as dead. He could not stand the thought that she might have been violated, abused, or tortured. He agonized over the fact that he had been helpless to protect his queen and people from the hordes of encroaching doom.

On top of that, his most trusted adviser had betrayed him, his best friend had forsaken him, his oldest friend was dead, and his kingdom was in ruin. What would be the purpose of going on when you knew all was lost? He felt thoroughly spent by the constant day and night fighting. For a time, his heart collapsed within him as he weighed up the odds that were mounting up against him. He felt his will to go on, drain out of him like water from a broken jar. As the dangers multiplied before him, his faith faltered, trepidation and trembling came over him, and revulsion overpowered him. The truth was that he was not only ready to die, but he was eager to end the terror that was consuming him, heart, and soul. His enemies were on the verge of celebrating his demise, and the power of darkness was set to exult its triumph over him. He wanted to scream a protest to Ammiz's God. He thought about falling on his own blade. A self inflicted death would be nothing more than a way to escape the evil that was about to befall him anyway. But that is not how he wanted to be remembered if there was anyone left to remember him. How was he allowing himself to think the unthinkable he wondered to himself? He thought about the flaying of the king of Skymount. That train of thought suddenly ended when he heard Ammiz's voice call out. Ammiz, as he often did, came out of nowhere. Coming through the rear entrance just in time to realize that things were about to go from extremely bad to utterly worse. Almost unthinkingly in an inspired moment, Ammiz shouted, to no one in particular, "Everyone, over this way!"

With no other option, Kondor, and the few still left standing moved back toward the sound of Ammiz's authoritative voice. The king remained steadfast where he stood, and the only thing separating him and death was himself. Sensing that the final kill was near, the advancing Norticlan warriors crowded in and circled the fringes of the chambers like bloodthirsty wolves, closing in on a flock of defenseless sheep. Anticipating the most opportune moment to seize upon and finish off their prey, the horde pounced. The only thing causing them to hesitate was an occasional last arrow shot into the heart of an advancing Norticlander. And then there was Kondor—still standing, still deadly. With the thought of what Zandor had done to their champion still burning bright in their minds, no Norticlan Warrior wanted to be the last one to die in the great siege of Edawn.

Kondor cautiously backed up, not daring to take his eyes off the enemy, and became so turned around that he could not tell if he was moving toward where the seer had last called out to them. Just in the nick of time, Ammiz once again called out, "This way, my king!"

The king took a moment, and a dark thought came to him, and he whispered, "My Queen is probably dead by now." The words did not travel farther than his own hearing. But his expression told his state of mind far more clearly than did his words. The king stared into the emptiness that was once his will to live and heard a faraway thought say to him mockingly. *The queen is dead!* By the time this thought completed, a deadpan look had settled over his face as if it would always be there, forever. "It is time…to leave this forlorn life." The king's voice was flat, devoid of emotion.

The tragedy unfurling around him was crowned with the sorrow of his losses. Life's bitterest sorrows all came crashing down on him all at once, accompanied by the shrinking down of his persecuted soul. It was as if every cycle of his life had come to a season of darkness that would only end with his death. He could not let anyone see him like this. With that realization, the king turned to face the inevitable destiny that awaited him. Revitalized by sudden rage, the king unexpectedly turned as he stiffened his upper lip, straightened his back, and tightened the grip on the handle of his sword. He let out a war cry that astounded his troops and momentarily confounded the pack of rancorous assassins. Again and again, his blade blazed a trail of Norticlan blood as he abandoned himself into the mayhem of battle. The wrath that raced fiercely through the veins within his body gave him inhuman swiftness and physical power. Instantaneously, he was joined by Kondor, and those still fit to fight. Those women and children still standing, recognized the hopelessness of the situation. They positioned their weapons defensively and backed away into the deeper catacombs. But the king instead advanced, attacking faster and deeper than the others, advancing recklessly. He swept his blade, fiercely cutting through flesh, blood, and bone with bewildering vigor and swiftness. Concerned, Kondor called out, "My King, what is your command? I can no longer guard your flank!"

The king spun awkwardly, delivering another fatal wound with an abrupt slice of his blade. With the unbalanced thrusts of his overstrained muscles, another two legged skunk fell. Then suddenly, as if he had run into a stone wall, his strength failed him. Physically and emotionally spent, he could not quite recover from his mounting mental plight. He just stood there, his body aching and his mind throbbing, too exhausted to even hold up his sword any longer. He felt the strength of his mind, body, and soul taxed to their limits. The Norticlan warrior standing in front of him stared with cold, hate filled eyes, momentarily frozen with surprise. And then suddenly, sure of his quarry, he moved into a kill position.

The Great Sword of Edawn hung from the king's hand as if it had become too heavy for him to lift. He loosened his grip, and the sword slipped from his hand and fell. As the blade hit the dusty, bloody stone floor, it bounced from the tip of its edge to the handle several times with the clanging sound of finality. As if caught in a dream in the slowest possible motion, the king saw the intense, bloodlust filled expression pasted on his would be executioner's face. The assailant resembled a giant vulture swooping in on its defenseless quarry. It was all right there ,unfurling at a snail's pace before his eyes. In only moments he knew he would be dead. To him, death had lost its sting in the midst of all the horror he had already seen.

The only thing that could have possibly stood between him and death was divine intervention. *Let the blow fall. I welcome its coming,* he thought as he fell to his knees. His eyes were large and round, but they might as well have been closed. As the savage slayer looked forward to the pleasure of the welcoming slaughter, he prepared to strike. The king's pupils enlarged, cold and glassy, fractured with bedlam. There was no one close enough to save him. The king's hair fell across his brow as he bowed his head and slumped his shoulders. He did not honestly want to die, but without his queen, he saw no reason to live. His fear of the unknown suddenly fell away. It was an odd peace. In battle, he had given everything he had left in him. It would be a quick, honorable death. Utter horror and hopelessness bolted over the soul of every onlooking Edawnian in the room like the agonizing sting of their sudden death. It was as if their resolve had all at once, suddenly and completely, shattered into countless pieces.

Meanwhile, deep in the entrails of the catacombs, Zandor prepared for the unthinkable. "This will be as painless as possible," he whispered. The unutterable words somehow passed his strained throat so that only the queen could hear.

Zandor's words struck the queen like a fist. The queen drew in a long, distressed breath as her heart raced. All she could hear was the beating of blood in her ears. This was it! She could feel her pounding heart in her breast so thunderously that she feared one of its chambers would suddenly burst. It was her final moment. She was not sure what she should do, but it seemed that remaining perfectly still and keeping her chin up, was her only option. With a sour feeling in his stomach, the king's righthand man bore his duties with all the courage he could rally. Zandor's right hand drove to his side and grasped the razor sharp dagger. As he drew his blade, it shrilled a whisper of irrevocability. Zandor could not help staring down for a moment at the blade; it was still smeared with discolored Norticlan blood. Not wishing to mingle his queen's royal blood with tainted blood, he carefully whipped the straight, double edged shank on his sleeve. He then gently placed his big, powerful hand over the queen's upheld chin. His thick upper fingers flattened around her mouth in case she had to scream. The strength of the entwined muscles in Zandor's hand astonished her. Zandor firmly drew the queen against himself and reached the blade of mercy into position for a quick, clean slash. Against Zandor's hand, the queen's jaw trembled as she clamped her lips tightly, swallowed hard, and bit down on her tongue to keep from crying out. She could feel the quickening of her blood rushing through her veins and heard its increased throbbing surge in her ears. Zandor felt a wave of nausea flow over him, and his heart too began to thunder feverishly with an irregular rhythm that forced the breath out of him. Somewhere inside him, the edgy composure that he had somehow managed to reinforce all this time cracked. Try as he may, he could not tap into the reserves of his fearless character. He closed his eyes for a second. There was a short period of mental blankness, and his arm seemed suddenly weak.

"King Ozzdon!" screamed Kondor when he saw what was unfolding, but hopelessly locked in battle, he was unable to come to the aid of his king. The king, like a shell of himself, having lost the will to live, just stooped there demoralized without a single inkling of regret. He would not grow old, and age would not weary him. He was ready to leave this world and to meet his queen, Zahra, in the next life. Nothing else mattered.

As if in slow motion, the Norticlander's blade arched back. Every sinew in Kondor's neck strained like wires just past their limits. The king's vision blanked. Sound receded. He dismissed the question of the multitudes that had died or who was dead and who was still among the living. The king was ready to feel the bite of steel. He did not fear his own death. He welcomed it. He was able to empty his mind of everything except for the cheers coming from the armies of darkness mocking his soul. Uncontrolled chaos ruled the minds and hearts of the king's men, as the sight of their king's suicidal surrender slew them. It seemed the air itself would break and split apart under their tense apprehension.

However, the scene of tribulation did not sweep Ammiz into its net. Having sensed that the king was about to do something rash, the seer had maneuvered himself unobserved, forward. He could not let what was about to happen, happen. Ammiz impulsively dropped the staff of age and immediately leaped from the shadows into action. He turned into a bundle of energy despite the screaming protesting of his knobby joints for the sudden movement. To everyone's amazement, friend and foe alike, Ammiz unexpectedly rushed forward and seized the Great Edawnian Sword from the stone floor. The battle sword felt too large for Ammiz's hands, but he clasped it as best as he could. The Norticlan assassin's curved blade arced back. The old man could see the knotted muscles in the killer's arms bulge as his blade came slashing down in a fiery arc toward the king's exposed neck.

Ammiz's fixed eyes fastened keenly on the weapon and just managed to raise the king's battle sword high enough to deflect the vicious, deadly blow on the very jagged edge of the last possible fleeting point in time. The swords made a clanging, grading metal on metal sound, sending sparks flying everywhere from the blades as they met. Never in all his life had the king felt death's chilling breath so close on the nape of his neck. The stunned assailant turned to face the old man, who carried no shield and wore no armor, and he laughed a roaring spiteful laugh. "Boys…women, now old men. What next…old women?"

From the background came an outpouring of laughter and a barrage of the most filthy language ever heard. The scared face Norticlander gave Ammiz an up and down look, rolled his eyes, and then said, "Come if you need me to ease your burden. Come, and let us get it over with, you foolish, old wine bag."

More filthy words and laughter went to and fro. The blunt skulled Norticlander flashed his sword about with a whooshing sound as he prepared to chop the old man before him into two pieces. With every swat of the Norticlander's heavy sword, Ammiz lost ground. One more blow and Ammiz would be no more. With a flash of pain burning in his bedimmed and enfeebled faculties, Ammiz mutated and made one last bold, breathtakingly move. His chest heaved, and his sinewy biceps strained with the effort of directing the lance he could barely grasp with both hands. He stepped forward into a tight spin. Ammiz moved faster than the ponderous brute could ever have anticipated. And with one lightning, fell swoop, Ammiz cleanly separated the Norticlander from his head. Sending it toppling end over end from its body with the proud sneer still twisted on its face. For that flashing moment, the old man's actions were as strong and as fast for that moment, as ever they had been in his long lifetime. The space all at once suddenly seemed deadly quiet. Everyone within eye shot on both sides began to wonder if Ammiz had supernatural powers. With sword still in hand, Ammiz unexpectedly reached out and forcefully pulled the king back and away just out of the reach of the stunned, and recuperating Norticlan forces. The king had lost the facility of self guidance and was lost in a knot of inter limbo. He whispered, "No...leave me. My queen is dead, my daughter doubtlessly so. All is lost."

"Your Eminence, I do not think you have thought this through. You must endure until at least you are doubtless until you are certain one way or the other."

The king turned as he pulled his arm away. "Believe me; I am sure—sure beyond any doubt." And there his words died.

By the time the king realized what was happening, they were standing at the mouth of an obscure hollow. Its opening was barely big enough for one man to fit through at a time. "This is what you have called me to?" The king asked as a look of anger flashed across his shocked face.

"We must live to fight on."

Then the king answered, slightly raising his chin, only his lips moved. "Who is we?"

"Whoever that is left of us. In here, a handful of men can hold off an army!" The seer insisted.

Ozzdon glanced into the cave, opening, "There is no way out!" We cannot afford to be trapped by these accursed cutthroats. It would be insanity!" Consumed in a fog of his ranting and raging, he looked like a man who was only barely holding himself together.

"If we dig in here, we can hold out. Everywhere around Zia, our forces have gathered and are converging on us as we speak. It is my hope and unwavering belief that any hour now that our reinforcements will come forth."

"I am so glad to hear that, old man! But in just a few moments, it is going to be too late."

But before the king could react, Ammiz had already stuffed him through the small opening. They had both disappeared down the hole of the hollow that was by then already half full. They were soon joined by the scrambling retreat of Kondor and others who managed to push and pull themselves into the cramp hollow. One by one, they disappeared down the hole like human moles. The broken spirits fled for their lives, bolting down the shaft as if crawling into their own grave. The last man was caught from behind before he could squeeze through. He was dragged back and ripped to shreds by the frustrated mob of Norticlan warriors. Inside dozens of Edawnian warriors were jammed packed, all around to the outer edges of the hollow. A few murderous assailants tried storming the small opening of the hollow, only to be sliced to pieces by the multiple blades that greeted them. The inner hole in the subterranean dead end seemed to be secure for the moment. Men burdened with war stood, motionless, reassuring themselves. Then suddenly, everyone inside the hollow turned and stared at Ammiz as if he had mystical virtues. They were all still shocked into silence at what the old man had done. Once again, like a beckon rising in the darkness, he had championed hope to the hopeless. The centermost sphere of retreat in the underbelly of the kingdom was their last sanctuary of defense. Ammiz stood there attending to the king as if he had only done what had to be done, and had been extremely lucky in having done so. He simply whispered, "The creator is faithful. He will not abandon those who seek hope in His compassion."

They all just continued looking at each other awkwardly, in

silent despair. A tense silence fell over the cramped unappealing space. Outside, controlled confusion reigned. A messenger reported to Dandork, "Lord Dandork, we have the king, and his men cornered."

Not quite sure of the foot soldier's babbling words, Dandork made his way to the forefront of his forces, down toward the inner hollow to investigate. He found one of his generals trying to the coax the insurgents out of the burrow. "We wish you no ill. If you will lay down your arms and come out, I will personally guarantee your safety."

Dandork produced a tight grin of satisfaction on his face when he realized that he held King Ozzdon exactly where he wanted him. He knew where all the catacomb secret exits were and where the king had sought refuge—there was no exit. Now all he had to do was flush him out and hand him over to Baddlock. Then it would only be a simple matter of slaughtering the rest of the resisters. While Dandork assessed the situation, he thumped his chin with his forefinger. The first thing he did was order a band of cutthroats to search out the women and children. He then pulled his top ranking general from the opening, who was still trying to coax the king out and asked with sarcastic contempt, "Did you think to ask them if they would hand you their hearts over on a silver platter?" He pulled the general away from the opening and concentrated on a plan to flush the king and his remaining men out.

"Why not starve them out?" someone asked.

"Yes,! Brilliant! Why oh why did I not think of that? We could all just camp around right here!" He screamed as he looked around for someone to backhand.

Those closest to him cowered away as they flinched in anticipation. Dandork returned to his divided thoughts, as the moment lengthened into a drawn out conundrum. The traitorous betrayer's eyes roved around the chamber and then dropped to the floor, when just then, an idea blinked through his mind. Finally, he spoke, pointing to a group standing around him and commanded. "Check those jars against the wall over there."

TOM ICON

The first man to reach the cache of stacked clay jars gave the one nearest to him a shake, and then shattered the jar's top with his long blade. He brought the blade to his nose and sniffed for a moment. "It is lamp oil, Master Dandork."

Dandork eye narrowed as he smiled maliciously and ordered the jars to be brought to the opening of the hollow. As the last jar of volatile oil was being carried to the hollow opening, Tigbone's stooped form appeared unexpectedly as he often did, hobbling along and carrying his right arm awkwardly. Upon spotting Tigbone's approach, Dandork asked bitterly, "What is it?"

"I bring important message direct from Mazter himself." Tigbone continued with an air of implied self importance, "The Mazter wills to know..."

Dandork could not believe the raving of this weak knee high dwarfling, this insignificant little string puppet who he had never before seen act in this arrogant manner. "What is it?" Dandork snapped as annoyance riveted through him at the untimely interruption.

With his round head drawn into his shoulders, Tigbone slowly and carefully approached Dandork and spoke out the message, "The Mazter must know news of the king." As he spoke, Tigbone looked around the underground cavity in dumb awe as he sucked up a string of drool that threatened to escape his mouth.

Dandork constrained himself before he spoke again. "You can tell our Master that he can rest assured that I have things very much under control here."

"Begging your pardon, Lord Dandork," the messenger accompanying Tigbone almost cut Dandork off in mid sentence. "The Master requires that you report to him personally," He said as he drummed his fingers on the armor piercing crossbow cradled in his arms, muzzle down.

The pale skinned, sunken cheeked, messenger volunteered no explanation. Dandork was enraged that he would be called away from the opportune moment only to satisfy Baddlock's whims. He had nervously awaited this very moment since the day of the ambush. He, at long last, had Ozzdon right where he wanted him. He knew that when one senses the unconditional defeat of the enemy, one must tighten the noose and crush that enemy. He genuinely feared King Ozzdon, and he would not rest at ease until he knew he was dead. Only his death could erase the haunting look that had pierced him to his core the moment their eyes met, and the king realized his most trusted friend had betrayed him. Betrayal without reason or cause was the greatest of all human miseries committed on a best friend. His guilt hung on his back like a blood sucking leech. By now, he was more than ready to cut him out of his life without a second thought of guilt or penance. But the look in those eyes that day, he knew it would forever prey on his mind. He was willing to do anything to end the torment that persecuted his soul and troubled his dreams.

Nonetheless, the only person he feared more than the Emperor King of Zia was the Wicked Warlock Wizard. "Yes, yes," Dandork finally answered. "I will be there at once." His voice turned as hard and as cold as ice as he looked at the messenger as if he could have strangled him. But just before Dandork departed, he turned to his most trusted henchman, drawing him near, face to face. Then he spoke in his ear.

"Take no chance. Allow no mercy," he said in no uncertain terms. "Pour all the lamp oil in the hollow and set them ablaze. If you can capture the king alive, very well, if not, dead is just as good. Do…not fail me, or it will be your miserable carcass that will be on the rack begging for death! For if we fail, that could put us all on the wrong side of the blade." With that, he turned making way for the messenger who fell in step beside him as Dandork hastened to bring word to his taskmaster, Baddlock.

In the dark hole of the hollow, with no second line of defense, it was as if a door of doom had suddenly clanged shut with the dreaded sound of finality. With dread worn faces, their swords in hand, the Edawnians crouched and huddled together like human moles. Each man was divided into his thoughts and breathing heavily, hoping against hope. One half crazed warrior blurted out, "The reinforcements should be here by now! Why are they not here?"

If only they could just hang on one more moment—one more hour. Just maybe, the long overdue reinforcements would, by some marvel, miraculously appear. Outside stillness fell. The unearthly silence provoked a moment of gasping panic as if they had already been sealed in their tomb. Out of the silence, another desperate soul blurted, "Maybe they gave up, and they are going to leave us alone."

Kondor stared the man down, forcing him to look away as he responded, "For all my life is worth right now, I would not bet it on the possibility of that ever happening."

That flickering speck of fool's aspiration was crushed abruptly, when someone asked, "What is that smell?"

Another answered just as abruptly, "Its lamp oil!"

Suddenly every eye bolted open with a start and then widened. The smell was unmistakable. It was a ghastly certainty. Hearts rent as the flammable lamp oil suddenly came gushing in from the opening above. Those who had been sitting gained their feet quickly only to stare at each other with looks riddled with panic. The king, who was slumped in a deep stupor, suddenly as if waking, wanted to rush Ammiz and wanted to grasp him by the throat and scream in his face. But instead, he just sat there and whispered, "Is this what you saved me for you stiff necked radical? To be roasted like a chicken in a frying pot!" His voice came up in pitch and then ended in a wounded tone.

"It was just an inescapable impulse of being who I am." Ammiz vehemently countered.

Forlorn men who had nowhere to run just stared blankly at each other as they turned pale with dread. Imminent Death made its presence felt. With every heartbeat, riveting shock grew among those hopelessly trapped. Kondor remained silent as the explosive mixture flooded in. The chances of dying were more real than ever, and for this, he had already prepared his mind. *We all live until we die,* the king thought. They were all about to die, but that did not mean he had to be afraid.

Desperately every man rushed to block the flow of the lamp oil with their hands. When that did not work, they removed their tunics and tried to stuff them in the hole, with panicky and irregular jerks, but the opening still leaked like a sieve. With his heart and soul still in a catatonic state, the king collapsed back into the corner, disillusioned and disgusted. Assailed with the question that kept pounding through his brain, *and this is what you saved me for.* "What now?" The king whispered, too tired even to be appropriately irritable. In his darkest hour, the king sagged evermore as he looked around the hollow at the gloomy, empty, blood, and gore stained faces. Their expressions showed the hopelessness of being in deadly combat for too long. And now the ghastly probability of dying more miserable than a rat was more real than ever. What about all the other thousands who had already died? Was living through all of this hell really worth the trouble. His mood turned instantly gloomier. With a heart sinking sense of disappointment, his eyes shifted behind his apathetic countenance as if a distant thought had suddenly crawled across his mind. As he focused his attention back on his queen, he wondered if she could all ready be dead. Had she suffered? He hoped that they would soon be together, where ever that might be. There glazed a remoteness over his sightless stare. And what about his beloved daughter? He hung his head in grief, and his endurance shrank another yawning degree. What had he done to deserve such misery?

Twelve
The Countermand

Zandor's thoughts darted through the recesses of his mind. His thoughts were drawn to Kondor. He knew his brother was in crisis in the same way one twin experiences a physical sensation of something that is happening to their twin. He searched his brain for the logic he was so sure of moments ago. Then suddenly, the remembrance of the king's last words pierced his mind. The thought of his pleading tone pulled him away from his own agonized thoughts. Instantly, there and then, there was no doubt about what he must do. A blackness like blindness suddenly came over him. He seemed to lose all sense of hearing as everything around him appeared to fall into dead silence. Time stood still as Zandor felt a loss of all contact with the real world. He drained himself entirely of all other thoughts as his fingers tensed around his dagger, and his hand took on a life of its own, passing beyond belief into raw feeling.

Not daring to breathe, and hardly daring to think, the queen's jaw muscles clenched and unclenched as her eyes widened and she swallowed down on a knot of anticipation. A tremulous jolt ran through her, threatening to overwhelm her as a twisted grimace spread over her face. Her lips shuddered as the blood was driven from her cheeks. She forced herself to breathe shallowly through clenched teeth, trying to steady the disquieting regret mounting within her. Zandor could sense her silent tears falling. As he drew his razored blade into position, he drew a deep breath to calm his heart. He felt a single drop of sweat run down his forehead and trickled down the middle of his face. Another droplet ran down the middle of his spine.

In the hollow, men who had seconds to live only stared at each other through the eyes of hopelessness. A closure that was sensed rather than spoken infused every soul. In a fleeting instant, Ammiz, who had up to that point been as solid as a rock, found himself in a unique moment of detachment. He had never given up hope, not even once. And even though his faith was wavering, somewhere in the old man's heart, there was still hope even now in the very darkest hour. He drew a shaky breath and stared from the outside in. He saw a grave conclusion that was looking more and more like the end of a long road. From the way things were looking, his decision had been a critically inadequate choice. The choice between almost certain death and probable death was now rapidly turning into inescapable death. The thought deductively bounced around in his head, *stay outside where our chances are slim to none, or crawl into a hole and be trapped with no place to run, or* The choice had been made, fate was cast, and it was history now, and he had taken an irrevocable step. He had led his king into what was looking more and more like the jaws of imminent, impending death.

The queen gasped when she felt the prickle of the sharp razor edge against her exposed throat just beneath her jawline. The full realization came that she was only a single muscular reflex away from death. Her chest rose to her deepening breath as she felt a swelling tightness in her belly. Zandor whispered in a choked tone as his hand grew damp on the handle of his lethal dagger. "I will soon see you in the next world, my beloved queen." There was an unfamiliar quaver in a voice, usually so sure.

In the midst of it all, at that exact moment in the heart of darkness, Abaddawn was in an ever proliferating fit of rage. Zuree had managed to cross the threshold where his evil was most powerful. The threat of Zuree's escape had shaken the pillars of darkness, and the underworld trembled. The prince of darkness wanted retribution! The smoldering smoke of his torment ascended forever and ever, casting itself upon the winds of chaos and diffused throughout the rift of lightlessness. The affront of evil had, for the present, been taken aback. The carpenter was rapidly advancing the maiden out of his evil reach and quickly taking Zuree out and away from his eternal clutches, in turn, foiling his last opportunity to free himself and his host. His last fighting chance was Baddlock. Having direct telepathic contact with the Wicked Warlock Wizard's internal soul, Abaddawn connected with Baddlock's collective consciousness and summoned his human pawn to him.

Just outside the keep's entrance, the horde of Norticlanders was gloating with greed like giant parasites feeding on the defeat and misery of Edawn. The fierce excitement of conquest and the insatiable greed for plunder was erupting everywhere as the invaders looted everything around them that radiated with gold. Baddlock, the vulturous monster, sat atop Nightmare, beaming with the intoxication of power while reeling in his triumph and gore. He had established a strategic foothold for his coming New World Order and the rule of the New Age. His spirit was devilishly lit up with lofty, godlike arrogance as he oversaw the ransacking of Edawn's treasures. His eyes were depthless mirrors dancing with fire that reflected the images of the devastation he had caused. The defecation of a buzzard raised his twisted fist to the heavens and proclaimed in a loud voice, "Edawn is mine and ever shall be." His words were distorted with malice as an explosion of evil elation emanated from his whole being.

By now, Dandork had reached the breached, front gate of the keep. He immediately mounted his warhorse and approached his high master to report that his moment of personal triumph over King Ozzdon was well in hand. As he approached, he noticed the Wicked Warlock Wizard was basking in the blissful euphoria of total power. Dandork's expression twisted when he saw Baddlock's visage unexpectedly shift awkwardly. As Dandork neared, he was farther surprised to see Baddlock spin around quickly as if someone had jabbed him in the rear with a long, sharp prod. Strange still, then for no apparent reason, he sat up abruptly as if a bolt had suddenly struck him. He forcefully yanked on his mount's reins, forcing Nightmare to reel violently to the left, sending both dancing sideways in a complete turnaround.

Tigbone, who had returned to Baddlock's side, was almost trampled as he stared on wide eyed at his master's odd behavior. Baddlock's high pitched squeal flustered the horses and confused the riders all around him. Then the Wicked Warlock Wizard peered around broodingly, angrily eyeing several of his surrounding generals suspiciously. Alarm overshadowed Dandork's face went he saw Baddlock bolt upright and heard his teeth grinding in rage as a poisonous mask of madness came over his entire visage. Everyone around the Wicked Warlock Wizard just stared back with gaping mouths, bewildered at what they had just witnessed. Baddlock's eyes and mouth suddenly widened as far as they would open as he slapped his two emaciated hands over the side of his skeletal temples as hard and fast as he could. Then he suddenly jerked vehemently, as if his eyes had unexpectedly been pierced with two red hot thunderbolts. His eyes rolled around in his head like two peas in a goblet. He instinctively lowered one hand to steady his warhorse. The other hand raked across the crown of his head and stroked the length of his face. "Uhnhhh!" He finally screamed at the top of his lungs as he reared up, ready to charge at whoever had dared to strike the unseen blow.

Dandork, by now, had rushed to his side and asked, "What is wrong, my lord?"

Baddlock was stooped forward like a sparrow who was about to fall beak first from its perch. Then an unmistakable voice only he could hear burst forth into his inner ear from within the deepest recesses of his black heart, *"Return unto me at once, without delay! I have urgent need of you. NOW!*

Almost immediately, Baddlock reopened his eyes, attempting to recapture some self possession as if coming out of a trance and trying to figure out where he was. In the next instance, he somehow managed to reclaim his composure. The following few words that came out of his mouth would change everything! In a hard reedy, nasal voice, his command exploded from his gaping mouth. "Recall our troops!"

Having heard this and thinking it had been a joke, everyone broke out laughing, including Tigbone and Darkon. Dandork was unsure if he should join in. But before he could, the laughter came to an abrupt halt. Just when in an even louder, more sinister voice that seethed with insistence, Baddlock let out another prolonged bloodcurdling scream, "It is of the highest priority that we return to Phantomsdeep immediately. SOUND THE WITHDRAWAL HORNS AT ONCE!"

As if a leash had suddenly tightened around everyone's neck, they all fell into an ominously quiet that left all speechless. Baddlock decree was so absolute that it made everyone jump with a rigid start. They were all instantly more than ready to follow Baddlock unquestioningly, unthinkingly, and unknowingly into the very fires of hell. Soon every general within earshot was echoing Baddlock's command except Dandork. All Dandork wanted to do was shout back, at the top of his lungs, *what the...have you gone totally mad...NO!* But instead, he held his tongue, biting off the words before they could leave his mouth, and thought better to choose his words more carefully, "Surely great one, you are making a joke."

Baddlock took his time to answer, "Does it look like I am laughing?" His lips snarled, and his eyes were fierce as his face blotched with rage.

Dandork still wanted to ask if he had gone stark raving mad, but the anger that still smoldered on Baddlock's face made him think that was a terrible idea. Instead, he thought best to try to figure out what could have possibly gone wrong in Baddlock's twisted mind. He heeled his mount into motion and came closer to Baddlock, with his eyes riveted quizzically upon a face that could have frozen one's blood. Eager to be rid of his nemesis, the king, Dandork, persisted, "The conquest of Edawn stands before you like succulent fruit at the peak of its sweetness. It just waits for you only to reach out and pluck it. Why stop now? Now that outright victory is yours, and King Ozzdon is at your mercy and the empire on its knees?"

Concerned with only fulfilling Abaddawn's bidding, Baddlock left the questions unanswered. Dandork looked around to see that every Norticlan general within earshot was in agreement and asked wryly, "Is that wise, my lord? Ozzdon and his entire court are in our iron fist. We must quickly crush them now, my lord."

There were many questioning Norticlan Warriors in the background, impatient for their share of any treasury booty that was to be had. Darkon thrust out a belligerent lower lip as he flexed and clawed his greedy fingers and joined in. "I say strike while the iron is hot. Deploy our troops where we can inflict the most damage and execute the death blow to end this now."

But the instant Dandork and Darkon had finished speaking, they both knew they had spoken out of line. Both turned to stone as Baddlock hissed at them like a venomous demon snake. The Wicked Warlock Wizard's prune face engorged with blood as he spun Nightmare back around with the fury of a slashing sword. His body stiffened with rage as his pale skin, sunken cheeks, and hooked nose ignited with anger. "Wh-what did you say?" His eyes were daggers, and his tongue was a two edged sword. "How dare you challenge my authority. The only thing that matters in this entire universe is fulfilling our rightful master's wishes. Nothing else matters. Nothing! Do I make myself clear? Baddlock nudged his steed toward Dandork and slapped him across the face as hard as he could with the back of his hand. Then he screamed, "Never is sooner than anyone will ever find any trace of you if you ever impede or question my authority to command this army, again. Damn Darkon and damn you too. I alone know what I am doing. Do you?" He stared Dandork down, forcing him to look away. "You have been warned."

Dandork and the others fell silent instantly. With a trembling hand, the Wicked Warlock Wizard reached up to press at his temple as he declared, "Our lord, the master of all, demands our immediate return. Sound the withdrawal at once!" Baddlock commanded with outraged annoyance and anger. "Do you have a problem with that?" Baddlock asked with a savage look that branded Dandork like a hot iron. The others wiped the look of resentment off their faces instantly.

"Yes, your Excellency! I mean No, your majesty! That is, I understand, your Worshipness. Your will is my command," Dandork blurted out as he wiped a trickle of blood from his lower lip. "At once, your lordship." Dandork submitted like a scolded dog. Without delay, Dandork signaled the horn bearers, and straight away, the horns of withdrawal sounded with a piercing blast throughout the kingdom.

By this time, the ill fated pack in the hollow was ankle deep in volatile lamp oil. The noxious fumes were overwhelming. In the wake of panic, one of the king's youngest warriors lost his nerve, threw himself before the King, and began to babble. "Maybe we can surrender, maybe we can bargain with Baddlock."

"Would you make a deal with the devil? Baddlock is never going to let us leave here alive," the king said with a harsh laugh as he pushed the crazed warrior away.

Ammiz stepped forward. "Given the ominous circumstances, we can sit here and hope for who knows what, or we can take our chances out there."

Sick with terror and dripping with sweat, they all continued looking at each other for an answer in silent, heart rending desperation.

Gathering all the courage he had left, Kondor bound to his feet, rising from his crouched position and said: "To hell with this, I am not going to die like a rat in this stinking hole."

There was a rumble of agreements as everyone in the hollow raised their swords over their heads and roared in defiance. All but the king who seemed bound in a troubled dream.

"What is your command my King?" asked Kondor

Whatever ends this humiliation quickest, the king thought to himself and reached for his sword. "I do not know about the rest of you, but I would rather die by the blade than to be cooked like a hare in a broiling pit." The only fear he now knew was not the fear that he would die. His greatest fear now was that he might live.

At that very same fragment in time, beneath the deepest recesses of the catacombs, the queen braced herself against Zandor the moment she felt Zandor's arm tense for the fatal stroke. *Be quick, be quick!* Zahra kept repeating in her mind as she felt overpowering panic welling up inside of her.

Then unexpectedly, she relaxed, feeling almost suddenly calm. It was an odd kind of peace, an enthralling sense of lull and quietness deep in her soul. She was a true queen, firm to the end. She drew herself to her fullest height resetting her chin in a proud line and stiffened her body to remain sturdy.

In the distance, the sound of approaching footfalls of marching boots clattered an echo of panic throughout the lower catacombs. The queen grit her teeth swallowed hard, and gave the faintest nod, signaling to Zandor that it was now or never. Somehow sensing what was happening and hearing the approach of the dreaded Norticlan search party, the women and the children began to gasp, and bitter weeping ensued. Instinctively, Zandor's sense of duty took charge. The command from his mind to his arm was instantly initiated. As the impulse to whip his dagger in a fiery arc coursed from one neuron to the other between Zandor's brain and arm.

In that precise instance, the unexpected happened. The sound of the goat's horn blast of retreat entered Zandor's hearing! Unfortunately, the goat's horn blast recalling the Norticlan force registered in Zandor's mind a fraction of a second too late to stop his blade's movement. Yet somehow, Zandor's slashing thrust was blocked at the speed of light, faster than the speed of thought by an unseen hand. If Zandor lived to be a hundred, he would never come to understand who, what, or how an invisible power interrupted his blade in its path.

He had to strain to hear it, but he knew now for sure he again had heard the Norticlan horns sounding a retreat. It was like an incomprehensible dream that could not be trusted, like the intangible controlling the tangible. Zandor was turned to stone where he stood. In the next heartbeat, he thought he heard the storm of approaching boots begin to recede as the horns continued to blast. Louder and clearer, the universal echoing signal for retreat reverberated throughout the depths of the catacombs. Was it just a ploy?

In the middle of the raging upheaval, the attacking Norticlanders everywhere stopped dead in their tracks to listen in disbelief as the horns of withdrawal sounded time and time again. For the most prolonged moment, astonished, they all exchanged surprised glances. The sudden oddity held the entire Norticlan horde in suspended animation. In the next instant, the Norticlan generals at the forefront of the hollow and those searching for the Royal Queen simultaneously and reluctantly ordered their troops to fallback.

In the underbelly of the kingdom, Zandor remained frozen against his own will. He was suspended within a matrix beyond the scope of his imagination. His arm suddenly, without any known reason, refused to respond despite his concentrated effort. He remained bewildered as he stared at his hand and how his impulse had been suddenly and miraculously intercepted. In the instance the horns had sounded, the unmistakable signal for a withdrawal his hand had been stopped. It could have been nothing other than divine intervention. Zandor's entire body remained motionless as the repeated blasts of withdrawal rebounded throughout the catacombs. As the roar of the swarming slayers died down to a crawl, the attack collapsed until the entire catacombs seemed deadly quiet. The silence was so total that the loudest sound heard was the queen and Zandor's thundering heartbeats from within. Several moments of silence passed until the queen finally whispered, "What is happening?"

When Zandor's last tremor faded, Zandor drew a shaky breath as he shuddered from head to toe. The blade slipped out of his hand with an awkward jerk as if it had bitten him. And then Zandor had a startling realization, and suddenly his whole being filled with an intense sensation of reprieve. One more split hair's breadth later, with one single muscular twist of his hand, the queen would have dropped slain at his feet. Zandor said nothing as he clutched at the sword at his side. Then suddenly he turned without a word and hurried out of the lower catacombs to investigate the meaning of the horns and the withdrawing troops. As he raced toward the corridor that led to where he had last seen the king and his twin brother Kondor, Zandor was amazed that he had not encountered one single Norticlander. As yet, it was still too soon for him to feel relief.

Meanwhile, the torch bearing Norticlan General guarded the hollow opening where the king and his men were trapped. He clearly heard the horns of retreat and ordered the full withdrawal of the men encircling the hollow. Again came the blast, and the commander turned and wondered at its underlying meaning. Once the monstrous throngs had all retreated, the torchbearer paused, looked down at the torch in his hand, and remembered the last words Dandork had spoken. He then turned and flung the torch at the hollow's opening. The flame twirled end over end as it flew through the air, reaching its intended target. And as it landed, it spewed its flaming sparks immediately igniting the volatile trail of lamp oil.

At the same time, the king was wondering why his miserable nightmare refused to come to an end! One disgrace was enough for one day. Still disheartened, but less so, preferring to just leap to the finish, the king grabbed his sword and howled, "To damnation with this, let us get it over with." And with that, he was the first to crawl crablike up the tunnel. He raced out of the hollow, ready, and willing to meet death face to face as flames licked at him on the way out. Though weak in numbers, they had left to them the strength of their courage. Ghostlike men who only had seconds to live, scrambled from a would be fiery grave, immediately following their king to face doom. Just when Ammiz, the last man to crawl out, reached the cranny's opening, the flame that had raced past him along the tunnel's floor reached the oil filled hollow. The igniting vapors within the hollow exploded with such a horrendous underground blast, its force shot out of the opening and propelled Ammiz through midair. The instantaneous combustion created a cataclysmic shock wave that expanded like a sudden rush of wind. The burst swept through the dark catacomb chamber, like a fiery subterranean whirlwind. Then followed by a blinding fireball flash that bellowed with a detonation that knocked the king and his men all off their feet and sent them somersaulting through the air. They were flung forward so forcefully that it knocked the breath out of all of them. The explosion caused the underground world beneath the kingdom to shake and quake.

Having heard and felt the horrendous blast with a stricken feeling, Zandor approached the chamber as the dust was beginning to clear. The sound of distant footsteps rushing away, echoed at a distance as the Norticlan army retreated across the outside keep's flagstone floor. The hearts of those that had managed to survive the blast resumed beating as they emerged from the smoke and dust filled ruins. They had not realized it yet, but for now, the worst was over. They had survived the darkest hour in the history of Edawn. For one mind boggling moment, Kondor found himself paralyzed with shock. And in the same instant, he wanted to laugh with a maddening sense of gladness for having survived. The others began to stir and looked around, bewildered. No one spoke. They just stared out of their heads at each other like stunned dreamers coming out from the middle of a nightmare. Totally at a loss. As if unable to recall what just had happened.

Aboveground, it had been just another one of Zia's many recent tremors as Baddlock impatiently waited for his armies to fall into formation. Once assembled, Baddlock pulled himself up straight and waved his hand haughtily with an exaggerated motion. Sparks seemed to fly from his fingertips. He addressed his troops, "Mark my words. The situation is well under control. All is as it should be. The conjunction is approaching its zenith, and the only thing that matters is the ultimate power that awaits us all. Every obstacle will be removed so that Abaddawn, the rightful ruler of this universe, may come forth at his will. And we shall return to complete our task with such a vengeance that the ground beneath Edawn will tremble from the onslaught of our armies, reinforcements, or not. At this time, the armies of the new order will march over Zia and spread across the heavens. And we shall all be as gods, masters of a new universe." The Wicked Warlock Wizard then heeled Nightmare in Dandork's direction and commanded, "Assemble one hundred of our fastest riders at once. Instruct Mossca and the rest of our forces to redeploy around the kingdom to ensure that none escape."

Just then, a chain of thoughts clicked in a comical place in Baddlock's mind. He threw his head back and ripped into a burst of crazed laughter from the depths of his gut. It was a dark, humorless, animalistic sound. It was Not a laugh at all, but more of a crazed exclamation, a laugh that grated like the irritating yak of a hyena. "Soon, I will return to crush the Edawnian Kingdom with still greater cruelty. Let them sweat it out. The more they bear, the better. It will make their final demise all the sweeter."

"Yes, my lord. Most assuredly. At once, my lord," was Dandork's only reply as he pounded his fist into his body armor.

When Dandork felt the dull rumble of the blast, the former Master at Arms was relieved that Ozzdon was as good as dead. Dandork rode into the midst of the Norticlan Forces and ordered the ram bearer to sound the horn that signaled the Norticlan cavalry forward. He pointed to different warriors and then beckoned them to him by rotating his right hand high in the air and then bringing his fist to his chest. The Norticlan commander's response was immediate. One hundred of the wildest among them, the most ruthless, battle hardened men that ever lived converged on Baddlock, Dandork, and Darkon.

"We ride to Phantomsdeep posthaste," the Wicked Warlock Wizard commanded.

Horses snorted and reared, stomped and whiffed, prepared for what they were bred for—the long, fast, grueling race against time. Mossca was left behind with his orders. A dust cloud was kicked into the air as nearly crazed warhorses neighed, whinnied, and squealed as they sensed the anticipation of the long, hard ride ahead. The Wicked Warlock Wizard pulled his golden dagger from his side and cut away the heavy armor from his giant warhorse. And everyone else did the same. The shrilling screams of his war stallion pierced the air as Baddlock dug his spurred heels, with a tinkling sound, deep into his mount's flanks. Nightmare wheeled about with a furious burst of restrained power, and as he swooped around, he sent Norticlan warriors caught off guard tumbling out of the way. Other Norticlanders barely opened ranks before Baddlock bounded forward and came barreling through, trailed by Dandork, Darkon, and his one hundred elite henchmen. Nightmare had no trouble picking up speed, as his muscled legs bulged, and he set off at a ground gobbling lope. As Dandork's plans for a decisive victory over Edawn unraveled, yet he was left with the solace that the king was more than likely dead. Shaken up troops closed up ranks again, giving each other curious looks as they watched Baddlock's detachment race away amid a storm of dust and thundering hoofbeats.

Baddlock took the lead with Dandork and Darkon at his flanks. The riders in black bobbed up and down to the rhythm of their racing horses. They sent their mounts plunging through the foothills toward the southern entrance of the Wazoo Valley as fast as they could carry them. Soon Baddlock was lost from view in a long dust trail etching the length of their trek across the Northern Plains. With reckless abandonment, the contingent rushed toward

Phantomsdeep at breakneck speed. Horses, specially trained for endurance, sped around turns and passages at full stride. Hooves pounded the rocky terrain as horses neighed and squealed, and their hearts were pushed to the brink of being run into the ground.

Through the clearing dust, Zandor came rushing upon the stunned, soot covered men, just as the last echoing footsteps of the departing troops died away. This time such silence was good news. In the deathlike quiet, Zandor's eyes quickly scanned the beleaguered faces. The measure of shock written on the faces of those that had survived the explosion was so profound. No one cheered or laughed, or even smiled. Zandor frantically looked from face to face, for his twin brother Kondor, while time seemed to pass with agonizing lateness. Out of all the faces on Zia, there was not anyone that he wanted to see more than his brother's. In a quivering voice, Zandor called out, "KONDOR!" He began to break a sweat as panic reached deep into his bowels like a fist and squeezed.

Kondor hastily got to his feet, his ears still ringing, his vision still hazy from the blast. He took a few unsteady steps forward as he brushed dust and stone fragments out of his hair. From within the scattered rubble, emerging from the mist of tiny particles in the air, Zandor saw the unmistakable figure of this brother, standing there. He was alive! Just the sight of him sent a chilliness of relief tingling up and down his spine. Neither twin could have hidden their childlike joy from the other even if they had wanted to. They ran to each other, both excitedly reaching for the other. Their embrace was powerful. Despite his attempt, Zandor could barely choke back his tears of joy. And Kondor, who was not very good at crying, was struggling to maintain his composure, but could not repress himself. Teary eyed, as he held Kondor's face in his hands at arm's length, Zandor asked, "Are you well? I was worried to death about you."

Kondor, forced back his emotions and asked, "Do you think you will ever stop worrying so over me?"

"No, I am afraid that brotherhood is a lifetime sentence," Zandor replied as he pulled his brother back to him, nearly squeezing the breath out of him over his roaring happily.

The king, who had remained silent for the moment, approached the two and asked, with a slight tinge of doubt creeping into his voice, "What…word of…the queen?" His lips were trembling as if he were readying a scream of anguish.

Zandor turned to his king and smiled as he placed a hand around his neck and pulled him forehead to forehead. "My king, as I live and breathe, the queen is well." In his telling, Zandor bit the corner of his lip as he felt a shuddersome unnerving coursing up and down his spine. To know just how close he had come to slaying his queen and having to have to tell his king he had done so, chilled him to the bone.

King Ozzdon squeezed his eyes together as a wake of relief that energized his heart came surging over him. He placed his hand on Zandor's great shoulder. Thanking him seemed so inadequate, but he did so anyway, saying, "I am eternally grateful to you. My good and faithful servant, I salute you mightily Zandor, the faithful Lion of Edawn." For he knew if there had been no other way, Zandor would have completed his ill fated mission.

Zandor bowed low. "I will forever stand ready to serve you faithfully, my king."

"How, can I ever repay the both of you?" King Ozzdon grabbed both by the neck and gave them a manly, brotherly embrace as the others joined in.

"Your wellbeing and that of my queen is my reward," Zandor answered. And he meant it.

Both twins beat their chests simultaneously in an Edawnian salute and bowed their heads respectfully. The king then turned to the rest of his surviving warriors and roared, "Well done, my Edawnian brothers!" The king suddenly turned and looked around suspiciously at the sudden strange withdrawal and said, "It is too soon to start dancing yet." Now with a reason to live, the king dispatched Zandor and Kondor to investigate the bewildering turn of events. "Be sure that it is not a trap."

King Ozzdon looked about him to see that his leadership of men had survived almost intact. The king then sought Ammiz out. It had been only Ammiz's faith that had saved them, but the seer was nowhere to be found. He had quietly slipped away to check on the wounded, with the hope of discovering life among the latest victims. Sometimes one does not fully realize what real courage means until it is almost too late. At times when one's whole world seems at the break of doom, a spark of faith can make the difference. Just then, women and children came up out of the recesses of the catacombs. They peered out from the passageways, trickling out of their hiding places into the upper catacombs. There they gathered among their men in jubilant clusters. Some emerged to rejoice others to mourn grievously. Among the women was the queen, still holding the same orphaned child in her arms. The king turned and immediately spotted his queen and very excitedly rushed to her as she put the child down.

King Ozzdon enfolded Queen Zahra in his arms in a deep, joyful, and holy embrace as tears of happiness filled both their eyes. The trauma of separation of not knowing the fate of the one they loved most had been replaced by joyous celebration. Only someone who had been brought face to face and looked into the eyes of death could fully know the soaring solace that they found in the warmth of each other's arms. The king entangled his fingers into the back of Zahra's hair and kissed her long and unfathomably deep. As his mouth took possession of hers, he tasted the sparks on the tip of her tongue. They both stood there, frozen in time. Neither of them ever wanted to have another scare like that as long as they both lived. Each heartbeat marked an eternal atoning for every hurtful sting of heartache and erased every tear that had fallen. If only they could feel this way forever...then the queen whispered, "The only other thing I could ever wish with all my heart is that Zuree is somewhere safe and sound."

Queen Zahra's love was the only fortress that protected the king's heart from the hopelessness that threatened to engulf him at that very moment. As they pulled themselves closer into the center of each other's being, they felt the strength of their hearts and soul bracing up against each other. Their love was stronger than it had ever been. The queen pressed her head against the solid, reassuring expanse of his chest, and the king rested his lips upon the crown of her head. There they found a sacred, unshakable refuge in each other's arms. And their souls were held up against the uncertain storm raging in their hearts for the only child they had ever borne.

Thirteen
The Armada

Zandor and Kondor hastily climbed the stairwell that led up to the Keep. The staircase was partially blocked with dead Edawnian and Norticlan bodies. Each Edawnian warrior's throat had been slit to assure that they were dead. In the keep, there were bodies everywhere the two stepped. As they shoved what was left of the battered keep's door open, they were surrounded by apprehension as deep as the pit of hell. They climbed awkwardly through the broken stone and bodies that were everywhere. Outside they found a stricken world, a kingdom ablaze, shrouded in smoke that billowed out through the numerous craters created by the brutal exploding pods. The uncanny stillness that greeted them was disturbing, as the gloomy outside world came rushing in on them. The deafening silence was too complete. Their boots tread on bone fragments with tattered ribbons of bloody flesh still attached. Their skin crawled as the dawning light crept over a landscape that had within a few hours become unrecognizable. They were met by remains of battered armor, a ruined boot with the foot still in it, and bizarre patterns of dried blood that lined the walls. A fog like smoldering drifted skyward and blotted out parts of the kingdom. A yellowish haze covered everything as if it was one immense death shroud diffused by the strange light of the gathering conjunction.

Zandor stood guard as Kondor climbed to the top of the only tower still standing. He was the enemy withdrawing into the foothills on the northern ridge. Farther to the North along the Wazoo Valley, he saw Baddlock's receding dust trail moving at an incredible pace toward the Northern Frontier. Kondor did not know what to think, but he somehow knew that for now, the worst was over. He turned slowly to survey the situation. Everywhere he looked, Kondor saw destruction, and there was no escaping the sheer vastness of its devastation. Then suddenly, in the far off distance, a movement to the left of his peripheral vision caught his eye. He turned quickly to see the most beautiful sight he could have ever hoped to have seen in his life. The long awaited reinforcements had finally arrived by sea in a way not foreseen by anyone. Kondor saw what looked to be the entire Xylenian fleet breaking over the horizon of the southern sea. It was an impressive sight. His heart leaped and overflowed with renewed hope that took his breath away, so much so that for a moment, he was struck speechless. From below, Zandor could see the excitement in Kondor's movements up above. "What is it? What do you see, brother?"

Kondor immediately recognized the Ziaian standards as they appeared like apparitions out of the fog. He could only point out to sea and stare round mouthed. Zandor had to race up the tower to see for himself. When he reached the top, his heart seemed to jump from his chest, and he stared spellbound, with excitement thundering in his heart. The twins riveted their field of vision on the breathtaking sight of the gigantic Xylenian Armada sailing toward the Port of Tranquility. The flotilla was approaching fast, very fast, converging on Edawn, coming from where the North, the West, and the southern seas merged.

The ship commanders had spotted the smoke of war and were sailing in at full speed ahead. The Xylenian flag fluttered majestically at the top of every masthead of every ship in the fleet. The finest vessels built to ride the high seas and bring new trade from throughout Zia had been transformed now into mighty battleships. They were monstrous, for their day, in every meaning of the word. Each ship measured one hundred and ninety-five paces long and thirty paces wide and weighing over seven tons. Each one crowded over five hundred men on the high seas. Every massive ship was escorted by several long, agile, and swifter assault ships that clung close to their transport vessels like a hard shelled crustacean. In the middle were the cargo carriers that were heavy laden with supplies, weapons, and horses. The transport ships were heavily fitted with thick steel armored plates, reinforced with thick oak wood and steel belts that crisscrossed along the waterline. The front of each craft was rigged out with a pointed, reinforced steel bowsprit, specially formed to ram through the side of any ship and added to the propulsion of the gigantic vessels. Each attack ship was heavily armed with massive long range catapults that stuck out of each vessel's outline like giant fortresses. Reinforced catapults that were designed for maximum range were mounted on pivoting torrents on either side of the floating slayers. From the ships, the Kingdom of Edawn came into view against the dim light. The glow of a new dawn was just on the verge of eclipsing the brightness of the gathering conjunction that was quickly sinking from sight just beyond the horizon.

By now, Zandor and Kondor were able to make out the banners and identify the armor and helmets they wore. But the twins were not the only ones that had spotted the approaching flotilla. From the nearby hilltop surrounding Edawn, the Norticlan catapult crews were already positioning their murderous catapults toward the southern seas. The catapults were pulled back, angled for maximum range, and loaded with the incendiary pot and explosive pods that had been left over. The Norticlan catapult overlords quickly lined up their sights, allowing for distance, ship movement, and windage. All at once, there was a sudden rumble and the thunder of launching catapults. The hilltop reverberated as the Norticlan lobbed their bloodletting payload of pots and pods sent hurtling southward in search of their targets. The discharged canisters rose on silvery trails across the vibrantly lit skies. Fed by the rushing air, the incendiary pots burst into red balls of fire. And the pods hissed as they pushed on, increasing in pitch until they were whistling round projectiles, screaming their terrible, awesome warning in all their vile majesty.

The shipmasters at the head of the flotilla, the biggest target in sight, had just enough time to see streaks of disaster headed straight for them. Onboard, alarm trumpets were at once blasting, and warning bells clanging as the first projectiles were seen approaching one after another. Moments later, the lead ship was pounded with three consecutive exploding pods, with a booming detonation and blinding, searing light. The impact made the whole ship shudder, sending a pillar of flames leaping from its blast center, spraying red hot splinters in every direction. Almost instantaneously, two more massive fireball strikes that engulfed most of the ship in an inferno from one end to the other. The pressure of the blast wave sent debris flying and sheets of fire raining down. The ship shook, shrapnel flew, and flames shot into the air. There were screams and showers of blood scattered in all directions. Then there was only smoke and obscurity and the cries of the injured. Widening puddles of blood formed under mutilated bodies and pieces of flesh smeared the deck. A sailor ran from the flames blindly, his eyes splintered with wooden slivers. The wounded were strewn everywhere, moaning, and screaming in pain. A warrior flopped about on the deck, blown in two, clutching at his open chest, uttering, "I am dead, I am dead," just before he closed his eyes forever.

The living rushed to their battle stations, stumbling across the dead as massive explosions continued to tear into the ship's lower decks. Another ear splitting crash of thunder sent streamers of white hot burning flames spewing everywhere like fountains of light. Men below were blown to bits or were burned alive in the firestorm that swept throughout the lead ship. Suddenly there was a loud whistling sound, like that of a gale of wind as water rushing in from the ruptured hull forced air through the ship's hatches and portholes. Within moments, the wounded battleship listed as it slanted away from the Edawnian horizon and began to sink. Dead bodies, along with the living rolled and fell overboard. Zandor and Kondor watched in horror as the once mighty ship sank on its way to settle onto the harbor's murky bottom.

At first, the fleet was stunned by what met them, but by now, all the other battleships' catapult crews were whirling their turret turning gears and positioning their catapults. Heavy metal munitions were already piled near every catapult. There were no deliberations and no questions; everyone knew what was expected of them. The here and now was the very reason they had come halfway across Zia. The arrival of reinforcements was that moment and the only reason they clung to hope. The exploding pods and incendiary pots that were landing all around them may as well have been raindrops falling into the sea for all the other Xylenian catapult crews seemed to care. The Norticlan catapult crews continued to strike repeatedly, daringly, desperately, but in vain. Fortunately for the Xylenian fleet, the winds were exceptionally favorable, for, without them, the incoming armada would have been as vulnerable as a pod of beached whales. As sails bellowed to the full with the prevailing landward winds, signal flags were hoisted, ordering the flotilla to head for the Edawnian southern shores at full speed ahead. The armada of redemption rode the southerly wind as fast as they could go, relentlessly slicing through the high sea as exploding geysers of water splashed all around the advancing ships. Now and then, a Norticlan pod found its targets, sending hardened oak ripping through the air and across the decks and fragments of hot metal slicing through everything in their path. As their intended target came within range, the signal flags came up the Xylenian battleship's masts, signaling the fleet to turn sharply into firing position. Once parallel to the coast, they lowered their sails and dropped their anchors. When the Xylenian ships came to a stop, they were facing the shoreline broadside and had a clear field of fire of the foothills beyond the kingdom. From the command ship, King Tydron, the Commander in Chief of the fleet, command with a shout, "Make ready!"

The catapult masters made their hasty calculated decisions on their targets beyond the kingdom and the distant hill encampment. The aimers turned the massive weapons with a spin of their wheels.

"Line your targets!" came the command from King Tydron.

Outlying ships mirrored the Command Ship's actions. Each ship, in turn, fired their sporadic test shots. The crow's nest observers reported the accuracy. Based on the trial shots, engineers with the best mathematical skills in Zia hurriedly recalculated target distance, catapult angle, catapult range, and tension.

Coordinates were quickly tabulated and dispatched. Every catapult was lined up on their latitude and longitude marks in correspondence with the new coordinates.

"*Loosen the catapults*!" shouted King Tydron.

Trigger lanyards were pulled. Outlying ships followed suit, and then suddenly, every armed battleship heaved everything they had as the fleet returned the Norticlan favor. The massive warships groaned and moaned as they simultaneously rocked back and then swayed forth. And while they were yet rocking and rolling, Tydron shouted, "Reload! FIRE AT WILL!" as if catapult crews had to be told.

Seeing the sinking of the lead ship from the hilltop made Mossca think he was about to pull off a devastating victory. But the utterly tumultuous instant later, diminished any such illusion. Catapult arms were drawn and set. Repeatedly, trigger mechanisms were locked, and iron balls loaded onto the catapult slings. Again and again, the long range catapults were fired, roaring and ripping the enemies' position. Iron globules filled the sky with a turbulent metal hail storm of pounding projectiles. Members of each Xylenian catapult crew worked in unison, each performing their specific job like practiced experts. The mark finders refined their catapult horizontal and vertical settings after every launch as they walked in their slaughterhouse barrage from every outboard direction. Wherever the deadly orbs struck, the enemy collapsed with their dying cries barking in their own ears. Wave after wave of iron orbs created a curtained salvo over the Norticlan encampment and surrounding hills. Ultimately Mossca was left, stunned in loss without Baddlock, Darkon, and Dandork leadership. The Norticlan warrior was known as one of the greatest, most brutal warriors accustomed to hurling themselves deep into the thick of any battle. But without someone competent to lead them, they were now unable to cope full scale deluge of crushing metal projectiles. The devastating return fire dwarfed their efforts to mount a counterstrike.

The fleet once again raised their sails, and as they billowed like giant puffy clouds in the sky, the Xylenian flotilla picked up speed and came about. Warriors of the Xylenian armies sharpened their swords, axes, and spears for the last time as they neared land. They were the ultimate assemblage of forces from every southern land, and chain of islands stretching a thousand zettas from northern kingdoms to their southernmost ends. They were volunteers from all walks of life asked to leave their safe, peaceful territories to go to a miserable probability in aid of their brethren. And Zia's finest young men had flocked to the recruitment centers, and there was no way the colossal ships could hold more. The massive transport ships did not slow as they ran aground. The disembarking trumpets sounded, and heavily armed troops from every part of Southern Zia debarked, scrambling over the sides of their ships onto longboats. Wind tossed spray drenched the reinforcement legions as they made their bumpy journey to the shores. Warhorses, mules, and yakoxen were disgorged, forced overboard to make their own way onto dry land. Thousands upon thousands of men of the naval flotilla came ashore, spreading across the beaches, swelling to over ten times ten thousand. By the time the battleships had weighed anchor and unfurled their sails, the Catapult Masters had turned the entire hilltop into a Norticlan death camp. The disorderly mass of chaos that was left of the barbarian's camp looked as if it had been pounded with a giant meat mallet. Mossca was hard pressed to maintain his ranks as the ground beneath their feet continued to shake and quake. Lower ranking generals began quarreling among themselves, and legion leaders started screaming curses at each other. And some of the foot soldiers had begun to scatter to the winds.

Eventually, the remaining Xylenian sea power crossed the threshold into the Bay of Tranquility and entered the port of Edawn. The turbulent incoming throngs of fresh, high spirited soldiers, their swords at the ready, stretched a defense line from coast to coast. And there would be nothing this side of heaven that could stop their influx. King Tydron quickly organized a land attack before the Norticlanders could regroup and strengthen their foothold. The overflowing Xylenian Cavalry gathered their big, rangy mounts. And drumming hooves thundered over the land as riders swung up onto their bare backs of their riding beasts amid a maddening swirl of dust and commotion. In the encampment, pandemonium continued to reign as several metal balls scored direct hits on the remaining incendiary stockpile. Flames quickly spread to the explosive pods and set off a chain reaction of massive explosions. Disorganized Norticlan combatants meant to surround the kingdom, reacted with apparent shock and confusion. Like goats without a shepherd, those who had not already begun to abandon their posts fell back in disarray. Most feeing Norticlanders gathered a few light weapons and provisions, taking nothing that might hinder or slow their retreat. As they high tailed it for the thick woodlands, they took flight as if they were being haunted by a pack of avenging angels fast on their trail, at last, come to claim their wretched souls. The ripped and rent wounded were abandoned where they fell or discarded by the wayside like pieces of rubbish when they could not go any farther.

The heaviest supply ships bearing the bulkiest equipment and massive armaments sailed into Edawn's deepwater ports and began to dock. Banners of different kingdoms from all around Zia rippled against the sky. The Xylenian flag with its golden eagle emblem and its red border fluttered majestically at the uppermost top of every mast. There were so many vessels that the docks of Edawn could not hold them all. Overflowing ships of the invasion fleet headed for the outer shores of the kingdom and dotted the southern coast of Edawn from end to end as far as the eye could see. Their numbers made them an unquestionable superpower. The Xylenian elite horse warriors quickly organized and drove up the hill. They rushed to encompassing the Norticlan position and gave pursuit with a vengeance. Young warriors eager to prove themselves in battle led the overwhelming strike force up the hillside. The swarms of the most hardened Norticlanders had already turned tail and run for their lives convincing the rest that they had no other choice. Mossca himself chose to serve his own best interests. He abandoned his post, ignoring the Wicked Warlock Wizard's orders, and fled for his miserable life. As the arriving cavalry came too close for comfort, Norticlan troops vanished without fighting back. When the horse soldiers gave chase, the barbarians scattered and bolted through thorn thickets, where not even a hedgehog could have gone.

As the pursuing Ziaian forces neared the foothills, they entered the valley of the shadow of death. Immediately the smell of slaughter and annihilation made its presence known. The foothills were foul with the festering bodies of King Ozzdon's failed retaliation. Under the hot sun, a faint breeze carried the smell of decomposing flesh. A mixture of sulfur and rot hung in the air like a mist of decay. A waft of wind carried flies everywhere, and the maggots had to be abundant too. Worms crawled in and out of decomposing flesh, and maggots thrived in festering lumps as flocks of vultures filled the sky. The advancing reinforcements halted for a moment in their tracks, waiting for the revulsion to pass. The blood was beginning to putrefy, and the stench lingered around like a veil. Everywhere one looked, the killing fields were filled with the bodies of the thousands of unidentified dead, rotting away in the open air, waiting to be buried. Broken weapons, equipment, and dead horses lay by the side of the lifeless.

The ground under hoof all around was caked with black blood. The mounted regiment commander tore himself away from the slaughterhouse and ordered the advancing pursuit to continue with an added vengeance. As the Xylenian forces made their way up the hill, they used their swords with such lethal vigor that the enemy fled in undisciplined disorder. Upon reaching the inner encampment on the upper slope, the Xylenian forces found it completely deserted. Young Xylenian riders triumphantly punched the air with their fist and roared victoriously. They saw most of the weapons, supply wagons, catapults, and armored turrets had been left behind, along with their stench of death, rubbish, and human excrement.

Then they came upon the ghastly scene of the tortured men. Their carcasses still hanging there left to tell their grisly tale. They could not believe men had been skinned alive, disemboweled, impaled, and tortured in the most hideous ways. The wails, still written on their faces, greeted them. Their flesh had by now turned green, and what could be torn away by the scavengers was torn away. The ever present of flies was massive, and maggot knots thrived in festering clusters. Repulsed men were sickened at the sight of man's inhumanity to man. Being tortured to death was no way for a warrior to die. The commander of the unit steered his mount slowly among the victims, and spoke soberly, "In all my life I have never seen anything so barbaric!" It was below even that of animalistic. Cut them down!" the horror struck commander commanded.

All wholly condemned the savagery. Every heart was enraged for what they had seen, and all demanded revenge for such atrocities. From the hilltop, sickened men surveyed the dismal graveyard scene of Edawn's failed retaliation before them. Shock riddled through the hardiest of warriors like a cold draft, leaving them chilled to the bone. The perusing horsemen, having heard the horns of reassembly sounding, gave up the chase of the retreating Norticlanders and returned to the main unit. Down below, there was bitter silence as the liberating armies stood astounded before the ruined remains of Edawn and her dead. The devastation of the Capital Kingdom that met their eyes required a moment to grasp. And there rose within each man's soul a soundless outcry of grieve. Their lamentation rose over the land, and reached up to the farthest skies of the heavens.

Up in the lookout tower, Zandor finally turned to Kondor and said with his heart beating with renewed hope, "Go and inform the king that we are saved. Tell him that I will gather the kings of Xylenia to him."

Kondor flew down the tower's spiral stairs as if on winged feet.

King Tydron, the Commander in Chief of the fleet before stood the gates of Edawn. What he saw was even worse than anything he had ever anticipated. It had been a devastating assault. Edawn's infrastructure was left charred and blackened with bits and pieces scattered everywhere. His skin crawled as the light moved over fragments of flesh, dried blood, and ruined structures. Thick tendrils of smoke rose in the prevailing winds like giant black fists ascending to the heavens. The vastness of the cataclysm shook the heart and boggled every onlooker's mind. King Tydron gasped, "This is inconceivable," His words did not do his feelings justice.

The oldest known kingdom on Zia, the foundation of civilization, the greatest empire on the face of Zia, lay in ruin, beyond recognition, and from all appearances depopulated. It's once mighty towering walls, fallen like dominos on a board game that had been played out to the death. The utterly ravaged kingdom within was scorched and consumed. It was as if a terrible fire breathing sea monster had suddenly risen from the deep and swept all of Edawn's opulence into extinction. To say it was a global catastrophe would only have cheapened the meaning of these words. There were charred corpses locked in a final struggle to live everywhere. There were bodies in the street, contorted in their final torment with the look of madness in their eyes. Amid the crushed bodies were those who seemed dead but were still alive, just barely alive, lost in the last fleeting moments of life. Then some had managed to hide from the Norticlan and were very much alive, yet they sat whimpering and crying like shattered shells of themselves. They bore the kind of wounds that did not shed blood.

To the North, the fields were stained of death as far and wide as the eye could see. No kingdom desecrated by such hostilely could have been despoiled to a more deplorable state. It was beyond belief that anyone could have survived at all.

Once out of reach of the demonic yonder world, Izz and Zuree stopped to catch their breath. As they realigned their energies, they held each other for dear life. Having come back from the gates of death too terrible to remember, Izz leaned against the stone passage wall and waited for more strength. Just to be in each other's embrace, where they both longed to be, made it all bearable. Without words, they regenerated their exhausted hearts. As they clung to each other, Izz's body heat kept her nice and warm. At long last Izz held Zuree at arms and finally whispered, "Let me see your beautiful face." She was a miracle in the flesh. The look on Izz's face said it all, but he said it anyway, "You are everything that I live for." Izz erased the lone tear of concern that had rolled out of Zuree's eye, wiping it with his thumb as it etched its way down her cheek. "We have little time. We must put as much distance between us and this unhallowed place."

Even after suffering such unspeakable torment and anguish, though Izz still felt crushed, his ever gallant spirit rose at this defining moment. The muscles of his arm and legs still quaked from the exertion they had just gone through. But he willed them to an iron steadiness as he pushed himself off the wall. Izz's love for Zuree invested stamina back into his spine and bestowed his flesh with unconquerable endurance. Even though they were, for the most part, free, Izz still felt captive. What they needed was for the cavalry to come riding to their rescue. But Izz would be the only cavalry. Ahead there would be many unknowns. Izz reached deep and fortified his heart with the backbone he might need to overcome any burden or threat yet to be encountered. And like all true lovers, they stood in the strength of each other's love, ready to face what was coming with a renewed sense of hope.

As if prompted by some unseen force Izz reluctantly turned his attention back to their daring escape. He stared where the path faded slowly, little by little to black, trying to fix on which way to go. Staring across the faint backwash of dimness, he could not see floor nor walls nor ceiling, nor anything. He tried to form a mental picture of a way out through the landscape of the world without light. As they took the first few steps hand in hand into the obscured shadows, their visibility was almost immediately reduced to zero. Still stunned and dazed, Izz thoughtfully pivoted around a center point in a half circle to the right, center, and left, looking down each ever darkening pathway. As Izz kept a perspective on time, he desperately tried to remember upon which way he must take through an infinite, impenetrable blackness that was blotting out his sight. He thought each step over carefully as snaking reflections of receding light ran down and up the sides in every direction. Izz stared in uncertainty until he finally sensed that time was of the essence; he firmly and steadily quickened his pace. They walked within the labyrinth, down the blind tunnel before them, focusing on the blotches of dimming light in the air. Beyond the yonder awaited only the utter shadow of darkness. At their backs awaited an evil much worse than the abyss they faced. Without any source of light, they had no other choice but to thrust forward. Together they navigated the uncertainty as flashes and flickers of fading light from the perpetual flames behind them faded little by little into the distance. Their path became one with the darkest of darkness as if the specks and patches of pitch black were the only things in the air. Every vestige of light shrank away as they were swept beyond the grasp of their sight.

Izz struggled to see in his mind's eye the way, the way back to the slave station, where they would find light, water, and perhaps even food. They made their way across the broken path of a silent, lightless world slipping deeper and deeper into the growing uncertainty. Now Izz's eyes were useless to him as he attempted to see in his head. All was shrouded in murky shadows, and even the shadows were cloaked in obscurity. He pushed himself forward, stumbling ahead, trying to retrace his steps, silently measuring off his passes. Disorientated in the lack of light, Izz, desperately fought to see in his mind's eye the way back to the slave station. The path back was hazy and indistinct in his memory. Almost every step of the way, they glanced back to see the last vestige of light disappearing until there was nothing but the darksome oppression before them. From this point they could not see beyond the tips of their noses. Any trace of familiarity was left behind them. With every footstep they took, the complete and utter murkiness deepened. Every black on black shadow that sprung up all around them merged with the lightlessness to close in on them and swallow them up in its all devouring nothingness. It became so darkened that it seeped into their very souls.

Primordial fears bubbled, gurgled, and seethed in the depths of their being. The inherent fear of the absence of light and its malignant obscurity first blinded then began to consume them.

Izz forced the bewitching scourge back and away. He knew that darkness alone could not harm them, yet Izz could have sworn he could hear knocks and footsteps all around them. Suddenly his body stiffened of its own volition as if refusing to take one more step until he could see his way. Try as he may, it was futile trying to place any reliance on any of his other senses, smell, taste, hearing, or touch—all were little more than useless in his present plight. Izz forcefully drove his feet forward like a blind man in strange surroundings. He arduously shuffled cautiously along, treading slowly, carefully, clumsily step by step guided only by his insight. Eventually, he stumbled into the cave wall and followed it around. As he led Zuree cat footing through the permanent obscurity, Izz tried to assure himself that there nothing to fear. He repeated over and over to himself, *Darkness is nothing but darkness only darkness* only darkness.

As if it would help, he blinked his eyes repeatedly to clear his vision to no avail. Izz then widened his eyes to drink in what light there was and found none. He saw before him only engulfing emptiness against a blanketed backwash of obscurity. The emptiness was broken only by flickering spots of inkiness that streaked across slashes of pitch black on black that ultimately dissolved into the utter void.

Izz paused for the briefest moment as if to catch his breath, thinking he had suddenly heard a unified scream of sheer anguish and defeat behind them. He glanced back at where the light had disappeared into the gate of hell behind them. Izz's thoughts were momentarily torn back to the unspeakable agony that had to be the eternal punishment of those souls that must remain damned and lost forever. What he thought he heard had only been the memory of their screams that followed behind him, echoing in his head. And all that remained evident of the inferno they had left behind was the diminishing stench of sulfur. Izz incessantly peered ahead, hoping for any indication that they were on the right path and only saw utter tar blackness staring back. Cautiously, Izz led Zuree as they groped their way in the complete pitch void. He felt along the wall, relying on touch alone, feeling for its edges before venturing the next step. As he kept one hand clasped to Zuree, he held out the other to poke around before him. Izz probed forward over the cave floor with the points of his booted toes, trying to feel the edges of each step. He hoped that if he kept his hand against the wall and took each step cautiously, he could fumble forward along the trail without plunging them both to their death.

Zuree's innate fear of the dark suddenly quickened and intensified her uneasiness as she stumbled forward after Izz. Unsure of her footing on the uneven floor, she tried to disregard the chilling grip of dread bolting up and down her spine. Her eyes were wide open, wildly darting about with anticipation squinting, peering trying to see anything. But she found only more velvety shadowiness as if her whole existence in the world of Zia had disappeared into a bleak black hole. A wild mixture of thoughts began to swirl about in her head. A strange dread of the darkness seemed to be trying to hold her in place as if her feet were dragging along the cave floor reluctant to move. She suddenly felt overwhelmed, afraid that her mind might submerge entirely within the unbearable torrents of an impenetrable, insidious sea of devouring blackness.

Izz urged Zuree along as he swept through the murky pool of unrelenting enigma, inching slowly through the passage, mind, and body on full alert. The farther they went, the more and more indistinct in his memory, the path back to the slave station was becoming. At best, his every effort to fix his position, every attempt to retrace his steps back to where he had come from, was failing him miserably. Each step, as if of its own will, became an encouraging triumph of faith as Izz quickly discovered that his sixth sense was becoming more reliable than his memory. He maneuvered slowly and purposely through the emptiness of the unknown relentlessly going forward, persistently onward. But in truth, he was clueless as to where they were much less going. He was not sure whether he was even still going in the general direction, or yet whether they were just going around in circles. With every step, the darkness seemed more and more like a judge set to punish them the instance they lost their way in its stifling blackness. If they were to get lost at this point, they would be returning to the surface no sooner than never. For all Izz knew, they were already hopelessly lost.

All was silent in the passageway, except for the sound of their own shuddering gasps of breath and the small pieces of gritty stone crunching and scattering under their shuffling feet. Every so often, Izz stopped to listen to what he thought might be something creeping up behind them. He could not stop feeling like they were wide open to attack from every direction as the unseen spirit of the underworld pulled the strings of his imagination. Never knowing if death waited to strike at them out of the gloom without warning, now and then, Izz looked back over his shoulder. Instinctively he attempted in utter hopeless to see through his sightlessness. He riveted his eyes, blinking, winking, and straining as if that would help. Wishing and hoping to see a vestige of something, a hint of a shadow, a suggestion of light. Hoping for some sign, anything that would confirm they were on the right path! Izz turned and looked toward Zuree, but again saw nothing but pitiless blindness, inwardly and outwardly.

Each moment was now stretching itself into an agonizing eternity. Were they hopelessly lost? Perhaps they were already a part of the everlasting damned and did not even realize it. And yet out of the alternative universe from the paranormal world, his extrasensory perception imagined a voice whispering like a ghost from another time, *You can run, but you cannot hide.* The scary voices faded away, back into the netherworld like a throbbing pulsation. Izz looked from side to side, whipping his head here and there, searching the gloom. But everywhere he looked, he only saw nothing but shiny black against the soot of a coal backdrop. Izz held up his hand but was not able to see it directly in front of the nose on his face. If only he could see something, whatsoever! He cursed the darkness. But only obscurity itself pressed back in on him black and claustrophobic. His eyes might as well have been wooden buttons sewn on a rag doll.

After what seemed like forever, with only the sense of his fingers and toes to send information to his brain, it seemed as if madness itself was closing in on him, as they stumbled forward in the eternal night. From time to time, a faint rumbling noise sounded as if the underworld was grumbling out a warning. Izz put his hand to the wall, and it felt as if all of Zia was fluttering, followed by faint shaking. Izz eased Zuree's death grip and asked, "Are you all right?" He smiled a smile she never saw, and she nodded back an imperceptible nod. She was still trembling as Izz continued to feel his way over the smooth surface of the trail, trying hard to persuade himself he could see something in the depths just ahead. But the reality was that he was powerless to see a fleck of a speck. However, Izz dared not stop. On and on they walked, hastened along as if by some unearthly power. Like a sightless man trudging through limbo, lost in complete disorientation, with no idea which way they were going. Yet Izz put his trust in the unseen force that seemed to be guiding them along. Zuree faithfully followed Izz through the haunting uncertainty of not being able to see what was just in front of their eyeballs.

As Izz and Zuree entered the next passage, they both simultaneously had an eerie, unyielding feeling that they were being watched. It was as if the source of all evil was just ahead lying in wait in the darksome gloom. And whatever was stalking them, seemed to have been only one step behind them every step of the way. All the while impressions of un-illuminant swirls howled around them like the long, painful cries of woe. But the fact was that if there had been anything out there, they were more likely to have bumped into it before they ever saw it. With eyes wide open, that might as well have been shut, Izz stared apathetically into the void he was thrusting them through. Relentlessly, ever onward, Izz waded through a river of darkness with only the wall as his slightest point of reference. It was impossible to be sure if the next step would not send them tumbling into a bottomless pit.

"What is that noise?" Zuree suddenly asked.

"It could be the sound of running water below us deep in the cavern. Maybe a waterfall, perhaps the falls in the treasure room."

"Treasure room...what treasure room?"

In the dark, Izz turned and faced Zuree and embraced her warmly. Zuree huddled up to Izz. "There are so many things I have to tell you, but for now, we must focus every moment on finding our way back to the world of the living."

With that, Izz turned, and they continued their struggle for survival. Instinctively, again and again, Izz strained to the utmost with inept eyes to pierce the absence of light. He struggled to see in his head the way back to the slave station, where they would find light and water for sure. But at best, the way back was hazy and vague, lost in the back of his head somewhere. Even if it had been etched crystal clear, in the pitch black, he might as well have been looking for a needle in a mountain of straw. Zuree alone continued to be the only source of illumination onto his path.

After an undetermined period of slow trudging, at long last! Up ahead, Izz thought he had caught a glimmer of sputtering shadows! Yes! There! In the distance, he saw against the darkest fog a beacon of light at the end of the tunnel. He thought he could see a row of minute, piercing, pinpricks of lights. It was the torches that lit up the slave station. In the distance obscurity, there was hope. Izz had somehow, at long last, miraculously located the slave station through the darkness. Sparked by renewed hopes of salvation, he turned to Zuree and reassured her, "Just up ahead, we will find food and water and torches to light our way back to the outside world."

They hastened their steps through the blurry darkness as the edge of the slave station came into unmistakable view. In spite of all, at long last, they had reached the slave holding cells. And Izz found himself back where he had started his descent into the realm of the damned. The room was dismal, except for the cold glare of the torch's smoldering fires burning within the confinement hold. As they approached Zuree, wrinkled her nose, and made a face. The smell in the slave hold was choking. The heat from the burning torches accentuated its ghastly smell. Zuree looked at the rusty chains that covered the gloomy walls, making the filthy cell an even more miserable place. The appalling conditions made it the vilest place she had ever seen and asked, "What is this place?" Her imagination thronged with images of her captivity.

Without answering, Izz took a torch from the wall and quickly rummaged through the area for food and water, and anything else that could aid them in their flight. At the end of the gloomy cellblock, Izz found a wooden barrel, and the stench, when he removed its lid, was vile. And he finally answered, "It is an inhumane place of slavery and degradation that should have never been allowed to be." He looked into the container and added, "I have found some freshwater—well, almost fresh." He then found a smaller barrel and removed its top. The stench that escaped it was more pungent than the overpowering smell of unwashed flesh that permeated throughout. "And a few scraps of food that are unfit for a dog," Izz added.

"I am so hungry I could eat just about anything!" Zuree said with a tone of urgency as hunger subjugated her body to the point of pain.

"Believe me when I say this hogwash is not fit for a pig. It would make an old goat retch." He assured Zuree. "These poor souls had to have a belly of metal," Izz said as he threw the ladle back into the swill. He found a few scraps of moldy bread and scraped the moldiness away as an emaciated gray rat scampered out of the shadows and ran past him. Izz broke a piece and tasted it. "It is not too bad once you managed to get past the impulse to gag," he said unconvincingly.

Zuree was so famished that her belly hurt. Feeling dizzy with hunger and thirst, she took a small piece of bread. Her nose distastefully scrunched when she smelled the stale crusted morsel of bread, as a look of revulsion flashed across her pretty face. But her hunger dominated her mind to the point of desperation. So she reluctantly held her nose closed with two fingers and eagerly crammed the bread into her mouth. She chewed a few times, scrunched up her nose, made a face, and gagged. A faint whine rose to her lips, and she had to spit the bread right out. She just knew she was about to be sick. It was the worst thing she had ever tasted. She wiped her mouth with the back of her hand and said, "I am not that hungry after all."

After tasting the water from the first refilled water skin to make sure it was safe, Izz offered Zuree a drink as he began to fill a second water skin from his satchel. Zuree wiped the dust and breadcrumbs from her dry lips, raised the water skin, and took a sip. She then drank long and deep. Her throat had been more parched than she realized. Her windpipe was so dry that to swallow, the water took a concentrated effort. There was a twang to the taste, but dirt flavored water was better than thirst. At least it was wet. Izz waited patiently, licking his parched lips while Zuree drank her fill and then some.

Briefly distracted, Izz found himself blowing fragments of cinders from around Zuree's closed eyes and caressing away blackened flecks of ash from her cheeks and hair. He watched a small stream of water run out the side of Zuree's lips, trickling down her chin, and her neck. Izz felt a sudden irresistible yearning to take Zuree in his arms and endlessly crushing his lips on hers. Zuree caught the odd expression in Izz's eyes as she slowly lowered the skins spout from her mouth. A look of stirring warmth came over her that made everything else seem meaningless and so, so far away. At that moment, Izz's thirst for Zuree was more powerful than his desire for water, but he knew that there was little time for matters of the heart. There would be a lifetime for that—if they lived. Izz took the water skin from Zuree, rushed a quick drink, and said in an anxious voice, "Now we must hurry, my love. Let us leave this place so we may live to talk about it another day." Izz stepped back over to the large ceramic water jar, and thrust his cupped hands into the water, then splashed water on his face and head. Its coolness seemed to clear his mind. Izz then took a torch from the cave wall and turned toward the darkness knowing that somewhere beyond the bounds of the blackness, there was life. "It is this way, quickly." He urged.

As they stepped toward the darkness ahead, Izz's keen eyes lay sight on something that seized his attention. "Look, Zuree!" Izz said excitedly, "Zappa has been true to his word. He has marked the way to our escape." Izz waved his torch in the direction the mark indicated. Its light shed an ominous, oppressive illumination that cast jagged, menacing shadows across the surreal rocky terrain ahead.

"Zappa? Who is Zappa?" Zuree asked quizzically as Izz hastily pulled her along.

Fourteen

The Landing

inally, Kondor had reached King Ozzdon, brimming with excitement he could barely contain. Nearly out of breath, he dropped to one knee as he clutched his trusty sword to his chest. His lips filled with the joyous message that poured from his overflowing heart, "My King we are saved, the entire Xylenian fleet has arrived. And Baddlock and his forces have retreated beyond the foothills without a trace."

"Our reinforcements…here?" the king asked, almost as if he could not believe what he was hearing."

"Yes, the Great Southern Armies of Zia have arrived. Even as we speak, they are routing the Norticlan forces."

The king gasped as a guarded expression washed over his face. Behind him, a spontaneous cheer of relief expanded throughout the catacombs. It was the measure of King Ozzdon's prudence that held him back from celebrating or hooting or smiling. He merely reached down and raised Kondor to his feet. As hope was renewed and morals were immeasurably boosted all around, King Ozzdon's focus was ahead of him now.

On the surface of the planet, the king emerged stony eyed, feeling like a caged bird that had been, at long last, set free. He had survived almost unscathed against all the odds. Yet beneath his superficial wounds, he bore more grievous slashes, deeper lacerations of pain, and anguish, and loss to the heart that would never be fully healed. Izz focused his mind and shutout all the perpetual remorse of conscience except for the mission before him. Between the paling of the receding conjunction, and dawning light of the rising sun, he could see revealed from every corner nothing but destruction. He stared out over Edawn's skyline as fury was building across his mental horizon. The king looked around a broken world, along the smoking landscape, and cringed. In renewed shock and anguish, the devastation came crashing down in all around on him.

Directly in the path before him, a young Edawnian had been hit by an exploding pod, blowing off his head and scattering his torso. Everywhere he saw crushed bodies, entangled bodies, and bloodied bodies. Every fiber of King Ozzdon's being was now screaming for revenge. He never imagined that it was as bad as it was. Rage, terror, and sorrow convulsed in his heart. The ambiance of devastation and death hovered over every emerging shadow. Even the sky above looked broken. Clay cold corpses lay blood, and mangled everywhere, and everywhere he stepped, death made its presence felt. Breastplates arrayed with the polished Eagle Crest that once gleamed in the dawning sun now riddled with arrows, still encased the men they failed to protect. His anger rose up from the mist like ghosts rising from pools of the blood of the dead. He saw the countless shattered men. His shocked eyes looked upon limbless torsos, blown off heads, chests ripped open, exposing the frail web of existence. Most were too young to see death like this. He looked upon the faces twisted in death. Fixed eyes glazed over with death were sightlessly upon him. And for a flash of a moment, he envisioned his reflective image among them looking inwardly back at himself.

Apart from the dead, the once magnificent palace was especially an appalling sight to behold. All around, columns that had once held up grand structures were now fallen into ruin, towers reduced into heaps of rubble, cathedrals shattered into piles of rubbish, and aqueducts pummeled until they were no more than drifts of dust and debris. Everything his forefathers had accomplished, everything that he had worked for so long had been lost in a fleeting moment it seemed. Its greatness was gone. Aghast, he stared in disbelief as if his heart had been taken and hacked into small pieces with a blunt, rusty meat cleaver. The palace's doom had ragged edges where whole sections had been blown away from its shiny exterior. But yet it still stood defiantly against the overwhelming cataclysm that had befallen it. The Ziaian insignia tattered and torn still fluttered from its soaring flagpoles. Waves of regret, sadness, and profound moral outrage washed over his spiritual vista as the weight of it all forced its way down into his heart. And in the end, he was overwhelmed. Stunned and teary eyed, he stood there frozen, thinking to himself, in disgust, *Were we so wicked?* "Had we strayed so far from the path of the Lawgiver that we had to be punished with the atrocious deeds of one lunatic?" He whispered weakly to himself in a dry, tortured voice. "Baddlock!" Recoiling from the bitter taste of having uttered that name, he screamed, "You son of a bloated warthog, I need to kill you myself personally. I need to feel your miserable life seep out of you by my own hand." The last words of his utterance were mumbled more to himself than aloud.

Like phantom spirits of the dead, bewildered and terror stricken, ghostlike men, only their eyes alive and glinting, emerged from the ruins to stand among the living. He saw those faces as he passed by, shells of themselves, empty faces murderously tired from being in continuous combat for too long. Haunted women bearing somber faces and traumatized children covered in the grime and grit started emerging in tattered groups from within the depths of the kingdom's underbelly. Grief stricken, they paraded themselves beneath the arched entrance of the Main Keep's crumbling stone. With mournful sounds, they came forth, bitterly weeping for the men they could no longer embrace. Those surviving warriors of Edawn who had lived through what they thought was their last hour, bolstered their spirits despite the gloomy shadows they cast. Those who found their families still alive burst into a mutual voice of shouts and cries of overwhelming reprieve. They hurried to embrace one another as the overwhelming exhilaration of being alive swept through them. Fathers on bended knees clutched their children, weeping with joy. Bewildered child shivered uncontrollably with elation. Pockets of spontaneous thanksgiving broke out. For them, the worst was over. The darkest day in the memory of Edawn had passed for now. The great outpouring of jubilance that, for the moment, had lifted their hearts and minds was unexpectedly shattered by the harsh screams of those who had suddenly come upon the dead bodies of their slain men. Countless wives, mothers, and children searched for their loved ones among the dead and dying. And upon finding them, they collapsed with grief, and they bewailed bitterly, and nothing could comfort their hearts.

The two bitter and sweet conditions of the heart collided and merged into one mystifying cast of mind; the exaltation for having endured a revelation of hell, fused with the brutal sourness of the frightening annihilation that had plucked so many from the living, without justification. Some women, incapacitated with the screams of <u>bereavement</u>, and loss, had to be restrained and protected from the sight of what was left of the ones they loved. In a world of torn flesh, some were so tattered that their bodies were unaccounted for. Children so cruelly orphaned cried without consolation. The king forced himself back toward self possession as he walked among the bereaved, offering comforting words of solace. Out of the surviving multitudes, one unified voice of anguish rose from the kingdom unto the heavens. Their voices rose together in grief and falling in the agony of its injustices and cruelty. Lamentation, such as had never been heard before, cast a great black shadow of bitterness over the late coming of the long anticipated reinforcements. What did the momentous redemption of the long anticipated reinforcements matter to those that wept? It was too little too late for those whose hearts that were pierced with so much pain. It meant little or nothing for those whose minds had been raped with so much wrong and sorrow. Of what consequences was it to those spirits crucified with mental scars never to be healed, never, ever to be forgotten?

King Tydron and the arriving reinforcements continued to be amazed that anyone could have possibly survived the cataclysm of the total obliteration before them. It was a scene of utter horror. The interior of the kingdom, place, galleries, and libraries was shred to bits in ways that a rational mind could not conceive. On top of the endless dead, and dying, the once pristinely, beautiful world of Edawn had been defiled beyond recognition.

TOM ICON

From atop the tower, Zandor could hardly believe that in such a short time, the deserted harbor had grown into such a vast military base. Spread before him there as far as the eye could see, were the swelling armies from all over the southern world of Zia, from every distant country, kingdom, village, and hamlet. He saw fresh, battle ready, and motivated men led by the noblest and most powerful kings of the empire. On the shore from every direction, troops fell into place. The multitudes were indescribable. And just when he thought there was no way the shoreline could hold more, yet the armies kept coming.

Tydron shoved his sword into his scabbard, heeled his riding beast toward King Ozzdon, and then reined his mount to a halt. He lifted his leg over the back of the powerful stallion and dismounted before the Emperor King of Xylenia. Bound by duty, Tydron took a few steps, executed the customary Xylenian salute, and knelt before his king, and pledged, "My sword, my men, and my life are yours, my lord."

King Ozzdon was then immediately surrounded by solemn faced kings from all the southern kingdoms of the Empire. Kings of great power, wealth, and dignity, impressed by their Emperor's dauntless, heroic survival, were ready and willing to follow him through the gates of hell if need be. In humble awe and amazement, they respectfully removed their royal war crowns dropped to their knees and lowered their heads in loyal homage to their rightful Emperor. Suddenly an eddy spread across the surface of the surrounding landscape as thousands upon thousands of gathering warriors bowed to their Emperor-King. Like a gigantic undertow rippling over a sea of humanity, in a perfect, concentric circle of splendor, heads bowed, and warriors knelt to the ground before their Emperor King Ozzdon. Horns blasted, trumpets blew, and every bell tower that remained standing was pealing loudly and echoing across the kingdom. The loyalty King Ozzdon commanded was a power born of nobility, and respect, not collusion. Filled with a mixture of overwhelming gratitude and veneration, King Ozzdon respectfully walked amidst the kings of Zia, urging them to rise.

The Empire had received a mortal blow, but there was no time to dwell on that. Ozzdon quickly came to terms with the reality at hand. His primary responsibility now was to rid the world of the one madman guilty of all these atrocious deeds. And each one of those that followed him, particularly Dandork and Darkon. This was his only reality, except for his daughter's well being everything else diminished to the back of his mind. In a loud, commanding voice, he called out, "I want all kings, warlords, noblemen, and the Council of Elders to gather in the Dome of the Great Table." The only public edifices that seemed sound enough to still gather in. "Take a moment to collect yourselves and meet me there as soon as possible." The King of Kings then called Tydron the commander of the fleet to his side, "Dispatch a contingent of your stouthearted men to gather the dead. Those within the kingdom must be taken to the smelters and cremated first as prescribed by our ancient war laws. Those who fell in the fields of battle must be cremated in incineration pits. The last thing we need is a pestilence on our hands."

"It will be done," was King Tydron's immediate response.

Baddlock's approach was spotted from afar off, from the peak lookouts of Phantomsdeep. The first watchman to spot Baddlock's party of a hundred announced to the towers below. "Lord Baddlock returns…with word of an early, overwhelming victory, no doubt."

The trumpeters on the main towers raised their goat horns and sounded the command to open the massive oak and iron fortified gates immediately. The prolonged horn blast conveyed the urgency for immediate action. The gate slaves were assembled and positioned. Two were set at every pace, on either side along the drawn out oversized tow chains. A single drumbeat was sounded, and the gatehouse drudges lifted the chains. The slaves strained and were beaten with long whips unmercifully until the inertia of the massive gate doors was broken. The gates moved slowly as the drudges were lashed most viciously to accommodate Baddlock's rapid approach. With brutal disregard for their horses, the hundred relentlessly pushed their riding animals at full gallop up Phantomsdeep's steep rampart. As one unit, the riders mirrored the natural action and movement of their racing mounts. Baddlock's party entered the gates in a cloud of dust but did not slow at the underground stables. Instead, Baddlock and his horsemen drove their riding beasts hard into and through the throat of the inner connecting caverns. As they raced through the subterranean labyrinth torches were grabbed on the run. Along their precarious path, on either side, the edges dropped off into the bottomless crevasses that lined the entire path.

Around a sharp turn, a horse and rider when down in a tangle. But no one broke their stride as they trample right over them. Another horse and rider were crowded off the edge of a cavernous drop, tumbling, just before horse and mount fell over the edge. The rider's wailed outcries and the horse's piercing shrills eventually faded until they were swallowed up by the depths altogether. At long last, the detachment had reached the innermost outskirts of the Altar of Abomination. Horses were pulled to an abrupt stop as they whinnied and bellowed to a halt. Baddlock quickly dismounted and commanded that everyone remain where they were. He disappeared into the darkness, seemingly vanishing through a secret passage that only he knew about. Abaddawn's outer lair was so secret that not even Baddlock's top generals knew its location. The Wicked Warlock Wizard rushed down the corridor of a long egress with his black robe swirled across the passage floor. Something vile and beyond all wickedness was afoot in those depths. As he descended in the darkness, there was the growing smell of foul smoke. At the point of reaching his intended destination, Baddlock grouped for something to fall back on, trying to reassure himself that Abaddawn would understand why he had not yet rid Zia of the carpenter.

The Wicked Warlock Wizard entered Abaddawn's throne room. There was an ominous deadness in the air, a reeking heaviness of ancient evil filled the air. It was a dark hole black as the darkest night lost in chaos beyond explanation. It was a dreary place beyond reality itself. Sensing the presence of Abaddawn, without hesitation, Baddlock dropped to his hands and knees and asked, "What is your bidding, my lord and master?

"I simply want to know..." Abaddawn's lips snarled, and his eyes were fierce as he spoke, "why oh why does the insignificant carpenter remain to be a troublesome thorn in my side!" Abaddawn was turning the air around him, amber with the panting of his uncontrolled rage. The demon lord's eyes widened, becoming cynical and ill tempered. The irises were fiery, and the pupils were dilating doorways, luring Baddlock into their delirium beyond.

"I sought to kill him and thought we were rid of him for good, but yet he lives. He keeps turning up again and again under some Devine protection it would seem. But I swear on my soul he will be dead before this day is done." His words flew out with a pleading urgency.

The demons masses all around only sneered. "I have heard your words, gate what you say carefully for what you speak will surely bind and yoke you! Abaddawn's voice turned as hard and as chilling as ice. The ruler of darkness continued, still in a rising fit of wrath that made the air around him quiver, "The maiden Zuree has been taken by that meaningless, peasant carpenter." Abaddawn's voice broke as he spoke.

And for the first time, Baddlock thought he detected a ting of fear. Was the great god of the underworld afraid? Abaddawn vented a long, foul hiss through his fangs that filled the air with a greenish stench as he continued, "Bring her back to me!" His voice sounded strangled. There is too much at stake to let one petty talking monkey, one pitiful little soul, destroy it all." Then his voice started to shudder.

With head bowed, Baddlock looked to the voice, coming from the nothingness of the darkness. It was an unholy place that had never been illuminated by the sun or shined upon by the light of the moon or stars. As his eyes adjusted to the lack of light, he saw the rest of Abaddawn's image. The Prince of Darkness sat enthroned, as gushes of flames engulfed an image that resembled a slimy, reptilian like toad. His wings were spread out like tattered, black cloaks, crumpled, hobbled, and riddled with holes. Every dark thing in hell surrounded and indwelled within his soulless existence. In the background and clinging to the roof and walls were the demon hordes. They were packed in tight in such numbers that one could barely distinguish one from the other.

"Bring me the maiden!" The fallen archangel demanded in no uncertain terms. Something desperate in Abaddawn's voice made Baddlock lift his head slightly. He cocked an eye and saw the beast fading in and out of focus as if from an unstable world. And the throne he sat upon seemed to be crumbling from its outer edges. Abaddawn red eyes angrily blazed as he blasted out an outraged blast of breath that seethed vapor out between his teeth and swirled before him. "Bring me the maiden before the conjunction elapses, and I will multiply whatever I have promised you a thousandfold." The father of lies promised.

Greed suddenly surged through the Wicked Warlock Wizard's heart like a deadly poison. Baddlock's gray eyes all at once widened like that of a wolf's for an instant and lit up with devilish delight as he rasped his sandy hands together.

Demons from all around were suddenly provoked, wild, intoxicated with the expectancy of victory, of a massacre, of unparalleled supremacy and grandeur. Many of their mouths dripped pink with the salivation of anticipation.

"They will be found headed to the western entrance by the Spring of Forgetfulness," Abaddawn instructed. "Kill the orphan!" The prince of darkness demanded in a voice that became louder and more insistent with every word. "Bring me his heart in pieces that his legacy may die with him." Abaddawn's eyes flashed from his shadowy face as a musty sulfuric haze drifted forth from his foul, fang filled mouth. "But, the maiden bring to me unharmed." Abaddawn continued, "Without the maiden, all is for naught. Her royal blood is more precious than all the gold in Zia. The opening of the dark gateways is fixed on exact rules with each complex order based on all the others. All must be done as one at the exact time within the matrix of the Great Conjunction. The maiden's blood must touch the black altar, at the precise moment in time of the alignment that we may rule and enslave humankind. If one cosmic altar fails to open, they will all fail. "We must not fall short."

Baddlock rose to his feet quickly and slapped his fist to his hollowed chest, "Your wish is my command, my lord and master." Baddlock repeatedly bowed as he backed away, eager to regain Abaddawn's favor and secure the added promise.

"Leave me now." Abaddawn's scary voice tapered off to a raspy whisper.

"Fail me not!" Baddlock heard as he turned to obey. But what he did not hear was, "Fail me, and I will crush your soul, and you will forever remain broken."

"Of course, your worshipness," Baddlock said anxiously. "Of course. It will be done this day." And as he dragged himself away like a disease towards its deathly deed, he could hear Abaddawn's fading voice in the distance.

"The world of Zia was always meant to be mine! I and I alone have the worthiness to merge the empire into a one world kingdom and call it to its greatness. The birth of the new cannot come to pass without putting to death the old. Out of disorder will come order..." Abaddawn's throne continued to crumble even as he spoke of victory.

Upon returning to his troops, the Wicked Warlock Wizard commanded Dandork to gather his most skilled assassins and riders. The first thing that came to Dandork's attention was the change in Baddlock's essence. There was a duller, more vacant look behind Baddlock's spiritually dead eyes. They were the eyes of a madman who had bartered away what was left of his woeful soul. He was deep under Abaddawn's influence than ever. As he barked out orders and everyone obeyed without question. Baddlock commanded Dandork again. "Bring the trackers forward. From here, we will ride around along the mountainside pass to the Springs of Forgetfulness to cut off and intercept our quarry. Darkon, you will proceed from here on foot, through the cave, take the trackers with you, pursue the two cave rats, and flush them out.

We will all meet at the secret entrance of the Spring of Forgetfulness."

For the first time, Dandork got the impression from the look on Baddlock's face that his plan for a quick victory was not going as well as he had led on, and could, in fact, be unraveling. The trackers, appropriately enough known as Slewsnouts, were brought forth on leashes, as one would control a pack of wild hunting dogs. Each strained against reinforced metal and leather collar fastened on thick leather straps knotted tightly around their necks. They were a subhuman half animal, half man, all beast. Every Slewsnout bayed with bound up fury ran around on all fours and snapped like dogs. Vapor wafted from the muzzles of the unimaginably vicious beast man like creatures. They drew back their black lips, baring their yellowed, twisted tusks with animal like yaps and grunts. Like upright warthogs searching for truffles, their pig like squealing, panting and snorting grew louder as they were driven, spider like, on knuckles and toes. They were bloodthirsty hunters of men and could track anything, over any terrain, better than any bloodhound. With howls of insanity, the Slewsnouts hurled themselves forward like crazed, screaming demons. They were led down the path leading away from Abaddawn's hidden throne. Each driver grabbed a torch as they disappeared into the deepening passage. The lead Slewsnout tracker caught a faint whiff of human scent and frantically searched out a trail. And the pack was off shrilling, squealing, and sniffing the ground. If the stalker had not been heavily bound, they would have, there and then, quickly left Darkon and his troops behind. The Slewsnouts barked and snapped with the savagery of cold blooded killers as they pulled their keepers at a grueling pace down the passage that led to the slave holding cells. As the beast men intensified the hunt of their elusive prey, Baddlock mounted Nightmare and headed back out the cavern entrance and out through the main gate. Dandork and a handful of selected riders followed close behind. Once outside, Baddlock's horsemen turned onto the narrow mountain passage that led to the Springs of Forgetfulness. Baddlock stayed close to the contour of the

Noragore Rim and maneuvered along the treacherous path that interlaced between the jagged cliffs and craggy projecting rock overhangs at a full stride.

Just when Izz thought things were falling into place, little did he know they were beginning to fall further apart. As Izz hustled Zuree down the tunnel, out of nowhere, his premonition flashed an image of hunting beasts tracking them and nipping at their heels. Like an icy hand of dread that gripped his heart, his sixth sense kicked in and told him that they were being stalked. He saw visions of snarling, salivating, sharp teeth, and in his inner ear, thought he heard animal noises, snarls, bays, and growls. He felt an achy feeling in his chest as his mind careened down an old familiar path of danger and despair. Like rottenness in his bones, the memory of Abaddawn crept back into his mind. The lord of the damned was there somewhere beyond the blackness, buried under the heaviness of darkness. Izz hastened his step. Even with the torch, Izz could barely see a few paces in front of him. Still, it was a lot better than black nothingness. Unexpectedly, there on the right side of the path, Izz spotted another one of Zappa's marks, pointing straight toward the dim glow of his torch. After what seemed like an ageless race against time, all of a sudden, up ahead, Izz could make out a hazy, silvery glare on the roof of the opening ahead. The mouth of the cave was barely visible as a fog of light shone with choking darkness that pushed in on its faint glow from every other direction. "There…," Izz uttered suddenly, "just ahead is the way out!" Izz turned to Zuree excitedly and kissed her deeply for a fleeting moment. Her dry mouth suddenly watered. "Come quickly. Soon we will be free, free at last!"

Dingy gray light filtered down as they hurried toward the opening. Suddenly out of nowhere, there came an unexpected tug of distraction. Terror gripped Izz's entire body as he realized he had heard something out of place so faint that only he had heard it. It was a deadened, but distinct approaching clipping and clopping on stone Izz listened intently as his pace slowed. Up ahead, the unmistakable pounding sound of horse's hooves beating on the rocky trail interrupted his next forward steps. Instantly, his blood froze in his veins as he focused on the mounting noises in the cave. The two of them slowed to a stop to listened for a while. It was the unmistakable sound of clicking hooves moving closer—moving in fast to cut off their lifeline to freedom.

With awful realization, both their hearts froze simultaneously. Izz could not move. He had been shot through the guts, bringing a groan to Izz's throat. That's what it felt like. He just stood there listening with great alarm and feelings of foreboding. Zuree could see in Izz's face that same feeling of inner brokenness she was feeling in herself. Neither had been expecting this moment. The cave floor and walls suddenly rumbled with the heart rending sound of riders. From the sound of swift rat a pan of hoofbeats on the cave floor, there had to be over thirty heavily armed men on horseback. Above the sound of the hoofbeats, the unmistakable sounds of neighing, whinnying, nickering, and sharp snorting confirmed to both that they were rapidly losing the race with the finish just in sight. So close and yet so far! With a groan in Izz's throat, Izz stepped back in the shadows and motioned for Zuree to do the same as he pressed her against the stone hedge of a boulder with his out searched arm. Heeding Izz's warning, Zuree stepped back as she raised the back her hand to her mouth in a questioning manner.

Izz craned his neck to look over the edge of the bolder. What met his eyes rooted in his greatest fears and caused his heart to wedge in his throat. The riders bore the Death Skull emblem! He saw them bringing their horses to an abrupt stop as their riding beasts swayed on wide spread legs. Zuree immediately tried to follow Izz's glance when he snapped his head back. Izz turned back to Zuree; an expression full of holes was frozen over his face. Zuree focused on Izz's face. His eyes were gripped in dread. There were no words to describe the startling expression screwed on Izz's face as he felt the thickness of dismay seize his soul. Zuree saw an eerie mask of intense fearfulness she had never seen before locked over his fallen expression. Had all their efforts been met with ultimate failure. She bit her bottom lip to keep from shrieking. Izz turned his head toward Zuree as if trying to decide which way to go and then made an expression indicating crushed hope. They stood, motionless, trying to calm themselves as they looked at each other with stricken panic. Izz leaned closer back into Zuree and stated the obvious under his breath, "We are in deep trouble." Anguish resounded in his voice. All at once, his firm and resilient appearance were lost as if the strength of his spiritual armor plating had suddenly fallen away.

Zuree knitted her eyebrows as she asked in an equally stricken whisper, "Whatever shall we do?" Her hands were shaking, her heart desperately hoping.

Izz raised a warning finger to his lips as he listened intently. He could feel the increasing tension pounding in his head, and then he heard a familiar foul voice. "I know they are near. I can smell their fear."

It was the raspy, evil voice of Baddlock the Wicked Warlock Wizard. It all suddenly seemed so utterly hopeless. They had stumbled headlong into Baddlock and his troops. Zuree looked up at Izz. His eyes were gripped in defeat. With their options quickly running out, Izz drew several quick, deep breaths as he thought surely things could not possibly get any worst, but he was wrong. To make an ever worsening situation even exceedingly worse, the sounds of growling, howling and high pitched whining was heard coming from the direction of the path they had just come from as the Slewsnouts had almost instantly picked up their trail. At that moment, it felt as though a legion of demons was about to pounce on them from all sides. Izz's thoughts were broken. He thought about dousing his torch, but he would not be able to relight it quickly. That would have left them virtually blind, and the torch was their only lifeline to the outside world. Thus far, their dwindling touch light had gone unnoticed for the twilight of the cavern opening. He wanted to run, but where? The opening to the outside world was blocked, and the passage from where they had come at the far end was filling with dancing torches led by animal noises that sounded like rabid dogs, wolves, or worse. They both cowered behind the rocks, any shred of faith they clung to evaporated as the wind went out of their sails. They looked at each other in silent desperation, breathing each breath as if it was their last, knowing that at any moment their torchlight would be spotted, and they would be discovered. For a moment, Izz raged in silence as a whisper escaped from his throat, "We walked right into their hands." Izz took several steps backward with the feeling that the end had come. Suddenly the immediacy of death appeared uglier, darker, utterly more certain than ever. Izz sensed that the chances of being killed were more real than ever, and for this, he had to prepare his mind. *No!* Hope penetrated the fog in Izz's mind. Their defeat was a thought he had to distance himself from forcefully.

"I am frightened!" Zuree whimpered. Her voice did not crack with brittle panic, but her heart was about to as she too heard the nickering and sharp snorts and the shrilling squeals of whatever was tracking them from where they had come. Her blue green eyes were shadowed with terror as she tried to blink back the tears that were pressing at their corners. But in spite of her greatest efforts to resist, her tears ebbed down her cheeks. She was not prepared to die.

All the while, Izz thumped the back of his head against the boulder and mumbled silently, "But...but...we were so close...too close to be cut off." He gritted his teeth.

By now, they could hear their assailants' gruff voices as they talked among themselves. Baddlock was so nearby that Izz caught wind of the stench coming from his hatred.

"Look everywhere! They have to be here." *I had him several times, and I let him escape. I have been paying dearly for that mistake ever since. It will not happen again!* Baddlock thought to himself.

Izz forced himself to calm down, to think things out. For nearly anyone, this would have been impossible—but not for Izz. For him, somewhere, somehow, there was still hope. As the intruders moved in from both directions, torch lights joggled, and their smoke waft in the darkness and all of Izz's faith was put to a hard test. The only foreseeable choice was to try and outrun them.

He looked here and there for any possible escape route. There! On the far end of the cavern in the dim light, Izz spotted an opening at the top of a steep incline. It was a long shot at best. But on the spare of the desperate circumstances, Izz saw they had no other option. It would be there and then or never. Instinctively, Izz grabbed Zuree's arm and urged her, "Come quickly, this is our only chance to run!" he whispered for her to get ready. Izz's dark eyes challenged Zuree to believe.

Zuree slowly nodded, trying to put on a positive expression but could only manage a pitiful contortion. Izz smiled a frail, almost apologetic smile as he brushed away a strand of hair. He kissed the top of her head. Then he turned to the tiny corner of hope in his heart. Not knowing any other way out, and without any clue, direction, or purpose, Izz intuitively bolted up an obscure footpath that led to higher ground with Zuree in tow. It had not been so much a rational choice as a desperate reflex for self preservation to save their lives. With reckless abandon, they yoked their wills. Their fervor, love, and devotion lined up with the others. Izz attempted to stay in the shadows as he tried to conceal the light of his torch as best he could. The two crept quietly toward the incline. Baddlock immediately heard their footsteps. Baddlock let his senses range over the cave entrance until he perceived the presence of the two. "There! There they are! Do not let them get away, you fools! Surround them! Cut off every possible escape."

Izz and Zuree suddenly dashed up the slope upward toward the top of the extremely steep incline. They had no other choice. Everyone heard the scuffle of distant footfalls and spotted their torchlight almost all at one time. Moving and working together, they scrambled up and up as quickly and sure footed as two wild goats. By this time, the Slewsnouts and Darkon's party were in sight and almost at once joined Baddlock's men. Baddlock was frantically giving commands, "You go there, and you there." As he pointed his spidery finger in the direction, he wanted to be covered. "Surround them, cut them off!"

When Darkon reached Baddlock, his face was pale, and he was out of breath. At his side were the Slewsnouts handlers and their subhuman bloodhounds. Having spotted Izz and Zuree, the beast men went into a frenzied craze and were all howling and snorting wildly. "Shall I release the trackers, my lord?" Darkon asked.

"No! You fool. Our master requires the princess unharmed. The carpenter you can do with as you wish."

Dandork unstrapped his crossbow from his back. Being the master marksman that he was, he would be the only one Baddlock would allow to fire upon Izz. Dandork placed the bow nose down on the ground, drew the string to the catch. He placed a razored, broad head bolt in the groove of the tiller, and notched it in the string. Dandork then choose a position over a nearby boulder and rested his elbows. He calculated his range, gauged his sight, and froze into place. On the coverless terrain, with his long distance, high powered crossbow, Izz would be the perfect target. The plan was simple, take Izz out, and they could do as they pleased with Zuree. Something like a smile glimmered in Dandork's eyes. "You are as good as dead." There was harshness in his whisper.

The click of the trigger sent the projectile on its deadly path. Izz heard the droning in the air as a heavy bolt went past, just narrowly missing his head. If Izz had not stumbled at that exact moment, the arrow would have found its mark—the back of Izz's neck. Dandork quickly fired again. However, because of the distance, while the arrow was on its way, Izz had intuitively hunched and stepped slightly to the side. The shaft glazed Izz's right cheek, slicing a deep gash on his face. An instantaneous charge of adrenaline dump into his bloodstream. He bolted like a hunted animal as he felt an overwhelming sense of terror fill his soul. Without stopping to think, Izz pulled Zuree in front of him, placing himself between Dandork's arrows and Zuree as one long range shot after another searched him out. "Run!" Izz bellowed. "Run for your life!" His voice already sounding labored with the effort he was making. At the mid point of the incline, Izz urged Zuree, "Climb quickly!" yelling at her like a demented madman as he half led, half dragged her, slipping with every step. Any hope of salvation waited at the top.

Izz of Zia

In sudden fear, Zuree vaulted as she turned and looked over her shoulder. Had it not been for the blind panic Izz felt at that time, he would not have had the stamina and incentive to climb such a steep incline as fast as he was. With all his might, he pushed Zuree along, struggling to reach the highest point where the opening awaited them. As they hastened up the slope, the broken rock made their footing uncertain. Zuree suddenly tripped. They went down together as another one of Dandork's deadly bolts narrowly missed Izz. Izz picked himself back up on his feet and thrust Zuree up and forward, as near to a run as the steep, slanted terrain allowed. Unmindful of the scrapes and bruises he was inflicting upon himself, Izz resumed the grueling upward climb.

"Just a little more, and we will be at the top." Izz drove Zuree along as fast as his depleted body could manage. With arrows zinging about them, fear empowered their flight. They united their two halves and moved on undiluted adrenaline that was pumping at full throttle. With lungs straining, Izz found himself moving much faster than he thought he could. His single thought was to get up the slope and out of harm's way as quickly as possible. Izz dared, not looking back or slowing down. He just kept running, doing everything he could not drop the torch. Zuree struggled in exhaustion, drawing long, choking breaths, stumbling, and falling several times. She glanced back at Izz and gasped, "I cannot go any farther! You are going to run me into the ground!" Zuree looked over her shoulder with pleading eyes, her face flushed by her effort to keep up the punishing pace. "I do not wish to hold you back. Save yourself. Go on without me!" She begged.

"No! You are bound to me, and I am bound to you." Izz had already made up his mind. He would rather lose his soul forever than leave her. That was the only fact he was sure of. "As long as we are alive, we have a chance! You must move, for the love of everything you hold, dear!"

Nearly at the top. Zuree gasped and choked, "I cannot...go on! Her worn out muscles felt consumed as if they were gradually turning to jelly and felt as though she would at any moment crumble from the exhaustion.

"No! You must go on!" Izz screamed. "I will not let you give up! And nor yet will I. Our lives have just begun with one and the other. You and I...are not nearly ended. I will not desert you. I could not live without you!"

The realization of what Izz must have been going through gave Zuree the hidden reserves of stamina and strength to stumble one foot in front of the other. Somehow drawing strength from his courage, with nothing left to give, she began to run again. It was challenging beyond imagination. On the verge of fainting, she desperately tried to quell her gasping as Izz like a madman, frantically, mercilessly continued to force Zuree up the incline, until they had reached the top. The remaining few paces took every bit of her last energy. At the top, the only option left to them was the cranny that led into the unknowable, if it led anywhere at all. That perhaps only blind faith could have seen. The hole in the wall was a tight squeeze. Izz realized that they could very well be backing themselves into a nook with no way out. Conceivably, it might be the biggest mistake they ever made, but with arrows raining down on them, at least they would not be out in the open. They crammed through the velvety curtain of blackness as far back as could be seen. Izz just followed his nose into the threatening, pure primeval darkness barely lit by the flicker of his smoldering torch. The tar black blindness stretched ahead, deepening into a cavernous world where the power of the sun had never and would never shine. Once Izz was reasonably sure that Zuree was safe for the moment, he handed her the torch and returned to the opening. With no strength to spare, Zuree clutched the torch as a drowning soul might grasp a straw. An intense whispered prayer of thanksgiving escaped her lips as she, at last, remembered to breathe.

Outside, Izz saw at least fifty men and half a dozen trackers moving frantically upon them from below. Under cover of darkness, Izz began to roll down the huge stone closest to the top of the incline as he dodged an onslaught of crossbow bolts. The first stone he toppled over caused an avalanche of numerous other large stones that came crashing down on their pursuers. Several archers and one of the Slewsnouts were crushed under the weight of the heavy boulders. Izz rolled down another stone and then another, but it was clear that Baddlock was more than willing to sacrifice all to the last man in the effort to kill him and recapture Zuree. Izz decided that his chances were better on the run. He rejoined Zuree in the passageway, where she waited, her lungs still straining and gasping after the hard upward trek. "We must move now, my love!" Izz urged.

Still desperately trying to catch her breath. Zuree cried, "Move, where?"

Izz gathered her near, and reassured her until she grew quiet, "There has to be a way out. There is always a way out. We have to keep looking." Izz moved forward, on the only path opened to them, knowing that it would not take Baddlock too much longer to reach the opening.

Ahead awaited the nocturnal deep and the fearful scourge of the unknown, but behind them, certain death hunted them. Izz moved forward, almost blindly. There was no other alternative but to cast themselves into a more profound, darker conundrum. It was an outside chance, a long shot at best. They followed the yellowish gleam of their torch as it shifted along the wall for what seemed like half an eternity. Eventually, they found themselves in an immense cavern enclosing one colossal floor space. Izz was filled with profound wonder and surprise as they stepped into the vast, echoing cavity. The roof, if there was one, must have been halfway to the surface. With disjointed thoughts, Izz and Zuree stood before a massive network of tunnels from where diverged dozens of passageways leading into the unfathomable reaches of the nameless unknown.

Although their minds were heavy with dread, there was no time for hesitation. If they took the wrong passage or stumbled over a drop off, they may very well never be heard from again. If they stayed where they were, their fate was sealed. With every step, vague alarm bells yawning from within rang out in Izz's mind and filled him with unfathomable anxiety. Perhaps it was just the normal unnerving of being hunted. Whatever the case, something within was driving him recklessly ahead. It was like entering the shark infested waters of the deep in the gloom of near dark. It was a gloomy place where one could not tell what may unexpectedly come at you out of its shadows. Still panting heavily, they quickly advanced through the cavernous chamber, they had no other alternative. They were suddenly met by a noxious ammonia odor that saturated the air of the entire huge cavern. There was nothing they could do but follow their fate to its end. Izz kept admitting to himself. *We have no other choice but to go onward. There is no other choice.*

The thick smell filled Izz's lungs, with an odorous reek of an eye stinging stench. Zuree wrinkled her nose as she breathed in the sour air that clawed at her throat and lungs. The overpowering foul smell was unbearable. A wave of coughing seized both of them as they entered deeper into the vast yawning. The rank air drawn into their lungs forced them to heave and hack as their eyes increasingly stung and filled with tears. Apart from their ragged breathing, all seemed to be secure for the moment. That is until suddenly the silence was broken by faint audible clicking and squeaking sounds and a shuffling, clamoring for space sound. Izz waved the torch in the direction of the overhanging darkness. As the glow of the flame passed across Zuree's face, he saw raw fear etched on her striking features. Izz felt her tremble and tightened her grip. There was nothing he could do but follow their fate to the end. From the recesses of the cave, the noise mounted and echoed off the walls of the vault, eerily amplified by its spacious expanse. But by now, he should have learned to expect the unexpected.

All at once, the air came to life with a vibration that began like the stirring of leaves in a quickening tempest. The commotion very soon burst forth in intensity into proliferating pandemonium. In an instant, they both knew that something was desperately wrong. They could hear from the depth of the cavernous roof a vibrating noise. It was as if millions of swarms of giant killer bees were taking flight just beyond the veil of darkness. Out of the dark, they heard a dreadful swarming sound. They could hear shrieking cries blurring out a woeful warning. The high pitched shrills escalated until the unbearable sound waves seemed to bounce back and forth and trill in their skulls between their ears. Izz again wondered if he had finally sealed their fates. Izz scanned his eyes across the heights as he focused on the haunting sounds. Far above them, the upper limits of the ceiling remained undetectable in the awful cobalt blackness. As Izz pressed his back against Zuree and the wall behind them, he turned his attention back toward the approaching sound. Less than a heartbeat later, his dagger was in his hand, feeling the same stomach revolving terror one gets when waiting for something horrifying to jump out of a nightmare. Zuree, who was biting her lower lip to keep from screaming, suddenly cried out on the edge of a complete emotional cave in, "Why is the ceiling moving?"

Fifteen

The Evasion

I n the kingdom of Edawn, fire brigades were formed to fight the blazes that burned everywhere. Hundreds were missing; many bodies were just too torn apart to recognize. Some were nothing more than dark bloodstains scattered in all directions. Others seemingly vanished without a trace. On the other hand, some were miraculously pulled from beneath tons of rubble without a single scratch. The dead from the inner kingdom that could be gathered were stacked in piles, heaped onto carts drawn toward the smelter yard leaving behind them dripping trails of blood and gore. The ghastly task of collecting loose limbs, pieces of the bodies, meat, and bone placed in whale stomach bags were left to the stouthearted. One worker reached down for a head, gently placing it in his bag. He closed his own eyes, waiting for the revulsion to pass. Then he shuddered as he moped his hands on his apron. The large furnaces were stoked to their highest capacities. Tall smelter chimneys sent up hissing jets of fleshy steam up along their vents. Heavy smoke belched into the air and mingled with the sickly smell of burning meat and bone. A procession of yakoxen carts bearing thousands of men's broken and twisted bodies lined the streets. The unidentifiable remains of men were burned first, followed by those that were horribly mangled. The dead bodies that were held in the arms of their crying families for the last time were pried away and wrapped in canvas. They would be the last to be carted to the smelter to be cremated. The sky filled with smoke and ash, creating a dreary sky under the rising sun as its dull glow arched across the sky.

On the battlefields where thousands lay slain and unburied, large pots of incense burned from one end of the killing field to the other. But it did little in the attempt to disguise the horrible, heavy smell that hung everywhere and clung to everything. Crews with faces drawn in nausea and perplexity, worked around the clock to gather the dead. Those that attended to the departed performed their ghastly duty with a kind of graceful obligation to their fallen Edawnian brothers, which released them any indignity. Scores of scribes walk through the open graveyard among the dead. Writing in some detail, they accounted for and tried to identify the victims of the bloodiest scene of carnage ever recorded. For generations to come, this would be forever remembered as the day when the lands of Edawn wept with the blood of men.

Huge pits had been dug and filled with anything that would burn. Then bodies of the countless were thrown into the fire pits, that their ashes may mingle with the natural dust of the Ziaian earth. It was a particularly gruesome task. Every time a rotting, maggot filled corpse was moved, an awful, gut wrenching, gaseous stench came belching out. If that was not bad enough, disgusting body fluids seeped from the decomposing corpses. The gruesome stiffness of the bodies made it easier to load them onto the wagons and carts. Yakoxen were used to drag the swollen carcasses of the horses that were laid next to their riders in separate fire pits. No one spoke; everyone simply stared into the flames. They had never seen anything so unbelievably tragic in their lives. So many dead, in the prime of their young lives. The promise of their powerful potential never to be regained. The crushing weight of all those deaths left no one untouched. Some that did not even know the dead fell to their knees and wept.

From every horizon that bordered, Edawn land troops began to arrive from the North, east, and west to join the southern kingdoms in ever swelling ranks. Throughout the day, Xylenian forces increased in numbers twofold each hour. The crowds were beyond description. And yet the armies kept coming. They came from near and far. They come from local hamlets, neighboring colonies, and distant kingdoms all over the Ziaian world. The true Xylenian patriots had voluntarily left their peaceful homes and families to come to a miserable land of death and gloom by the tens of thousands. Around the kingdom, the arriving troops were busily setting up over crowded camps as tent cities of thousands of canvas shelters sprung up everywhere. It seemed that there was no way the Edawnian lands could hold more. And still, the armies kept coming from every direction. Food courts were set up with tables that held enough food to supply the immense growing armies around the clock. But very few that had seen the devastation had an appetite to eat. On the beaches, the flood of supplies continued to pour in at all hours of the day from the transport ships. Dock cranes worked none stop unloading heavy equipment, and supplies.

Within the kingdom's walls, a knot of the noblest of Noble Kings surrounded their Emptor King Ozzdon as he quickly took charge bringing the Ministry of defense to order. "We must all now do some tough thinking. The outcome of words and a strategic plan is in this council. But the ultimate outcome of this war will be in the hands of our troops, so let us be quick with our words. There was an overwhelming rumble of agreement throughout the gathering. The unified voice of confidence in their Emperor-King bolstered Ozzdon's courage despite the long shadow he was casting. Still shaken but in full control, the king continued, "What Baddlock wants, he will do anything to get. It is clear that he does not care what he destroys, who he corrupts, who he murders, or mutilates to make sure of it. Total retaliation, at all cost, is the only path Baddlock and the stains of maggot defecation that have chosen to follow him have left us!" His words came in fuming, measured tones. "Thankfully, this day, the Celestial has empowered us to stand against evil. We must now do not what we want but what we must. When a transgression of this magnitude goes unpunished, the world is left broken. When an immoral wrong is unavenged, the Heavens look down on us with reproach. No one knows how long we will live, nor when his time comes. All that we will leave behind our short lives will be the honor, pride, and the respect those that come after us will feel when they remember our names."

A chant of unanimous agreement rose from within the group. Speaking slowly and deliberately, the Emperor-King continued, "You are here, as I am, for no greater reason than to defend our way of life and to protect those that we love from the despicable evil that has come upon our lands. You like I am here to stand up to deliver justice. You are here because you men of nobility want nothing less than to eradicate this malignancy that threatens to infest the whole world of Zia." Every ear and heart hung on King Ozzdon every word. "Now is the time for Baddlock and his misguided misfits to account for the unprovoked atrocities they have so mercilessly inflicted barbarity on countless innocent and helpless people. He has returned to the ancient fortress of the beguiled seekers of darkness. We must strike at the heart and pull them out at the root like the weeds that they are. The terrain is treacherous, and Phantomsdeep's defenses are formidable. Baddlock and his forces will be at their full force there, armed with weapons that will inflict great losses upon us. Zandor will take command of the kingdoms of the West, Kondor, the kingdoms of the East, Tydron, the kingdoms of the South, and I shall command the Northern Armies. And together, we shall grind these festering, cankerous sores into the dirt until hell is the only place left for them to hide."

Meanwhile, in the deepest recesses of Zia, Izz was riveting his attention, as he stretched his torch up as high as it would go. But he saw nothing, but the suspended darkness. The dismal light of his feeble torch sought out the source of the movement but did not come close to reaching its source. There was something there moving like ebbing waves on a skyward sea of inkiness in the darkest night. As Izz peered anxiously, the strange, intensifying noises continued to emanate from the blackness. Sounds that ranged from clicks, ticks, smacking, to whispering trills similar to that of descending wings, amplified. Then, as the sound of flight grew louder and louder, all at once, a black shadow of a cloud began to descend from above. The reddish tint of flashing teeth reflected off of Izz's torchlight. The black on black cloud began to spread as though it were burning from within.

Zuree, who had still been waiting for her stomach to calm down, felt her heart jump to her throat. She would have screamed, but her voice was locked, clogged in her throat. Only a high pitched wail managed to escape. Izz swept his torch along the cave floor, revealing massive piles of droppings. Each heap was seething with millions of shimmering, black dung eating beetles. To add to the frightening ambiance unfolding all around them, the crawly creatures were now trying to crawl up their legs. Zuree leaned back against Izz's shoulder. Her lips soundlessly moved as she drew a shaky breath. Out of the darkness, something brushed her face and fluttered away. Something warm and furry. Zuree suddenly let out a blood curdling scream that unnerved Izz as he waited for something too horrible to imagine to come upon them. The creepy chittering sound soared and reverberated off the walls as both swatted away slimy crawling bugs that were climbing up their legs.

Unknown to Izz and Zuree up above in the recesses of the cave just beyond their sight, there were millions of big, furry vampire bats roosting. They restlessly hung from their toes on the canopy of the cave with their dark, slick hided wings folded up tightly around them. Everything about the firry beasts was creepy and scary. From their weird, contorted faces with their beady, creepy, fiery red jeweled eyes and wrinkled, prominent noses right down to the membranous leathery skin stretched between their webbed fingers. Each one was about the length of a man's arm from the armpit to fingertips. Izz and Zuree had, without knowing it, stumbled into the roosting den of the largest concentrated colony of vampire bats on Zia! The entire colony had been suddenly confused by the receding light of the retreating conjunction and the glow of a new sun that had not yet reached its full strength.

At first, only a small shift of the more restless vampire bats began to come gradually into view. Then there was more and more movement, as the first one then ten fluttered down into view then hundreds then thousands. The horror rapidly escalated as the gargoyle like creatures came forth fluttering out of the dark nooks and crannies of the deep. But little did Izz and Zuree know that that was only the initial wave. Suddenly from every conceivable perch, crack, and crevices, there was an erupting movement of yellow, red, and brown hairy bodies. Then tens of thousands burst into flight then hundreds of thousands exploded into a storm cloud of winged bat creatures. All at once, the main wave of bloodthirsty flying rats with all those beating wings were screaming, swooping, and diving everywhere. From their high roost, millions dropped into the lower parts of the chamber as they spread their black, bony webbed appendages to ride the warm currents across the caverns. Their long awaited emergence had been delayed by the passing brightness of the gathering conjunction. But now its disappearance over the horizon triggered the long anticipated exodus of their nightly hunt.

Izz could feel the breeze from what seemed like trillions of wings flapping, with a very unearthly resonance. But he should have fully known that nothing should have dumbfounded him by now. The increasing turbulence swirled from high up the cavern roof and came down to rustle through their hair. Izz felt Zuree shudder and tightened her hold. There, just at the edge of his vision, he could barely make out the ghostly emergence of the main colony pouring from the upper ceiling like black smoke from a raging firestorm. Dense plumes of flying mammals spiraled into the lower cave, departing in a mass exodus for their nightly search for blood. At first, the main flow made its way toward the quickest exit only to encounter the strange intrusion of Baddlock and his men. The sound of stomping boots and howling Slewsnouts, along with the flashing torches, caused the colony bank in the opposite direction. In their wildly unpredicted flight pattern, Izz noticed the horde of bats flying back closer and closer toward them. Then more and more of the small, furry creatures converged out of their usual pattern of flight. On their alternative flight path, they began rushing past on muffled wings.

Izz stepped forth as the first of the storm passed close

enough to let him feel the brush of their wings against his face. Izz cringed and felt a fierce sense of impending disaster as some dreadfully scary vampire bats who had young lashed out in angry agitation at the intrusion. A dense swarm of blood crazed bats whirled and shrieked above the two in a synchronized confrontation. Their upheaval escalated like an enormous swarm of killer bees around their disturbed hive. The onslaught of angered, blood hungered beasts was everywhere, bounding in and out in frightful swoops from every side at once. They could feel their hair being tugged and felt the pouncing bats scraping over their heads. With their razor sharp teeth, angry bats cut nasty little gashes on any exposed skin. Zuree cried out. Her voice was brittle with panic. Clicking little jaws filled with flashing, sharp blades, screeched and shrieked like an ever maddening storm. It was a chaotic nightmare. The creepy encounter of violently flapping wings and swift, razor sharp slicing fangs left both overwhelmed. Izz pressed Zuree against the wall, lamenting for having taken this route of escape. Zuree cried out again, and again, "They are everywhere!" as Izz tore the beastly blood drinkers from her.

The swarm continuously emitted high pitched squeaks from their spiky toothed mouths. As one bat after another was slapped from raw, red wounds, teeth snapping angrily bore their enraged grimace. The massive throngs were all over them, striking at their faces as they screeched on passed. Suddenly pain knifed up Izz's arm from the wrist of his hand as razor sharp teeth bite deep. He snatched his hand back, reflexively trying to wiggle the vicious creature off. The varmint lost its grip, fell to the ground, and Izz stomped on it as it squealed and squirmed and bit at his boot. He clamped his teeth on his lower lip until the excruciating pain subsided. Both had endured at least a dozen inflicted bite wounds, from each of which blood began to stream. The vampiric fiends used the fleshy, strange outgrowths around their mouth's lower lip as grooves so that their tongues could then suck the blood up as they frantically clung on with their sharp, curved claws. Izz's hands were slippery with blood as he scrapped the trembling, razor sharp fangs away from Zuree. All the while, he was trying to ignore the pain of horrible the needle like teeth and claws that were cutting through his clothes and had begun to gnaw and suck on his blood. With sharp teeth snapping a fingers breadth from her face, Zuree screamed, "They are eating us alive!" All the while, trying to contain the cries of pain and horror, she could not help. Her greatest fear was that her screams would lead Baddlock straight to them.

Izz incessantly batted away at the blood feeders with his blade and swatting them away with his torch. But for every few he scraped away, more razored teeth rushed in to redden their nasty little maws on their blood. No matter how valiantly Izz fought back, the unholy monsters were not going to let up. In Izz's incoherent struggle to resist, he refused to yield, urging Zuree to fight the torrents of attacking bloodsuckers. She would have fought on, but her arms and legs were overburdened and ineffective. Zuree felt so tired, and at this point, what did it all matter. Trembling, she stooped into a crouch and in doing so, lost her balance. She was very close to throwing up, on the verge of fainting. Zuree fell and rolled up into a fetal position. Her face came in contact with something furry. She would have been utterly horrified had it not all seemed so far off and illusory. In Izz's losing battle as if drawn by an unseen hand, he stumbled across a crack in the stone wall. He instinctively shuffled Zuree into the crevice and shielded her with his own body from the onslaught.

As he warded off as many flying rats as he could with his torch, Izz pulled a blood sucking creature off his neck. A chunk of his flesh tore away with the nasty little bloodsucker. Through it all, Izz had managed to hang on to his trusty dagger for the time being. With Zuree safely out of harm's way, in blind desperation, he wielded his blade and wildly struck at the attacking squall. Izz sliced bats out of the air in mid flight and kicked them away from him as they fell relentlessly, snapping their teeth in their last throngs of death. Vampires with crumpled and tattered wings dragged themselves away clumsily as flesh eating beetles swarmed over them. The dead, rat like, winged creatures with their; spiny backs, long pointy ears, sharp fanged teeth, and their weird, buggy red little eyes looked more revolting dead than alive.

Trembling with disjointed thoughts, Izz gathered the last of his energy to lash out at the vicious creatures that endlessly swirled all around them. He thrust his bloody dagger again and again and again as darting bats dove down at him with their razor keen teeth. One after another, the cries of slain bloodsuckers became fading shrieks of agony, and then slowly but surely died away. Izz intermittently wielded his dagger until it hung in his leaden and useless hand at his side, seemingly too heavy for him to raise. He backed himself up against the cave wall to keep himself from falling. Izz watch in astonished surprise as the main bat wave suddenly formed itself into a huge long, twisting snakehead. The cluster of shadows then forged a fist like a flood extending along the length of the cavern. Within moments the horizontal mass thickened into a tornadic swarm that began to pour out through an alternative passage on some sudden exodus. It was an unbelievably awesome and spectacular phenomenon to witness. Izz's view was suddenly eclipsed as it seemed that the entire bat colony began to fly across his field of vision. The massive departure darkened the cavern the more, and the draft it created almost extinguished Izz's torch. The entire colony began to disperse in one direction, screeching and clicking, driven by their delayed, primal instinct to feed. Millions and millions of bats disappeared into the shadows pouring out of the roost, looking like a black deluge silhouetted against the darkest night sky. Within a few minutes, the elongated black smoke like a cloud of flying mammals trickled into a receding stream. When the chamber finally cleared, Izz came forth from the entrance of the hollow to surmise the situation. He turned to Zuree and offered his hand as she had just begun to regain her equilibrium. Izz's voice rose with overflowing excitement as he beckoned, "Come, we must leave this place immediately."

Still, not quite altogether, "Leave where?" Zuree moaned in a voice thoroughly vexed as she threw Izz a questioning look.

And then she followed his pointing finger with her eyes to where the bat colony had disappeared. Izz took a deep breath before answering. "The bats, they know the way out. We must follow the bats." He finally responded in a gruff whisper.

Knowing that Baddlock and his murderous band was sure to enter the bat cavern at any time, Izz wielded his torch toward the path they had come. As the torchlight lit a path across Zuree's face, he saw resignation fixed on her beautiful features. Still shaking, she looked into the depth of Izz's eyes, wishing she had only half of his endurance. His dark eyes made him seem invincible as they challenged her to gather her strength. Zuree stood, wobbly on her feet. "I think I am going to be sick!" Zuree managed to whimper a moment just before she proved herself right.

After giving Zuree a moment to relieve herself, he asked, "Are you all right?" She nodded still lightheaded, but less so. Izz urged, "We have precious little time."

Having heard the looming Slewsnouts, Zuree could not see that she had any choice but to agree. Shuddering, where she sat, she frantically massaged her numb legs and feet until sensation returned. She frantically tried to stand on her quivering legs, but when her knees threatened to buckle, she was forced to sit back down. Her body reminded her of how punishing the ascent had been. Her muscles were almost too taut and sore from the climb to let her move. "Give me a moment." Zuree woefully mumbled. Her voice was a feeble croak, yet it managed to echo off the stone walls around them.

Izz continually peered back from where they had come, unable to shake the feeling that at any moment, Baddlock and his men would reach the entrance to the vast cavern and come crashing in on them. The twisted expression of exhaustion on Zuree's face was very painful to look upon. But Izz did not have a moment to spare on empathy. To hesitate, meant sure death or worst. The deranged baying of the Slewsnouts stalking them could be heard coming closer and closer. A wild, hunted look flashed in Izz's eyes as he seized Zuree under the arm and like a madman, unceremoniously hauled her up on her feet. Zuree felt as if she could not possibly put one foot in front of the other. Her feet seemed to drag along as Izz guided her forward. Gradually renewed strength coursed through Zuree's blood vessels, as Izz clasped her hand. Their hands locked as he shepherded her forward. Zuree had no vigor left for running but somehow found her footing and began to quicken her steps in tow. When Izz paused to fix his bearing on the exiting bat swarm, the torchlight shone on his arms, Zuree gasped, "You are bleeding!"

Izz had numerous bleeding cuts and scratches on his face and arms. The injuries were not severe enough to cause blood to flow freely, but only to trickle slowly. "I do not have time for a little bleeding," Izz said as he tugged on Zuree's hand and led her toward the tunnel the bats had taken.

Baddlock's approaching steps sent pebbles cascading down, the incline, scattering to tumble among the rocks below. The distant sound marked the Wicked Warlock Wizard's path of advance. The thought of Baddlock's revolting presence transformed Zuree's repulsion into revived energy and did not hold Izz back any further. "I will follow anywhere you lead come what may." She said without a second thought.

For a fleeting moment, Izz stood at the entrance of the threatening unknown through where the last of the bats were disappearing. He suddenly got the strangest feeling, just like the one he felt when he had entered the subterranean world for the first time. Izz listened to the distant fluttering of the millions of receding wings as their sound wove a backdrop into the foreboding dread that bubbled deep in his primitive subconscious.   H   e looked frantically around carefully but saw nothing to fear, yet fear coursed through him the more.

"What is wrong, Izz?" Zuree asked in a distressed voice.

"Nothing... I was just wondering why the bats came this way and not the other more obvious way from where we came." It was a mystery that was left unanswered. Izz guessed. "It is as if they are evading some unspeakable predator." Izz tightened down on Zuree's hand and pulled her along as he followed the path the bat cloud had taken into the mysterious darkness of the tunnel.

No sooner had Izz and Zuree disappeared into the tunnel when Dandork, Darkon, and a few other Norticlan warriors entered the cavernous bat den followed by Baddlock. Huffing and buffing, Baddlock asked between gasps, "Where have they gone?" he raged. "Bring our best Slewsnout tracker forward immediately."

The lead trackers were brought forth, drooling through forcefully gritted teeth, sniffing and dribbling like rabid dogs searching out Izz and Zuree's scent. However, the subhuman bloodhounds could not seem to pick up their trail in the guano filled cavern. The rest of the contingent entered the bat cavern, with their torches blazing, and their Slewsnouts howling, whining and snorting. The echoing sound of the imminent threat seemed to kick Izz in the stomach as it entered his hearing. Suddenly confused, Izz lost his bearing. His nerves were rattled and threatened to unravel as each echoing sound seemed to be coming from everywhere. He felt his frustration rising as he looked frantically around for the escape route. Izz knew he needed to calm down, he told himself as he stared outwardly into the murky gloom. He was confronted with several openings branching off in different directions, and he had no clue which way to run. Izz could feel the throb in his temple, and his vision seemed to pulsate with every thundering thump of his heart. He looked to see if Zuree was all right. Her blue green eyes were shadowed with dread. If anything happened to her, he did not know what he would do. "There has to be one way out," Izz insistently said as he kept sailing the flame of his torch before him. Just then, he spotted a straggling bat as it whizzed by. "This way!" Izz pulled Zuree forward purposefully.

The tunnel wound, turned, and at long last emptied into another large chamber. Izz saw the tail end of the bat exodus disappearing up through the ascending center of an almost perfectly circular vent. Izz hurriedly led Zuree toward the midpoint of the chamber. Izz was intently looking up to mark the bats exiting path somewhere through the faintly lit ceiling. As Izz was anxiously staring up, something like divine providence stopped him dead in his tracks. Izz gasped at the unexpected terror that abruptly seized him by the roots of his spine. He stood frozen there, pressing back against Zuree's advance. Iced over, shuddering, teetering, and tottering, daring not to move a muscle.

Confused, he wondered why his foot refused to take the next step. Why had he inexplicably been suddenly seized by such absolute fear? Then Izz looked down! So fixed was he that he did not notice the sheer drop he was about to step off. With no way of knowing they had unexpectedly run up to the sheer edge of what was the yawning drop of an ancient volcano vent. Horror filled every fiber of his being as he precariously balanced himself between life and sure death. He suddenly felt as if his stomach was floating in his chest. For a fleeting moment, his liver and spleen within seemed to dangle on their connecting ligaments. A free floating sensation shifted around as if attempting to rebalance. Izz dare not even breathe as he felt the certainty of death shoot from the tips of his toes to the top of his head. And then seep deep into his groin and tighten around his buttocks. Ever so carefully, Izz arched back and held his arms out, still tottering for a hair raising moment. He eased back, pushing in reverse to block Zuree from pressing any closer.

After backing off, Izz cautiously glanced down and found himself standing on what looked like the brink of a bottomless abyss. Izz's lips parted, and an odd little sound of shock shuddered from his throat as he withdrew farther, stumbling backward in heart quaking in terror. Just one more fingers breath and that would have been the end of both of them. Once he had backed Zuree away to a safe distance, Izz cautiously edged himself toward the gaping vent shaft as he pushed Zuree even further back. A wave of lightheadedness rolled over him as he craned his neck over the rim of the drop off with his lungs still gasping, his heart still thundering. Izz looked up and then down as he blinked and squinted with strained eyes. He carefully turned his gaze to look up, searching for the top of the vent only to realize there was no way up and no way down. Above he saw the last of the bats disappearing through the vast throat of the volcanic vent. He quickly looked around. They were in a large vaulted chamber with no exits except for the vent and the opening they had come in through. He suddenly concluded the worst had befallen them. They were trapped! "Impossible!" Izz groaned inwardly to himself, as he shook his head in disbelief.

Zuree could see in Izz's face the unmistakable look of dejection. Somehow he had lost his protective armor, his endurance, and his faith all at once. That same inner brokenness began to trill through her own heart. Going up or down or back were not options. Every way of escape was closed. Suspended where he stood, Izz knew he had pushed his luck as far as it would go. And now, where were they to turn now that they had gone too far? Escape was a foregone conclusion, and that forced Izz to the next conclusion that was frightfully alarming. It all meant that they were as good as dead or probably worst; this was not as much an intuitive conclusion as it was a rational one. Still gulping for breath, his senses numbed with exhausted resignation, Izz had been slashed through the guts one too many times. That's how it felt. An overwhelming feeling that something terrible was about to happen rattled over Zuree. Disheartenment sent tiny cracks that shattered into a million fragments throughout the loose ends of her feeble willpower to go on. Feeling suddenly weak, Zuree ponderously inched toward Izz. With a voice that was close to cracking, she asked, "Izz, what will we do? I would rather know the worst."

A half hearted smile played across Izz's parched lips, contradicting the forlornness so apparent on this face. For the longest time, the knot in Izz's throat would not let him speak. Panic clogged his senses. His expression grew dark, and then he fell silent and downcast. He just stood there deflated, lamenting with bitter disappointment, with his shoulders slumped as he stared down into the abyss. Why did misfortune seem to ambush them at every turn? There was afar away look in Izz's eyes as he carefully took stock of the vaulted chamber trying to decide what to do next, which way to go. He was standing at the edge of the drop, but his heart was down there, somewhere at the bottom of the deep chasm. There was no place to advance, no place to retreat. Izz's heart made a hollow thump of defeat, almost stopping with the awful realization that there was nowhere to run, and he knew he could not hide it from Zuree. Acutely aware that they were hopelessly boxed in, a haunted look, hollowed his eyes that stared out blankly at nothing. Updrafts of warm air currents rose to the roof of the volcanic chamber to thrash black strands of hair about his face. As Izz stared into the vent that burrowed into the center of Zia as deep as the heavens were high, he suddenly somehow realized it was the same vent from which he had fallen. Below Izz thought he could make out the web in the depths. At the lowest pin point, bright flashes of magma, little more than a blotched pool of molten rock, waited for his fall. It's wavering pressure boiled with sizzling noises, as gases erupted with wisps of caustic, yellow white smoke.

Hoping against hopelessness, Izz looked up, anticipating some magical path of escape, some inkling of expectancy. High above, beyond the shadows, he could see around puncture hole through poured dim rays of light filtering down. The thin stream of illumination that shone straight to the bottom of the abyss was the sole link to Zia's upper crust. From this point, the sheer vertical vent was the cavern's only alternative entrance and exit to the outside world. How could they possibly get around this? Despairing certainty once again crashed in. They were hopelessly cornered, stuck somewhere between the ends of heaven and hell. From a distance, the bloodcurdling baying of slobbering Slewsnouts and the sound of stomping boots resounded throughout the adjoining bat roost. Izz glanced instinctively toward the way they had come. Zuree's eyes followed his gaze. The encroaching sound was still a ways off, yet it echoed all through the stone walls all around them. Time was not on their side. At once, Izz felt that all too familiar foreshadowing of overwhelming panic and doom once again coursing through his mind, stalking him like a death sentence. But this time, what he felt went beyond fear. He was ready to die a hundred deaths. His fear beyond fear was for Zuree.

Having heard the distant footfalls, Zuree felt a bewailment began from the pit of her bowls. *I am very afraid!* Her lips were parted as if a scream were about to boil up and wail forth. But before Zuree could utter a sound, Izz quickly silenced her with a long, deep kiss sealing her lips. "Do not fret, so Zuree," Izz whispered across her trembling lips.

Frantically Izz returned quickly to look up and down the vent trying desperately to formulate a plan that had no existence. Izz recklessly scoured the lower perimeter walls, here and there, high and low for an escape route down. But all he could focus on was the memory of how he had fallen. He knew that Zuree was quite incapable of climbing. Again and again, only black clouds of forlornness rose up from the depths bringing up with it feverish desperation that completely and utterly exhausted his strength and disjointed any shred of endurance.

In the remoteness of the bat roost where they had come from, the bat dung covered ground offered Baddlock's party a cloaked scent to follow. Hysterically the manhunters searched throughout an unrecognizable labyrinth of stone corridors that honeycombed its background. The Slewsnouts hurried along from side to side madly, trying to pick up a track on their prey's scent through the shadow haunted cavern. It would be just a matter of time before they were discovered. Nothing mattered now except for the precious, fleeting moments left to them. Izz's body trembled, and his heart shivered. The despair he felt was unbearable as if some demon's talons were squeezing down on his throat, while mercilessly driving a slowly twisting dagger into his heart. And in the back of his mind, he could have sworn he had heard the princes of fools laughing. Izz's broken heart imploded, shaken to the depths of its core. He could find no solace. NO! There had to be a way out. There just had to be. Discovering no solution, Izz once more abandoned his last vestiges of hope that just seemed to keep bouncing back into his heart again and again. And sure enough, it came bouncing back one last time. For the last time, he desperately looked around, deliriously trying to figure out what if anything he could do. Suddenly overcome in a monumental moment of wretched anguish, and incredibly insurmountable uncertainty, something inside of Izz snapped. Izz ran his fingers through his dirty, tangled hair. And then unexpectedly reached his arm out, and allowed the torch to roll off his fingertips into the recess of Zia's deepest interior. Izz watched in helpless dismay as the torch tumbled end over end until its light disappeared into the depths. Seeing this, Zuree gasped, "What have you done? They are coming this way, Izz! Zuree croaked in utter confusion. We have to save ourselves!" Then her voice started to quiver as it waned, "What will we do without a light?"

"It would have only led them straight to us." He whispered. Izz turned, looking more lost than she felt. She could tell from the look of despair that broke across his face that things were bad, really bad. Izz said nothing more, but through his silence, Zuree could sense his inconsolable heartbreak. Unable to bear her seeing him this way, Izz's gaze twisted away as he deliberately tried to hide his desolation. He closed his eyes for a moment, weary even of breathing. Zuree reached for Izz shrinking against him from behind. She wrapped her arms around him, put her head gently on his back, and whispered, "There must be something…"

Izz shook his head with resignation, "You do not want to know." Izz said in a strangled, almost inaudible whisper that faded with crushing anguish. In his rising desperation, for a time that lengthened for too long. Izz thought of throwing himself and Zuree into the abyss. Anything would be better than letting Zuree fall into Baddlock's hands. The creeping thought leaned him farther and farther over the edge until with a start; he shook off the unspeakable notion. No—that would have been the coward's way out. Besides, he knew too well what waited for their souls down there. Realizing the end was just around the corner, he seized the here and now. Izz gasped a deep breath, turned and drew Zuree by the arm, and pulled her into the shadows. He hoped that the darkness would somehow conceal them, offering them more time. But by now, the light source from the returning conjunction was shining almost straight down the vent much brighter than before. In a harsh whisper, unable to keep hopelessness from his voice Izz lamented, "It is over!"

"What can we do?" Pleadingly Zuree looked up into Izz's eyes. There she found only a mortified look in Izz's eyes that merely unsettled her furthermore. "There has to be away. We need to find it...before...it is too late." Zuree mumbled. But it was already too late, and as of that moment, any illusionary hope only seemed would prolong the agony of the inevitable.

Izz choked up with a woeful response like an echoing that emanated from the craterous void in his soul "Grow wings." Was all Izz could think of saying at that moment. He tried to laugh, attempting to lighten the grim mood, but there was nothing funny about it.

From the near side of the bat roost, the onrushing, savage barking of the advancing Slewsnouts sounded from the next chamber. Behind them came the muffled footfalls against the stony ground striking a hard warning like the rumbling drumbeats of foredoom, loss, and defeat. The two of them ensnared like two doves with their feet caught in the same trap. They only stared blankly at each other in inconsolable silence. She wanted to beg. *Do something!* Her lips moved without a sound. What could he do that he had not already done? An apathetic smile played across Zuree's lips. Both stood there at a loss for words, not sure what to do next. Izz knew Zuree's safety would soon be threatened. The approaching footfalls made it clear what too quickly would unfold if he did not come up with something fast, very fast. They listened with increasing despair as the insurmountable dangers came closer and closer to discovering them. Baddlock distant voice could be heard shouting, "Check every nook and cranny."

The ever deepening feeling that the end had, at last, come engulfed and overshadowed them like a death shroud that settled down into the depths of their souls. Izz reached out with a special touch and a distinctive glance of compassion. He gathered Zuree into his arms and held her close. They huddled in the semidarkness, attempting to comfort and inspire courage in each other. Her eyes locked with his and his with hers. Izz was numb, stricken by, haunted by the struggle he had fought for life and lost, and his bleakness reflected in Zuree's eyes. Izz's muscles felt depleted, his bellyached, and his throat was so parched that he could barely swallow. His body aches prompted him to remember how backbreaking that fight had been. Zuree's face was smudged, lined with exhaustion, and her hair was tangled in disarray. Her sleep deprived, dark ringed, blue green eyes were so moist and glinting with grief now that she could only barely see Izz. A suggestion of a bittersweet smile played across her lips, eclipsing the trepidation so evident in her beautiful eyes. Something like a pained smile twinkled in Izz's eyes and attempted to drop into place on Izz's face as he brushed a strand of dirty blond hair away from her face. Izz looked upon Zuree at her worst, and still, he loved her with all his heart. Both lapsed into a profound silence as they continued to smile lopsidedly at each other, united by their perplexity, fear, and troubled minds. They could both feel the dark presence of death crowding in on them. As they stared at each other in wary silence, the atmosphere grew strangely hushed. Whatever happened next, they would face it together.

As the planetary alignment came around one more time for its final configuration, the approaching apex of the Great Conjunction drew the attention of sky gazers, astronomers, seekers, rulers, and demons alike, who all waited breathlessly. The phenomenon excited the keenest interest. In the unimaginable dance of interplanetary bodies, no one could predict the orbit pattern each planet would take nor what changes they would bring. But no principalities waited with more expectation than the underworld. At every dark, inner dimensional stronghold where a black, rough hewn, round stone stood polished as smooth as a precious gem they waited. A red electromagnetic fog covered the aura of each black marker of damnation. Around each Black Altar, powerful dark energy crystals were placed strategically, encompassing the altars in signs of every spiritual wickedness. The stonework glowed, signaling the expected moment when vast expanses of space shifts would trigger a complex series of events. Events that could momentarily interrupt the space time continuum, from the whirl of the tiniest molecule in the microcosms, up to the spiraling of the vastest galaxies in the universe. The alignment, in turn, was believed would open the receiving and sending vortexes throughout the darkest corners of the super cosmos. Everything could forever be changed in an instance.

Descending like a gathering storm, multitudes of Abaddawn's multidimensional legions continued to assemble and lay in wait at the center of each spacious domed enclosure. Each altar station was a defiled chalice ever filling of vile evil, whirling with wickedness. Endless spiraling plumes of liquid fire continued twisting down toward the lower underbelly of utter oblivion. The fallen sat on their haunches, flashing their teeth at each other. Frothing, wailing, and hissing while they watched, and they waited. It was the pinnacle time for the conjuration of conjurations in the wickedest sense of the word.

At the same hour, Ammiz was once again in his study with his countless charts, calculations, and diagrams before him getting caught up with his work. Only reluctantly having left the wounded after being reassured that they were in the capable hands of the fleet's medical staff. Only then had he been persuaded to take a desperately needed rest. Ammiz knew he badly needed to rest, but instead, the way maker, true to his nature, returned to the odds and ends of his reckoning, probabilities, and possibilities. He sat there wondering about Izz. It had been three days since he had descended into the belly of the beast, and Ammiz questioned what his circumstances were by now. He felt a seed of tribulation he could no shake sprouting deep within his soul. He noted his frustration but not the reason and began to wonder if Izz was safe or even still alive. He raised a hand to his face. There were still traces of blood from the many wounded he had attended still encrusted under his nails. His hand began to shake uncontrollably.

Ammiz turned his thoughts back to his computations as his concern for Izz ran in and out of the back of his mind. He needed to know the exact time the Great Conjunction would reach its pinnacle or at the very least, an accurate approximation. The seer revisited his latest predictions scattered across his desk. It was like a jumbled jigsaw puzzle with hundreds of pieces that needed to fit together in only one way. He focused his concentration, trying hard to riddle the conundrum bouncing around in his mind and trying to align his spirit with the vibration of the approaching conjunction. Suddenly a pattern of connections sparked and interconnected from some unknowable source of understanding. Out of his reasoning, a pattern sparked a link between several calculating mechanisms and observations he had committed to memory. Out of nowhere, a true and full understanding became crystal clear in his brilliant mind. Ammiz whispered, "The Great Conjunction will come to its zenith during Zia's next rotation." No sooner had the revelation come to the visionary when he felt the stable hand of foreboding reach out and grip him. He keenly sensed Izz's mysterious presence and knew somehow that he was in grave danger and was about to meet with some tragic calamity. Ammiz shuddered at the image in his mind as he uttered, "Great Creator of all things, I come to You with heart bowed. I ask You for Your divine protection for the young carpenter. Surround him with Your divine hedge of fortification. Encompass him about with Your strength." Then his thoughts returned to Izz, "Young master never, never, ever, surrender!"

As Izz and Zuree prepared their hearts for the worst, neither could ever begin to imagine any vestige of hope left to them. All hope receded, sucked away by the bizarre hopelessness of their encroaching circumstances. The blood from their faces completely drained as the gravity of their grave predicament slew them. As they huddled ever closer together, awaiting the unfolding tragedy to sweep them away. Zuree whispered, "Hold me tight!" There was a pitiful plea in her voice.

Izz squeezed Zuree tight as if being closer to her would somehow make everything right. His clinging embrace sent an intense rush of courage surging between them. Zuree felt the power of his love, and it sustained her in her greatest moment of weakness. Clearly, at a loss for words, numbed by the reality of the situation, Izz fumbled for some last words. He opened his mouth.

His voice forsook him. All thoughts of comfort failed him. Izz knew any words of consolation would not lessen the terrifying truth of what was about to occur. He let a few moments pass in mute grief. Again he tried to speak, raising his chin slightly; only his lips trembled. His faith, energy, and will had already gone further than humanly possible. He could barely think what he thought much less say it, but it was useless pretending otherwise. Choosing his words very carefully, Izz forced himself to put into words slowly and very carefully, in a hushed whisper, "It will all..." He struggled to steady the quaver in his voice, "It will all be over soon." He finally said mournfully. His voice resounded with a gloomy note of finality. He grimaced and tried to control his runaway emotions.

Zuree sensed the depth of his heartache and said nothing, but only rested within his arms and nodded mutely. Izz finally broke down as he spoke of his overwhelming happiness of spending his last moments on Zia with her. Understanding the concept of eternity and that consciousness would survive the death of the body, he said, "My last dying wish is that when you reach the afterlife, you will find me there."

"I will seek you out, far and wide, throughout a hundred worlds and an eternity of lifetimes," Zuree vowed. She was somehow mystified, wondering why she was not trembling, lamenting, or shedding frantic tears. She should have at least been grief stricken at a time like this, something, but she only felt numbness. Gone was all the foreboding, along with all the torment. There was not a single trace of fear in their countenance. They were free of any feelings except for the love that they shared. Their last breath on this side of eternity would be peaceful. They held each other for dear life, soul mated in a way that was undying, absolute, and irrevocable, both almost losing sight of the graveness of the moment. If this were to be the last day in their universe, they would make the best of every fleeting moment fate allotted them. Izz took Zuree's hand and squeezed it gently as he lowered his forehead to hers. He closed his eyes and shook his head, a melancholy smile twisted on his lips. "If only..." He did not finish his sentence before his voice deserted him. Izz swallowed dryly and attempted to speak once more. He wanted to say how sorry he was for having let her down. In a throaty murmur, his lips parted, and only a peculiar, mournful noise emerged from his windpipe. Zuree tightened her grip on Izz's hand and squeezed it reassuringly. "It is all right," she whispered, "I do not fault you." And that was the honest to goodness truth.

For a magic moment, everything in the universe felt as it should be, for the briefest juncture, anyway. They shared a beautiful, fleeting moment. Izz held Zuree in a fierce embrace enshrining her closeness as her whole body instinctively pressed against his. Both refused to permit the encroachment of the ugly certainties that were crashing in on them to infringe upon their last bittersweet moments. Both knew the end was overdue, even wishing it would, at last, be over. Why could it not just be over, *why, why, why*? Like drifters in a dream, they lost sight of what was real. It was as if they were entering a bizarre duel world where good and evil existed side by side, swaying back and forth, colliding with triumph and defeat. At least they were together. The beautiful moment had eased their minds, but only for the moment. How could it all have come to such a dismal end? Both took a deep, shuddering breath at the same time as if the whole world of darkness had suddenly forced its way back into their waking continuance. Then Izz remembered Baddlock's soul sacrifice plans for Zuree. The disturbing question he scarcely dared to envision was of what Abaddawn might be capable of doing to her pounded through to his mind. The thought sickened him. He could not bear to think of her suffering. What he felt now for Zuree was dread so voluminous and painful that the sheer anticipation of it was crucifying him. Cold beads of sweat ran down his forehead and burned in his eyes. Izz attempted to reason out by what logic he had managed to console himself. And why should he be at peace with death? As he resisted fear and doubt from the inside out, fear and doubt worked on him from the outside in. He searched to recapture a positive thought, any thought. Vengeance of eternal fire wanted him dead, but he wanted to live. He wanted to scream an angry protest to the Creator. Instead, he prayed. Casting out all fear and doubt, Izz took a leap of faith. "If you truly do exist as Ammiz the Great Seer says you do...Please, please do not desert us, " *Save us or kill us quickly.*

They were still drawing and exhaling breath, and if they were still breathing, they were still alive. And Izz was going to fight to keep them alive with his last dying breath. He abruptly held Zuree at arm's length and suddenly blurted out as if waking from a nightmare within a nightmarish dream. "We were not meant for this. There must be some way. We have only to find it!" He expectantly turned again searching here and there, on the right, on the left, high and low. Looking back from where they came would not have done any good. Again, he looked everywhere, fiercely hoping for some hint of an escape path. He looked up expectantly all along the length of the smooth face of the domed vault. His mind struggled for a way out but found no conceivable escape. Everywhere he looked, the way was closed. The fact was that he had done the very thing he had dreaded the most. He had led them both into a dead end death trap. Guilt hung on his back like a coal black leech. Why could he not just accept the fact that there was absolutely nothing he could do about it now. Exasperated for having hoped against hope, a sense of being misled overshadowed him. Before, there had been only absolute hopelessness. Now, the undercurrent of total betrayal by a God he had put his full trust in slapped him in the face and sucked his soul more rooted into the pit of devastation. His only escape was to admit that there would be no escape. He had dared to believe, dared to hope, only for disheartenment to knock him down again. In an acute fit of desperate frustration, utterly feeling forsaken by fate, Izz reached up and slowly dragged his hand downward, wiping the sweat from his forehead. He stopped his hand at his eyes and whispered, "There is nothing" his hand continued downward and paused again, leaving one eye exposed, *We could run and hide, but they would only hunt us down.* Izz gave Zuree an empty, blank look as if nothing was really of any consequence anymore. His hand moved yet farther down until he held his chin between his thumb, and his fingertips, *I would rather die like a man...here and now, but what about Zuree?* He thought in agony. He would have gladly died a thousand times in her place if only he could He dropped his hand to his chest to wipe the sweat on his grubby tunic. Without thinking, his fingertips felt and traced the outline of the object that hung down from around his neck beneath his garment. A tug of distraction penetrated the fog in Izz's mind when he realized what it was. He smiled weakly to himself. It was his eagle whistle nested against his chest, still bound around his neck. In his haste to leave Edawn, he had forgotten to remove it.

As he rolled it around restlessly between his thump, pointer, and index finger, he felt its emotional attachment. He remembered how many times when he ventured out that his two Crown Crested Eagles would secretly follow him hoping for a treat. For an extending moment, Izz was lost somewhere between where he was standing, and a distant point beyond the remote cavern's depths. His dark eyes were fixed, devoid of any expression. Zuree stared at him blankly. His thoughts were a million Zettas away. Zuree was waiting for him to return from his thoughts when she heard faint voices and footsteps approaching the entrance of the vent and felt a powerful impulse to pulled Izz back into the semidarkness. "Izz they will discover us any moment, what now?"

Izz left her question unanswered. She gasped, feeling more alone and unprotected than ever. Zuree looked in the direction of the voices and caught a glimpse of lights and shadows swarming around the entrance from where they entered. She could feel their evil presence closing in. Their heavy sweated bodies boots stomping, dashing and darting to and fro, and their eyes were wildly searching. An expression of helplessness ripped across her face. "You know the most frightful is not so terrible when it is at last happening." She whispered as she attempted a pained smile.

A grumbled voice pierced the silence, "Search everywhere, leave no stone unturned, no shadow unrobed!"

Suddenly a great weight seemed to close in around them from every direction. The chamber echoed with the sound of

Baddlock, Dandork, and their Norticlan troops. The Slewsnouts were converging in as they came nearer and nearer to discovering them. With a start, Izz shook off the awful lethargy, not realizing how long he just stood there, transfixed. He stood there at the edge of time as if returning from a beaconing spirit world. The thought of Baddlock's approach made Izz's skin crawl. He urgently tried to master his emotions, not wanting to reveal any weakness, but despite his brave front and despite his great effort not to show his fear, he was terrified for her. He reached for Zuree and buried her face into his chest next to his thundering heart. She collapsed against him completely motionless, as she listened to his heart booming in his chest and her own heart answering its call. Somehow she felt safe in Izz's arms. She felt enraptured as if a spell held her. As the atmosphere around them grew thicker with danger with each passing moment, the impending peril only served to increase their love to soaring heights. The moment stirred something in both their souls that would forever refuse to return to its former state. Zuree's fortitude was kindled anew by the life or death love that blazed red hot in the turbulent heart of the man who now embraced her. Izz's body trembled with a strange consolidation of fear and exhilaration, rage, and compassion all at once. Neither wanted to die, of course not, who would, especially not now that they had so much to live for? Izz gallantly tried to pull himself together for Zuree's sake. He cleared his throat, swallowing back his near tears. "We may have but a moment left to us, my love…" His voice sank into a whisper. The utterance of his most profound fears did nothing to elevate either of their bleak state of mind. "But, my eternal love for you will go on living forever." His heart poured out as he felt the tears; he had fought so hard to still form, and fill his eyes. However, because of the profound love woken between them, he was not ashamed to cry. In what might be their last few moments in this world, Izz clasped Zuree's face with his hands in an eternally loving embrace as tenderly as he would the most delicate flower. He drew her face close to his. His tenderness created a little island of solace in the encroaching storm. Through his tears, a smile glimmered in his eyes. "I will never forget how beautiful that day was when my eyes beheld you for the first time."

As Zuree recalled the day and the moment Izz spoke of, she cried a tear, and he gently wiped it away. Zuree reached with her hands and pulled Izz's face yet closer as he gazed down upon her. "I love you Izz. I will always love you." Zuree breathlessly whispered. She surrendered all, merging slowly and unconditionally against Izz, heart, and soul.

Their bodies were still trapped, but their spirits were sent soaring. Well aware that precious time was ticking by, Izz closed his eyes, looking almost as if he was in pain. He covered Zuree's face with one tender kiss after another. The wheels of time stood still, and with every heartbeat, they lived a hundred lifetimes. The moment had room for nothing more, and nothing else mattered. In another space and time, their souls expanded endlessly into infinite dimensions that only the lucky few could have been able to transcend in a thousand lifetimes. True love was the mysterious and sublime grace that could only be shared by two that had become one in the spirit of love. Zuree's stone, which was nested safely against her bosom suddenly, brightened, glowing despite the smudges and grime that covered it. As the stone shone like a miniature sun, its shimmering pulsation tingled against her skin. The amulet brightened until the stone was discernibly beating its pulse of white inner power. The stone's magic filled the air they breathed. Unexpectedly, a sizzling, blue spark jumped, and took flight, and shot out through the vent's opening. Baddlock's excitedly voice reverberated, "There! What was that? Every one this way, now!"

Zuree quickly grasped the stone tightly in her hand to mask its power.

Sixteen
The Dawning

utside, on the surface of Zia, the sun was beginning to rise out of the East. The dawning conjunction was well on its track across the sky toward its appointed pinnacle. Once the six sister planets entered the gravitational pull of Zia, the parent planet, like gigantic moons they entered an accelerated orbit around their sun. What had once been only pinpricks in the vast backdrop of the sky were now billowing globules of bright neon radiated. As planetary alignment approached their imminent apex, their combined light soon rivaled the brightness of that of the midday sun. The closer they came to their vertex, the faster they orbited around the sun, and the quicker they came around again. The celestial indicator of infinite time brightened and further intensified as it entered the final countdown to its ultimate zenith. As the eternal cosmic clock aligned into its pinpoint position, the seven planet's gravitational pull interlocked. Each world began their dance in which one heavenly body existed for all and all for one and the other. In a state of intertwining forces, the combined mass between each body in proportion to their orbit created the teetering possibility of misalignment. There was the potential risk of a negative influence casting all physical matter within its gravitational path into an actualization capable of tearing space and time to shreds. The fixed prance of planetary masses aligned along its integral elliptical path. The impending conjunction entered its most unpredictable state in which it would ever increase its capacity to rip itself apart into a billion fragments, crystallize into one single mass or complete its cycle as it had every thousand years without a hitch. Very soon now, if darkness had its way, a fissure in the order of the megacosm could potentially strike a note in the symphony of heaven that was never meant to be. It would be a cosmic upheaval, one that could eternally swell to the ends of time, and resound to the ends of the universe. Either way, for the minutest fraction of time, gravity, the unseen force that rules over the galaxies would hold the seven sisters firmly in place in which time anything could happen. It was fully believed by those imprisoned in the underworld, according to the dark secrets from the other side of time without end, that Zuree's blood would set them free. Zuree's bloodstain on the stone marker at that exact moment would trigger the cauterization within the collective conciseness of perpetual darkness. It was believed that this would permit wickedness to disrupt the absolute intricacy of the universal matrix. In that instant in time, for a fractured instance the powers that kept the darkest demons, bound might be breached. Blood was the most powerful medium in the physical world, and all that was needed was the pure blood of the royal virgin spilled upon the Black Altar of Desolation. And for that fleeting instance, at long last, the oppressive shackles of Heaven would be loosened and cast aside for the briefest flash. A wormhole in the magnetic continuum that protected Zia from total darkness would then be created that would spread from Zia to neighboring worlds. One world after another would fall like domino columns falling throughout the temples of the heavens. Paving the way to and fro, from one forbidden black altar to the other. Chaos would reign as portals along the pathway first made by the fallen who first attempted to overthrow and to rule the womb of the universe.

Back down, below in the bowls of Zia, Izz and Zuree were still momentarily lost in each other's embrace, breathing each breath as if it was their last each counting off the *moments* until they died. Suddenly Zuree felt Izz's spine straighten as Izz abruptly opened both eyes, breaking the powerful spell that emanated from within them. It hurt to be alive. Out of desperation, Zuree cried out to Ammiz's Creator in her agony. In the same instance now that Izz had gotten over the fact that they were both going to die. A gloomy curtain was drawn aside so that Izz was able to think clearly. All at once out of nowhere as if guided by an unseen essence that defies description, a voice seemed to call out to him from above. Sensing the Creator's call, Izz withdrew from Zuree's embrace and for no apparent reason, slowly turned his head instinctively glanced upwards to the top of the vent opening. Zuree tensed when Izz unglued himself from her and turned towards the vent.

Zuree's eyes abruptly followed his gaze as Izz intently stared at the vent's edge with sudden inexplicable hope. In an inspired moment, Izz suddenly froze, with his eyes shifting upward to the farthest reaches of their sockets as if sensing the imperceptible. A great notion came to him. It was something he did not have thoughts or words to explain. Oblivious to Baddlock's encroaching approach, Izz slowly leaned over and craned his neck towards the upper vent in anticipation. His senses gave no reason. Zuree stared at him blankly. There was a longing look in Izz's eyes that unsettled her. She had no idea what he was doing. He just stood here fixed, listening, and staring intently, with a suspended look on his face as if tuning into some spiritual music that only he could hear. It was enough to tear them both from their tempestuous thoughts briefly. Several moments passed, and then Izz shook his head as if it was full of mental cobwebs. And then he nudged over the vent's drop as far as he dared to. Thereupon the mystical call seemed to direct his attention to the vent's soaring opening. Izz was momentarily blinded by the flash of the imminent conjunction coursing down the vent's shaft as the Great Conjunction advanced on its universal path towards its fulfillment. Izz had to shield his eyes with his hand against the intensifying light that shot down through the vent and temporarily dazed him. As soon as he was able to focus, he looked back up the length of the vent. The opening was just a tiny circle above him. It was like looking through a keyhole. Izz scratched a nonexistent itch on the top of his head. In the wake of the approaching conjunction, he imagined that he had spotted the silhouettes of two tiny dots. There, barely visible, two specks as small as grains of sand, hovering and circling at the rim of the vent's opening. Two black points against the ever brightening clear sky circled just beyond the edge of the volcano's overhanging crater. He continued to look up the vent with a sudden new sense of concentration. A faint movement in the sky registered in his mind. It was at that moment that a small, almost forbidden ray of hope first blossomed in Izz's heart. A dark cloud seemed to lift as sparks lit Izz's thoughts like shafts of light from a brightening beacon penetrating the dense fog in the back of his mind. Izz's spirit and soul accepted the fact before *his* mind did. "Do you see what I see?" Izz asked in a voice that was an intense whisper. It was the excitement in his tone that commanded her complete attention.

In the center of his perplexity, his face lit up, and the look of total dejection that had plagued his countenance moments earlier seemed to fall away into the depths of the abyss. Zuree's eyes went to where Izz was focusing but saw nothing. He had a strange expression washed over his face as if he had just become conscious of something. Could it be! That chance was slim, no none. Was it his imagination, a trick of the blinding light, or deception of his distressed hope. The possibility defied reality. They could have been shadows or wisps of smoke. Izz held his breath and was almost afraid to hope too desperately in the face of hopelessness. He was a drowning man reaching for a straw of a chance. It was a crazy, one chance in an infinite likelihood. But when a man is sinking to the bottom of despair, when he is going down in a sea of hopelessness, he will defiantly reach for that straw. Izz's heart leaped as a thought occurred to him, *Could it possibly be, Fina and Bolo?* Izz wondered as he reached down and lightly ran his fingers over the length of his whistle. Cold beads of sweat ran down Izz's forehead and burned his eyes.

Within a leap of faith, a new sense of encouragement began to form in his mind and thunder in his heart. What were the chances that they would be there at that exact time? There was no way but yet, and yet; there was something that was circling up there. Izz fell into a trans like silence. Then he was suddenly hit by an impossible impossibility. His mouth flopped open, as he stared transfixed at the circling specks. His tempestuous hope wanted more than anything to believe that it might be Bolo and Fina circling above, somehow sensing that he was down there. He was struck breathless with his heart wedged in his throat, transfixed. Frantic to believe, his subconscious projected what his extraordinarily keen eyes could not perceive. And his conscious mind filled in the rest, so well that he did not know he was doing it. YES! YES! Getting excited, Izz began nodding his head enthusiastically as his optimism mounted to new heights, "Yes, that is it...It has to be!"

Zuree only stared in wide open mouthed surprise as she had seen his face flicker through an odd range of expressions, from despair to hope. "What is it, Izz?" She asked, unable to keep despair from her voice.

Not quite sure of what to believe, Izz hesitated. There had been too many heartbreaking disappointments. He could not bear the possibility that he might be allowing his hopes to soar only to have them dashed again. Faith was the only pillar that held his crumbling world up, and he began to pray against impossible odds, *Please! Please, let it be!*

When Zuree noticed the flickering of anticipation in Izz's eyes, she dared to feel a glimmer of promise spark within. Hope beyond hope became the new reality Izz could not shake. In that same instant, he could have sworn he heard high pitched eagle screeeeeeeeech and the dull and distant flutter of wings amplified by the hollow of the volcano's opening. Izz had an impulsive explosion of unexpected insight. His immeasurable intuition seeped inwardly through his mind as if following the one path that was their only way out.

All of a sudden, the depths of Zia rumbled as its internal balance was threatened to be pulled off its axis by the gathering conjunction. From the epicenter came a loud grinding and scraping of stone upon stone as tremors shifted deep in the bowls of Zia. Pebbles pelted the heads of Baddlock's troops as white dust filled the air. Strong, sharp ground rolling shook all of Zia's foundations. At the entrance of the vent chamber, Baddlock was pressed with the awareness that the conjunction was fast approaching. The Wicked Warlock Wizard intensified his efforts to locate Zuree, desperate to find the final key that would set chaos in motion and unleash the universe onto its cataclysmic path. A course set in motion that would shake the bedrock of the cosmos and make him master of Zia.

The entire cavern trembled and moaned from deep within the vent, reverberating off its walls, reaching up to thunder from the vaulted ceiling. Narrow cracks appeared in the vent floor, where its vibration rumbled through Izz's boots. Izz precarious footing on the vent's rim became a balancing feat on the knife's edge. At the last possible moment, Zuree pulled Izz back as the ground continued to rumble. The instability of the cavern magnified the uncertainties of the already impending treats. But his unusual thought kept boomeranging back to what he thought could be their only salvation. And so yet, Izz clung desperately to his hope against hope as his spirits continued to lift, and his heart began to race. When the last tremor faded, Izz drew a deep breath, searching for calm, reaching for certainty, trying to align his thoughts. He could hear footfalls and scattered grunts and murmurs closing in on them. The vaulted chamber was becoming increasingly hostile, further reducing their chances of surviving with every passing moment. Baddlock was closing in for the final assault, somehow knowing he had maneuvered his quarry into an inescapable corner. Inwardly Izz's faith was raging. From the outside, his disbelief was crashing in. Izz's conscious mind froze for a moment considering the craziness of the idea that was sweeping over it.

What he hoped he had seen might have been a straw in an infinite sea, perhaps just that. Perhaps his despair was causing him to imagine things, but what did he have left to lose? While crisscrossing his mind for answers, in a state of confusion, a faint undertone in the corner of his skull ebbed a wild shot in the dark. His thoughts ceased to swim about and began to lineup unto the same path. His face suddenly lit up as if he had just remembered something. Before his Doubts could double, Izz grabbed at his last fleeting hope, reaching under his tunic into a concealed breast pocket. With a jittery hand, he fumbled for and found what he was looking for. His jaw tightened, and his dark eyes narrowed as he fished out his eagle's whistle and began to blow on it as hard and as long as he could. Zuree feared he had taken leave of his senses. The blasts echoed off the walls of the volcano vent and rose to the crest of the volcano's crater. The sound waves were picked up by the rising volcanic gases and carried to the volcano's mouth. The sound of the familiar whistle register in the senses of what was ever in the heavens above. Zuree looked quizzically at Izz, and unthinkingly, thought he had fallen off the deep end of desperation. She whispered under her breath to herself, "My poor dearest Izz."

The shrilling whistle instantly drew the attention of everyone within earshot. Having heard the whistle blasts, Baddlock dispatched his search party in the direction the whistle had sounded from. "What is that fool doing? Has he taken leave of his senses?" Baddlock asked wonderingly. "He has led us straight to him." All of sudden, out of nowhere, Baddlock was heard to scream, "There! They are over there! My, my, how far the little varmints have managed to run so fast?" However, for the moment, Izz and Zuree were still just out of range of the deadly crossbows. Baddlock continued to scream frantically, "Through here, quickly," as he pointed to the corridor that would lead them to the vent.

Izz and Zuree were at once unnerved by the voice they were horrified to hear. The moment they had awaited—dreaded! Crazy as it had to have seemed, there was nothing left for either to lose. In a leap of faith, Izz put the whistle back to his lips and again boldly blew out one piercing blast after another. Through the twilight from above came an answering screech that only Izz was able to perceive. If not for the keen, far seeing eyes of the birds of prey focusing on what the gathering conjunction's reflecting light beams had illuminated at the deep end of the vent, both might have gone unnoticed to the other.

In amazement, Baddlock questioned, "What is that fool doing? Blowing a toy whistle? Calling us to exactly where he is!" Baddlock laughed out loud. "I will personally reward beyond their wildest imagination, the man who kills that imbecile. But the girl fetch her to me alive and unharmed. QUICKLY!"

From above, the two black dots circled sharply and seemed to maneuver into a fixed, tightening pattern suddenly. As miraculous as it might seem, it was indeed Bolo, and Fina summoned to the vent by a Divine Force. The pair focused their incomparably sharp vision, much keener than any other creature on the face of Zia into the crater far below where they spotted Izz and Zuree. The two masters of the sky circled several times in ever tighter loops, accommodating for the limited opening of the volcanic vent. The pair focused and fixed their maximum concentration on their targets down in the crater far beneath them. Then they pivoted once to set themselves, stiffened and tilted their heads. Dipping their right wings, one after the other, the cloud riders banked sideways. Then in one instance, they both barrel rolled, spiraling quickly and lurched down headlong like dropping for a kill. The fastest creatures on the planet fell into a plummeting dive straight down into a brain numbing plunge. The two tucked in their wings and feet, fixing them rigidly, gravity did the rest. Their descending spiral tightened as they entered into a steep vertical pitch, on the edge of what was possible. The rulers of the sky and mobility thread the eye of the needle, down the throat of the volcano. They pierced the air at a blinding, death defying speed, locking into their stealth, diving form perfected in play and hunting. They shot downward in a straight line, plunging earthward like two falling meteors entering Zia's atmosphere.

The two Descended at lightning speed in their perfect surge, a dual, rushing sound began to drone as the spiraling two fixed their acute tunnel vision on Izz's figure standing at the bottom of the vent. The rushing sound grew until the intonation of their feathered wings was a steady low pitched whirr. The droning increasingly echoed back upon itself from the volcanic stone walls all around, like a stormy wind howling down a funnel. Faster and faster, they plunged, cutting through the thin layers of warm rising smoke as the air screamed past their forms. At an ever increasing speed, fearlessly, they bolted down like lightning from the sky.

And still, they accelerated slashing the air too fast for the human eye to follow. Descending so quickly that Izz's eyes could only move fast enough to catch a streaking blur. They swooped down closer and closer. The sound of the air being displaced by the speeding bolts of feathers, flesh, and bone reached the howling pitch of a growing tempest. As the twosome dove, their slicing flight path smeared long, silhouetting shadows along the vent's walls. Everyone within the chamber heard the amplifying currents of air as they whistled a high pitched shrilled through ruffling feathered wings. Izz and Zuree watched breathlessly as Bolo and Fina's shadows fell across them. Their descent drew closer and closer at an alarming velocity, dangerously close to the end of the vent. As the duo careened towards the bottom of the vent, their wings began to unfold to rein in the air in the vent. Bolo's earsplitting screech resounded from inside the vent and echoed throughout the cavern. What could that unearthly sound be, everyone in Baddlock's party wondered?

Zuree lost her breath in shock when she caught sight of the two descending crested eagles as their great wings blocked out the light. How were they to stop once they reached the chamber? In the flashing light and a flurry of wings, the chamber went almost completely dark. In split second timing, just before crashing Bolo and Fina instinctively pulled out of their dive. They unfurled their enormous wings capturing the air, bellowing to full capacity like the gaping sails of a ship in a blasting headwind. Strong, warm, dry whirlpools of air wafted outward, almost knocking Izz and Zuree flat to the cave floor. They shielded their eyes against clattering turbulence, of voluminous wings and dust. A kind of loud, swishing sound filled the volcanic cavity. At the last possible instant, the eagles spread their mighty, flapping wings wide, suspending themselves upon the air currents to soar around the chamber once in a graceful arc. They slowed for a landing extending their yellow feet and gracefully touching down before Izz as they furled their expansive wings. Izz peered through the fracturing light as it shone through the cloud of dust. Almost in total disbelief, he opened his eyes to see Fina and Bolo standing stationary before him. The two rotated their heads nearly a full turn, as their yellow eyes gazed out from their deep sockets, over their long, curved beaks.

As they adjusted their eyes to the dim light, they took in a panoramic view of the volcanic cavern. Unable to trust her eyes, Zuree was stunned beyond words. Astonishment immobilized her. She could not believe her eyes, but there they were two giant crowned eagles descended from above like a violent storm. She could only stand there frozen where she stood, still, staring with her mouth gaping open in amazement. Izz's eyes grew wide as he excitedly uttered his relief, "Yes! This is it." At first, Izz whispered the thrilling words, then he almost shouted them at the top of his lungs, piercing into the gloom, "Yes, yes! This is the answer to my prayers!" Izz repeated over and over again as he threw up his hands and looked skyward in gratitude.

It was a stunning miracle! An unimaginable wonder! Here, at last, was the hope he believed for, a greater hope than he had ever dreamed possible. Izz, once again, was filled with excitement and energy. His eyes radiated back from the shadow of death to sparkling life. As the three life forms eyed each other with chilling mutual respect, Izz jumped towards Bolo the male eagle and threw his arms around his neck, "I am so glad to see you two," as he reached out and stroked Fina's head and neck. Suddenly the barking of the oncoming Slewsnouts jerked Izz's thoughts back to the immediate danger closing in around them. With Dandork in the lead, the Norticlan sharpshooters each carrying powerful crossbows and a fully loaded quiver over a shoulder swiftly moved in. Spinning swirls of dust at their boots drifted across the cave floor as they rushed in. Shouts and footsteps seemed to be coming from all directions. "Shhh," Izz cautioned as he peered out to see Baddlock taking great care to surround the outer perimeter of the volcanic chamber. Baddlock took every precaution to block what he thought was any possible exit, cutting them off from any conceivable escape. The Wicked Warlock Wizard was not about to give the two the slightest opportunity of getting away from him this time. Still, out of the range of their crossbows, Baddlock commanded, "Move up quickly, you dolts!"

Only extreme urgency of the mounting threat prevented Izz from kissing Fina and Bolo from beak to claw. While still holding Bolo around the neck, Izz turned and called, "Zuree come quickly, we have but one chance and one chance alone, but we must act now!"

Zuree did not say a word, just looked up at Izz for what seemed like the longest time. She had no idea what he was proposing. As though someone lost in a stupor, Zuree remained frozen there unable to move as she stared at Izz vacantly. Her face was puzzled. Then the unthinkable registered. Her eyes bulge in surprise, and her face lost its color as she took a step back, and unwittingly shook her head. Her analytical mind reeled in stunned disbelief. With a signal glance, Izz read her conflicting emotions. Her fear was plain to see. "Quickly," Izz pleaded, "there is not much time!" Aware that Baddlock's huntsmen would soon be upon them, Izz implored, "This is the only way…there is…no other way out. It is our only option. It is now or never!" There was a note of desperate urgency in his voice.

Lingering indecisively, Zuree tried to keep her legs still, but they kept backing her away as misgivings assaulted her mind. Zuree gave Izz an odd hesitating look, focusing her stare on his with an expression of, *Are you completely out of your mind*, written all over her face. Then she flashed him a quizzical look as she stammered, "Are you joking?" Her voice was almost breaking. *You had better have a different plan in mind.* She was thinking.

What Izz was suggesting frightened her almost as much as Baddlock plans for her, if not more! It was ridiculous. The only thing slightly more preposterous would have been to suggest jumping into the fiery abyss to escape Baddlock. And if it were not for the graveness of the situation, it would have even been almost laughable. Zuree continued to shake her head in disbelief and only gazed back at him suspiciously, but the serious mindedness in Izz's eyes told her not only that he was not joking, but that this indeed was their very last and only hope. Zuree just stared blankly, attempting to weigh the odds logically. She could not even think about it without a tautness twisting inside her chest. A thousand doubts and anxieties pierced her heart. She was too afraid. "Zuree!" Izz insisted as he extended a pleading hand out to her. There was an unnerved edge of necessity to his voice. "You know I would rather cut out my own heart than hurt you."

She knew she did not have time to wonder whether or not it was a good idea. And even as she resisted, she wanted, needed, demanded Izz to persuade her. She needed the same kind of hope he had. Finally, she grabbed on to hope and yielded to his resolve. She knew she had a choice, take her chances on Bolo, or face a certain horrible death. She almost determined that death would be less frightening, but certainly not at the hands of Baddlock. She drew in a deep breath through her nose, held it for a few seconds then released it through her mouth, knowing that Izz was right. With uncertainty, she grudgingly submitted as she nodded in half hearted agreement. With uneasy eyes, she swallowed hard as she nervously wrung her hands, and approached Bolo with all the courage she could rally. She tried with all her courage to repress her fears.

"He has got a very gentle spirit inside. You have nothing to fear. I assure you." Izz urged encouragingly enough as he stroked Bolo's breast.

"How assuring," Zuree said, trying to keep her voice from shuddering as she began to feel a tentacle of hope.

Izz took Zuree's hand, pulling her in next to Bolo. "Mount him as you would a horse, Izz instructed as he prepared to boost Zuree onto Bolo's broad back, "He will fly you right out of here. You will see."

He did not sound too sure of that. Zuree thought as she cocked her head and shifted her eyes towards the waiting bird. Her stomach was so knotted as her toes and fingers crawled with spider like tingling. She cautiously came closer and felt the overwhelming size and power of the majestic and proud wild beast. Zuree made a face as if she was going to be ill. Bolo was much bigger up close than she expected. She sucked in doubt like a last breath as fear eclipsed her resolve. Two opposing forces struggled madly within her. She looked at Izz and could not help but stared at him as if he had taken leave of his sanity.

"We can stay here and most assuredly die, or take our chances on the eagles!"

Zuree needed a third choice, but there was none. It was either push her fear aside or die an uncertain death. Suddenly at that instant, Baddlock's patrol poured forth, coming into sight. Their torches reflected across the rock formations as their smoke slowly drifted upward. They cast their grotesque shadows over the walls and domed ceiling as they rushed forward. Their path would lead them straight towards the vent as they intently searched out their prey.

"They are almost here! The birds are our last hope!" Izz had not intended to shout at her.

"No! I cannot believe this! It is insanity," she mumbled in a shaky voice, "There is no way you can be serious!" She had every right to be concerned. Zuree sensed a glint of uncertainty in Izz's eyes as he gave her an expectant look. She chewed on her lower lip as she stared at the White Crested eagle with misgivings. She assumed an even stiffer posture as she nervously positioned herself between the two massive birds. The two eagles seemed to sense it too and snapped their beaks with nervous energy. Zuree quickly gathered all the courage she could manage and stepped forward with her jaw set firmly. She distrusted this. But she was going to attempt it anyway as she surrendered to Izz's will, only because it made brutal sense. Zuree could somehow feel his hopefulness pouring into her. It was almost easy to believe Izz while she was heeding his voice and staring into his eyes. It was a slim, almost reckless hope, but the only one left. Izz seemed confident enough. Zuree shut her eyes and breathed in deeply for a moment, trying to reassure herself that Izz knew what he was doing. Izz felt her tremble as she reached her hand toward him. With an encouraging expression pasted on her face, she put her full trust in Izz. She reached out a shaky leg, obediently setting her foot in Izz's interlaced hands, and stepping up. As she almost lost her balance,

"Are you sure that this makes any sense?" She protested weakly, but she knew she had no other real option nor any real excuse. Her anxiety escalated. She sucked in a breath and began to breath faster. She looked down at him; her expression was perplexed. "Izz?" Her voice sounded croaky, frightened, and on the verge of tears.

"Quickly!" Izz urged vehemently.

She was fighting the inertia that weakened her knees. Zuree pressed the flat of her hand against Bolo's big wing and tightened her clinging hold on Izz's neck as she resisted wave after wave of panic. Bolo stood still as she eased one leg over his sizeable bulk, almost not daring to let go of Izz's shoulder. Finally, Zuree disengaged her death grip from Izz. She felt a rippling shudder as she straightened her trembling shoulders and aligned herself on the eagle's broad back. Bolo's muscular back was wider than she expected, and straddling it forced her to strain her legs into a tense, uncomfortable position. The heat rising from Bolo's powerfully built body surprised her. As Zuree mounted her full weight on Bolo, Bolo cocked his head, looking mystified and uneasy as he felt a load on his back for the first time. Bolo twisted his big head around, glancing back at Zuree, catching a moment of eye contact as if in protest. Just looking at the huge bird's sharp beak caused Zuree to lose her breath as her stomach knotted. "Easy Bolo, easy." The one who spoke all the languages of all living things quickly reassured the male bird that this is what was expected of him.

Zuree was desperately making an effort, not to be terrified and failing miserably. Dark thoughts almost forced her to reconsider her commitment, but she said nothing. Zuree dug her fingers deep into the top edge of the bird's feathers, holding on for dear life to the base of Bolo's wings. Izz looked pointedly back at Zuree while sustaining his self assured front of encouragement. His masked eyes were deep pools of unshakable certainty, trying to keep his mounting anxiety in check. As Bolo shifted his balance Zuree weakly frowned in hesitation as warning bells began to blare inside her head. She ignored the tightness in her chest and decided not to resist fate farther. Izz knew that a bird of Bolo's size could not directly bound into flight, especially with the additional weight. The massive eagle needed a running start, tree, or hilltop. The only other logical option was the drop off of the up drafting vent. So before Zuree could realize what was about to happen, Izz hastily maneuvered Bolo to the edge of the abyss. Bolo initially protested leaping sideways, almost unseating Zuree. But Bolo had learned to trust Izz since the time he was an eaglet. Izz forcefully guided the giant bird into a readied position; feet set wide, with its upper body slightly angled downward into the vent. "Everything is going to be all right, you will see." Izz kept assuring Zuree. Izz gently nudged Bolo closer to the edge of the sheer drop off. Zuree groaned. She craned her neck at the last instant to look down into the utter drop. Suddenly the fear of falling filled her breast and knotted in her belly. Izz quickly distracted her for the moment and looked deep into Zuree's blue green eye and said, "Say you believe in me."

"I believe in you. In you is where my only hope is found." She proclaimed, and she tried to smile as she desperately tried to hide her mounting fear.

"Are you ready?" Izz asked.

Zuree hastily brushed at a loose strand of hair that clung to her cheek as she moaned, "Izz, I have a bad feeling about this!" Her voice was shaky and broken. Her nerves were taut like ropes sustaining an overbearing load about to give way.

"This is going to work! I would not let you do this if I had any—real doubts. You will see." Izz insisted.

Zuree felt a crawling trill of antsy like sensations that started from the tips of her toes up to her spine and through her to the ends of her fingers.

"Hold tight!" Izz instructed.

Zuree let out a little whimper. Her back turned ridge, and her heart thundered even harder, pounding out such a savage beat that it was almost painful. She squeezed with her legs and clasped her hands on even tighter. Zuree was as pale and terrified as could be, but she kept her lips turned up in the faintest, broken smile. Suppressing a shudder, she lined up her back, squared her shoulders, and held her head up, trying as best she could to control her overwhelming foreboding. At this moment, the last thing Izz wanted was to knock the bottom out of what little assurance Zuree was groping for. Maybe it would have been fitting for him to mention how potentially dangerous this could be. But as it was, their necks were on the chopping block already. However, he did need to be sure Zuree was ready for the unexpected. "Brace yourself for this one." He admonished, "We cannot be exactly sure how this is going to turn out."

Zuree did not like the sound of that unnerving statement. "I am not so sure this is such a good idea, Izz!" The overwhelming panic was evident in her voice.

"Have faith," Izz reinforced, dispensing any doubts lying in wait in his mind, and quickly moved before Zuree could lose heart. Izz pulled Bolo near, and as he stroked his feathered head with one hand, he pointed to the opening at the top of the crater. Bolo cocked his majestic head skyward, then turned back to Izz as he blinked with understanding.

Zuree's lips moved silently, *This is going to work, this is going to work, this is going to work,* mouthing the words over and over until she almost believed it.

"Just hang on tight, I will be right behind you, trust me." He assured attempting to avert her from hysterically becoming spooked in the final moments.

Zuree looked anxiously at Izz as her chin came up, and she nodded a quick acknowledgment. Then he gave her a solemn nod back, admiring her grit. She gave Izz a last sidelong glance, and caught, out of the corner of her eye, a hint of mounting concern written on Izz's face.

As Bolo anchored his talons on the steep edge of the abyss, Zuree saw the play of inconsistent expressions intensifying across Izz's facial features. The look in his eyes, the tense set of his jaw, the twitch in his cheek unsettled her further. At the defining moment, Izz unthinkingly cringed. Yes, he was fearful. But, he was more scared of the alternative that awaited. Zuree also knew the alternative too well, and so held her tongue. As Bolo leaned into the point of no return, every inch of her body resisted. Zuree began to breath faster and faster. Her face flushed red as she desperately tied to control her crucifying fear. The hair on the back of her neck rose instinctively, and at once, she felt as if the inside of her stomach lining was covered with prickling goosebumps. Her heart was by now violently slamming inside her chest. She felt herself shaking, her bowls churning, and all out terror was only a breath away. She tried to saddle herself down, forcing her trembling thighs together. Everything was happening too fast to think things out. Zuree thought she was going to be sick to her stomach, but she swallowed hard and forced back the nauseating sensation. Izz breathed a silent prayer as he prodded Bolo over the side of the yawning vent. He hoped with all his heart that the eagle could harness the thin, up drafting thermal winds created by the vent. Zuree's body went completely rigid. As she looked down the yawning drop, her heart leaped, and her eyes nearly popped out of her head with fear. Zuree let out an elongated scream, "NOOOOOOO!" having lost her nerve, wanting to change her mind, at the last instant. But it was too late and was swept down and away.

Izz said a silent prayer, begging for one more miracle if there was any chance at all. Izz's stomach lurched as Bolo launched into the deep. With a whishing clatter, Bolo unfurled his massive feathery wings. But instead of taking flight, the bird instantly plunged, awkwardly, straight down. Izz heard Zuree breath suck in as her eyes widened. Something in Zuree's lower bowls jumped to the top of her chest cavity. Izz saw her face twist as she emitted a scream, so loud, so hard, and so painful that he thought it would sear her throat. Zuree blared a blasting sound she had never made or heard come out of her before. She could not believe the scream was coming from the mouth in her head, from just below her bulging eyes and entering back in through her ringing ears. And it would not stop until she felt her heart leap to her thorax chocking her off. Zuree looked up at Izz with hysteria etched across her face. As she continued to plunge, she found her scream again, "IZZZZZZZZZZZ!" her last cry was high pitched and panic stricken. She started to raise her hand toward Izz but dared not. Her hands seized Bolo's neck feathers for dear life so tightly that her knuckles whitened bloodlessly.

As Zuree's echoing scream descended into the depth with her, Izz's spirit collapsed. He dropped to his belly at the edge of the vent's brink. His own heart quickened and leaped with a great thud as he watched in horror as Bolo was losing his fight to take flight. With one wing up and the other down, ineptly flapping maddeningly, Bolo plummeted on a downward path. His wings were a furious whirring flurry of motion unable to generate enough lift to equal that of his and Zuree's weight. The updrafts from the flames deep below were creating turbulences, and Bolo was finding it impossible to adjust. The mighty bird was wildly grabbing at the thin air, trying to correct his angle of flight with violent, desperate flurries of forceful wing thrusts. As Izz watched Bolo's wings buffet in the turbulence, he felt his skin break into a cold sweat.

With the tension of the moment, As Zuree's amplified cry disappeared entirely into the void, Izz shouted her name in a raw whimper, "ZUREEEEEEEE!" and then stared blankly, with his heart plunging after his beloved. He held out a trembling, outstretched hand to her, bellowing out her name again and again until his breath caught in his throat, and he let out only a strangled gasp. Izz flipped himself face up, filled with speechless terror, wishing he had been the one that had fallen instead of Zuree. He had not had the time to think about the possibility—that Bolo would not be able to carry Zuree. Izz slapped his hand hard to his forehead. He drove his fingers through his tangled hair and jerked as if to rip it out by its roots. He had had just enough time to catch a receding glimpse of the stricken look that had stretched over Zuree's beautiful face. A look he had never seen before, eyes wide, transfixed with shock, her teeth closely clinched. Her tortured look still engraved in the front of his mind, her hysterical tremor still ringing in his ears. He slid the back of his trembling hand down, clasping it over his mouth in trembling disgust as his heart slammed inside his chest with a dreadfulness he had never known.

And his soul collapsed in agonizing pain just when he had begun to dare to believe. He had staked Zuree's life based on nothing more than a fleeting hope, and now he could only tremble as he repeated, "No Zuree, No! No! *No!*"

In the depths of the vent, Zuree was fully aware that she was falling without resistance or without slowing. Try as he may, Bolo could not break out of his free fall. The master of the sky dropped helplessly even though the eagle's strong breast muscles were desperately flapping its wide open wingspan. Bolo frantically flapped his wings downwards, attempting to lift upwards. In the confined space, the strength of the updrafts was in flux, and Bolo had virtually lost all control of uplift. Zuree did not have the time to do more than gasp in breathless shock. By now, Zuree's hands were trembling so violently that she could barely keep her grip. Scared to death, the blood drained from her face, and nothing but overwhelming terror registered on it. As she felt herself falling off the deep end of Zia, her skin grew suddenly cold, and her heart froze in midair, despite the rising heat of the vent.

Above Izz just lay there, motionless, wholly numb. There was a strange delay as if reality had taken a few instances to reach his mind. Then all at once, as if for the first time, he felt the full weight of what had just happened. The shocking stunned silence, an ominous prelude to the waking of the almost unbelievable tragedy, suddenly overshadowed him. A throaty moan sawed its way up Izz's throat as he emitted half stifled shrills, between half murmurs. "You were so eager to be a godlike hero...that you abandoned all sound judgment." In any case, in a fleeting thought of logic in the corner of his mind, he understood beyond any doubt that they had no other alternative. "I had no other choice!" His voice came undone. His sight blurred. His eyes welled with stinging tears that leaked from everywhere behind his eyes. Madness burst forth with quaking sobs as Izz cried out like a wounded animal, uncontrollably and inconsolably. Izz's spirit and soul smote him simultaneously as his heart broke apart. Shaking his head in resignation, and trembling from head to toe, Izz cast fistfuls of dust upon his head and wept bitterly. "I had no other choice! I had no other choice! I had—No—Other—*Choice!*"

Izz lay there waiting for and welcomed his own end to come for him as he whimpered in very short, shallow gasps of terror. He could not bear to live one more moment without Zuree. As Izz gather his strength, he decided he would be better off joining Zuree. At least their remains would be together. And just as Izz was ready to throw himself over the edge after Zuree, eager to face his own death eye to eye. As he prepared to cast himself down out of the depths, he heard the dull flapping clatter of distant, billowing wings. He stopped wailing, and while he was still sniffling and sobbing, he ran his forearm across his face brushing away at the blurry wetness to see below him, Bolo suddenly emerging out of the chasm through the swirling smoke. Izz's eyes sparked with sudden vitality. He flinched, and his heart leaped as he reeled back from the brink. Bolo had intuitively ruffled his wing feathers to twice their usual size and stretched them out as far as he had been able to. And his giant wings had finally caught the density of air pressure rising from the centermost pillar of warmed up drafting, air. Bolo's wings were heaving and erupting like the sails of a mighty ship. Flying against the thin sky, Bolo banked, and there Zuree sat firmly riding the massive bird as one might ride upon the wave of a raging sea.

Izz was trembling now, thanking unseen angels, unable to contain the exciting current of emotions coursing through him. His grief had instantaneously turned into ecstasy, astonishment, and reprieve. The look of wild elation burst upon his face as the rhythm of joy beat steady and faithful in his heart of hearts. A crushing weight had been lifted from his shoulders. So happy was he that for an instant he thought he might leap and soar through the air straight into the heavens after Zuree as Bolo carried them pass him and skyward. There was no greater wealth, no greater bliss, and no more priceless gift better than knowing that his only true love was alive and well—for the time being anyway. Suddenly the blunt truth of actuality reared its ugly head once again as a flight of zinging arrows smashed everywhere, and the reality of his perilous plight dawned all around him. Baddlock jaws slackened with amazement, his mouth flopped open with disbelief, and his eyes widened with dread and wonder at what he was witnessing. "Shoot the bird down!" He shouted with maddening urgency.

His crossbowmen fumblingly responded to his orders, immediately reloading and nocking arrows to their bowstrings. "Begging your pardon, my lord, but will that not endanger the princess?" Dandork asked.

"An injured princess is better than no princess, you moron. Bring the bird down now!"

Bolo instinctively dipped a wing and veered sideways as a volley of arrows came at them. Zuree strong legs braced against the tilt, her mind still recoiling from what she had just experienced. By the third time Dandork and the Norticlan marksmen had loaded and elevated their weapons, Zuree and Bolo had reached the upper ceiling. As her insides crawled back and finished realigning themselves to where they belonged, Bolo had accelerated into full flight. Bolo tilted his head skyward, beating his mighty wings desperately as he pulled up into a vertical flight pattern. Zuree's fingers dug in, clinging on for all she was worth. The majestic bird's commanding wings snapped into an ever quickening alignment. And with an explosion of wings that shot them forth, Bolo carried Zuree straight up into the vent. Zuree crouched forward, digging her heels in forcefully, holding on, bracing herself against the frightening gravitational pull of Bolo's upward surge. It was simply unbelievable! The spectacular creature's wingspread was so vast it momentarily darkened out the light in the cavern as the grand bird rose straight up ever higher through the red mist. And Zuree was lifted on eagle wings as the air raced past her ears with gale force. Zuree looked down to see Izz looking back up at her in wonder. She saw how his face shone with relieved happiness for her. Zuree's long golden hair flew in the waves of the rushing currents as she beckoned to him with one outstretched hand. Finally, she lost sight of him as she disappeared into the upper vent. Baddlock just stood there frozen in time, looking like a child whose candy treat had suddenly been snatched away from him.

The Wicked Warlock Wizard clenched his fists and flew into a loathsome outrage. "You nitwits, you let her get away. To say you were dumber than jackasses would only be insulting the jackasses."

Izz was smiling broadly, almost dancing with glee as he saw the king of birds continue its steady rise out of the range of even Baddlock's crossbows. He stared skyward as Bolo ever adjusted the angle of his wings towards the surface, as he steadily gained altitude. In no time, Bolo and Zuree were well into the uppermost vent, caught in the rising thermals that were rapidly carrying the majestic bird and Zuree spiraling up higher and higher. "She is safe from your wicked clutches, Baddlock!" Izz yelled out, disregarding his inconsequential circumstances.

Hearing this immediately, Baddlock turned his full frustrated wrath on Izz. "Kill that loud mouthed carpenter, or I will personally kill all of you with my bare hands."

Several Norticandic bowmen nearest the vent scrambled to get a shot off at Izz. As Izz ran towards Fina, he heard the sound of shattering rocks grinding under heavy boots as archers were spreading out and swiftly converging in on him. Upon reaching Fina where she was, obediently standing there as if tethered by submission, At a running start, Izz quickly swung himself up on Fina's back, with one mighty, fluid surge. Fina sidestepped and recoiled until she finally accepted the indignity of being mounted. Fearing he may have delayed too long, celebrated for far too long, Izz firmly fixed himself. Fina appeared to feel the lateness of the moment also. The female eagle chocked her head toward Izz and looked at him with impatient eyes as she was filled with the impulsiveness to take flight. Fina was eager to leave the strange world that was so visibly becoming increasingly hostile with each passing moment. With half opened wings, Fina readjusted her balance against Izz's weight as he prodded the bird with his knees towards the edge. While the vultures circled, and the hyenas closed in, every thickening instant drastically reduced the likelihood of their escape tenfold. Izz entreated *Just a few more moments*. "Just give me half a chance," he begged, the Giver of second chances as he called to Fina, "It is our turn, girl."

Fina fixed her footing, unfurled her expansive wings, spreading them wide like a canopy, and cast herself over the ledge. She twisted away, launching into thin air without hesitation. And just like her brother, Fina struggled to adjust to Izz's weight as they both dropped awkwardly towards the center of Zia. A n d e v e n though she was the bigger of the two giants, she too went into a crazy downward spin. The air beneath her wings had no upward element. Below, Izz could see the glowing red gulf of hell boiling over like a great thundercloud filled chasm, pierced by fire and chaos. As they plummeted, Izz thought he had suddenly seen a monstrous cyclonic eye leap from the depths below, burning itself into the back of his mind. The eye seemed to be drawing them down into its fiery grasp. Fina attempted various combinations of wing angles with varying upstrokes and down strokes. She tried anything and everything, attempting whatever to produce an uplifting force and reduce their falling speed. With long flapping bouts, Fina pitted her skills against the changing turbulent forces of the vent. She struggled to maintain her balance and regained control, but the altering updrafts and Izz's weight kept pushing and pulling her down.

Finally, at the last possible moment, Fina tilted her wings at just the right angle in unison with her fanned out tail feathers, and her descent decelerated. As they slowed, Fina harnessed the superheated thermal airs created by the increasing heat rising from the volcano's internal inferno. Fina's expert ability to utilize the almost nonexistent updrafts allowed her to stop dropping. Suddenly Fina's wings transitioned to the thin air currents whirling upward in the vent. Just in the nick of time, the scorching air served to empower Fina's wing beat to counteract the inertia of upward motion. Having carried a much heavier weight, but never on her back, the cunning bird quickly adjusted the weight load and redoubled her efforts for the upward climb. Fina and Izz began to rise gradually.

Soon they would be out of the lower vent if things did not suddenly take a twist for the worst should a downdraft materialize unexpectedly. Izz and Fina slowly but steadily gained momentum upward. All the while, the noble bird remained calm and focused, a formidable embodiment of grace and power. For the time being, Izz's distress began to ebb away as they gradually claimed. But it was only the calm before the storm. Izz looked up and saw Zuree and Bolo high above them, riding the lofty heights of the upper waves of thermal currents. He could see their outline in the ever brightening light from the vent opening. Now they were a mere tiny, black dot against the brightness of the gathering conjunction. The sight lifted and flooded Izz's spirit with relief, and he felt an overflow of gratitude. Halfway up from the lower vent, Fina had finally managed to yoke the rising thermos to produce maximum lift. The most enormous flying creature in Zia swept into a steep upward slope as her massive wings beat an increasingly faster rhythm that ever accelerated their rate of ascent.

Izz was almost too scared to find out what waited above, just knowing that Zuree was safe was all he needed to know for now. But just maybe they had a chance. An inner voice of hope sounded in his heart. *Do not be afraid.* But just as he had feared, it was already too late. As Izz and Fina neared the chasm's rim above the clamor continued, and by now, the vent was well within the range of every deadly crossbow bearing marksman. The luminous conjunction nearing its climax already flooded the upper chamber to the point that it offered only the slightest element of concealment. In the brightening half light filtering down, Dandork and the wary Norticlan expert shooters had heard the heavy beating rhythm of ascending wings. They had already taken up positions on the rocks that surrounded the vent. Dandork was sure that he would be the one to score the kill shot. He was merely counting off the moments until Izz's came into view. Knowing that he could hit a flying sparrow at thirty paces, left little doubt in his mind. The carpenter was as good as dead. Baddlock could already picture himself removing Izz's head off his shoulders and presenting it to Abaddawn in appeasement for his failure to recapture the princess.

He could hear the slashing sound of it and smell Izz's fresh blood as it oozed out of him. It was certainly only a matter of a minuscule passage of time.

As Fina, gain height Izz could hear the commotion of siege above him as he urged Fina on. He knew that they would in all likelihood be shot down, but he would die fighting for his life. It was not the end he would have chosen, had he had a reasonable choice. But still, he clung on to the outside chance that they still might make it. And that is what he focused on, yet even if he perished here and now, his preeminent mission had not failed as far as he was concerned. Beyond the present reality—it would be okay. As they reached the opening, Izz felt himself stiffen. Fina's wings surged with power and began to lift him into the open. He took a deep breath and flattened himself over Fina, pressing his chest and head against her shoulders, becoming one. At length, Fina came into full view from the misty lower vent. Like a mystical phoenix rising from the ashes, Fina spiraled upward, looking at the strange humans that stood in place with bows drawn. Their assailants lay in wait perfectly, still ready to strike with weapons that could rip through anything, including armor, muscle, and bone. The first shots were, however, hurried, and all but one narrowly missed hitting its target, just barely grazing Izz's shoulder.

On the other hand, Dandork took his time, having propped the stock of his crossbow on a stationary rock for stability. His keen eyes were searching for a kill shot for his arrow. The arrow was positioned in the bow's flight groove. His arrow was nocked, his crossbow string pulled taut, finger on the trigger. He rested and snuggling his cheek onto the crossbow's butt. Dandork held his arm out steady and aimed with his body. With his eyes unflinchingly fixed, he took careful aim at Izz's heart. He was such a clear target for his deadly arrow. He took accurate consideration of the sight breeze and the movement and rotation of the bird. He was as good as dead. Dandork's eyes narrowed and filled with malice as he drew a bead on Izz's heart. He held his target in the center of Fina's rotating flight path. He let his finger linger on the crossbow's trigger contour, then he steadied it and took up the slack of the triggers. At that range, he could not possibly miss dropping Izz with one shot. But just at the very moment, Dandork released his arrow, all at once, and out of nowhere, a storm of returning bats came flooding through the upper vent.

In their haste to escape the brightness of the gathering conjunction, the bat hordes came overflowing back into their subterranean underworld in a state of confusion. As the flash flood of bats came rushing in, Fina was the first to collide beak first into the blizzard of incoming vampire bats. Izz clung on for dear life as he was pummeled with the heavy blows of crashing bat on his head, chest, and shoulders. This influx of bats caused the deadly arrow to veer off its intended target. As the bats entered their roost, they were already agitated by the confusion of their untimely exit and return. And reentering their den to find it overrun by intruders agitated them to new heights. They immediately began a vicious attack against the trespassers, frustrating the archer's line of fire.

Despite Dandork's surprise, and obscured vision, he quickly reloaded and already had his firmly pressed finger against the release mechanism as he once again hugged the crossbow up snuggly against his cheek. Dandork took a deep breath, stroked the trigger once, and then began to slowly, deliberately and very gently squeeze, as he whispered, "Bats or no bats I am your death carpenter." Suddenly something furry struck Dandork face, screeching, squealing, and biting with razor sharp teeth. Reflexively he flinched. In doing so, he jerked his trigger finger. There was a solid click, ping, and a whirr. The loosed arrow was off along its flight path with a hiss streaking along its nearly perfect trajectory. The instant Dandork dispatched his arrow, and he immediately knew his shot had been slightly hooked. It would hit its mark but not exactly where he intended. "You will take my arrow to your tomb." He hissed as he swatted the bloodsucking bat with his free hand. But for every bat he swept away, another few sets of tiny jaws darted in to redden themselves on his flesh.

Izz had heard the familiar, ominous, metallic clicking sounds that sounded simultaneously from every direction all at once. All along their steady, spiraling path, the deadly arrows made a whistling sound as their whirling blades sliced through the air towards Izz and Fina. Like a bolt of fast lightning among a hail of other arrows, Dandork's death sentence pierced through the air. Three arrows suddenly flew pass Izz's head, just inches wide of their target, too close for comfort. And just when Izz was starting to feel good about his odds, unexpectedly out of nowhere, the arrow bearing his name found him. Its wicked point and shaft slamming into him with a dull meaty clunk. Slightly off its mark, Dandork's arrow pierced Izz's flesh with the hard jolting impact of a sledgehammer that knocked all the breath from his chest. The pain scorched Izz's body like a blazing bolt of lightning. Izz felt the arrow's sharp point enter, biting deep as he heard his flesh rip! His back violently arched, as he felt the arrow entered his chest between his shoulder blades. A splattering of blood gushed out bright red like water to stream into the rising thermals and down the vent drop. Izz wheezed and clutched at his chest. The impact of the blow shivered up Izz's spine and back down. His body contorted in agony as he almost passed out from the unbearable pain. He struggled in vain to let some air circulating through to his lungs. He immediately crumpled onto Fina's back.

The excruciating physical pain which seized his body was like nothing he had ever felt before. He doubled over in convulsions and wanted to shrivel up into a fetal position. The sudden shock came in great throbbing waves, for a moment threatening to rob him of consciousness. Izz could not make a sound. Again he almost passed out. He doubled up, and tears poured out of his eyes. His muscles gradually unclenched. Now he could cry out for the sheer pain of it. The pain was too great. Torrents of blood poured out freely from the wound, running along the shaft of the arrow, dripping in beads onto Fina's back. Then his whole body contorted, arching violently backward as he felt one shivering spasm of pain after another. Izz's eyes rolled back in his head as the look of agony took over his face.

As the second barrage of murderous arrows fired from different directions across the chamber. Fina immediately sensed that her master was in grave peril. She raised her crest and valiantly turned to fend off their attackers as she let out an ear piercing screech that shook the cavern and alarmed all those within the vent. Her wings propelled her like a trapped hornet about the cavern as the archers fired their arrows at her in saturated patterns. With her wings, she swatted arrows away and shielded Izz from additional harm. And suddenly, Fina's whole body was buffeting and shaking madly as several arrows abruptly slammed into her chest, stealing her breath away. Izz felt Fina's body shudder as steel tipped bolts buried themselves deep within her, but her wings did not miss a beat for an instant. Fina squawked, flinching and rearing away in pain. Whoosh! An explosion of wings sent her banking and angling sharply to the right and then sweeping to the left. Fina quickly regained control; her attention was fixed as she gathered speed maneuvering in a soaring, looping, zigzagging flight pattern. The agile bird flew twisting through the air threatening to unseat Izz at every turn. Fina shrieked in excruciating protest at the bite of steel, but the embedded shafts did not slow her down. She bent her neck around her wounded chest and plucked out the arrows with her beak. In an earnest attempt to protect her keeper, she was ready to swoop down on whoever had struck the blow.

Knowing that Fina was prepared to defend him to the death, Izz commanded, "No!" as he drove her upward with his legs. In response, Fina immediately swooped around with an explosive upward stroke and beat her powerful wings with an enraged burst of fury. Then she banked sharply and blasted into a skyward flight toward the vent opening at an unbelievable climb. Surprised archers were sent stumbling back with blinding winds and dust and bats rushing past their faces. Izz dug his heels into Fina flanks causing Fina to quicken the beat of her wings through the storm of incoming bats. Fina's wings erupted into a sudden, blinding blur and picked up speed as Izz clung to two handfuls of Fina's back feathers and to sheer life itself. Despite her grievous wounds, she maintained her mighty strokes and somehow kept flying upwards. Fina moved sharply skyward, and with attention fixed, she accelerated steadily ever soaring upward through the volcanic vent. Below, the black cloud of incoming bats began to spread through the recesses of the vent. The sound of wings grew louder as their shadow fell across the chamber.

Izz could not catch his breath to utter a sound as he clutched at his blood soaked tunic to feel the point of the bolt protruding through the middle of his chest. He reached back, but the arrow was just out of reach of his fingertips. He could only double up as tears of pain came streaming out of his eyes. The blades of the hardened steel tip had ripped past his back ribs, just narrowly missing his backbone and heart. Its impact had gashed out a sizeable chunk of flesh that splattered a considerable blood pattern in the front and back of this tunic. The arrow's shaft felt like a red hot iron burning in his chest. Izz's eyes bugged and fluttered, and widened with panic as pain splintered through his brain. Throbbing agony forked through his chest equal to a piercing, red white poker. The sting stabbed through him like a long pruning needle driven down his spine from his neck to his tail bone. His muscles gradually unclenched, allowing him to catch a shallow breath and to blurt out a scream. "Aaaaaaahh!" Izz let out a lingering, nerve chilling cry in anguish so horrific that it startled Fina. On the verge of losing consciousness, Izz concentrated on clinging on to Fina's neck with both hands as he wheezed and gasped for breath. He was flung into the most excruciating, truest agonizing pain he had ever experience. The unendurable throb was indescribably beyond what anyone could ever imagine knowing. Izz squeezed his eyes closed.

Yowl! Oh, it *hurts.* It *hurts so bad!* Izz thought as he flew out of his mind and temporarily lost his ability to think. Then suddenly, everything seemed to decelerate into slow motion. The deadly arrow was lodged next to his heart, within a breath or two of narrowly hitting it and just barely missing any major blood vessels. Massive amounts of adrenaline were released into his bloodstream, causing his central nervous system into a sluggish mode. The red stain spread on the back of Izz's tunic as streams of blood jutted out, running in glossy crimson streamers from his life threatening wound. Then in front, a blot stretched rapidly, becoming a bloody blotch across his chest.

Sensing the urgency of Izz's plight, Fina entered a vertical path that required the eagle to exert a greater ascending force to maintain the upward axis. As Fina's wings, swept skyward, her powerful downward thrust strokes pitch her body higher and higher along the length of the towering vent. All the while, far reaching arrows continued to threaten them. Both Izz and Fina were severely wounded, but the power of the beast within kept Fina climbing heavenward until she reached the safety of the upper vent for her master's sake.

Before being overwhelmed by inrushing bats, Baddlock had heard the rigid, "Whack!" of a bolt striking flesh. He had seen that Dandork's arrow had pierced deep into Izz's mid back. As he shrouded himself with his heavy cape against the bats, his face broke out in a menacing grin. Dandork turned to Baddlock, protecting himself against the bats as best he could and shouted, "He is as good as dead."

"How can you be certain?" Baddlock asked from beneath his cape.

"The arrow had to have pierced his heart or lung or both. Besides, my arrow was laced with poison. Even now, he must be feeling the fiery tentacles of the toxin's grip. Soon enough, its bitterness will crush his heart. And on top of that, there is no known antidote."

Baddlock might have allowed Zuree to slip through his fingers, but no matter what happened, at least he could be assured that Izz was as good as dead. His voice raised jeeringly, "May you enjoy the noxious rot of your love shriveled up and alone in the wasteland of your grave."

Izz strained his dimming eye to see Zuree and Bolo nearing the outlet of the vent. That was all that matters anymore. He gasped as the toxic poison spread throughout his bloodstream with a dreadful feeling of chilling deadness. Unable to sit up straight, Izz frantically clutched and sunk around Fina's neck, reeling as his life's blood drained away to soak Fina's back feathers. Izz's face seemed anesthetized with death, and his mouth drooped open. Aware of a sense of urgency, Fina, despite her injuries, slapped her wings against the rising thermal winds as she fixed one eye on her rider and the other on the vent's lofty crater. The only thing that kept Izz from blacking out was the searing pain that coiled throughout his body. Every pulsing heartbeat sent blood erupting and pounding with unbelievable pressure in his skull until he thought his head was going to explode. He could feel the waves of jerking nerves involuntarily shooting pulsing spasms, coiling throughout him. His breath was becoming hot, fast, and sporadic. Each breath he took in brought a new heightened jolt of pain up from the center of his body. He groaned and bit down on his lip to keep from crying out, which forced tortured moans from his throat. As the cloud of returning bats began to clear, Izz sat up slightly, with blood still oozing down from his wound. As white hot pain continued to shoot through his body, he reached under his tunic to feel the glint of steel protruding just below his right beast. He withdrew his hand and squeezed the sticky blood that trickled down from his fingertips. He coughed violently, and red froth bubbled from his lips.

Izz knew he was mortally wounded.

Izz could feel the poison tingling in his bowels. His mouth was wet, and he could taste blood running down his throat. With spasm after spasm, life poured out of him. Izz was rapidly losing the control of his body, and his breath was coming up shallow and in short gasps. He pitched forward just as though he was about to pass out. Izz could feel himself dying. He slumped forward into a shadowy world of obscurity as if hanging on to life by a frayed thread. The staggering loss of blood and the venomous potion circulating through his bloodstream sent him careening in and out of a murky world. Izz drifted back and forth into enchanting dreams from which he knew not if he would ever wake. The trauma of massive blood loss induced hallucinations. He slipped from the eagle's neck several times, and each time, Fina adjusted her angel to balance Izz in the center of her back. The image of the wicked flaming eye came crashing back into Izz's brain, and he heard laughter in the fringes of his mind. Dreams surrounded him as everything collapses into chaos as Izz struggled against the throbbing pulsation that wanted to kill him. Izz wanted to stay alive if only to kiss Zuree goodbye. Izz imagined a voice whispering from a paranormal world in an alternative universe. "You can run, but you cannot hide." Izz resisted from the inside out, as the forces of darkness worked on him from the outside in. From moment to moment, Izz pleaded, *Just one more moment. Just one more moment. Just let me see her one more time hold her, kiss her...one more time.* And the demon presence receded back into the unseen.

Seventeen
The Zenith

ventually, Zuree and Bolo reached the crater's mouth that unfolded into the light and out to the opened air. The sensation of flight during those first spiraling moments had been terrifying. Zuree could now see the outline of rays from the light of day, shining down from the vent's entrance into the crater as Bolo climbed steadily towards its source at the end of the volcano's throat. Zuree looked straight up. She saw no darkness, no repression, gloom or doom. What she did see were beautiful, blue, freshly washed skies. And light! Beautiful light from the blissful Celestial Heavenly Realm. Half blinded in the brightness; she savored now the first breath of fresh air. Her heart was thumping so vigorously to know she was still very much alive. Zuree glanced down into the breathtaking depths to see Fina's outline in the cascading light indicating that Izz and Fina were rising from the mist. Not having an inkling of what had befallen Izz, she exclaimed, "We made it!"

As Bolo rode the updrafts on his spiraling upward flight path, Zuree, at the same moment was gasping with relief as the crisp, clean air of the surface surrounded her. With one mighty surge of power Bolo crested over the rim of the crater and into the open sky. The brilliant, half blinding light of the outside world pierced Zuree's pupils like the flash of an intense lightning strike. A rush of clean, crisp, pure air, swept over her face sweet and refreshing. Its breathtaking fragrance rejuvenated her in a wash of blessed relief. She inhaled deeply and filled herself with its delicious and refreshing stimulant to the senses. She basked in it, as she drew in one deep lungful after another. The rush of the wind swept across Zuree's long hair as she gazed out across the wide valley beneath a vast cauldron of swirling blue clouds. The sight lifted her spirit, which brought a great flood of gratitude and relief to a heart that had finally settled back into her chest. Zuree straightened her shoulders, raising her head thrilled to at long last be escaping the aura of despicable wickedness.

One by one, she shed the weight of every evil thing, that had been so intent on destroying her. Zuree emptied herself of the foul fear that plagued every waking moment since that night she had been taken from her room. She went on with a lighter heart as her body became one with Bolo's powerful rhythm and the oceanic sky as far as the eye could see. She became accustomed to the buoyancy of flying as her racing heart began to return to its regular rhythm, and her entrails finally crawled themselves back to where they belonged. Zuree's mind was still reeling from what she had seen and experienced in the bizarre world she had just left. She drew fresh air deep into her lungs as the restless air streams swirled her golden hair before her eyes. A silent prayer of gratitude escaped her lips. She was thankful to be out of the demonic world of death, beholden to have escaped the aura of evil. She paused for a moment to drink in the freedom of being emancipated.

With long, muscular wing beats snapping fully like bellowing masts, Bolo circled the jagged peaks and launched himself over the Noragore Ridge. He instinctively veered due south, immediately slanting towards where the distant Kingdom of Edawn lay. The blissful, sparkling sunshine lit the heavens before them. As Bolo ascended away from the vent's opening like a bird flying out of a cage, his heart soared with the physical pleasure of the cool wind as it ruffled and swept past his feathers. Zuree's eyes fluttered from the sheer gratification of being free. She tried to banish the terrifying images of a world that was increasingly becoming nastier with every passing moment.

All at once, before her next breath, Zuree's attention was forcefully drawn to the fiery awesomeness of the gathering conjunction. Zuree's eyes attempted to adjust to the overpowering brightness of the light fully. She was suddenly spell struck, like an owl, bewildered in the daylight. She brushed a stray curl out of her face as she shielded her eyes from the unexpected dazzling phenomenon. Through the blinding glare, Zuree was able to discern that the abnormality was coming from a cluster of bright orbs. She wondered what this occurrence suspended in the vault of the sky might be. Could the pure, white rays of light, sunny, strong, and warm upon her face be the fabled conjunction? It could have been no other. The globes appeared as if superimposed suns hovering in the vast trek of their displaced paths. She stared utterly entranced, gazing from one brilliant orb to the other. She had a sense that they were whirling stars that seemed to have loosened themselves from their fixed path. It was the most beautiful light she had ever wanted to see. Seemingly hung on nothingness, they were, foreboding, humbling, disturbing, and awesomely amazing all at once. As the mechanical indicator of all endless time etched towards its vertex Zuree continued to scrunch up her eyes in the ever increasing light that shone with the power of a thousand new stars. The brilliance dazzled Zuree's vision so much that she had to squeeze her eyes shut and bury her face into the nap of Bolo's soft neck feathers. It took a few moments for her smoky, rimmed eyes to readjust, and her sight to finally normalize to the blinding light. When at last she was able to reopen her scrunched up eyes wide enough to see anything, she looked down.

Zuree was unprepared for what met her vista. What she saw made her stomach flip flop, and she felt a sharp tug as her stomach's bottom seemed to drop out. The entire world of Zia seemed without warning to suddenly plunge straight down and tumble away from the crest of the volcano summit beneath her. Just like that, the full panoramic view of the terrestrial sphere unfolded like a flourishing tapestry that came rushing in on her in total. Altogether she felt a tingling sensation rise from within her groan. The rush of adrenaline from being thousands of feet in the open air over a limitless, breathtaking drop apprehensively overwhelmed her. It was absolutely and unbelievably amazing. Her grip tightened and was sure, and she could feel Bolo's back muscles flexing with the strength of iron as his broad stately wings billowed. The air raced past her ears with gale force as Bolo gracefully harnessed the tremendous currents of the prevailing winds. The majestic king of the sky fixed his attention, yoking great bodies of air as he moved sharply southward. Bolo steadily accelerated his airspeed as the saw tooth peaks of the Noragore Rim began to fall back and shrink into the distance at a fantastic speed.

Zuree repeatedly craned her neck back to search Izz out. She shuddered with the feeling that they were finally free, that is until she gasped with the awful premonition that something was not right. She recalled Izz's last warm embrace. It was an embrace she was beginning to fear she would never feel again. The intuitive possibility was like a cold hand on her heart. An inner feeling of worrisome despondency was displacing her buoyant outlook.

Meanwhile, Fina and Izz climbed upward into a world they were about to reenter. A world in which they were about to escape the grasping clutches of the underworld. Izz's glassy eyes widened as he saw sparkling sunlight through a wall of gray exhaust fumes. Finally, Izz felt the power of daylight like the light seen against closed eyes. Izz's gasping eased as even the smoky air around him seemed to taste defiled. Despite his grave condition, there was an enticing of hope in the fresh air and the radiance of the unwavering sun that shone through his tightly locked eyelids. Fina was in poor shape, but strength from within kept her going on a steady spiraling path surface ward for her master's sake. At long last, Fina finally crested the protruding rock face summit of the crater, clambering ahead ,just managing to jostle over its edge. For the moment, the tension in the air ended as Izz clung on to the belief that he could make it. In the outside world, the light was so intense that Izz could hardly see the summit of the crater's ridge through squinting eyes. Izz had been so long in the lightless dark that the fiery, reflective glare of the eternal sunlight blinded him. Even though his eyes were closed tighter than knotted cords, the sun's rays felt harsh and unnatural, burning his eyes and skin so painfully that it made his head hurt.

As the poison coursed through Izz's veins, Izz was whisked toward something he wanted so desperately to forget; he was suddenly seized by something very bizarre. Distant demons began to laugh, heckling and growling and cackling with joy, taunting Izz. He was no longer contending against flesh and blood, but against principalities, powers, and spiritual wickedness. Izz's head was on fire bristling with the sickening sensation of blood loss. Izz was wary of proceeding and afflicted with an unquenchable thirst and eternal hunger. He was too disconnected to think straight. What was once right side up was now upside down. A dreadful thought entered his mind. An utterly out of touch with reality, feeling of wanting to go back into the darkness overpowered him It was almost as if preferring the nightmare to the brightness of the outer world. Izz drifted in and out. It was like dying. He began to assume he must be dead.

Then suddenly, in a blinding flash, the brightness of the gathering conjunction blazed wildly upon Izz's dimming retinas. The waking sensation at that moment was almost devastating. It shone out with an intensity that extended to every far reaching horizon. Behind Izz's closed eyelids, the glow of the cresting conjunction changed from red to white, whiter than the whitest snow. Its light was amazing, humbling, and scary all at once. Ever closer, the conjunction neared its zenith. The light grew and grew, blossoming, filling the sky from one end of the valley to the other. The light brightened out of every corner, thicket, nook, and cranny in Zia. The shadows of the tall trees below grew deeper, and at first, became more clear cut. Then, spreading wider, they lose their distinctness of outline in the brightening tide of oblivion until every shadow below shrank and ebbed and faded away.

Fina's grim condition was worsening with the end of every downward stroke. Bewildered by the sudden extreme brightness of the day and weakened by blood loss, Fina struggled on when she had nothing left to give but for the sake of her keeper. Izz focused his weakening strength on hanging on to Fina's neck with both hands and breathing in as best he could. The White Crested Eagle seemed to sense no hesitation about which direction they should go as she sailed south through the sky, over the blurred landscape of earth below. The yellows, greens, and deep purples were so deep they could have been a hallucinatory kaleidoscope. Fina spread her wings wide to float upon the uplifting currents from the sun beaten ground below. Feeling the updrafts through outstretched wings, Fina found her rhythm.

"Well, girl, you seem to know where you are going. "Izz whispered as she seemed to cock her head back to fix one watchful eye on her rider.

All along, Zuree kept looking back over her shoulder, expected Izz come through the clouds at any moment. Her mind blocked out the possibility that anything terrible could have befallen him, and she remained hopeful that he would be coming into view soon. Zuree knew she would never, ever be able to get the horror that they had been through, out of her head. But all that was behind them now, and if only her luck held out, she would soon be home with Izz and in the presence of those she loved most. Zuree looked south past Bolo's wings and shoulders. In the remoteness, she could see the distant sea. She wondered how her mother and father were coping with no news. She questioned what they must be going through and what it all was doing to them. Never sure always having to wonder. She thought of the cruel uncertainty they must be having to endure. But soon, all that would be over.

In the ever brightening sky, Zuree took in ever deepening breaths of fresh air that carried in them the scent of sun lit pine trees. Unexpectedly like an encouraging omen, a flock of geese in perfect formation arched across the blue heavens half a zetta up in the sky. Beyond the flock, a vista of mountainous peaks stretched away until they finally disappeared in the haze at a remoteness that seemed impossibly far. Bolo expertly utilized the thermals that rose up against the mountain. His huge wingspan mounted the heavens high above the Northern Territory, maneuvering him in boundless, effortless flight. The majestic monarch of the sky soared proud and serene on the winds that carried them over the beautiful mountaintops toward Edawn. Puffy low hanging clouds became fleeting mountains that rolled away on either side. Under the gathering conjunction, the view was amazing, and the sensation of flight was exhilarating. With that thought, she looked back longingly, over her shoulder, though still sensitive, tear stained eyes, hoping to catch a glimpse of Izz. She knew she had seen him climbing out of the vent. Where was he, and what was keeping him? Seeing little more than blotches and patches of shimmering light, She once again buried her face in Bolos rustling neck feathers. Zuree could not even think of Izz without a constriction descending into her chest. With a gust of disappointment, a thousand thoughts and uncertainties swirled through her head.

In the act of faith, Zuree did not know how, but somehow, beyond hope, beyond certainty, she believed that everything was going to be okay. The strength of the sun on her face meant another day, and she found solace in her hopefulness. Zuree allowed herself a moment of absolution. A look of reprieve broke across her face. Because of Izz, she had been able to slip out of Baddlock's grip like a butterfly out of a closing fist. The baptism by fire was over. Her living entombment was all just a bad dream now. She felt all its ugliness fade and slip away behind her. But she knew the smells and sounds and sights would be forever etched and left to echo in the annals of her mind forever. Half blind in the ever brightening light from the blurred green earth below, Zuree thought she could faintly hear the rushing sound of water. It's trickling flow seemingly singing, as it carried within it sparkling waves of dancing of light. She had gotten away, escaped certain death, and nothing else mattered...nothing except Izz.

Once more, Zuree lost herself in the canopy of the sky as Bolo sailed through thin wisps of whitish clouds. The temperature seemed to grow cooler as the light mountain mist embraced her, and its damp morning moister chilled her to the core. Zuree's teeth clattered. Confounded and overwhelmed by the brightness of the climaxing conjunction, she coiled herself over Bolo and buried her chest against Bolo's powerfully working shoulders. As she warmed herself up with the heat steaming away from Bolo's determined body, rushing air fluttered fuzzy feathers around her face. A warm knot settled in her stomach as Bolo continued his commanding southbound flight. Not a moment went by without Izz crossing her mind. But Zuree could not even think of him without a tightness coiling inside of her chest. Again Zuree looked expectantly back. And yet, a hundred doubts and anxieties pierced her heart every short moment. In an urgent whisper, she called out his name, "Izz...!"Then she shouted against the onrushing wind, "Izz, where are you?" Zuree knew she had seen them climbing out of the vent; she just knew she had. Where was he and what was keeping him, she questioned, yet again. But come what may, Zuree believed she would feel her arms around him and once again kiss the wonderfully warm taste of his love.

At the same time, Fina was trying her best to keep up the grueling pace. The crisp, clean air had an effect in clearing Izz's head as the breezy wisps of the wind evaporated the drops of cold sweat on his face. His frantically beating heart was the thing that assured him that he was still alive. Fina's flight path was wobbly, and the rhythm of her wings was inconsistent, but for Izz's sake, she was unwavering. Every stroke of Fina's great wings agitated the arrow's shaft lodged in Izz's back. Each movement was agony. Every beat kept up the scornful rhythm of pain that racked throughout his body as if it were multiple knives stabs inflicted on his back. Izz's face was misshaped with anguish. And with every wing beat more of his life's blood trickled from his fiery wound onto Fina's back feathers. He had lost a lot of blood. Fina's back by now was covered with his sticky, dry blood. Izz could barely think through the excruciating pain. Yet he tied to stop the flow of blood. He managed somehow to tie his woven belt around the grievous wound as best he could. But despite his best effort, he could feel the sickening sensation of himself dying.

As Izz was struggling to stay conscious, all of a sudden, his attention was forcefully jerked toward the gathering conjunction. All at once, each sphere of light appeared bigger, brighter, closer to each other, and closer to Zia than ever. Each one of the seven sister planets, along with Zia's moon, seemed to line itself up directly in front of the sun polarized by the apex of their gathering. The cluster of heavenly bodies seemed to stand still in the sky. They seemed to line up so perfectly that they formed one huge frenzied system pulling against each other, dancing an intricate dance into a whole different orbiting pattern. The planetary zenith had arrived and this would be the deciding moment in the time continuum. Time just stood still as the conjunction seemed to hang there, suspended in eternity. Then unexpectedly, the internal electromagnetic storm from within exploded as if a Devine Hand had touched a flare to a cauldron of oil in the sky. Unbound by time and space, suddenly, a dazzling light pulsed towards every horizon, across Zia's broad expanse to the North, to the South, to the East and to the West possessing itself of everything. Izz was coherent enough to realize that he was witnessing the Great Conjunction that for so long Ammiz the Seer had so often detailed. It was as if the whole universe was simultaneously interfused with the unfathomable, red blaze of a giant iron sphere in a furnace. Its radiant blinding flash exploded with the magnitude, and the fury of its nucleus burst forth like a thousand angry suns shinning from one central point. It's golden edges poured out, stretching across the cosmos like a spring wind. Its brightness seemed to burst right out of the celestial realm with one powerful light a hundred times brighter than the brightest of days.

At the same time, up ahead, Zuree clasped her hand to her mouth. The radiation of light and extreme heat that had struck like a bolt from the blue had blinded Zuree's vision. The tremendous flash of the perfect conjunction had been enough to cause Zuree to go temporally blind. The overwhelming brilliance of light at the Zenith of the Great Conjunction appeared like a disk of bright molten silver. Suddenly it glimmered more brilliant than the most radiant sun had ever shone before. The pulsating phantasm created the most astonishing effects that one could ever imagine. The eyeful fluctuated in all the colors of the rainbow, emitting great bursts of electronic multi colored flashes of light. Her hand seemed on fire as her coming of age stone caught the light and burst forth to answer its call. Its blue facets brightened until it lit the air all around her. The Great Conjunction's immense dynamism surged throughout the globe of Zia, and swept over its inhabitants, from the mountains to the valleys, from the deserts to the sea.

As the noonday sun once again reached its Solar Maximums, the congregation of planets seemed ensnared by the magnetic abnormalities of their proximity. They appeared to advance forth, ominously as if to crash upon Zia with their massive blazing weight. Ammiz the Seer had been waiting at his window just in time to catch the full bloom of the astonishing planetary spectacle. With round, dark glass lens dawned, the old man was ready to bring his spirit into line with the vibration of the universe. Amid an ever changing number of infinite calculations, the phenomenon excited his keenest interest. At long last, the mechanical indicator of all conquering continuums unbound by time and space locked into its perfect apex, and the Keeper of Time struck the hour. And Ammiz was astonished by the omnipresent curiosity as it began to unfold in its entire extraordinary splendor. He could sense the power of the Creator. It was poetry with breathtaking beauty. Everything within the universe at once seemed to fit together, interwoven in singularity. Both the Beginning and End were nearing one and the same. The last day became the first and the first day the last. Zia, one of a billion, billion specks in the greater cosmos, however insignificant, was no less than any other in the vastness of the deep universe. Zia reflected a glimmer like a many faceted diamond into the immense darkness that swept the heavens to its farthest reaches, shimmering, sparkling, and splashing across infinity and beyond.

Then Ammiz's thoughts turned abruptly to Izz. Had Fate allowed him to fulfill his destiny? Had he rescued the Royal Princess from a doom worse than death? Or would Zia be drawn into the grasp of the dark path, collapsed under the forces of unimaginably dense gravity. Would Zia be squashed into a degenerated mass the size of a moon, ball, fist, particle? Or sucked up along with any trace of light into a black hole to vanish entirely?

On the other hand, perhaps the cosmic clock might be turned back to the beginning of chaos. As it may be, the whole clustered solar system's structural and mechanical settings could fly off in all directions, shooting flames down out of the blackened sky. The seer's vision was startling. Only the next few moments would tell.

At that exact instant, were fulfilled, the ancient astronomical writings inscribed, and calculated by the charts and textbooks of the stargazers. That which was predicted by the great Book that Reveals had come to pass. It was the event Zia had been anticipating for a thousand years. Disciples of the Stars were swept off their feet, by the confirmation of such a fantastic anomaly, and they threw themselves on their faces. It was particularly significant to them that the miraculous prophecy had been announced in advance. The event consecrated Ammiz's greatness in their eyes and hearts. And now, after the fact, they believed his ominous warnings.

Around the Kingdom of Edawn at the same moment, the thronged armies were incapable of explaining what they were staring at. They clamored in pandemonium as courageous warriors dropped nervously to their knees. Some were filled with a fear that threatened to extinguish the very fabric of their collective mortal souls. The light even eclipsed the interior of the Dome of the Great Round Table, where King Ozzdon shielded his face. He narrowed his eyes against the luminous glory of the conjoining planets that filled the whole of Zia. In the core of his soul, there was one cosmic certainty, and that was that Ammiz had been right in his tireless efforts to counsel him. The seer had repeatedly warned him to take measures against the threat of madness about to befall Zia. In anguish, his thoughts were drawn to Zuree. What was the fate of his beloved daughter? And what of the carpenter?

On the surface of Zia, from every corner, whoever turned to look upon the oddity was star struck. All who witnessed the spectacle were all at once held spellbound. Those that stared at the center of the conjunction were transfixed like children staring at a concentrated beam magnifying its light in a crystalline, water filled globe. While they yet stared, the conjunction entered a state of turbulent flux up surging in awesome fragmented waves of energy. The immense multitudes throughout Zia stood froze, awestruck looking up at the sky, enthralled by something they had never seen, nor could ever explain. Villagers had already been perplexed by the wonder of abnormally lengthening days and shortened nights. All had been dumbfounded by nights that had turned unbelievably into midday. And now men and women came out of their abodes into the brightness of the brightest day ever witnessed, to observe the latest phenomena. At the zenith, most feared the worst, and many expected the end of Zia at any moment. Its light appeared to shoot skywards to the farthest reaches of the universe, to beacon throughout the cosmos. And for that fleeting moment, the entire universe seemed to pulsate with the overpowering brilliance of oneness. But just as soon as the zenith came, the conjunction began to dim and started to come to its end. Many, as if awakening from a dream, went about their everyday tasks as if the Great Conjunction had never been.

The retreating Norticlan Armies fell back, one arm bracing their fall, and the other held up in a guarded position. Some held up their shields up as if it would do anything to protect them against the imposing fiery sphere of light that appeared to devour the sky. It stirred even the dullest imagination. Many cried out in fear, speculating that it was the avenging God of the Valley Dwellers who they had ruthlessly pillaged and murdered for so long. Could it be the God their many victims had cried out to under their heavy handed torture, come to avenge them? There was wailing and gnashing of teeth as the power in the heavens seemed would at any time detach itself from the sky and crush them with its oppressive and luminous power. They felt the pulsating of its great heat upon them. And they believed that something ultimately powerful had gathered them before the foothills of Razorback Gore to blot them out altogether. They raised their spears and arrows to the sky when they thought the air itself would suddenly burst into flames and consume them.

Baddlock had the sensation at that same twinkling that something was utterly wrong. He looked up the vent throat to where he had last seen his prize disappeared. In a blinding flash, it appeared as if the sun itself had whirled out of its place. The phantasmic specter looked to be unbound from the heaven and falling towards Zia just as if to scorch him to a cinder with its vast fiery brightness. The Wicked Warlock Wizard's eyes widened, his face twisted, and his body seemed to contort. The overwhelming power of the light flooded the vent cavity all around him. It was astonishing, frightening, humbling, demoralizing, condemning all at once. But because he was deep in the underbelly of Zia, he was not exactly sure what was what. But he could very well have guessed that all his evil dreams had come to not. Then out of nowhere, a bloodcurdling wind like cry began to wail. It was a harsh howl from the bowels of the deep, out of the demonic universe of the dead.

The moment the entire unseen spirit world in the dark universe had anticipated for at least the last thousand, thousand revolutions of the Ziaian sun was finally at the threshold. Imprisoned demons, the worst of the worst, stood clustered closest to the pedestals of condemnation. Here is where the material realm intersected with the spiritual. And here is where they were found clustered waiting, desperately waiting for this moment. They crowded in where portals and posted tunnels between universes from different dimensions were expected to open. The moment to unleash their powers of abomination and desolation had come. The fallen that had self destructed awaited to be reborn. The era of their punishment would soon be over. The hour had come. The demon world knew the time was fast approaching. They were excited, and they were frenzied, they drooled at the thought. They had waited so long and wanted it so bad. All would once again be theirs and more. They were eagerly dancing, mocking, celebrating, and cheering wildly. They were energized heckling, drunkenly. They were frantic, and they salivated at the contemplation of soon, exacting their hatred of humankind for replacing them on the hierarchy. The unified vision they had reverberated across the centuries was finally coming true. They had all come out of their hiding in countless numbers and were still trickling into overflowing.

Layer upon layer they, clung to the walls and ceiling like a swarm of insects. Their accursed breath mixed in noxious vapors that obscured their faces. Non flesh creatures that were once the wisest and powerful of overwhelming exalted beauty, those that radiant brilliance and utmost knowledge were waiting, desperately waiting for the approaching moment. Streams of demons filled the chamber with a churning, sooty perpetually swelling overcast of spirits with their black, leathery wings. Each devil had his position, his role, his own level of authority. The excessive numbers grew tense and agitated, pushing and shoving, jolting, and riotously coming to blows. The huddled masses more numerous, riotous, and cocky than ever, caroused, exchanged elbow jabs and jolts as they crowded in.

Everything was in readiness. The time of imprisoned oppression was over. And the whole universe very soon might bow before its new altered reign devoid of love, light, and hope. The moment of truth had arrived. It was time for the grand finality. All made ready, posthaste. The star gates within the dark altars began to fluctuate erratically between dominion and temporal alignments within an unsystematic ebbing pattern. The Altars were seemingly shuffling through random combinations, attempting to locate the open window. Demons were arrogant, wild, intoxicated with the expectation of triumph and celebration. Archfiends worshipfully kissed the highest point of the Dark Altars.

Evil spirits laughed, cackled, taunted, danced, and cheered deliriously. Solid walls of the sounds of countless thousands of clicking talons, and beating wings in applause rose in pitch and intensity. All that was needed now was the precious blood of the One. Abaddawn, the once super being perfect in every way with unprecedented authority and glory, knew the time was here and now. But with the princess quickly slipping away from his clutches, there would be no sacrifice, no reprieve, no liberation, no nothing. The momentous event could have come to them no other way. Suddenly the edges of each black stone throughout the sinister cosmos sparked and flashed as the two realms synchronized at the climaxing Zenith. And they waited and waited. When nothing happened at the anticipated moment, the demon hordes became restless. Suddenly the restless beasts grew tense and agitated. Impulsively an overzealous, high ranking demon of the sixth hierarchy filled with arrogant impatience became outraged over the indefinable peculiarities of having to wait past the appointed hour. With his fists stubbornly clenched and squawking, the impulsive hellion cast himself upon the Dark Altar. The rogue tried to force himself through the alternating windows that had not completely unlocked, yet to the bestial brute, the porthole seemed penetrable. The demon managed to stick his head through the black stone as it undulated. The oscillating window abruptly vacillated, ripped apart, and then forcefully slammed out of existence. The stone threshold closed around the stunned Arch demon's neck with the sound of a massive gate slamming. The demon thrashed about hideously, trying to free himself then dissolved in a choking red cloud of smoke. As black magic drained from the air, demons closest to the gateways crumpled, decayed, and disintegrated to dust.

Instantly demons of all ranks throughout the universe felt the systematic failure that had descended, and they all knew that they had been defeated. The malignant spirits all around were stunned and looking for answers, but none had one. Immediately the boiling red and yellow tinted mantle overhead quickly turned into acidy pitch blackness and began to settle down upon the demon throngs. In the same instance, rising gray vapors of dust rose from the cave floor and sent the two colliding clouds swirling within the midst of the bereaving masses. Some looked like frightened jackals with nowhere to hide as if apprehended by an overpowering spiritual force. Bewildered and blinded, demons, fell to the ground, staggering about, trying to find an exit. The hellions fled blindly, shrieking in all directions. The demon horde all around was traumatized. Their hollow hearts shank and trembled. Some expressed their frustrated fury upon the lesser demons around them. Suddenly, as if colliding with a speeding wall, multitudes found themselves bound under a weightier bondage than before. Some of the higher ranking demons withdrew reluctantly like a pack frightened vermin they cowered into the farthest, darkest corners. Some fluttered into the air like terrified crows grasping after elevation. The total assemblage suddenly broke away in a hissing, whining, and wailing terror. Had their master Abaddawn met with some great and mysterious calamity, as to cause a catastrophic glitch in the fabric of the evil matrixes? Or had he merely been deceiving them all along? Alas, it was not meant or permitted to be, and hence, all the principalities of darkness were defeated by one man of flesh who defeated Abaddawn the infamous Lord of the Damned.

In the same hour, the throne upon which Abaddawn sat suddenly split in two from top to bottom as a surge of flames engulfed it. The ancient creature that was once the most beautiful began to fragment. Baddlock had failed him, and his fierce anger for him was inflamed. Hatred spewed from his yawning mouth, and Abaddawn's bewailing was loathing, venomous, spewing death, and hate. His bid for a gladiolus victory had expired as the conjunction began to separate, and his hopes for victory withered and crumbled to dust. His very brief triumph was only displaced by his monumental defeat. His plans to become his own god were ordained to fail from their inception. Even before time was time when he first hatched his scheme in the self serving blob of greed, that was his heart. What did you lack? You who dwelled in the presence of the Most High, who feasted at the table of the elect, who was blessed in every way?

Meanwhile, Izz had been left squinting in the extraterrestrial light. Momentarily roused by the dazzling light show that had forced him to raise an arm to shield his glassy eyes until the brilliant light had begun to fade. Then suddenly, the powerful aura of the Great Conjunction in all its splendor dwindled. Each planet's centrifugal force edged themselves out of the other gravitational axis and flung each other back into their eternal astral paths. The Great Conjunction once again abated back into the brightness of midday, its ominous luminosity destined to return someday unimaginably far into the future.

Still stunned by what Zuree had just witnessed, as she regained her sight, she repeatedly looked back, straining her vision in the Conjunction's afterglow. Time after time, she scanned the sky behind her, wishing to grasp a glimpse of Izz. *Where are you, and what is keeping you?* What could have gone wrong was the question that kept bouncing around in her head? Zuree Attempted to ease her anxiety. She fixed her eyes ahead. She tried to focus on the vast expanse of the green forested canopy beneath the clouds. It was a sight she could not quite get used to. It was amazing and terrifying in the same instance. Yet the sight stirred hope in her as she looked back at the Noragore Mountains falling into the distance behind her. As the strange new day lit her way, the breeze gently caressed her face and danced gracefully in her hair. For a fleeting moment, Zuree realized that she was living a reoccurring dream she had dreamt many times when she was but a little girl. In her dream, she had flown like a bird at the top of the world. The dream had seemed so real then, and now her dream had come true! She had touched the sky and seen what only eagles see. Zuree's vision stretched hazily up towards the unseen, and the infinite provoked her mind. She wondered at the many enigmatic mysteries that must lie just beyond the clouds. It was all so thought provoking but all so incredibly frightening all at once.

As Fina flew awkwardly away from the Noragore Rim and the ruins of Skullsdoom, her chest wounds further weakened her with every stroke of her wings. Below the jagged barren terrain of the Waste Lands of Woe was gradually being replaced by lofty, pine covered hills. The farther Fina got away from the Northern Range, the freer Izz felt. He let out one gasping breath of relief after another. He had entered the world of eternal darkness and returned alive with his beloved—at least for the moment; he was still breathing. Behind him, those things that had brought him so much pain, heartbreak, and despair dimmed away into the past. He was leaving behind the terror of the underworld, leaving behind all the horror of the lost, and with it all the threats of eternal damnation. He had saved his beloved from a fate worse than death by the virtue and strength of his love. And in doing so, he had inadvertently saved the world of Zia, perchance the universe. But now, he was in the fight of his life and sadly, losing miserably. And as the conjunction slowly faded, so did his strength.

Izz concentrated on hanging on to Fina's neck with both hands sticky with dry blood. He could feel the toxicity of the poison spreading throughout his organs until it had reached his beating heart. He could feel himself dying. Each movement of Fina's flight path was an agonizing jolt. In his frailness, Izz breathlessly called out to Zuree, "My love, I am sorry I may not make through this one." Then gradually, he slumped down until he hung limply against Fina's neck who was struggling to keep him upright. Every wing beat was like a whiplash laid across his bareback. Izz tried to sit back up, weakened by the loss of blood he failed and slumped back down. His face was misshaped with unbearable agony. He could no longer sustain himself. Izz thrashed about unable to keep his balance, and his weak grip began to slip. It was a miracle he had been able to resist as inhumanly long as he had. Izz's body swayed gently as if in a tranquil breeze. Sounds became muted. He drifted until he was a fragment, just a figment of his own imagination. He carried Zuree's smile in his heart.

All at once, everything went black. Fina's gaze slowly turned to look back at Izz. He had let his hands fall to his side, and his predicament became even more precarious than hers. Izz weaved in a circular pivot reached the tipping point. By now, he was just a shell of himself, so light that a stray breeze rolled him off Fina's back despite her best effort to keep him mounted. Izz tumbled over on his side, flying off Fina's flank. He was swept into the sky and plunged straight down towards the rocky terrain below. Suddenly startled Izz's body contorted as he awkwardly grabbed for Fina but only grasped two fists of thin air. There was utter bewilderment in his eyes as horror twisted his pale face. A scream clogged in his throat. He gasped for air, but only a faint wail escaped his gaping mouth as he plunged to earth like a falling angel.

Just ahead in the upper air currents, Zuree had no way of knowing what had just happened. As Bolo steadily careened Zuree closer and closer towards Edawn, suddenly out of nowhere, Zuree felt a pang of fear. She looked longingly back at the black mountains of the Noragore Rim as they fell awesomely away into obscurity. All her beliefs were put to a hard test. She clasped her hands to her mouth and shouted against the rushing of the wind, "Izz, where are you!"

Despite her pain and loss of blood, Fina flipped in midair, pulled her wings in, and plunged towards the ground, dropping at speeds exceeding faster than she had ever plunged before. Racing against time, Fina thrust herself downward faster and faster in a dead defying dive. Mere moments remained before Izz would spatter onto the rocks that were coming up blindingly fast. With wings straight back, Fina arched into a sharper, instinctive hunting swoop horizontal to the ground. The spectacular creature was followed close behind by her flickering shadow as it flashed across the rocky landscape, just a breath beneath her bristling maneuver. And at the last possible moment, without room for error, the rider of the wind, extend her talons as the fastest living creature on Zia soared faster than at any other time in her life. With one dazzling downstroke, she was tracing a brilliant streak of lifting force across the rocky terrain. Fina reached for Izz inches before he splattered on the stony ground. In a stabbing flash of a twinkling, Fina snatched Izz away from the jaws of death for the second time in so many hours that day. She was ever so careful not to pierce Izz with her eight razor sharp talons as she gently scooped her master up and away. FOOM! With an explosion of wings, Fina returned high into the lofty sky where the sky was thinner and easier to navigate. After regaining attitude, Fina continued where she had left off on her arduous journey, back to the Kingdom of Edawn. Unbelievably the overlord of the sky unrelenting gave when there was nothing more to offer. Upon the rush of the wind with one mighty blast after another, Fina beat her wings like tattered black canopies fluttering as they sliced through the air. She carried Izz up and over the wide valley, while he dangled limply from her talons like a broken rag doll caught in a tizzy driven wind.

Along Bolo's and Zuree's steady southward path, a hash wind began to blow through a white fantasy world of clouds. Bolo spread his wings wide at a new angle to soar against the increasingly resistant wind force. Below the mighty Megacon River snaked along the Wazoo Valley and through Razorback Gorge, the highest mountain canyon in the world of Zia. Before them, the heavily wooded basin of the Ebony Forest waited. Somewhere to the East lay the Kingdom of Skymount from which a strange dark cloud rose. Over the green forested hills, rural roads and remote cottages appeared and vanished behind their stealthy flight path. Ahead, the southern shores of Edawn loomed imposingly nearer and nearer, its beaches arched around a shoreline rapidly expanding as they approached. From these heights, the land beneath them seemed tranquil and a peaceful, lush, fertile, and paradisiacal world. But as they dropped lower,

Zuree was alarmed to see that the beauty of the landscape was covered with splotches and scorched patches of burnt ground. Zuree's thoughts filled with dread, again turned to Izz as she continued to crane her neck back, looking over her shoulder for any sign of Izz. With piercing eye, she searched the northern skies, again and again, seeking any sign of Izz in the distance. Try as she may Zuree could not shake the premonition that something had gone terribly wrong. Weighted down by apprehension, she feared for Izz's safety. When she turned to look back towards the South again, she saw increasing signs that all was not well with the Kingdom of Edawn ether. As she passed overhead, below she saw tall, ominous, black clouds of smoke billowing from settlements down in what was once a pristine valley. She saw what was once a peaceful land that now had been torched and was still smoldering. Where there had once been the greens of fruit trees and gardens of vegetables, there was now only upheaval and the force of destruction. Bolo snapped his wings forward, and the surrounding patchwork of farms, fields, orchards, and roads became a blur beneath them. Zuree squeezed her eyes tight, unable to believe the glimpses she had seen between the clouds of a desolate scene below her.

From a great distance to the East, Zuree's eyes caught a clearer sight of Skymount, just a faint shimmering on the horizon. She could see the kingdom like a smudge pot still spewing noxious red like smoke rising into the air to hang over the horizon like an eerie, thick vaporous cloud of doom. The kingdom itself seemed shrouded in devastation and engulfed in the stillness of death. When the smoke filled air began clear up ahead, Zuree could tell by the highlands below that they were nearing the boundaries of Edawn. At long last, she was back within the borders of her own world. It was a sweeping view of a world she had never seen before, not even from the highest towers of her father's kingdom. As they flew into the wind, it whistled in her ears, carrying an eerie sound mixed within the tinge of strange sights and odors. The echos of mourning and sights and the smells of battle were everywhere.

Below, Zuree looked about her in all directions as they past scenes of horrifying devastation and destruction after horrendous devastation and destruction. Zuree just stared numbly at the tattered, gnarled landscape that encircled Edawn. Great charcoal drifts of ash and smoke reared up in the air, stirred up as Bolo's wings caused currents to whirl as they hovered closer to the ground. The smoldering soot choked Zuree and made her eyes water. Through the eerie nightmarish haze that covered the landscape, she saw the giant catapults. Jutting masses that looked like jagged metal and wooden monsters reaching a fist to the heavens. She felt sudden knotting in the pit of her stomach, a strange sensation she could not quite place. She thought she heard, in the witching, wailing wind that seemed to moan, the ghostly, echoing cries of those that had died and the weeping howls of their inconsolable loved ones. Then all at once, she saw the brokenness of the kingdom of Edawn on the horizon against the bay. Columns of black smoke plumes rose from within the kingdom's walls and were carried out to sea by the air currents. The silvery towers that once proudly glisten in the sun and stretched toward the skies were now heaps of rubble. Of the seven, only one stood. Just beyond the kingdom, she saw the Xylenian Fleet docked in the bay, but did not recognize them until she got closer. An ominous feeling of trepidation came over her, and her heart trembled. She whispered to her self, "Izz…what is taking you so long?" as she remorsefully searched the cloudy skyline behind her. With a heavy heart, she reluctantly went on.

The burial patrols spotted Bolo in the northern skies first. Warning trumpets sounded their unwelcoming alert, and the entire Xylenian army readied for battle. Forces in the kingdom moved to the Northern Wall, thinking that it could be a surprise attack. In knotted tension, everyone awaited orders from their leadership.

Meanwhile, in the Dome of the Great Table, King Ozzdon stood among his kings, general warlords, noblemen, and the Council of Elders of Zia. Before him lay, a mapped out war mock up of Phantomsdeep and a detailed layout of its defenses provided to him by Ammiz the Seer. The king took charge, "Our most formidable opposition will be the fortress walls. The Seer Ammiz has seen these walls and has assured me that they are almost as thick as they are tall." Several Warlords presented their proposals of action. They all agreed that a catapult assault should be their first plan of action. The king took a long hooked stick and moved his catapult pieces into their positions. "I agree, our first move will be to deploy our catapults and sling launchers along the northernmost ridge line, and unleash a torrent of devastation. Own catapults should most certainly breach their gate, if not their walls. But if all else fails, we will have to assault the walls with our climbers, battering ram and diggers. With our established base of catapult fire, we can support our troops if need be. At the same time, we will deploy our battering ram, and assault their gate. At the same, time while we move our traction trebuchet, ballista, and our towers into there ready positions."

Tydron spoke up and volunteered to storm the main gate with Baddlock's own dragon battering ram. The king moved Tydron's board piece into play. Zandor then Kondor volunteered to lead the flanking wall attack. The king moved Zandor and Kondor's pieces forward. "Zandor, you will assault the western wall, and Kondor, you will assault the eastern wall."

Zandor and Kondor both nodded firmly. Just then, the warning rams were heard, and the king turned to his twin generals. "Go and see what this is all about and send word to me immediately."

The twins rushed to the main keep's top. From the northern tower of the kingdom, the keen eyes of the watch who had been monitoring any possible movement of the enemy, or the lack thereof, was the first to sight Bolo as he approaches from the North. "A White Crested eagle approaches from the North, and it appears to be carrying a rider" The tower guard called down to the wall guards.

Zandor was one of the first to reach the keeps deck. "It could be one of the Baddlock's tricks," Zandor warned and motioned to a group of archers to position themselves along what was left of the Northern Wall and the upper levels of the keep.

"The rider appears to be a woman, General Zandor." The watchman on the tower called down.

"Take nothing for granted," Zandor commanded as Bolo neared the outer wall and motioned for a defensive response as archers trained their longbows on the incoming eagle and rider.

From the skies above what Zuree saw next was all too immediate, and all too painful to understand. She saw faraway bright furious red stains and the horrible sight of men lying scattered everywhere over the killing fields. Men who were sprawled in contorted positions like discarded tin soldiers strewed out as far as she could see in all directions. She saw the cremation fires and the endless succession of carts and wagons, stacked with the dead, moving along in orderly processions. The once faultless countryside was now a cankerous covered world of death and annihilation. A faint cry escaped from her quivering lips. Zuree was having difficulty believing what she was witnessing. In disbelief, Zuree cradled her head in her hands as she shook it in bewilderment and shock. Nothing could stop her frightened tears from falling on Bolo's neck feathers as she cried, "Why has this happened? Why? Why? Why!" She asked herself through trembling lips.

The sight made her heart implode and fall from its place. She saw the Xylenian armies surrounding Edawn. However, it was not yet clear to her who was the conqueror and who was the conquered. As Bolo and Zuree neared the Kingdom of Edawn, it spread out below and came into focus before them. Bolo dipped lower and approached what was left of the northern outer walls, now mostly laid waste. There were more and more traces of battle and slaughter throughout. The stale smell of smoke and death burned her nostrils as the black swirls ascended into a blood red sky. As Bolo swooped down, the kingdom below became an indistinguishable lattice of shattered byways, avenues, alleys, districts, and neighborhoods. Up and down the main boulevard, moving steadily, horse drawn carts still carried the dead to the smelters. The streets were strewn with devastated buildings and ruinous debris, blighted with gapes and gouges everywhere. The quadrant around the keep was strewn with wreckage and rubble like confetti across the courtyard. As Zuree stared in disbelief, the spirit of death and destruction wrapped its arms around her.

As Bolo hovered over the keep, everyone below could hear the quickening of Bolo's feathery wings and see the cascading of his shadow over the keep's deck. The keep's century blinked his eyes against the glare of the sky, then suddenly exclaimed with a hint of doubt in his voice, "It is the Princess Zuree!

To be continued
in Tom Icon's final book, *Izz of Zia:*

THE

BLOOD

ATONEMENT